FATE OF HELHEIM

ANNABELLE HUTSON

ANNABELLE HUTSON

CONTENTS

For a 15 year old me.
This is quite the upgrade from handwritten pages on legal pads,
hm?
Wait til' you see this werewolf, girl.
I love you.

CHAPTER 1

"Everything is fine, Mom." I rolled my eyes and debated throwing the phone across the room just to stop talking.

"Have you been going to church? Pastor Bryan says he hasn't seen you in a while."

"Why are you still talking to Pastor Bryan? You haven't lived here in four years. Anyway, I don't have time to go anymore. I'm on duty at the Sanctuary on Sundays now."

"Can't they change your schedule? You have to make time for the Lord, Anais Sutton." My full name made me flinch.

"No, Mom—"

"Can you at least sign up for a bible study on a different day after work?"

"I'll think about it. It's late; I need to get to bed." I pushed her off the phone just to stop her scolding. I hadn't believed in God in a long time, but my mom didn't know about that.

"Alright, alright. Please think about it."

"Goodnight. Love you." I was ready to be off this call.

"Love you too," she sighed.

I hung up and chucked my phone into a plush comforter laying on my floor rather than where it belonged on my bed. The sigh I heaved emptied my lungs completely, and I reached for my weed pen. I wanted the next thing I inhaled to be pure relaxation so I could detox after talking with my mother. I was not going back to that church, not even if she tried to come from California to make me.

Raking a hand through my dark brown hair, I grit my teeth as I felt the frizz and waves. I'd spent forty-five minutes straightening it that morning, but the snow all afternoon while I was at work foiled my efforts.

Plopping down in my desk chair, I sipped on my vape, starting to space out at the fairy lights and fake wisteria plants hanging in my room. A few vined plants hung from my bookshelves full of tattered paperbacks, and on the walls were a few paintings I'd bought in Italy beside pictures of family and friends. My bed was a mismatch of sheets and blankets; as long as it was clean, it would work for sleeping. I was renting my apartment, so while I did what I could to make it cozy, it really wasn't much of a step up from my dorm room in college. Certainly the cleanliness level today rivaled that of 'a pig sty,' as my mother would say. Dirty clothes littered the floor and formed an impressive mini mountain on my desk chair. Glasses of water sat on every surface, gathering a layer of dust, and the sheets were rumpled on my bed. I promised myself that by the time I was in my thirties, I'd have my shit together enough to have a grown up bedroom.

For the time being, I loved my mid-twenties broke-trash aesthetic.

I felt the knots in my shoulders and gently rubbed them. I debated calling Dan to come over and give me a massage, but he would want more and I wasn't in the mood. Church talk did that to me, put me out of the mood for almost everything that was fun. I was supposed to be online to play games with Kerri, but I had sent her a text canceling as soon as I picked up my mom's call.

Looking outside at the dark Canadian winter night, I sighed. I felt like I was sighing too much lately. My mom just wouldn't let it go. I hadn't believed in God in a long time. I had not been to bible study since before my parents and sister moved to Los Angeles for Dad's work. I had conveniently been put on Sunday breakfast duty at the wolf wildlife sanctuary I worked at, and I kept the shift since I was in college, but she still kept harping about it.

I eyed my shelf of fantasy books; my mother, and Pastor Bryan for that matter, would highly disapprove of each one. A shelf full of magic, full of witchcraft, full of escape. Reading was always my escape from the pressures of my very religious family. The books called for me to come look at them, to smell their pages and reminisce on their stories.

Caving, I walked from my desk to the shelf, running my fingers over the bindings as I reflected on the stories that saved me, carried me through my childhood. Fae, teenage witches and wizards, vampires and werewolves. I used to read them on cold winter nights like this one. The wind would whip snow against the window of my bedroom, and I would be camped out under my comforter, my flashlight illuminating the pages of whatever book I managed to sneak from the library without my mother noticing. Occasionally, my father would find them when he raided my room, and I'd paid fines for several that he destroyed in rage.

After flopping down on my bed, I reached for the blankets to tug them up over my body. I always liked to daydream about being in those stories, falling in love with High Fae and having magical powers somewhere far away from my mom, somewhere magical and sheltered away from all the problems I faced here. Sighing again, I rolled over, squeezing a pillow to my chest and hitching my leg up in my favorite sleeping position. My eyelids were already heavy, and I knew it wouldn't be long before I was dreaming about my knight in shining armor coming to save me.

When I became conscious of my dream, I was in a familiar setting: in the woods in the snow. I wasn't exactly sure where the woods were; I thought they must be the woods where I played as a child, but occasionally they felt like the ones near my apartment, where I regularly ran now. I'd had this dream enough that these woods felt as familiar as both in real life.

I loved this dream.

My feet itching to get to the best part, I began running through the heavy falling snow, leaping over logs and ducking under frozen cobwebs to leave them intact. They looked like small chandeliers in the forest, so I left them undisturbed. Thick snowflakes stuck in my hair and on my eyelashes as I clambered through the winter forest.

This dream was always in winter, no matter what season it was in the waking world. Snow always fell; sometimes it drifted in delicate gentle flakes and sometimes it was a torrential blizzard. I followed a small incline, intent on getting to my favorite part of this dream. I could hear it now, calling for me: a lonely howl piercing the air. I followed the sound, climbing toward the melody until I came over the rocky cliff edge to see the beast waiting for me. A massive black wolf stood there, larger than any I had seen in real life, with yellow eyes that found me as soon as I came into view. I smiled at my dream companion.

Any time I had a nightmare, I often had a dream of the wolf when I next slept. Everything about the wolf was comfortable; I had walked with it many times since it started appearing shortly after my nineteenth birthday.

I crossed the distance to where it stood at the base of a large boulder the size of a two-story building. I reached out to pet the wolf's ruff, as I always did in this dream, and admired the jet black, shaggy fur that hung from its lean and powerful body. Stepping away, I walked ahead, turning to look at the wolf behind me. I smiled, encouraging my friend to join me. The wolf obliged, walking to my side as we set off through the forest. I could tell my companion was more agitated than usual tonight, the flattened ears and quick pace clues enough. The wolf wanted me to follow.

"What is your problem tonight?" I asked, and the wolf paused, eyeing me with concern before hustling forward and impatiently waiting for me to catch up. The wolf's gaze was on something in the distance, downhill from us. I looked through the trees ahead to see if I might catch a glimpse of the castle today.

Sometimes, through the trees on our usual trail, I thought I saw a castle in the distance and a city by a river down below. It was always hard to see in the dim cloudy light, and many times the blizzarding snow blocked me from being able to identify what lay more than ten feet in front of us.

Today I could see the castle the clearest I'd ever dreamt of it. In the distance, the massive grey castle rose above a city set on the water, mountains surrounding on all sides. I looked at the wolf, who was watching me intently, its paws inching toward the city. I had never made it there, to the end of the trail, though I tried many times.

"Is that where we are going?" I asked.

The wolf snorted, its breath hanging frozen in the air between us.

"Let's go then." I began descending the hill before us and the wolf came to my side, allowing me to steady myself against its body as we picked our way through the snowy underbrush. The wolf was sure-footed wherever we went, its strong paws sturdy and made for moving through the forest. It was still in a hurry, although it patiently kept pace with me to make sure

I got down the hill without tripping over my feet and rolling down face-first.

I followed the wolf who, now that we were down the steep incline, walked ahead several paces, eagerly looking ahead and darting its eyes back to me with anticipation.

"I'm coming, I'm coming." I waved it off dismissively, hurrying my steps to catch up. The wolf snorted, and I swear it looked like it was smiling at me, its mouth twitched up, before it bounded ahead a few steps and waited for me again.

We walked through a never-ending stretch of forest. The wolf's eagerness was not abating, although it slowed enough for me to catch up as the trees became more dense, blocking more light. The snow began to pick up, and wind whipped at my face, feeling so real I almost opened my eyes—but I wanted to stay in the dream with my wolf. As the storm darkened the sky above us, the wolf's ears twitched up, and it watched through the trees with alert anxiety. Its agitation was rubbing off on me, and I walked closer to its side, worried about what it heard.

A rumbling that sounded like thunder swept through the forest, and I looked to the wolf, who paused to sniff the air. Under my hands, I felt the wolf's fur stand on end. Its hackles rose on its back as it looked around us with a wild expression. The wolf was seeing things I was not, hearing things I couldn't, and its agitation made my heart race.

There was a presence ahead of us, somewhere beyond my sight. We both could sense it. The wolf's ears flattened to its head, and a deep growl shook me to my core. I took a step back from the snarling beast, but it stayed at my side, putting itself between me and whatever lay before us.

I wanted to ask the wolf what it saw, knowing very well my companion never responded with words, but I kept quiet, my mouth failing me. The temperature dropped and I shivered, coming closer to waking with each breath.

Without warning, a huge crack of lightning struck a tree to my right with a blinding flash. I was thrown out of my dream and into the very real, cold, knee-deep snow of a forest. Panting, I looked around, completely dazed and disoriented by the light. It was bitterly cold, and I couldn't feel my fingers. I could barely feel my silky pajama set clinging to me, soaked from where I had landed in the deep snow. As my eyes adjusted to the darkness, I saw glowing red ahead of me. Embers. Burning on a tree split in pieces by lightning.

I tried once again to get my bearings, but it was so cold. My eyes shut, the embers ahead becoming fragments of red light. Just before dark nothingness consumed me, I heard footsteps and saw two dark, tall figures approaching my side, standing over me.

"Hm. So this is the one?" a deep male voice said.

"Yeah. Why is she out here?" a woman's voice responded.

"I bet they were trying to get to her before we could."

"You're probably right, and if that's the case, they can't be far. Let's get her out of here. Something's wrong with her—let's take her to the hospital."

CHAPTER 2

M y eyes roved around the room, trying to get my bearings as I took in the fluorescent lights above and steady
beeping coming from a machine near my head. I groaned,
lifting my arm to see the plastic band around my wrist and the
tube protruding from my hand, confirming that I was indeed
in the hospital.

"Welcome back to the waking world," a nurse with a kind
smile said as she gave a gentle knock and entered the room. I
noted the deepening purple under her eyes and the hunch in
her shoulders as she walked to my railed bed. She must've been

working overnight, and it was morning now by the look of the light outside the curtains.

"How are we doing? Any feeling in your fingers yet?" she asked as she checked the machines near my head before turning to me. I looked down at my discolored fingers on both hands, starting to feel the 'pins & needles' feeling in all of them.

"Yeah… Kind of hurts," I said, my raspy voice surprising me.

"I'm not surprised. You were about to get a nasty case of frostbite with that hypothermia. But I'm glad you can feel something, that's what matters." She smiled, gently taking my hand and examining my reddened appendages. "I'm going to sit you up." She raised the bed under me so I was upright.

"Do you know what happened?" I asked, biting my lip as she tried to bend my fingers slightly, making the pain intensify. I cringed but allowed her to continue working my fingers one by one. I had no memory of why I was here, although based on my history, I was wondering if I was sleepwalking again—a nasty habit I'd developed in my teenage years.

"No one called. A man brought you into the ER; he was carrying you." Her eyes flicked to mine, and I saw the curiosity boiling beneath. "He said he found you out in the woods at Hemmings Park. Said you were collapsed in the snow wearing nothing but pajamas. Do you remember anything?"

"I was...." I tried to remember. "Just dreaming, I think."

Something was blurry about the memory of the dream, as if it was wrapped in thick cellophane that kept me from seeing the whole thing. I remembered going into the woods and walking with my wolf, but I wasn't sure why the wolf had been upset, or if the lightning I'd seen was even real. I couldn't tell her about the wolf. I'd only ever told Kerri and my mother, and both thought I was wacky.

"Well, I was dreaming about walking in the woods ... but that's all I remember." She nodded sympathetically, walking to my feet to inspect my toes. I sucked air between my teeth as the tingles turned painful when she bent the appendages. I looked down to see I was in a paper hospital gown, my wet pajama set heaped on a chair next to me.

"Who was this man? Did anyone get his name?" I asked.

"He was tall with blonde-ish hair, and honestly he was carrying you like you didn't weigh more than a feather. It was impressive. If you don't know who it was ... you should. If I wasn't married..." She sighed, clicking her tongue dramatically before looking at me with a suggestive smile.

"Does anyone take note of that on intake? Did anyone record who he might be?" I asked, starting to curl and uncurl my fingers as they hurt less to show her I could use them. I doubted it was Dan. He had dark hair and wouldn't be able to carry me twenty feet, much less to the hospital. Who would even find me in the middle of the woods anyway?

"We usually ask for an emergency contact, but honestly, once we took you back, he disappeared. We found your emergency contacts in your cell phone and called your mom, Sweetie." She gave me another sympathetic smile. "Well, if you're feeling better, you're all set to go in about a few hours. I'll start getting the discharge paperwork together for you."

"Thank you, for everything." I smiled, albeit weakly, to show my gratitude at all her hard work.

"Oh good, thank God you're awake!" My best friend Kerri sidled into the room holding a coffee in one hand and tupperware in the other. "They called your mom and she called me—oh, I'm her ride home," she told the nurse, who nodded and exited out to the hall.

"What the hell happened?" Kerri hissed at me as soon as the nurse left, turning her deeply concerned stare onto me. I rolled my eyes, loving her with all my heart but wishing it was anyone but her and her judgmental glare here at the moment.

"I honestly don't remember, okay? I was in bed, having the dream about the wolf like I always do. It got weirder than usual, and I…" I trailed off, remembering just a flash of waking in the woods and seeing a burning tree ahead of me.

"Maybe you hit your head or something. Maybe the wolf dream will finally be over." Her tone turned playful as she set the soup in front of me and pried the lid off. I sent a little prayer to whatever powers that be, hoping it wasn't the end of the dream.

"Eat up, show them you're good, and let's bust out of here." She started typing on her phone, texting my mom no doubt.

"Kerri, did you hear anything about this man that brought me in?" I asked, curiosity gnawing at my chest.

Her fingers paused on the keyboard and she glanced up at me. "No, I didn't. It's weird though. I hate that he didn't leave any information so I could thank him for saving my idiot best friend."

I sighed, a flash of frustration at my fuzzy memory and the lack of information in my mind.

"Seriously, eat and let's go." Kerri handed me a spoon.

That evening, Kerri stayed the night, making grilled cheese sandwiches and heating a can of tomato soup for us to share. We sat in front of the TV binging our favorite period romance, then fell asleep on the couch, not waking until the morning light created rainbows across us from my mosaic window hangings.

"You're absolutely sure you don't remember anything?" Kerri asked me for the millionth time as she pulled the orange juice from the refrigerator.

"I would have told you eight hours ago if I did." I groaned, checking my fingers, which felt nearly back to normal today.

She paused her bustling in the kitchen and planted both hands on the counter, staring me down. "Anais. We both know you're prone to sleepwalking and also doing dumb things when you're fully awake. So my question to you is this: were you being dumb?" I rolled my eyes at her condescending look.

"Probably, okay? Probably I was being dumb. But I *was* sleepwalking, so it wasn't really my fault." I picked at the pancakes on my plate, and she scowled at me, not reassured by my confirmation but settling for it for the time being.

"I have a job application I'm working on. I want you to help me with my resume tomorrow at Roast." I nodded, wishing I had my favorite butterscotch latte from the coffee shop right now. Roast was where we spent most afternoons on days I wasn't working at the sanctuary.

"How is it going with Dan?" she asked, her tone soft. I glanced at her warily. She never wanted to talk about Dan, or any of the men I dated, other than to poke fun at them or tell me they were not good enough for my attention.

"It's okay. I haven't seen him for a while; he's been busy." Dan was a dating app match up that had been on again, off again since college. He could never decide if he wanted something serious, and every time he broke it off, I swore him off for good. Yet every time he called late at night, I found myself in his bed at 2:30 in the morning. The past few times I kept it hidden from Kerri, not wanting to listen to her dragging him for a half hour. I never had much luck dating someone long term; Dan was the closest I had come to realizing my dreams for my love life.

"What is 'a while'?" she asked, the distaste for him visible on her face. So easily masked just moments ago, my best friend couldn't keep her true feelings from her face or voice very long.

"I really don't need your judgments right now, can you hold it to yourself?" I snapped.

"Yes. You already know my thoughts on him, but if it's what you want." She sighed.

"It's not what I want. Of course I want something real, I have forever—you know that." Kerri had always been my support growing up, my very best friend. She always listened to my dreams of love and read the cheesy romance stories I adored, even long after she told me she would rather read about two women together.

"I do know that, which is why I think you should stop wasting time on fucking *Dan*." She paused before turning back to where she was rinsing plates in the sink.

I sighed heavily, rubbing the last of the sleep from my eyes as she clanged dishes around to load the washer. She didn't press the Dan issue any more.

"What about you?" I asked her. "Have you been seeing anyone since Janine?" Janine had been her long time and first serious girlfriend in college; they broke up a little under a year ago. Kerri cried for weeks, destroyed several sets of plates in the parking lot of her apartment complex after buying them from Goodwill, and then had a serious online hook-up phase.

"No, but I'm ready to start dating someone seriously again, I think." She offered a smile to lighten the mood. "We're going to have to start traveling. I've dated every woman in town at this point. I need broader horizons and a bigger sea with more fish."

Kerri finally left late in the afternoon with a reminder to meet her at Roast in the morning. I waved her out the door and tried not to cackle when she comically slid on the ice by her car. It was around 4:30 in the afternoon, the sun getting ready to set in the winter sky. My least favorite time of the day.

I went back inside. Normally, I would go for a run at Hemmings Park at this time of day, but after my hospital stay, all I wanted was extra warmth and something to eat. I flicked the TV on, scrolling to my favorite garbage reality show to keep me company as I bustled around the kitchen.

Not having much in the way of groceries this evening, the only option was breakfast for dinner. I made my favorite childhood breakfast: egg tacos. My dad made them every day for me when I was in high school, and I smiled, thinking I should call him and let him know I'd got home safely.

Settling in on the couch, I devoured both tacos and some sauteed mushrooms and spinach I'd made earlier in the week. I called my parents, letting them know I was okay and telling them it was just a bad sleepwalking episode. They were skeptical of the story, just as Kerri had been, and my mom reminded me to lock my door to keep myself inside tonight.

"I can unlock doors in my sleep, Mom. That's how sleepwalking works—you can do normal functions."

"And I'm saying it sounds to me like the devil lured you out there and tried to take a nab at you," my mother snipped, making me lean away from the phone to escape her sharp, exasperated tone. "If you would just pray before bed, Anais, that's how we stopped it before. Don't you remember? When you were nineteen, right before we left Vernon?"

"I don't think that's what stopped it, Mom. I just go through periods like this. This time was just the worst one, but I didn't drive anywhere and someone did find me, so it could have been worse."

There was a moment of disappointed silence, and I could picture her on the other end of the phone line, lips pursed, eyebrows knit together in disapproval, and frown lines deepening. "Well, I will be praying for you, Anais, and I hope that's enough to save you next time."

"Okay Mom. Thank you." I ground out the appreciative words even though I didn't feel them. She was being condescending, disguising it as concern and prayer. Typical. "I need to get to bed. I'll talk to you again in a couple days. Love you."

I hung up the phone and dropped my head into my hands. I took a few deep breaths to calm my nerves before I grabbed my laptop, pulling up my editing software and opening my most recent batch of photos from the sanctuary.

Hours later, I woke up with a start, the TV still playing one of my favorite shows. The golden eyes of a beautiful white wolf from the sanctuary stared out at me from the screen. Groaning, I sat wrapped in my blanket and debated just sleeping right there on the couch.

What the nurse said about someone carrying me into the hospital rushed back to my mind. I wished someone was here to carry me to my bed.

I sighed and stood, shuffling around the room to unplug the fairy lights and double check my door locks. Finally I scooted off to my bedroom, still thinking about the strange man. I wondered how he found me out there, in the dark, in the middle of the night. I also wondered why I couldn't remember any details except the flash of lightning.

When I had woken up for that brief moment and saw the burning tree, I had not recognized the forest around me. The nurse said it was the park by my house, but I must have been very deep in the trees. I hadn't seen any familiar trails. Then again, it had been dark and I was disoriented from the lightning flash.

The itch from the plastic band on my wrist reminded me of its presence, and I ripped it off Hulk-style, tossing it in the trash before I flopped down in my desk chair and plugged in my laptop. I needed to do some research to see if there were any records of weather anomalies last night.

CHAPTER 3

After stomping the snow off my boots at the door, I took a moment to appreciate the warmth and comforting smells of my favorite coffee shop. It was a newer store in town, frequented by the college students and remote workers in the area. Deep, luxurious scents made my mouth water every time I walked in the door. As I looked for an open table in the familiar warm-wood interior, my nose took in the day's roast with hints of vanilla and butterscotch for winter. I noticed an unfamiliar man behind the counter. My usual barista was Zeke, a friendly albeit shy young man who usually was halfway through making my butterscotch latte before I walked in the door.

Today, the man behind the counter was stunningly handsome. His strawberry-blond waves and trim, well-kept beard framed his bronzed face, with full lips and stunning ocean-turquoise eyes. He stood fairly tall, my eyeline meeting his chin if I stared straight ahead. His broad shoulders gave way to muscular arms bulging under a long-sleeve shirt rolled to his elbows to show bronzed and veiny forearms. He smiled with perfectly straight, white teeth as I approached the counter.

"Hello, what can I get for you today?" His voice was warm and deep, matching the rich smells of the coffee around us. Everything about him was inviting, enticing. He was a drop of California summer sunshine in the bleak Canadian winter. My voice caught in my throat for a moment before I could respond to the beautiful stranger.

"Ah—a butterscotch latte please." I stumbled on my words a bit as I squinted at his name badge. "Thanks, Mag." Such an odd name, I wondered if it was short for Magnus or if he was truly named after a loaded round of ammunition in a gun. Either was possible where we lived in the rural countryside.

"You got it. Name for your order?" he asked.

"Anais." I rummaged in my bag for my wallet, finding it sandwiched between my computer and one of the hard drives where I hoarded all my photos for the wolf sanctuary.

"Oh, okay. Zeke told me about you when he trained me yesterday." My head snapped up at his words.

"What did he tell you?" I felt my cheeks reddening.

"He said you were the butterscotch latte girl and to always make sure you had one in your hand." He winked, making my cheeks tingle as I blushed impossibly deeper.

"That's why he's the best." I watched a smirk play on his lips when he took in my reddened cheeks. He took the cash from my hand, and as our fingers brushed, he shocked me with static electricity.

"I'm sorry," he mumbled, embarrassed as I jumped back from the counter. My finger prickled from where the shock stung me. I gave a little shake of my hand, an image of the burning tree after the lightning strike flashing to mind.

"No worries." I raked my hand through my hair in exasperation before taking the coins he gave me and dropping them in the plastic jack-o-lantern tip jar that sat on the counter year-round.

I walked to a table toward the back to wait for Kerri, setting my bag down in the seat next to me and pulling out my computer. I could feel Mag's focus on me across the room as he prepared my coffee, and I tried to ignore it as I opened my laptop to start my work.

"Anais." The way his rich voice called for me nearly had me stumbling from my chair to the counter for my drink.

"Do you work at the wolf sanctuary?" Mag asked as I approached and wrapped my chilled fingers around the warm ceramic mug, a beautiful fern made of froth delicately swaying on top of the sweet drink.

"What?" I asked.

"The wolf sanctuary. OWS." He nodded toward my laptop sitting on the table, several Okanagan Wolf Sanctuary stickers on it.

"Oh, yes. I do." I shook my head, trying to get myself together.

At that precise moment, Kerri swept into the shop, her eyes immediately darting between me and Mag with blatant curiosity and then narrowing on Mag. She walked to my table, putting her stuff down and sitting in the chair across from mine, opening her own laptop.

"Zeke didn't mention that one." His voice dropped as he leaned on the counter.

"That's Kerri, my best friend. She'll have one of these too." I tapped my mug with my finger. "And a little tip," I whispered as he leaned in so we would be out of Kerri's hearing range. "She's for the ladies." I looked at him expectantly. A grin spread across his face as his gaze moved over me like an elevator.

"Well, that's all right, all I really care about is who you're for." He winked, sending me shuffling back to my table with a flush creeping from my chest up my neck.

"Who is that?" Kerri drawled with feigned disinterest as I sat across from her at the table. I kept holding my latte in my hands, seeping all the warmth it offered as I sipped on it.

"His name is Mag; he's a new barista, apparently," I said.

"I'm not going to lie to you, Anais. That is the most beautiful and breathtaking man I have ever seen." Her words captured my full attention, because Kerri rarely ever pointed out the attractiveness of any man to me. Looking back over his powerful frame, I noticed how his toned muscles flexed against his t-shirt and in his neck as he worked. His beard caught the afternoon light from the window, lighting up like a flame in the sunlight.

"If you don't get his number before we leave today, I will. And I do not guarantee I won't use it myself." A serious threat coming from her—she hadn't dated a boy since we were in middle school. She had kissed a boy named David behind the bleachers in the sixth grade, and that was the last boy Kerri had been interested in.

"Who knows what his story is. Maybe he's not single. He's probably not; he moved to Vernon and looks like he's from Southern California, or maybe Florida. No one just moves to Vernon for any good reason. It has to be love." She raised an eyebrow at me, not buying my story as I talked myself out of going to speak with him again.

"There's also a good college here, so don't forget that. You always count yourself out too soon, Anais. Seriously, go talk to him. He keeps looking at you. I need to find a new design for my nails anyway. I have an appointment this afternoon. Go. Shoo." She waved me off as she pulled out her phone and began scrolling her nail inspiration pins.

I took a deep breath and allowed my attention to wander back to the coffee counter. He was already watching me, and he didn't look away. He winked at me again, making my heart flutter weirdly in my chest. I had such terrible luck with dating in this town I wasn't sure I could allow myself to think about it. So many awful first dates—did I dare take a chance on this one? I blushed and tucked my hair behind my ear as my eyes dropped back to the latte in my hand.

"Ow!" I yelped.

Kerri had kicked me with her boot under the table. Now, she motioned with her head to go to the counter. "Okay, I'm going." I huffed, taking my latte with me so he wouldn't see my shaking hands.

"So"—I leaned on the counter, watching him clean the espresso machine parts in a small sink—"are you new around here? I've never seen you before."

"Zeke did say you were a regular, so I believe you would know all the new faces around here." He smiled graciously.

"I'd say that sounds accurate." I returned the smile.

"I am new." He paused to grab a bar towel and start drying the machine parts. "I just moved in with my sister, Tora. We're students at the college; I'm here on a hockey scholarship." For a college hockey team, the one in Vernon was fairly good, and everyone in town attended most games. It was unusual for someone to join this late in the season, but there could be any number of reasons for it.

"Where were you before?" I asked, curious how someone so sunkissed could be a hockey player rather than any other sport out under the sun.

"Somewhere a whole lot sunnier than this." He laughed as if he was reading my thoughts. "It's brutal up here, how do you survive?"

"Well, butterscotch lattes help." I smiled, looking down into my cup.

He laughed at that, keeping his eyes firmly locked to mine as he said, "Winter is sponsored by butterscotch lattes and your boyfriend then?"

I blushed a deep crimson as I replied, "I don't have a boyfriend."

"Quit lying to me," he teased.

"I'm not lying! I really don't!" I yelped.

"Well, that's a shame for the men in this town, but it works in my favor, now doesn't it?" I shied from his intense eye contact. He was poised as though ready to leap over the counter at me any moment.

"Oh, does it?" I asked, trying to push down my nerves. My stomach was twirling, my heart racing. I had never been very good at flirting.

"The men here are not interested in the most beautiful girl in town? Yeah, I'd say it gives me better odds to win her affections. At least I hope it does?" He raised an eyebrow at me.

"I suppose it does." I covered my mouth as a girly giggle completely unlike me escaped my lips.

"So, what does a guy have to do to get the most beautiful girl in town to come watch his hockey game on Friday?" He was leaning forward and watching me with such intensity that, if the counter hadn't been there and the coffee shop wasn't full of people, I would think he was about to kiss me.

"It's not too difficult when that's all there is to do on a Friday night around here." Raking my hand through my hair, I dissuaded myself from closing the distance and pressing my lips to his. We just met, and I was never so bold. In fact, I often had trouble identifying flirting and often missed cues that Kerri would point out to me later when she asked why I had spurned a guy's advances. Yet something unexplainable drew me to him, and I wanted to touch him, to be near him, to run my fingers through his beard.

"Well?" Kerri asked as I approached our table once more.

"Well, I got his number," I responded with a faux-casual shrug of my shoulders. "He plays for the college team and I'm seeing him after the game Friday." Kerri nodded her approval, looking over her shoulder at the barista, who was now welcoming and taking the order of another customer. Her eyes swept over his broad shoulders, studying his muscular back as he turned toward a cabinet to refill a bottle of syrup.

"I have never seen a man that attractive before. It's like he showed up overnight. I would remember seeing him before." She squinted at his back.

"He says he's here with his sister." I raised an eyebrow, curious to see if I could pique her interest. Her attention snapped back to me at that information.

"Is this sister going to be at the game?" she asked, leaning her arms on the table.

"I will ask and let you know." I sat down before my laptop once more. I pulled up Kerri's resume and began to work on it as she went back to scrolling her pins for nail inspiration.

I tried to concentrate on my work, but it was impossible with the hypnotic eyes watching me from the bar counter. I couldn't help but look up every few minutes to find him watching me work. I tried to keep the flush from climbing my neck, but the longer he watched me, the harder it was.

Something about him seemed off. It was more than just that he was too beautiful, too much like a model from California, to be slumming it in this frozen tundra . He moved fluidly behind the counter, as if he had already memorized where everything was. Several times he pulled a cup from what seemed like thin air.

Also, Kerri was right—he had just shown up in town out of nowhere. Usually all the new faces in town showed up in the fall when the college was beginning classes, and they left to head home for the summer in late spring. It was not normal for newcomers to appear midyear, especially not for new hockey players to show up midseason. He must be particularly good.

Every word I spoke to Kerri felt like he was listening, like he could hear me from across the room even if I whispered. I felt that every movement I made, every time my chest expanded and deflated with breath, was being watched. It made the back of my neck prickle, but I blew it off as the feeling of butterflies with the beautiful new stranger so near.

CHAPTER 4

On Friday night, the stands were full for the game, bathed in the light of the setting sun. Every winter, the college team set up a full hockey rink on the frozen lake in town, breaking from their indoor facility for the fresh air. We were one of a few colleges where the players could play outside; most didn't have a body of water that froze deep enough to support all the players.

The teams were already out, skating around and warming up before the game. We'd already watched the refs do safety tests on the ice, determining the lake was indeed frozen enough for the game to be held here. Now the players were stretching and doing warm-up drills together.

It wasn't hard to spot Mag in the lineup. He was taller than nearly all the other players, and his tan face stood out even under his helmet. On the back of his blue and silver jersey was the name 'Thorson' and the number nine.

"Mag Thorson." Kerri read his last name from his jersey.

"That's my brother." We whipped around, coming face to face with a woman who looked just like Mag but impossibly more beautiful. Long strawberry-gold hair the same color as his flowed freely down her shoulders, catching the sunlight and making it look as though her face was wreathed in flames. Her turquoise eyes and brilliant smile matched his too, and she looked like the sun had come down to earth in a human form. She was taller than both Kerri and I, just a few inches short of Mag. She wore blue jeans tucked into winter boots similar to mine and a sweatshirt from the college underneath her winter jacket. Her shoulders hunched with a shiver as an icy breeze blew by; obviously she was not used to the cold temperatures of her new home yet.

"I'm Tora." She offered a hand out to me. Kerri stood slack-jawed at my side as she took the woman in. Everything about her was almost ethereal, her hand long and slender, the skin perfectly smooth and bronzed, just the same as Mag's.

"Anais, and this is Kerri." I shook her hand before nudging my friend to say something. Kerri finally shut her mouth but couldn't look away from the beautiful stranger.

"Ah, so you're Anais." She smiled brightly at the name. "My brother was saying he was hopeful you would come by today. He wanted to catch you after the game to say hello." I blushed at the information that Mag had already mentioned me to his sister.

"Well, I'm glad you're not playing so we can say hello now." Kerri was back on her game, her eyes brimming with lust as her gaze swept over the woman. "Sit with us." Kerri offered her arm and Tora linked hers through without so much as a second thought.

My attention shifted back to the ice, looking for Mag. He was over at the bench talking with his teammates, but he looked up as we passed, giving me a subtle wave that I returned. I sat on the other side of Kerri, watching as the players skated out on the ice.

Kerri was admiring Tora's nail job, holding her hand delicately as she made flirty comments about each one and Tora giggled, flirting back just as much. I settled on the cold bench, watching out over the ice as the players skated into position for the coin toss.

Mag was a superstar. I actually googled him on my phone after his sixth unbelievable shot on goal. There was barely any information about him; the only thing I could really find was an article written by the Vernon Journal that said he was a transfer from Arizona State. The coach of Vernon's team expected him to be great, and the team was "lucky to have this caliber of player."

"How long has he been playing?" I asked Tora, incredulous as we all cheered for yet another goal from nearly across the rink. The clock was ticking down, and Vernon College was about to win by a hefty lead.

"He actually picked it up more recently, but he's pretty good, yeah?" Tora's expression was proud but unsurprised at her brother's performance on the ice.

"No shit, he's fantastic!" Kerri loved hockey and was one of Vernon College's most loyal fans. She had been to so many games I don't think she kept count any more. "Exactly what this damn team needed. Hopefully he can whip the rest of those yahoos into shape too."

In the final seconds, Mag took control of the puck once more and made a completely unreal shot. The puck was moving so fast it actually tore straight through the back of the net and bounced off the boards before careening into a cluster of trees not far away. One particular tree shook violently, my indication the puck found a mark. My eyes snapped back to the net, which looked like it was … smoking? I thought I saw embers, and it reminded me of the tree split in the forest from my sleepwalking adventure. It had to be an illusion, a trick of the light on the red poles securing the net or something. I shook my head, trying to destroy the illusion in front of me.

Whistles pierced the air and cheers rose from the crowd at the great win. Mag was skating around in circles with several teammates, cheering and whooping along with the crowd. I blushed, not believing this extrovert was so interested in me.

"C'mon, he'll want to see you!" Tora grabbed my arm and pulled me down the bleachers after her. I tried to keep the blush from my cheeks as I felt many eyes in the crowd watching me approach the star player.

"Good game, brother," Tora greeted Mag as he skated over to us.

"That was pretty good, no?" His expression was one of great pride, and his eyes locked on to me as I approached the fence. "Hello gorgeous." He grinned at me, making my cheeks flush red.

"You were amazing," I said a little breathlessly.

"Well, thank you pretty girl," he said, nearly purring with pride.

Tora and Kerri were making eyes at each other off to the side, having a silent conversation about us as Mag's gaze swept over my face, coming to rest on my lips. Self-consciously, I flicked my tongue out over my bottom lip. His eyes fixed to the movement. I felt my stomach drop, and invisible butterflies swatted my heart with their wings in my chest.

"Do you two want to go grab burgers with us?" Kerri's voice sliced into the tense moment, and we reluctantly broke eye contact to look at her.

"Yeah, I'm starving." Mag winked at me, flashing a grin, before skating off to get his boots and gear from the bench.

"I think he might be starving for something else." Kerri's low voice was dry, and Tora snorted, biting her lip to keep in words.

"He does like you." She shrugged at me, a knowing smirk tugging on her lips. It was too hot in my winter jacket at this point. I was utterly sweaty under all my layers from the blushing and intensity of Mag's stare from moments ago.

"I want to get out of here before Pastor Bryan tries to come over and talk to us." Kerri mumbled to me in a low voice, pulling my focus from how flushed I was. My head began swiveling, wild eyes looking for the man. I hadn't realized he was here, and I didn't want to talk to him either. I spotted the old church crew on the other end of the bleachers, preoccupied by taking selfies and chatting together.

"Yup, let's skedaddle."

Mag returned with his gear, and we made for the parking lot quickly so we wouldn't get caught by the church crowd.

"The last goal you made, where the puck went *through* the back of the net? That was insane," Kerri blabbered. "I've never seen someone hit a puck hard enough for that to happen."

"I saw it hit a tree across the lake after. I bet it's stuck in the trunk." I smiled, sipping my milkshake as Kerri dipped her poutine fries in the gravy swimming at the bottom of the basket.

"Maybe we should go check after dinner," Tora said suggestively, nudging Kerri's arm. Kerri, in turn, nodded eagerly.

Mag chuckled. "Alright. You two go find it, and I'll take Anais home."

We cleared our table, returning our trays to the stack before heading out into the freezing cold evening. The sun was long gone, darkness fully enveloping the outside world. There were no clouds tonight, offering a rare view of the stars in the late winter. I shivered as wind blew into my jacket.

"Better hurry if you want to find that puck—you'll need a torch," Mag told Tora, who nodded. We all knew the two women had no intention of finding the puck and every intention of playing tongue hockey together.

Mag opened the door of his jeep for me, ensuring I didn't slip in the icy parking lot before he went around to the driver's side. It wasn't a long distance from the restaurant to my apartment, but the drive felt like it stretched on for hours in the awkward silence.

"So, how are you liking Vernon so far?" I finally forced words from my throat, feeling sweat starting to bead on the back of my neck. He was so handsome, I kept having to tear myself away from staring at his beautiful jawline.

"It's nice. Cold, but nice." He smiled, reaching over to place a hand on my knee while he drove. I tried to ignore my body's instant reaction to his touch, the desire that coursed through me. I'd never felt that for anyone before, an instant lust. "It's not so much the place as the people." His eyes slid sideways to mine, making my cheeks flush, and I dropped my gaze to his hand on my leg.

When we arrived in the lot for my apartment complex, I tried to open my door but he stopped me. Getting out, he came and opened my door, helping me climb down from the jeep. As soon as I stepped out, he closed the door and leaned in, pinning me against the vehicle.

"Do you know how hard it was to concentrate on playing that game today with you there?" he whispered.

"You're sure it wasn't your adoring fans and the local news being there that made it hard to concentrate?" I asked, feigning innocence.

"I could care less about those things. All I care about is a certain set of hazel eyes that I can't stop thinking about." He brushed my hair back before leaning in to place an intense kiss on my lips. Sparks flew through my body, and I found my fingers tangling in his shirt, tugging him closer.

He chuckled when we broke apart, my eyes fluttering open to look up at him.

"Is it fair to say that I've also been on your mind since we met?" he asked.

I nodded, a dazed look plastered on my face. He chuckled again, trailing his thumb across my cheek. Watching with large doe eyes transfixed on his lips, his perfect smile, I stood breathless as he leaned in to kiss me again.

"Come on. It's too cold to keep you out here," he whispered when we finally broke apart. It was plenty warm between us, but I let him walk me to my door and kiss me one more time. I watched him walk back to the jeep and pull out of the lot with a small wave.

CHAPTER 5

"You work here?" Mag asked, pulling the jeep in the lot of the wolf sanctuary. Okanagan Wolf Sanctuary, known as OWS most often, was a piece of property on the outskirts of Vernon where the owner Gladis and volunteers rehabilitated injured and abandoned wolves as well as rescued wolf-dog hybrids that were surrendered.

I'd started working here in college, finally not needing a parent's permission to volunteer with the animals. Back in high school, I would volunteer to put the wolves' dinners together, clean empty pens, and help Gladis with office work. My mom thought wolves were evil creatures and discouraged me from my love of the beasts any chance it came up. She wouldn't even allow us to have dogs growing up, despite me asking for one every birthday and Christmas.

"I have for a long time," I said, getting out of the jeep into the muddy gravel lot. The snow had turned to rain today and was melting the great white snow banks around town. I could hear yips and barks beyond the walls of the sanctuary. Since I started working with the residents, I came to know the animals as friends. I had photographed each a million times, and they were all over the sanctuary's social media and website.

I couldn't wait to introduce Mag to the wolves I had come to love. Lexus was my favorite, a four-year-old pure white wolf-dog surrendered two years ago after she ate the interior of her owner's luxury car. They had gone into the store to buy something, and in the span of fifteen minutes Lexus tore both front leather seats to shreds. They brought her to the sanctuary that day, and ever since she had lived in the back corner of a large enclosure.

I took in the familiar scents of the wet forest, the gravel crunching as Mag followed me in through the side door of the sanctuary.

"Hi Gladis." I stuck my head in her office, finding her at her computer like always. She smiled at the screen, finishing her current task with a few more clicks before she turned to us, peering over her square glasses.

"Hi kids." She looked over my shoulder at Mag, and her smile faltered for a fraction of a second. "Who is this, Anais?" She motioned for us to walk in the door.

"This is Mag, my— "

"Boyfriend." He cut me off to my surprise. He gave her a winning smile, his whole being still glowing handsomely, warm and bright as in the sun even under the fluorescent lights.

"I didn't know you were seeing anyone, Anais," she said, her voice oddly cool. She was usually so vibrant and warm; she had welcomed me with open arms the day I started volunteering. I had never told her about Dan, but she always insisted on trying to set me up with one of her nephews. I politely declined each time, insisting I was perfectly happy the way things were and would run into the right person at the right time. Now here I was, introducing her to the right person who had found me at the right time.

"He found me. Just like I always said he would." I smiled, leaning into him. His arm wrapped around my shoulder, pulling me close. She nodded slowly as she looked him up and down.

"Are you sure you don't need me over the long weekend?" I asked before we left to feed the animals.

"No, Anais. You deserve a break, and I hope you take some time to relax and do something fun," she said, marking her desktop calendar with my absence as a reminder.

She plastered a fake smile on her face and told us to have a great visit, reminding me to give Jade, an elderly female wolf, extra salmon oil on her food for immune support. Gladis turned back to her computer and waved us off absently as she immersed herself in her work once more.

"She seems nice," Mag said quietly as we rounded the corner, heading for the supply room where the wolves' dinners were ready to be prepped. I could feel his skin sparking with anxiety, and tension filled the air between us.

"She's just protective of me." I playfully pushed his arm. "Be your charming self and she'll warm right up—just like every other lady in town," I teased as I pushed open the door to the storage. I walked to the long table and grabbed a stack of bowls, setting each out on the counter to be filled.

"I don't know..." His tone changed, more nervous with the familiar tension of anxiety starting to show. It made me turn to look at him. "Wolves and dogs, they don't really like me. I'm more of a cat person."

"You've been around wolves before?" My curiosity piqued. They were mostly found in cooler climates, and he definitely was not.

"Yeah, my dad's buddy had one. It was an awful creature—it actually bit his hand off." He looked at me with wide eyes.

"You're joking," I said flatly. He pulled me close as I was about to walk past to get the meat from the refrigerator. I wanted to snort with laughter, knowing no wolf could be that powerful. Sure, they could do some damage, but what he was saying was improbable.

"I wish I was, Ana." His arms wrapped around my back, and I slid mine around his neck. Inwardly, I cringed at the new nickname. I'd always hated when people shortened my name without asking me. I loved my unique name.

"Were you joking when you told Gladis you were my boyfriend?" I whispered, my sight glued to his soft pink lips. Ever since he'd said it, I'd felt the flapping wings of butterflies in my chest.

"I would never joke about how I feel for you," he purred. "Is it okay to call you my girlfriend?" I couldn't help the smile that broke out across my face. It was all I wanted, to be in a perfect relationship with an amazing man like him.

"More than okay," I whispered, bouncing up to my tiptoes to close the distance between us and kiss him deeply. My eyes closed, his beard tickling my face. My heart soared above us, complete elation flowing through my body.

We finished prepping the meals, and I took him to deliver them. I decided to start with Lexus; she was my special wolf friend and she absolutely loved me. I knew she could ease his nerves about the wolves with her goofy, friendly attitude.

She was a hybrid of a grey wolf and a husky, but she looked like a white wolf with vibrant yellow eyes. As a puppy, she had been taught to play fetch, and she still enjoyed it. I'd taught her to bring the ball to the side of the fence. I reached through with a plastic ball-throwing arm and launched it over the top of the fence, deep into her enclosure. It was a game we played for hours when I came to visit.

"Lex!" I whistled, opening the gate and placing the food just inside. I closed it again, waiting for her to come over and begin scarfing down the food the way she always did. Nothing moved in her pen before me. I began scouring the treeline, looking for her bright fur among the trees. It was always harder to spot her in the winter when there was snow on the ground.

I scanned for several minutes before I saw her, and when I did, I flinched back from the fence. She was laying low to the ground about fifteen feet away under a snow-heavy fern, her teeth completely bared. She was staring at Mag. She looked terrifying and completely feral compared to her usual self.

"Lex, it's okay. He's not going to hurt you." I frowned at the hackles raised on her back, every hair on her body standing at nervous attention. Her tongue licked her shining teeth, and she made a low, threatening growling noise. I turned to Mag, who was just as locked on to the animal as she was to him. His eyes blazed with defiance, daring the animal to strike at him. I wasn't sure which unnerved me more, my animal friend reacting this way or him looking like he was ready to attack the wolf right back.

"Okay, okay everybody." I placed a hand on his chest, pushing him a step back. He backed away but didn't break his eye contact with the animal. Neither one was winning at the moment.

"I told you they don't like me." He finally shrugged with a forced, sorrowful smile. "I wish they did but they really don't."

"Well, then I don't know if I can like you." I shrugged back.

"You don't mean that." He reached for me but I danced beyond his reach with a playful smile. I was trying to play off how shaken I was that Lex had reacted that way to my new man. I trusted animals more than people—they were better judges—and for Lex to react the way she did was disturbing to say the least. I tried to shake the feeling, the elation rushing back to me as I remembered Mag in Gladis' office calling himself my boyfriend.

"I do. Animals are the best judges of character that there are."
I allowed him to catch my hand and tug me close.

"I believe you might be the best judge of character there is.
Your friends adore you, and this town is like a movie where
you are the main character." I blushed, the heat dashing my
cheeks and intensifying as he gazed at me. He knew the effect
he had on me.

"That's kind of what it's felt like to me too since meeting
you," I breathed. "The star hockey player I met at my favorite
coffee shop. It all feels a little too perfect." I smiled as he leaned
in to kiss me softly, his lips sending small electric bolts through
my body.

A snarl ripped through the air, and I stumbled, falling backwards onto the ground as Lexus slammed into the chain gate.
She was snarling and snapping her teeth at Mag, her eyes completely feral. She looked rabid, with spit flying in all directions
from her wild jaws. I didn't recognize the animal before me
at all. She gnashed her teeth against the bars of her enclosure,
trying to free herself to get at Mag.

"Are you okay?" Mag helped me from the ground as Lexus
kept attacking the door. My legs were shaking from the shock
and surprise of Lex's attack, her dangerous teeth burned into
my mind. I wiped dirt and gravel from my hands, wincing at
the bite of the rocks on my palms where I'd fallen.

"I'm fine. I seriously don't know what is wrong with her.
I'm so sorry." I stood, looking puzzled at the animal I had
come to love so much. It didn't make sense. She liked the
men who volunteered here. I had never seen her, or any of
the wolves here at the sanctuary, act so viciously toward any
person, volunteer or guest. Lex had stopped jumping on the

chainlink and was now barking and snarling at Mag, all her fur standing on end. Her hackles were still raised and her tail was completely bushy, trying to make herself look larger than she was as an intimidation tactic.

"You don't need to apologize." He shook his head. "Let's get you out of here. I'm upsetting her and I don't want you to accidentally get hurt."

I was beginning to question myself as I listened to Lex snarl as he spoke, remembering Gladis' hesitation when I'd introduced her to Mag. She was a great judge of character too. I couldn't understand what about him made all of them uneasy.

"C'mon," he insisted. I let Mag lead me away. We turned down the trail between Lexus' pen and another wolf's. Lex was chasing us along her pen, barking and baring her teeth at us the whole length. I jumped as, on the other side, Romeo—an older male wolf—slammed into the metal chain link, snapping his jaws and howling at us.

"What the actual fuck?" I said, pausing to observe the animals' behavior. I was more curious at their reaction than afraid now. Romeo was just as agitated as Lex, and the only difference today was Mag's presence. The male wolf threw himself against the fence, baring his fangs toward Mag just as Lex was doing on the other side.

"What is with you guys today?" I asked the wolf, who did not react whatsoever to me, keeping its full attention on Mag. Mag stood, sizing up the wolf with his arms folded across his chest protectively.

"Anais, let's go," he insisted.

I started walking once again toward the double doors. I had to get Mag inside, away from the animals, so they could calm down. I couldn't fathom what about him was setting them off, but something about it wasn't right. I would finish serving the wolves' meals myself. Hopefully they would not be so upset if it was just me.

"I've never seen them acting like that before," I said, trying to keep my hands from trembling as I picked up the other food dishes. "I'm going to finish passing out their dinners and then we'll go. Why don't you wait here."

"Can't Gladis feed them?" he asked, looking concerned. "I don't want them to hurt you."

"If you stay in here, I'm sure they'll be their normal selves. I've fed them multiple days a week for years," I told him.

"They're wild animals, Anais. I'm worried about you." He shook his head.

"Just wait here. I'll go feed them and be back before you know it." I picked up several meals and set out as he sighed in defeat, his arms folded across his chest.

I walked to Romeo's pen first, seeing his dark grey fur coming through the trees as he eyed the bowl in my hand. He did not lunge, did not snap his jaws, simply flicked his tail back and forth. I set down the bowl and pushed it into his enclosure, and he waited for me to retreat before approaching. His normal behavior, what I saw most days. So it really was Mag's presence.

Lexus, in her pen next door, had eaten the whole bowl of food and was now rolling around in the dirt playfully, as if she had not a care in the world. The rest of the pack was calm and mellow as I fed them and checked on each one. Each animal seemed glad to see me, and I felt as though they were checking on me just as much as I was checking on them.

"Anais, are you alright?" Gladis hobbled from her office, leaning heavily on a cane behind me as I finished with the last animal. She was an older lady and had a bad knee from an injury when she was younger. She loved the sanctuary with all her heart, the animals and the people. "I saw what happened on the camera with Lexus. It was so strange."

"It was. I've never seen her like that before. I'm shaken, but I'll be okay. Did you see Romeo too?"

She nodded. "All of them started going crazy in all the pens. They were running back and forth. I was worried about you, dear." She squeezed my arm. "I know you're tough, but that was a shocker."

"Gladis." I lowered my voice, leaning in so she could hear me. "About Mag, I—"

"Listen to me. You know I love you, and I'm very protective of you, but you need to take me seriously right now. Something is very wrong with him. I'm sorry to have to tell you this. The pack didn't trust him and I got a bad feeling in my office. Something is deeply wrong, and the wolves can sense it. I think you need to get away from him. You deserve an amazing love story, Anais, but this is not the one."

We stared at each other as I took in what she said. Gladis usually didn't give me advice unless I asked for it specifically. She was the only adult that knew anything about my life growing up here, and I often considered her a mother figure. This warning was serious, and it was out of love and concern.

Disturbed, I could only nod. Sympathy brimmed in her expression before she turned and shuffled back inside to her office. I was left standing and looking at the wolves. I wondered if Gladis and the wolves sensed something about Mag that I didn't, if he was actually dangerous.

It was so strange. Of course wild animals were unpredictable, but these animals had lived here for years, and generally we could predict their behavioral patterns well. Yet the only one who predicted that behavior today was Mag.

I took a last lap through the enclosures, checking on all the animals one more time before heading back to the storage room where Mag was still waiting. He was texting as I came in and looked slightly distressed at his phone.

"Everything ok?" I asked him.

"Yeah." He looked up, running his hand through his hair as he took a deep breath and let go of whatever was stressing him.

"I'll clean up and we'll get out of here, okay?" I tried to shoot him a flirty wink.

He nodded, a tight lipped smile on his face. "Sounds great."

I loaded the dishwasher with the dog bowls and cleaned up around the feeding station. "So, is it that way with all dogs? How did you know that's what would happen?"

"Yes, it's all dogs. It's like they're hardwired to hate both Tora and I. That's how they usually react, so I just try to avoid them if I can. I was just hoping it might be different if you were there; they seem to like you quite a lot. Felt like they were trying to protect you or something." His tone was probing, and I wondered what reaction he was trying to get from me. This whole day was strange.

Maybe I introduced him to the sanctuary too soon. Gladis' warning ran through my head for the third time since I'd talked to her. This sanctuary was my sanctuary, my refuge for years from family and social pressures. And now my sanctuary, my refuge, my haven, was rejecting my new boyfriend loudly. I wasn't sure what to make of it.

CHAPTER 6

P *lease don't notice me. Please don't see me.* I silently begged the universe for a break. As soon as I entered the grocery store, I spotted the table where Pastor Bryan was standing with several of my old friends from the church. It was late winter, so the church was running their recruitment booth inside rather than out in the fierce weather. I attempted to slink past them unnoticed. If my mother really had talked to Pastor Bryan recently, then surely he would stop me if he saw me passing.

"Anais!" I cringed at his overly-friendly voice calling for me. *Fuck.*

I was completely and fully spotted. I plastered on my church smile that took years of practice to perfect before turning to face him. "Pastor Bryan, I didn't see you there!"

"How have you been?" He came in for an uninvited hug and my spine snapped straight as he wrapped his arms around me, squeezing me to his chest. I tried not to cringe at the smell of coffee breath and Irish Spring. He was mashing his chest against mine, something he'd done too many times over the years. After an unreasonably long moment, I tried to pull away and he reluctantly let me go. "I talked to your mother this week. She said you might be interested in a bible study on Wednesdays?"

My face was already hurting from the fake-friendly smile and keeping the animosity from my expression. I folded my arms over my chest as his eyes grazed me from the neck down. At his words, the color drained from my face and a high-pitched laugh came squealing from my throat.

"I'm really busy these days; I'm not sure I have time for anything like that." I was sweating with nerves, beads of it forming on the back of my neck.

"That's too bad. We really miss you! I know our Heavenly Father misses seeing you around church too." He nudged me with an elbow, reminding me how uncomfortably close he was still standing. Again his eyes traveled down, trying to get a peek past my arms. His body heat was uncomfortable, and when he spoke I felt his breath on my face. "You know, we're thinking about adding a service on Fridays after work. Do you think you could make that?"

I would rather shred my own face off with a cheese grater than spend another bible study with Pastor Bryan ever again. Over his shoulder, I could see the girls I used to be friends with huddled close as they whispered, casting side-long glances and snarky giggles in our direction. I missed nothing about this world, and while my life was more lonely and less busy now, I found peace working at the wolf sanctuary and spending time with Kerri.

Kerri had grown up in this same church and was a fellow victim of Pastor Bryan's predatory behavior. She stopped attending long before I did. Every Sunday morning, she snuck out one of the back doors to smoke cigarettes behind the warehouse where church was held. She tried to convince me in sophomore year to join her, but I'd known my mother was keeping a close eye on me. I was the goody-two-shoes who kept going to church events throughout high school until Pastor Bryan had made clear his feelings about the LGBTQ community in my senior year. I never went back after that, and Kerri and I spent our first Sunday together not in church or at work, but drinking ourselves under the table at a Mexican restaurant with fake IDs that Kerri got for us.

"So, Anais? Friday services, we'll see you there?" he asked.

I snapped back to the present and blinked a couple times.

"No, Pastor Bryan. I'm sorry, I—" I stammered.

"She's got a date." My cheeks rushed hot as Mag put an arm around my shoulder. I looked around, bewildered, wondering where he'd come from. It seemed like he had materialized at the opportune moment.

I wasn't sure if I was glad he was here or not. I knew Pastor Bryan would call my mother and report that I turned down Friday service. He would also tell her that a man said I had a date, and that's why I couldn't make it. Both of my parents took celibacy until marriage very seriously. My dad had taken me to every Dad & Daughter dance the church threw to promote chastity. Not that it worked—I certainly wasn't a virgin, but they didn't know that. They would not take kindly to finding out I was dating a man they had no idea about, much less that he was keeping me from church.

The Pastor's eyes were wide as he took in Mag, sweeping over his broad shoulders, muscular neck, and perfectly bronzed skin with faint freckles spattering his nose and cheeks.

"Ah." Pastor Bryan pursed his lips. He looked annoyed, irritated that Mag had interrupted the pressure he was putting on me. "I don't suppose you'd want to join us for Friday service yourself?"

"I don't suppose I would," Mag said with such coolness that all I could do was stare at him in awe. "I believe we had plans to make pizza that night, didn't we?" I just nodded, wordless as I stared at my savior.

"Sorry, we'll have to catch you another time." Mag shouldered his way between me and Pastor Bryan, who stood just as slack-jawed as I was. He nodded, looking dumb as he finally shut his mouth and stepped back for us to be on our way. Mag guided me deeper into the store before looking down at me and removing his heavy arm from its steering position on my shoulders.

"Are you okay? That dude was creeping on you so hard." He threw a glare back toward where Pastor Bryan had returned to the table and was shuffling awkwardly through papers as the younger women giggled and gossiped. They were looking at Mag with gaping mouths and sneers that did little to mask their intrigue in the handsome man.

"Yeah, he's…" I didn't even know where to begin. I was rubbing my eyebrows with my fingers, wishing I could just teleport home before my phone began ringing.

"Hey." He gently tilted my head to look up into his eyes. "It's okay. I won't let him get you."

My smile was weak as I silently wished someone had been there to say that to me years ago. I would take it now. I was thrilled to have it now. Suddenly, my doubts from visiting the sanctuary melted to the back of my mind.

"Let's do your shopping and I'll walk you out so he can't stop you again." I nodded, my heart hammering as I pulled out my phone with shaking fingers to view my shopping list. No call from Mom yet. I took a deep breath and tried to settle myself. I may be shaken after any interaction with the Pastor, but I needed to remember who I was. I didn't go to church or bible study anymore. I didn't believe in God anymore.

My phone began screaming the Imperial Death March the moment my tires hit the apartment parking lot. I grit my teeth, pulling into my space and debating not answering. If I didn't, she would just keep calling and leaving me voicemails of her disappointment. She'd also call Kerri and start pestering her for information. She might even blame Kerri; she was never a fan of Kerri's 'sinful lifestyle,' but she and Kerri's mom were very close.

I heaved a sigh as I looked at my mother's caller ID before sliding open my phone.

"Anais, Pastor Bryan just called me." Her tone was clipped.

"And what did he tell you, Mom?" I couldn't keep the exasperation from my voice. I was in for a fight and we both knew it.

"He said he invited you to several events, and you said no to all of them. And then he said there was a young man in the store who said he was taking you out for a date this Friday."

I sat there regaining control of myself before I responded. "Yes, I have a date." I hissed into the phone.

"I hope you're being appropriate with this gentleman? Where did you meet him?" I knew she'd always planned for me to marry one of the boys from church. It was a great disappointment for her that I was still single at twenty-six years old, working at a wolf sanctuary and barely making enough to cover rent and ramen noodles. Unmarried, no children, and getting into all sorts of bad influences without her around to 'guide' me to the Lord.

"He's a barista at the coffee shop, and he plays hockey for Vernon College," I told her.

"Not that dark coffee shop where all the employees wear black and that one girl has the tattoo of the demon goat? Anais!" she screamed through the phone. I pulled it back from the side of my head to keep her from rupturing my eardrums. I'd always admired the employee's adorable Baphomet tattoo on her shoulder. Most of the time she kept it covered, but the one day my mother had come to visit and we went to the shop, it was hot—the middle of summer—and the woman was wearing a tank top. That was three years ago, and obviously my mother had not forgotten.

"Yeah Mom, I go to that coffee shop all the time." I rolled my eyes.

"For goodness sake, Anais. I don't suppose this is a man of God then?" she snipped.

"I don't know, Mom. We haven't talked about it yet." Her annoyed snort on the other end of the phone brought a smirk to my face.

"Well you should, Anais. It's very important to find a man who will put God first in his life. That's how you'll know he's on the right path—if he's right with God first and foremost."

"Okay Mom, good talk." I unbuckled my seatbelt so I could hang up and get the groceries inside.

"Anais, please tell me you're still being faithful in your own way. Even if you aren't going to church physically, you should still have a relationship with God. Do you pray every day? Are you still wearing your ring?" She was talking about my promise ring, the one I had sworn to my father to wear until he was giving me away at my wedding.

The ring symbolized my virginity and sexual purity in the name of Jesus Christ. Kerri and I had made a night of throwing both of ours into the Okanagan Lake several summers ago. Right after I'd had sex for the first time with my college boyfriend, we'd set a bonfire on the beach and got completely wasted on strawberry-lemonade-flavored vodka. The neighbors checked on us because of the loud obscenities Kerri screamed when she launched her ring high and far over the water.

"No Mom, I'm not wearing it anymore." The dead silence on the other end of the line was uncomfortable enough to spur me on. "I'm twenty-six years old, Mom. I am an adult person, and I've had sex." Her gasp made me want to both cringe and give a triumphant whoop.

"Anais! You promised your father and I—"

"Well, I also promised Jesus my heart and walked that back too, Mom! Things change." I was coming close to shouting.

"Are you saying you're not Christian anymore?" She was screeching now.

"Nope, I'm not. I'm not a Christian. I don't believe in God. What do you have to say about that, Mom?" Tears were sprung to my eyes, and I hastily wiped them away as they dribbled down my cheeks in the silence that followed.

"You were baptized as an infant, Anais. You will always be baptized, no matter how far you stray from him. You'll never be able to undo that. Your soul will always belong to God." Now her voice carried obvious triumph, and my tears burned as they became more angry. A wet sniffle sounded from my nose, and I realized I was physically shaking with rage.

"Hm. I guess I haven't sinned hard enough then. Well, Friday should take care of that. Instead of going to church, guess what I'm doing? I'm having that man over to make pizza at my apartment. And you know what? I'm gonna fuck him, Mom, and Kerri's going to fuck his sister. That should be enough debauchery to get me out of God's good graces." I yanked the phone away from my ear as she erupted into unintelligible screaming that cut off as I pressed the button to end the call.

"Goddammit!" I screamed, slapping my steering wheel hard enough for the horn to give a short beep. A passing runner jumped on the sidewalk ahead of me. I gave an apologetic wave before letting my head fall against the top of the wheel.

It had finally happened. I'd snapped on my mom. I'd revealed pieces of what my life was like now that they were out of it. I supposed I should rent an Airbnb somewhere for a few days, since my mother was likely to fly all the way up here just to get me back in line. Slowly raising the phone again, I pressed ignore on a call from my dad and pulled up my texts with Kerri.

Me: Big blow up with my mom. Don't answer her calls. Bring butterscotch ice cream.

Kerri: Fuck. OMW!

Sloppily wiping my tears and snot on my sweatshirt sleeve, I slid out of the front seat of my car into the icy air. It burned my nose, the tracks of my tears freezing painfully on my cheeks. The sun was starting to set over the bare trees as I hauled my groceries inside.

"You actually said that?" Kerri was trying to hide her proud grin behind her hand as I finished relaying the story.

"Yeah… My dad has been calling me all evening, and she's even trying to get my sister to text me about it." My younger sister had texted soon after, asking if I would call Dad so they would stop arguing. I knew my mother was behind it, trying to manipulate both her and I.

"Don't fall for the guilt trip, even if they use Kaylee." Kerri stabbed at her slice of cheesecake with a fork, the grin descending into a scowl within fractions of a second. "Everything you said is totally fair and justified as an adult in her twenties. I just wish fucking Bryan had been there to hear it." I imagined the way she was mangling the cheesecake with the fork was what she wanted to do to Pastor Bryan's junk. We hadn't talked about what happened with him for a very long time, more than ten years now. We both knew we could talk about it if we wanted to, and we trusted one another enough to talk about it still, but we both preferred to leave it undiscussed.

"So, are you going to fuck Mag on Friday?" she asked, curiosity brimming in her tone.

"Yup. If not for me, then purely out of spite towards my mother. But mostly for me," I said.

She smiled, sympathy, pain, and love all shining in her eyes as she reached out and took my hand.

"Sisters forever," she said. It was what we always said when things were hard for either us, ever since we were young girls growing up across town. A reminder that we were a chosen family and loved each other unconditionally. We hadn't had to say it in over two years, but here we were.

"Sisters forever."

CHAPTER 7

"Come on in!" Kerri welcomed Tora and Mag into my apartment. They both looked tall in the room, and I admired Mag's height as he locked eyes with me. Electric pulses through my whole body as eye contact stirred the butterflies in my chest, and my heart beat a bit faster.

We had spent the day cleaning and getting ready for them to come over. The time included Kerri dressing me, because in her words, she did not trust me not to wear my yoga pants and stupid, oversized t-shirts with wolves on them. So I wore my favorite pair of jeans and a cute pale-blue top embroidered with pink flowers that reminded me of the women's dresses in our period drama.

"Hey there, love." Mag leaned in, surprising me by pressing a kiss to my cheek as he placed a bottle of wine in my hands. A shiver ran down my spine as his soft beard brushed my face. I wrapped an arm around his neck and hugged him before he leaned away. He was so tall and broad-shouldered, I felt small in his arms as he wrapped them around me.

"Thank you so much." I inspected the bottle of wine when we broke apart. It was a nice riesling from a vineyard I'd never heard of. "You didn't have to." I smiled up at him and he reached out, tucking my hair behind my ear, pausing to let his fingers brush my chin as he studied my lips.

"I wanted to. You have the pizza, so I'll bring the booze." I took his hand, and he followed me to the kitchen, where Kerri and Tora were already getting out glasses and digging in my drawers for a bottle opener. I glanced at Tora, dressed tonight in a casual outfit with a tank top.

I tried to identify what about them might set the wolves on edge. Skepticism began creeping into my thoughts, but I pushed it away as the conversation with my mother rushed to the forefront of my mind. I was going to sleep with him. Tonight. I reminded myself not to point out any more flaws with Mag for the rest of the night.

"Okay, show me how to do this thing." Mag grinned, flouring his hands at the counter where I dumped out the pizza dough. Mirroring his grin, I handed him a piece of the dough and started showing him how to shape it, gently stretching and pressing it out with our fingers.

"That's pretty good!" I checked for punctures, gently folding the dough over any I found to keep the sauce from leaking out the bottom.

"I am obviously learning from a professional here." Mag took a deep drink from his glass of wine, leaning against the counter as he observed me. His eyes trailed down over my backside when I leaned forward. "You said you have been to Italy before, right?" He glanced over my shoulder at a photograph of Kerri and I holding up pizzas in a restaurant in Naples. I nodded, remembering the tour we'd taken after graduating high school. I wiped my flour-covered hands on my apron before grabbing the container of homemade sauce and my glass of wine.

"I absolutely loved every single pizza I ate there. Salud." Our glasses clinked together, and I looked at our new friends bringing fun and life to my kitchen on a Friday evening when I would otherwise be binging Netflix and ignoring texts from Kerri about how lame I was for not going out drinking with her.

"Oh my gods, I have always wanted to go there!" Tora squealed. "I would just die to see the Colosseum, and I bet the pasta is just..." She imitated a chef blowing a kiss. Kerri was watching her with a lazy smile, obviously infatuated.

The four of us laughed, drank, and ate all evening long. Mag was all over me, flour covering both our arms and streaking our faces and clothes. We left handprints of flour on each other, barely able to keep our hands to ourselves long enough to make all the pizzas. By the end of the night, he had one of my handprints on his chest and I had one of his on the ass cheek of my jeans.

"Okay, you two are a mess," Kerri announced, waving her finger at Mag and I. "We are going to go back to my place for the night." Tora nodded and handed car keys over to Mag.

Color rose to my cheeks as I looked at Mag, who was grinning excitedly. It had been a long time since I was intimate with someone new, but the way he calmed my nerves gave way to excitement at the thought of him staying. Plus, I had been looking forward to it all week after the fight with my mother. Somehow, having him stay over was just more fuel for the fire, and I was ready with matches. My heart flapped its invisible wings, sending waves of elation through me.

When the door shut, I looked at Mag and his hungry expression had returned, scanning my body from head to toe. Without a word, he crossed to me and slammed his lips to mine. I whined in anticipation. His tongue pressed its way into my mouth, claiming it as his. His hands slid down my waist and around my backside, stopping below both cheeks of my rear. In one swift movement, he lifted me so I was entirely off the ground.

"Oh!" I gasped against his lips, looking into the blue pools of his eyes.

"Is this okay?" he whispered, and I nodded, biting my lip.

"More than okay," I breathed. The next second, his lips were back on mine. My legs wrapped around his waist, and I felt how hard he was as he pressed his body flush against mine.

He carried me back to my bedroom, softly lit by my fairy lights. Laying me down on the bed, he climbed between my legs.

"You"—he paused to kiss down my neck toward the edge of my shirt—"are the sexiest pizza chef I have ever seen." His hands fumbled with the edge of my shirt and I pulled it over my head, moaning as he instantly brought his lips against my bra line. He kissed down my chest, down my stomach, to where my jeans were fastened.

"I'll do that. Get your shirt." I was panting, desperate for him. If I was honest, I had been desperate for him since he rescued me from Pastor Bryan at the grocery store. Him saving me from that situation was the hottest thing any man had ever done. When I thought back to him saying 'I don't suppose I would,' the back of my neck prickled with an intense heat.

Maybe someday I'd be brave enough to say something like that to the Pastor.

Mag was pulling his shirt over his head, revealing the most perfect six-pack of abs I'd ever seen. Magic Mike could never. They were defined, hard-packed, and perfectly bronzed, just like his face. In awe of his physique, I ran my fingers over his skin. He felt oddly warm, like he maybe had a fever.

"Are you feeling okay?" I asked. The pandemic had not been long ago, and I was still wary of illness being passed around, especially during the winter months.

"I feel fantastic," he murmured, grabbing my hand and guiding it over his body. I had never touched someone so muscular before; it was slightly intimidating seeing how powerful his body was. "Let me make you feel fantastic too," he purred before his fingers slid between my legs.

"I never got to thank you for saving me at the grocery store the other day," I said.

I was sitting up in bed while he looked through my bookshelf, tipping his head to read the spines. He'd occasionally pull them out and flip through them, chuckling or snorting as if he was actually reading the full stories that quickly.

He smiled over at me. "No problem. It wasn't hard to save a beautiful damsel." My cheeks flushed. "Do you know that man?"

"He was my Pastor growing up." I groaned, flopping back on the bed and throwing an arm over my eyes. "I was in an evangelical church with my family, who are very Christian. I actually had a huge fight with my mom when I got home from the store, because he called her and told her about you."

His eyebrows raised in interest. "Is that so?"

"Yeah. She thought I was still a virgin." I laughed, reflecting on her shocked silence that day.

"Ah, well, that you are not." He sat on the edge of the bed, leaning back as he looked at me. I blushed as his smirk brought back memories from just hours ago.

"No. I told her I'm not. I also told her I don't believe in God anymore." I sighed, not sure why I was telling him all of this. I expected him to run screaming any moment when he realized exactly how damaged I was.

"You don't believe anymore?" Mag stroked my hair, frowning ever so slightly, but a smile was not far from his face.

"Well, no. I'm sorry I'm talking about this, if it offends you."

"It doesn't offend me." Now the smirk was back, and he was watching me carefully as I sat up crisscross, the sheet pulled around me. "I think it's interesting to talk to people about their gods."

Curiosity sparked in my chest at his tone. "Why is that?"

"Do you believe in other gods?" he asked. His deliberate words made me lean forward as I listened.

"I… No… I guess. No." His smirk did not falter, and his eyes flicked back to the bookshelves.

"Do you believe in all those books?"

I couldn't contain my snorting laugh. "Those are all fantasy stories. Vampires and Fae. I don't really believe there are witches and wizards, no." One eyebrow rose as if he didn't believe me. Or knew more than me. "What is that look about?" I was starting to get defensive, worried he was judging me for the books and for believing in any fairy tales during the course of my life.

"Nothing." He shrugged casually.

"Do you believe in other gods?" I pulled my knees to my chest, watching him cautiously, curious about his smirk but not enough to actually ask him about it.

"I suppose I do." His smirk cracked into a grin as he admired his own hand, as if it was proof enough for him that God existed.

"Multiple?"

He nodded and looked me in the eyes, biting at his lip.

"It's okay, you don't have to tell me about it. I don't believe in any of it."

He regarded me for a moment. "Just because you don't believe in it doesn't make it untrue."

My eyes rounded as I questioned who I'd let into my bed. "Well, what is a god to a nonbeliever?" I squinted at him.

"Still a god." His confidence in those words shook me to my core.

"But if no one believes in them—"

"They're still a god." He shrugged.

We stared at each other as I contemplated kicking him out or asking him what the actual fuck he was talking about.

"Okay, I'll bite. What are you talking about?"

He took a deep breath and held his hand out, palm flat and facing the sky. As I watched with skepticism, a shimmering—like heat waves—radiated from his skin. I watched as a blood red rose appeared in the middle of the shimmering, the flower resting on his palm. Gobsmacked, I stared at the rose. He made a motion to offer it to me and I shrunk away.

"What the fuck?" I yelped as I leapt from the bed, grabbing my sweater from a chair and pulling it over my body. If I was going to kick out this gorgeous magician, I wanted to be fully clothed in front of any prying eyes who live for the complex drama.

"Anais." He grabbed my wrist with his other hand, and I tried to remember the self-defense training class that Kerri made me take in high school. "Please just listen. I can explain." His tone was calm, as if he had expected this reaction from me. He still held the red rose in his hand.

Having an out-of-body experience, I sat slowly on the bed, my eyes locked on him. He took my wrist and flipped my hand, placing the rose in my palm. It felt real, like a living flower rather than a fake, and I could feel the velvety petals on my skin. Small veins ran through each petal, telling me the flower was real and living. Not to mention grown somewhere far away from the Canadian winter where nothing bloomed.

"I'm an Aesir god. Do you know what that is?"

I wasn't even sure he could register the shake of my head, it was so slight as I stared at him with dinner-plate sized eyes.

"It means I am from the Norse realms. I'm from a place across the galaxy called Asgard. My father's name is Thor. Have you ever heard of him before?"

"Like the movies? Like … Chris Hemsworth is your dad?" This man was delusional—that was the only explanation. I didn't have an explanation for the rose I'd watched appear out of thin air—the only thing I could think was I was delusional as well.

"Not exactly." He patiently stroked a finger over the rose still sitting in my hand. He was perfectly calm, not acting strange in any capacity as I questioned him.

"You mean to tell me you are actually an alien? From another planet."

"Not an alien, a god. From Asgard, which is a different realm."

I wasn't sure how to ask him to further prove it, not sure if I would believe anything more he might claim as proof. I couldn't explain what I'd seen, but I was sure it was some kind of magic trick I just wasn't understanding.

"Where did this come from?" I asked slowly, brushing my thumbs over the rose's petals once more.

"From my balcony at Asgard Palace."

A snorting laugh of air pushed through my nose. "A palace?" My voice was disbelieving.

"Wanna see it?"

My heart thudded loudly, blood rushing in my ears. I considered it for a moment.

"Let me guess—you've got a white van outside with some candy in it, and we'll go right there?"

He smirked, holding his palm flat out in front of me once more. The shimmering heat waves stretched several inches from his skin before a Snickers bar appeared, sitting in the center of his palm just as the flower had.

"I don't need a van for candy. And I don't need one to get to Asgard."

I snatched the candy bar from his hand, inspecting it. The wrapper was crisp, just like it was plucked straight off the grocery store shelf.

"Do you believe me?" His eyes were intent as they looked into mine.

"Hell no!" I unwrapped the candy bar and shoved a good sized bite in my mouth before getting up once again to find my phone. Kerri needed to know about this insanity.

"What would you need as proof to believe me?" he asked, and I turned as my brows furrowed together.

"Probably a signed note from a psychiatrist that you're not certifiably insane. I don't know how this little magic trick here works"—I motioned to his hands—"but I'm not falling for it."

He was full on grinning like a crazy person now, and I wondered for the first time if I should be scared of this man. He already proved his physical strength when we'd been together. My stomach did a flip at the memory, and my core pulsed in response. If he really wanted to hurt me, he'd had plenty of opportunities to do it by now.

"What if Tora told you the same thing? What if we both showed you Asgard? Just for a few days over the long weekend?" I opened my mouth to protest, to say I had to work, but Gladis had given me the long weekend off already and Mag knew that. "We could leave this morning and be back by Monday night."

"You're going to take me where?" I asked.

"To the realm of Asgard," he repeated.

"No," I said with a shake of my head. "No way, I just... How?"

"Using a mode of transportation between realms called a seam," he replied, his voice still even and unwavering.

I let out a long breath, considering him. He remained calm, stoic, waiting patiently for me to agree or kick him out of my apartment.

"Fine, take me. Do you have a spaceship or something? Maybe a rocket that needs to be launched?" I said sarcastically.

He rolled his eyes but couldn't keep the smile from his face, absolutely thrilled I'd said yes. "I told you, we'll take a seam with Tora."

"Won't the other gods care that a human is in their midst?" I raised an eyebrow.

"No; we haven't had humans in Asgard for a long time, but no one will care. They'll be interested in you and Midgard more than anything."

"Midgard?" I frowned at the strange but familiar word.

"It means Earth, the realm of the humans," he replied.

"How many realms are there?" I asked.

"Of Norse descent, there are nine." My eyes rounded once more. Nine realms?

"Call Kerri to let her know you're coming with me. I don't want her hunting me down when you're not here. Then pack some stuff and we'll swing by to pick up Tora before we rip a seam to Asgard."

I glanced around the room, not sure at all what I should pack for an intergalactic trip. Or a kidnapping. Whatever this was about to be.

CHAPTER 8

"Really? The whole weekend?" Kerri's whining came through the speaker of my phone as I hastily shoved random clothes into a bag for the trip.

"That's what he said." I shrugged even though she couldn't see me.

"Well dammit, what am I supposed to do? Tora didn't invite me." She huffed. "I wonder if I wasn't good enough or something. Can you ask her and find out when you're there?"

"Yes, I will corner your one-night stand and ask her to declare her feelings for you." I wished I could be there to see the eye roll I knew Kerri was giving me. At some point, she would permanently damage her sight with how often I made her do that.

"And he said you can't take your phone?" Her voice became skeptical and reminded me of Gladis' warning the other day at the sanctuary, the undercurrent of her tone telling me she was sensing danger. But she wasn't about to tell me not to go.

"I can bring it, but we're not going to have service." I tossed an extra shirt in my bag after it passed the sniff test.

"Where are you going again? Can you at least send me your location so I can keep an eye on you?" She sounded more worried by the moment.

"I'm really not even sure, somewhere just north. Mag's family's house or something. I'll send you a pin." Mag told me we'd be traveling to Asgard from a house in a town about an hour north of us. If I dropped the pin of my location to Kerri, it would show me there until we came back on Monday evening. I would just leave my phone there for the weekend—she'd buy it until I came back. When I lied to Kerri, I had to be vague. She could smell my lies miles away. I had not told her where we were going, figuring Mag's supposed 'God-hood' wasn't something to go shouting around town about. Kerri would think I was the crazy one for believing in it on any level.

"Okay, well, call me if you need anything." Her tone turned even more serious. "And don't be dumb."

"It hurts me that you think I'm so stupid," I pouted.

"If it makes you feel better, I'm dumb too." She paused and I heard her take a deep breath on the other end of the line. "Janine called..."

"And?" I asked.

"And she wants me to come over tonight. I dunno Anais, I want to go… Is that awful of me?"

I took a deep breath. It had been hard for Kerri to get over Janine, and I knew she was still in love with her.

"Whatever you do, Ker, I love you. I support you, and I will always be on your side." She took a deep breath on her end too, sounding a bit shaky. "Do you want me to stay?"

"No, absolutely not. You go, have fun with Mag, and I'll talk to you when you get back. Just don't forget to drop me the location pin when you can."

"I will. I love you. Talk in a couple days," I promised her.

"Love you too." She sighed before hanging up.

So Kerri and Janine were getting back together this weekend, and I was going to visit another 'realm' supposedly. Intergalactic travel, to the realms of Norse mythology. Which I knew nothing about.

I pulled out my phone, doing a search for Asgard and the Aesir, clicking on the first basic article that came up. It was entirely about gods with super powers, the sons of Odin, giants and battles, and Valhalla—the equivalent of heaven for those believers who died in battle.

There wasn't any possible way this was real. I read a simple description but didn't have time to go in depth on any topic or story, of which there were hundreds. I spotted a link to a god named Magni and followed it, assuming it was supposedly Mag. The website displayed a short description of Magni and his brother, stating he was the son of Thor and his name translated to "mighty." If he was making all of this up, at least he'd picked a god who appeared to be on the good side to impersonate.

As I scrolled the page, an image caught my eye: a painting of a giant black wolf, a massive serpent, and what looked like a female grim reaper attacking the city of Asgard. In the background, smoke filled the air. Beautiful golden buildings were in flames, and the water the snake was emerging from threatened the city from the other side. Seeing the wolf reminded me of the story Mag told me at the sanctuary, the one where a wolf bit his friend's hand off. The wolf in the painting was certainly large enough to do so. Something about its wild yellow eyes made the hair on the back of my neck stand up.

Finally I began searching up how to travel between the realms, seeing a rainbow bridge called the Bifrost as the mode of transportation. The photos all looked like a magical rainbow bridge from a fairy tale, or they were stills from the Marvel movies about Thor. Frowning, I turned my attention back to my open bag on the bed and wondered again where we were really going.

Maybe it was mushrooms. Maybe we were just going to be tripping in a cabin all weekend. I could see that happening. How else would we get to another 'realm'? Why else would he believe he's the son of a god? And a god himself? Unless he planned to kill me, which also still felt like a real possibility.

'Were you being dumb?' Kerri's voice was always in the back of my head, the voice of reason in my chaos or, many times, the fuel on the fire spurring me on. She was both the angel and the devil on my shoulder, as I was on hers. She couldn't know about the truth this time though; she would never believe me. If Tora didn't trust her enough to tell her, then I would keep my new boyfriend's secret for now. Probably I was being dumb.

I missed the first three calls from my mom that morning as I prepared to leave, and had a minor cardiac event the moment I saw the notifications on my phone. I debated not answering on the fourth ring, but if I disappeared for three days, she would absolutely be here by the time I got back.

We hadn't spoken since our fight earlier in the week, and there was no doubt she was calling to check in after my threat to sleep with Mag on Friday night. I had made good on that threat, so she was in for a bad Saturday morning.

"I've called you three times," she snapped.

"I'm sorry. I'm going on a trip, and I've been busy getting ready to go." I forced my voice to remain even.

"A trip? Where? I didn't know you were going anywhere this weekend." She sounded highly suspicious.

"It's spontaneous, Mom. My boyfriend asked me to come visit his family home up north." There was silence after I dropped the b-word. The last time I used it was with my college boyfriend, who she hadn't liked either. We'd had a big fight back then too. I ended up lying to her, telling her he never stayed over and we'd never had sex.

As far as I knew, she still believed I was a virgin until that last phone call. Not that it mattered. There was so much pressure put on sex, on chastity until marriage, in my family. I learned everything I knew about it from reading and talking with Kerri. When I'd had sex with my college boyfriend, I expected it to change me completely, but the next day I was just the same as I ever was. Maybe a dash more defiant toward the church than the day before.

"Boyfriend, hm?" I could perfectly picture her disappointment on the other end of the line. Her pursed lips, her furrowed brow, her hand on her hip as she glared out the window over the backyard.

"Yep. Boyfriend. So you can tell Pastor Bryan he can stop creeping on me and trying to hug me all the time. Next time you have one of your little chit chats." My voice sounded sharp.

"What has gotten into you, Anais? You're such a sweet, nice girl... Why are you being so difficult all of a sudden?" She sounded disgusted with me.

"That's the problem, Mom. This is all pent up. I've been thinking this shit for years. It took you moving away, not suffocating me into conforming to your life, for me to finally be honest about who I am. I can be a real person and have my own thoughts." Sweat was dripping down my temples as I finally gave a voice to the truth.

"No—we've moved away and you've been corrupted by all the damn liberals up there. It's Kerri, this new boyfriend, the demonic coffee shop, that wolf place you work at with *that woman*. You're surrounded by bad influences, Anais." She was spitting; I could hear it on the other end. I smirked at her dig toward Gladis. The two had only met one time, but they deeply disliked one another, especially when it came to me. Gladis knew my mother was always pressuring me about religion, and my mother knew Gladis was who I went to for advice. When Mom found out Gladis was a Pagan, she called her a witch.

"Okay, and?"

"And they're leading you from God. I am debating if I need to come and drag you down here so you can be put back on the right track."

"Mom, I'm twenty-six years old. If you do that, I'll never forgive you." I huffed.

Her voice softened on the other end, morphing into her manipulative church voice. The one she always used when she talked about God to me and my sister, trying to entice us to join her way of thinking.

"You can still ask for forgiveness from Him, you know? No matter what you did with this boy. He will forgive your sins, and you can go back to church. No one has to know what happened…"

My head dropped to my hands and I wiped the sweat from my temples.

"Mom, it's 2023. Literally nobody cares that I slept with him." Tense silence followed.

"God cares, and the church men will care. Evan Meekerman will care—I thought you always kind of liked him?" My brows knit together as she brought up my church crush from eighth grade.

"Mom, Evan Meekerman has got two women in town pregnant and frequents the gentleman's club on the west side of town so often he has a points card. I don't like him. I haven't liked him since I was fourteen!" I yelled into the phone.

"Well, Pastor Bryan says he still attends every Sunday," my mom said with a sharp edge in her tone.

"I don't give a fuck what Bryan says. He is a predator too, and I will be glad if I never see him again," I growled, anger pricking my skin all over.

"Anais!" she yelped.

"You should be ashamed of being friends with him, Mom," I snarled. "After what he's done to so many girls, and maybe the boys too, I don't know." I'd told her before about the Pastor, but she hadn't wanted to hear it and wouldn't listen.

"Anais—" Her voice was softer, she wasn't screaming anymore, but all my pent up fury kept spilling out of me. I was raging too hard to listen to her anymore.

"What he did to Kerri, what he did to me, Mom! And you didn't listen, you made me keep going there. I'm done. Do not come up here, do not call me again, and do not talk about the church or God to me again."

There was a moment of very tense silence. I wasn't even sure she was still there; all I could hear was my own heavy breathing and the blood rushing in my ears.

Her voice was quiet but even when she spoke. "I will pray for you Anais—"

"Oh, fuck off!" I screamed, hanging up the phone. I stood panting and seeing red. I couldn't catch my breath. I couldn't get enough oxygen into my lungs, my chest heaving air in and out rapidly. The panic made me shake, the rage made me hot, and I was starting to feel sick to my stomach.

Fuck it. Wherever this *dude* was taking me had to be better than here. If I got murdered by this guy, then that's the price I'd pay, but I needed to get out of here. I needed to get where my mother couldn't reach me, where I could escape my past for a while. And who knows, maybe Mag could make me believe in some sort of god again, even if it was under the influence of drugs.

"Everything okay?" Mag's voice was gentle behind me. "I heard you yelling. Did you fight with your mom again?"

My breath finally slowed as I tried to regain control of my emotions. Dammit, he probably heard all of that. This was pretty heavy stuff for a new boyfriend to be dealing with. Then again, he was the one running around claiming he was a god, so maybe he could deal with it. Maybe it was destiny, because he was the best one to help me heal from this. I clung to the idea, hoping I was right.

I hadn't realized tears were welling in my eyes. I looked away as they began spilling down my cheeks. I caught them with a sweatshirt sleeve as I stared out the window.

"Tell me again what Asgard is like." I sniffled. I felt him take my free hand and gently tug for me to look at him.

"Let me show you." He gave me a reassuring smile as he swiped my tears away with his thumb, caressing my cheek.

"You don't need to pack anything. We have everything you need there. We'll dress you in the clothes of Asgard, and anything else you need, I can summon it. Let's go. I don't want to waste another moment with you down here like this." He pulled me firmly but without any viciousness, urging me to follow him.

"Okay." I let him lead me from the apartment, shutting off the lights and double checking the locks as we went. He walked me out to the car, opening the door for me and then getting in himself.

"Next stop will be to get Tora, and then off to Asgard." I nodded, using what was left of my time with cell service setting up out of office emails and texting Kerri about what just happened with my mom. I wanted her to know in case my mom called, although I doubted she would dare to call Kerri after what I'd said about Pastor Bryan.

CHAPTER 9

"So you're telling me you're for real, actual gods?" I gaped at Tora, who was confirming everything Mag told me this morning. I sat in the passenger seat next to Mag, with Tora in the back, speaking to me over the center console.

She proudly held her hand out. Familiar golden, shimmering heat waves appeared above her palm, then she held a picture frame in her hand. It was the photograph from my kitchen of Kerri and I with our pizzas, the same one we'd looked at just last night.

"How…?" I was speechless as I stared down at the frame.

"I saw it when we were there last night. We have magic to summon just about anything. If we know where it is, if we picture it in our head, we can summon divine magic fibers from the world around us to create an exact replica. That picture is hanging still in your home—you just have an extra copy now." She beamed as I stared dumbfounded at the picture frame.

This was insane, but that was the third time I'd seen that magic trick. I was starting to feel like Santa Clause was real again, curiosity and wonder sparkling in my chest the way it did when I was a little girl. I looked between the two beings sitting next to me, thinking how it made complete sense that they were a god and goddess they were so perfect in every way. It was slightly intimidating sitting next to them.

"How are we going to get to Asgard?" I asked, looking between the brother and sister. "Please don't tell me there's actually a rainbow bridge somewhere."

Mag was driving us deep into the woods, and he reached over, placing a hand on my thigh as he continued steering down the road. "You did some research, huh?" He chuckled. A smile played on his lips, looking excited and perfectly content, perfectly casual.

"We're going to take a mode of travel called a seam," Mag responded with a reassuring squeeze of my leg. "It's a lot faster than the old Bifrost and easier to use. What else have you researched?" he asked curiously, his eyes sliding between me and the road ahead.

"I just did a tiny bit really, like five minutes' worth on Google." I blushed. I didn't know anything about Norse gods, and I'd looked at a general webpage about it. It was a reckless decision to come, to trust them, but who would enlist their sister to kidnap a girl? If anything, I trusted Tora not to lead me astray. Plus, they'd really shown me magic, real magic. No matter how I tried to convince myself it was a trick, I watched them pull objects from thin air with golden heatwaves. It was going to be fine, nothing was going to happen, and we would be back by Monday. Outside, the snowy forest was passing by, and I wondered what would be different about Asgard.

"Will I be able to breathe?" I asked, suddenly concerned since we would be traveling through … well, whatever we were traveling through to get there.

"Yes, there's oxygen in our realms," Tora responded, not judging me at all. I expected one of them to laugh, but neither did. Tora watched me, waiting for me to continue. I felt empowered to ask my questions with her straight answers.

"Do the gods speak English?" I asked.

"Mostly. We all spent a lot of time studying different languages. We've been alive for hundreds of years, and we don't have a lot of things to do other than learning about the human world on Midgard." Tora's tone was reassuring and Mag nodded as he watched the road ahead.

"*Nine* realms, and you're saying keeping up with the humans on Earth is the most interesting thing you have going on?" I asked skeptically.

Mag didn't respond, and neither did Tora. He pulled the jeep down a driveway, plowing through deep snow toward a small cabin that looked dark and completely unused.

"This is your house?" I looked at the empty shell of a cabin sitting before us.

"We own it, but we don't use it. It's just where we're departing from today. We updated the magic from the Bifrost to be
able to rip a seam in the fabric of realms, allowing us to travel
from one to another. I'll show you what I mean when we get
to it." He looked at me, reaching over the console to take my
hand as Tora exited the vehicle. She walked to the side of the
cabin and paused, waiting for us.

"Do you trust me?" he asked.

I nodded.

"Do you believe in gods again?" he asked with a mischievous
smirk.

"I'm starting to," I mumbled, feeling a blush heating my
cheeks.

I followed him from the car, taking a quick moment to send
Kerri a pin and a message telling her we'd made it and she
wouldn't be hearing from me until Monday. I left my phone
on the passenger seat in case anyone pinged it. If anyone did,
they would see I was where I said I was going to be. I doubted
the phone would work in the realms of the gods anyway—and
if he was going to kill me in the forest instead, at least Kerri
would have the location to search for my body.

"Tora has just torn a new seam a little ways from the cabin,"
Mag told me, leading me through the trees. "See it there?
Where the trees are split unnaturally and it looks like a mirror."
He pointed ahead of us, where Tora was standing. I didn't see
it at first, but Tora reached out, grabbing the air and pulling
the world back like a curtain. Beyond was darkness. It looked
like a prank show, and I bounded forward to inspect the seam.

"It's just out here? What if someone finds it?" I asked, gesturing to Tora to put the curtain back, admiring the way it was so subtle in the trees. A secret hidden doorway in the world.

"We can seal it again when we leave and reopen it when we come back." Tora smiled as she watched my brain process what I was seeing.

"So, we just step through it?" I asked Mag, turning to look at him.

"Together," he smiled, offering his hand. I took it, my heart beginning to race as Tora reached out to take her brother's hand.

"Going somewhere?" The mildly bored voice dripped with icy coldness behind us.

All three of us whipped around. Tora stepped forward, putting herself between the stranger and where Mag and I stood. The woman was slightly taller than me but shorter than Tora. Dressed in black, a hood and mask covered her face, two pale blue eyes faintly glowing from the shadows. Two braids of long, white hair hung down her slender frame, and although she was slight compared to my companions, she stood confidently, unafraid and unimpressed with them. She folded her arms across her chest while she waited for a response.

"Hel." Mag spat the name, and her eyes narrowed as if the stranger was smiling behind her mask. "We're on our way to Asgard, and no, you're not invited." The stranger snorted, unamused by his joke.

"Who is she?" I whispered to Mag as Tora slowly took several more steps toward the stranger, summoning a lethal-looking sword to her hand.

"A fucking snake. She's the Goddess of Helheim, the realm of torture. And that's her *pet* guard dog." He nodded toward another figure stalking out from the trees behind the first. He was taller than everyone, including Mag, a lean figure dressed in tones of brown and green. Standing tall, he fixed Mag with an annoyed glare before rolling his eyes and crossing his arms as well. He too wore a hood, but his amber eyes flashed in the winter landscape around him, and no mask covered his handsome face.

"I'm a Lieutenant, at least get it right. Sheesh." The strange man's tone was almost playful, his voice warm. "And really, Mag? You can't remember my name after all these years? We've been alive for hundreds of years together; you'd think at some point he'd remember." The strange man pouted with an over-exaggerated expression at his female companion, who rolled her eyes and shook her head at him.

"I know your damn name, *Jerrick*," Mag hissed, making the man's harassing smile widen to reveal perfectly straight teeth. I tried to get a better look at him, thinking I saw long fangs in place of his canine teeth. Mag grabbed my arm, stopping me from approaching, and pulled me back toward him.

Hel's blue eyes narrowed once more, flicking between Tora, Mag, and I. Tora crept closer to the two strangers—Hel and Jerrick—her blade glinting in the cloudy light of the day.

"That's enough," Hel snapped and flicked her wrist toward Tora. Tora dropped to the ground, screaming, clawing at her head. She cried out, tears springing to her eyes and running down her cheeks. The stranger was nowhere near her, and yet Tora cried as though she was being viciously attacked, trying to cradle and protect her head from an unseen threat.

"Stop it," Mag seethed. He made no move toward Tora on the ground. My heart raced in my chest, wondering what she was doing to Tora, why Mag wasn't making more of an effort to stop her from hurting his sister. I couldn't understand why he was protecting me rather than going to her, or why this goddess Hel was so much stronger than them.

The man, Jerrick, watched me from the other side of the clearing. When my eyes met his, he smiled a friendly smile, unlike the teasing one he'd flashed at Mag earlier. It was warm and completely out of place with Tora's screams as she writhed before him on the ground. I shied away from the frightening pair, suddenly more grateful for Mag's protection. I felt like a child, stepping behind Mag's shoulder before peering out at the lieutenant again. He was still smiling, but he wasn't showing his teeth anymore, his expression almost sad at my response.

Hel let go of her invisible hold on Tora, and the golden-haired goddess lay panting on the ground. She wept in relief at the apparent disappearance of her pain. I watched her, eyes round with fear as Jerrick approached her and crouched down. Lacing his fingers into her golden hair, he forced her head up as he whispered something, then let her head fall back to the ground.

"I don't think you should be taking what isn't yours, Magni. This wasn't the deal." Hel growled. Her eyes found me again, scanning me as though she were checking for injuries. I shivered under her gaze.

Mag smirked, and the look made my stomach churn. He looked frightening. Ominous. Unlike any state I had seen him in so far. "Everything is mine to take. That is the whole point of this, deal or not. You need me; no one else will do what you want. So I'll have my fun."

"He'll kill you," she responded, a threat by all means.

"He won't do a fucking thing," Mag snarled back, "just like you won't right now either. I'm the only one who can get her into Asgard and we all know it." I wondered why the Goddess of Hell wanted me in Asgard, and who 'He' was. I'd have to ask Mag more about it when we got away from the devil and her giant minion, who was blocking us from leaving.

"That's true, but he's still going to kill you if you do anything to her. And this wasn't the plan we were discussing. For what you've already done, I bet he wants you dead. If you hurt her anymore, I promise to flay you alive before he does." Jerrick's tone was deadly serious. I frowned, wondering what Jerrick thought Mag was doing to hurt me. Mag was nothing but protective, sweet, understanding, and kind. Who was this Jerrick person to be threatening Mag on my behalf, anyway?

"Why the hell are you arguing over me like I'm not here?" I demanded. "And who the fuck are you? Talking about me like you own some part of me."

"Sorry," Jerrick mumbled, looking genuinely ashamed as his eyes met mine. "We wouldn't have to be here if these two did what they were supposed to"—he threw a glare at Mag and Tora, who was now back on her feet—"but you can't trust them to do shit right."

"Fuck you, you fucking mutt," Tora snapped at him, brushing her hair back from her face.

"You wish you could, Tora." He snorted, his tone playful again as he wiggled an eyebrow at her tauntingly, making Tora redden with anger.

"Should I know who you are? Who is 'he'?" I started asking questions.

"He's—" Jerrick started, looking at me with intensity. Suddenly, I felt I needed to hear him, to hear who 'he' was. I dialed in on the man with amber eyes.

"I'll tell her later," Mag growled, cutting him off as he pushed me behind him, away from sight of the other two. "You two," he addressed them, "can't do anything for now. You need me, so I'll do whatever I please. Just slink back down to home, and you'll know when we're ready for you."

Hel shook her head and Jerrick gave Mag a threatening look, but neither made any further comments.

"We'll be going," Mag said, taking my hand and leading me toward the seam. It was only a few steps behind us.

Hel raised her hand, and Tora flinched at the movement. "Do not forget who I am," Hel hissed at us. "You want to be the King, but I have been a Queen for a millennia. Since you have not been keeping your end of the bargain in regard to her, I may not keep up mine either. If you hurt her in Asgard and he kills you for it, I won't stop him. Deal or not."

"He will do nothing as long as I have her, and even when I don't," Mag snarled, but I thought I detected some fear wavering his voice as he spoke. "And neither will the two of you."

"Hello? I'm right here. You can stop talking about me like I'm not," I snapped. No one acknowledged me.

Mag reached out, grabbing my arm and Tora's and pulling us backward through the seam.

It was awful. I felt as though I was free falling through a compression vacuum. I couldn't breathe, darkness streaked with bright colors whirling past so fast I thought I might be sick if I could gasp air. I closed my eyes, but as soon as it all started, it ended. I felt solid ground beneath my feet once more, and could feel the heat of the sun rather than the frigid winter I was in before.

CHAPTER 10

"Welcome to Asgard," Mag whispered in my ear, and I opened my eyes to blinding daylight. I blinked to adjust to the bright afternoon. We stood on a balcony of white stone that overlooked a magnificent city made of the same stone with gold accents. Streets stretched out in every direction below us. The balcony was attached to a magnificent white-and-gold palace that rose high into the air, almost as tall as the mountains surrounding the city. A breeze with a hint of ocean saltiness tousled our hair, and the distant crash of surf and cry of gulls drew my attention back to the view. Beyond the city, an ocean waved in the distance. A long rainbow bridge stretched from the middle of the city out above the water. Much like the movies I'd seen, a massive domed building sat at its end.

Surrounding the city on the land side was a horseshoe of enormous purple mountains, some snow capped in the distance. Other castles gleamed on the mountainsides, spread out and soaring over the city. Trees spotted the mountains between the dwellings, and magnificent gardens could be seen even from where I stood. Plants covered some rooftops completely. Everywhere around us, and on every balcony in sight, a plethora of plants and flowered vines grew, making it look as though small jungles were intertwined with the buildings in the close quarters of the city. The colors seemed more vivid here, the sounds softer and melodic. I could hear laughter and music coming from the streets below and smell both the salty ocean and crisp mountain air in the same breath.

Our balcony was also covered in plants, flowers blooming everywhere over white stone laced with gold adornments. The thick stone handrail provided a place for me to lean so I could look over the side of the castle down into the city streets far below.

"Come. Let's go to my room and get you dressed like a proper Asgardian." Mag held my hand as he led the way toward the interior of the palace. All the entrances and windows were paneless, open to the warm outside air. The interior of the palace looked like it should be freezing, its walls made of a brilliant turquoise stone that matched Mag and Tora's eyes, but the warmth followed us through the halls. Gold filled every seam and crack of the building. It adorned every bit of hardware, every door frame, every piece of furniture in sight. The furnishings were large, made for much larger beings than me, and each was upholstered with rich velvety red fabric or made of fine, heavy wood. Even Mag looked smaller than he was against the palace walls that soared high above us.

We stopped at a huge door. Carved on it was a depiction of Mag, or a figure I assumed was Mag, with lightning bolting all around, striking the ground where he walked. A flash in my mind reminded me of the tree in the forest, split in half with burning embers glowing in the night.

I shook the memory from my mind, following him inside the room. It was a grand bedroom, with a private open-air balcony overlooking the city. An arched doorway and two tall, arched windows without glass opened over the balcony and the city beyond. Potted flowers and trees provided shade to patches of the balcony. They bloomed everywhere, colorfully framing Asgard below as a magnificent painting as the sun shone through and warmed the stone tile floors.

To one side of the room, there was a massive golden four poster bed with red and gold drapes hanging around it. The bedding looked plush and comfortable, the bed made and waiting for him—by servants, I assumed. I had not seen anyone else so far, but I wondered who ran the household duties of Asgard Palace. I cringed at the thought of servants, or even worse, slaves. I hadn't asked much about that before we'd left, and I was reconsidering now. Magic, I told myself. They must use their powers to keep it all looking this way.

The other furnishings in the room were just as large as the bed, and sun beds lay out on the balcony. Drapes of crimson adorned the golden walls carved with intricate knot pattern designs.

On the other side of the room, a large pool of blue water sat in a marble tub that was half inside the bedroom and half out on the balcony, the water steeping in the Asgardian sunshine. The stone-carved heads of several medium-sized cats protruded from the wall over the indoor part of the pool. Their jaws were open, and a steady stream of water dripped from their jaws between fearsome fangs.

"We don't need any doors or windows, it's so warm most of the time," Mag commented, walking to the doorway of the balcony and looking out over the rainbow of plants and the beautiful day beyond. A few lazy clouds hung unmoving in the sky, looking so much like cotton candy I wasn't sure they weren't tinged pink.

Trying to take in all of the fantastical splendor at once, I followed Mag to the balcony. The sunshine warmed my cheeks as I crossed to a familiar flower grew on a potted shrub. A red rose, just like the one he had given to me to prove his power. This one was just as lush, with ruby red petals warmed by the sun.

"That's where I got it from," he said behind me. "They have grown out here every day of my life. I've had them since I was a little boy. I love them, and I wanted them to be the very first thing you saw of Asgard." He smiled, taking the one I was admiring and pulling it from the stem. He brushed back my dark waves, sliding the stem behind my ear so the flower sat against my head.

"They're beautiful," I mused, running my fingers over the petals, listening to the rustle of them against my ear. I turned to him, studying his brilliant strawberry-blonde hair shining in the vibrant landscape. He looked like a flame here, radiant in the daylight. He looked like he belonged here, definitely born and raised in the sunshine and the blue skies that matched his eyes.

"Nearly as beautiful as you." He lifted my chin and leaned in to press his lips against mine. "I can't believe you're actually here. I can't wait to show you all of Asgard. After I have my way with you, I'm going to take you for a walk in the city." He kissed me more intensely this time, his tongue sliding across my bottom lip.

"Have your way with me?" A soft snort escaped me, though a thrill jolted through me at his words.

He tugged at my sweater, pulling it over my head. Already needy for him, I began unhooking my belt as he spun me to face the city. He pulled down my pants and placed a firm hand on my back, bending me over the stone railing. Trailing two fingers between my thighs, he leaned over and purred in my ear, as if he were one of the big cats on his bathroom wall.

"It looks like you're ready for me, hm?" he asked, feeling how slick I already was at the thought of him. I gasped as he gently inserted a finger, stroking me, making me whimper for more. I rocked back to meet him, begging for him as he drew his hand away.

"This is the best way to see Asgard." He groaned as he slid into me, one hand still on my back, the other on my hips as he thrust forward. I looked out over the city, feeling the length of him within me. My sight was hazy with lust, but I tried to appreciate the view as he found his rhythm.

"And you are the prettiest thing here," he panted. "Oh Gods, Anais, you are taking me so well." I could only moan in response to his praise. The sun, the smell of the roses, the feeling of him—it was too much, and I descended into decadence, letting shudders consume my body.

"Ugh, Mag!" I whined, and he took my hair firmly between his fingers, pulling my head back to look at him. He slowed, relishing every shiver of my body as he made me shudder with pleasure over and over again.

After an afternoon of cuddling—and a few more romps around the balcony, the pool, the floor, the dresser, and finally the bed—he pulled me close as we lay between the silky red sheets.

"What was that today?" I demanded gently, rolling over in bed to look at the magnificent god stretched out before me. "I know it was Hel and that guy, but what was she talking about?"

He tensed at the question, suddenly eyeing me warily, as though he didn't trust me entirely. "She's the goddess of torture, charged with making eternal life miserable for those sent to her realm of Helheim. Which is most people, since you only go to Valhalla if you die in battle. She's obviously an evil, vile creature who wants to kick start Ragnarok." He sighed, admiring me in the afternoon light.

"But who was the 'he' they kept mentioning? Why don't they want us to be together?" I frowned. "Why is 'he' going to kill you? Over *me*? Aren't you worried about that?" I put my hand on his arm, thinking how I'd be terrified to receive a death threat from the lieutenant of the realm of Hell.

"They're talking about Fenrir, Hel's brother. He's a prisoner here in Asgard. They think *you* can free him, and they want me to have you set him free to start Ragnarok. They want him to kill my grandfather, Odin, and then destroy Earth—and all the realms except Helheim." I stared, wondering what on earth could make these gods of the underworld think I would ever free such a monster. Why would they think Mag would want me to allow his grandfather to die?

"I would never free him. I would never do that to my home," I assured him. He raised an eyebrow and I noted a tiny frown that tugged at his mouth before being replaced by a smile. "Why would they think I would?"

"Of course you wouldn't, darling," he mused, ignoring my question. I opened my mouth to repeat the unanswered question, but Mag cut me off. "Enough end-of-the-world talk. I would like to take you out and show Asgard the most beautiful woman Midgard has to offer," he said, pulling back the luxurious sheets to stand.

My eyes narrowed on his back, my brain trying to work through why he was avoiding this conversation. I tried to brush it off, but it still nagged me at the back of my mind.

"I want to see everything," I said, deciding to change the subject as he crossed the huge room to a closet and pulled a beautiful red flowing dress adorned with gold embroidery around the waist and bottom.

"And you will, don't worry," he purred, again reminding me of the sculpted cat heads on his bathroom wall. "Come put this on, Ana." He waited for me to join him and take the dress, my fingers skimming over the fabric after I slipped into it.

I admired the dress in a mirror near the bathing pool. It clung to my curves, with a slit in the leg and a strappy top that exposed my arms and shoulders to the Asgardian sun getting ready to set soon. I smoothed my fingers over the embroidery, admiring the detail. The dress came with a pair of red shoes embroidered with the same intricate patterns as the dress.

"You look stunning." Mag's arm wrapped around from behind me. He too was wearing red and gold, but where my dress looked elegant and delicate, his clothing resembled armor plating.

"Not as stunning as this place, as Asgard." I sighed, looking out behind us at the city, and he chuckled.

"Asgard is a special type of stunning, I think." He took my hand and led me toward the hall. "Let me show you how stunning she can be." I took his hand and we whisked out the door.

The castle walls were well adorned with paintings and tapestries, some depicting Thor fighting giant serpents, and Odin the Allfather battling a pack of wolves. A particularly nasty wolf caught my eye in the painting of the Allfather. All black, it was larger than the wolves behind it. Its eyes, wild and yellow, sent a shiver down my spine. I'd seen those eyes on the webpage when I researched Asgard this morning. Somehow, they seemed even more familiar now, like I'd seen them before.

I hurried on to the next painting, a beautiful woman holding a basket of apples with an eagle swooping over her head. In almost all the depictions of the gods and goddesses, there was a lean, handsome man somewhere in the image, with red hair and a strong striking jawline. His horned helmet gave him away as Loki, the God of Mischief. I could thank Disney for my limited knowledge there.

We walked all through the palace. I wanted to stop and admire each piece of art, but Mag insisted there would be time later—now it was time to go out into Asgard. I followed him to a cavernous entryway leading out to a massive plaza. Buildings lined the plaza, with towering columns providing shade to porches where Asgardians dined outside. In the center of the plaza was an enormous golden statue of Odin the Allfather sitting on his throne, his back to the palace as he looked out over Asgard. He wore a winged helmet and held a tall spear in his hand. At his side, a woman leaned on his shoulder, watching out over the city as well.

"That is Odin the Allfather, the King of Asgard, and Frigg, the Queen of Asgard," Mag explained as he saw me staring at the statue. "This is the Palace Plaza. We carry out all sorts of festivities here: a festival every solstice, all my father's victories abroad, sometimes public punishments if necessary for traitors of Asgard." I couldn't imagine what someone would do to be publicly punished on these beautiful streets in front of all these people. From the corner of my eye, I thought I saw a smirk flicker across Mag's face as he reflected on the idea of punishing people here, but by the time I got a good look at him, his face was calm and blank.

People milled about the plaza and the streets that led deeper into the city. There were restaurants, vendors, blacksmiths, and more lining the streets. Mag fit right in with the people of Asgard, beautiful and tanned, the skin of gods kissed by the heavenly sun. While I stood out in appearance, my dark hair and pale skin a stark contrast to the Asgardians around me, it was as if I were invisible on the streets. No one bothered to pay any mind to me or Mag, which surprised me. They cared so little that their royalty walked among them.

The streets were all made of white stone, marble, and gold. Everything in the city was luxury and decadence, every business clean with an immaculate window display for their goods. I could have wandered the streets for hours, and perhaps I would when I had more time to spare. Mag insisted that I would need to spend more time exploring later because now it was time to go to the palace to feast with the rest of the Aesir.

"This place is beautiful," I told Mag as we walked.

"It is, isn't it?" He smiled, seeming content as he looked around, but I felt as though his eyes had a sharpness as he surveyed the street. "It is, but it won't always be. When Ragnarok happens, everything will be destroyed." I frowned at the thought, wondering how soon he thought that might happen. It looked like it had taken hundreds of years to build a city so grand, and Odin had been alive for more than a thousand years. Surely Ragnarok was still far off, past my mortal life. Although who knew how short my mortal lifespan would be compared to a god.

"Well, when are you planning for that to happen?" I asked.

"Sooner rather than later," he responded, watching my eyes carefully as I listened. I remembered the conversation this morning with Hel, and how Mag had told me she wanted Ragnarok as well. They'd discussed some sort of deal. "Once Ragnarok happens, Tora and I will flee. We intend to survive so we can come back and rebuild Asgard City." My brows furrowed as I thought through what he was saying. We were climbing the stairs toward the palace, toward his room. He'd mentioned needing to get something there before we went to dinner in the feasting hall with the other Aesir. I had yet to meet any other Aesir gods since being here.

"Ragnarok will be the end of Odin and your father, right?" He nodded as we turned down the hall toward his room. "So you would inherit the crown then, of Asgard? You would be the Allfather?"

The thought crossed my mind, wondering if it was possible he could be plotting Ragnarok. Would he really scheme after power like that? Was he power hungry enough to doom Asgard City? The city is so beautiful, I didn't understand how anyone could purposefully destroy it. Then again, the royals on Earth went to great lengths to gain power. My mind turned to conspiracies about Princess Diana.

I thought about what I really knew about him, and a blush burned my cheeks as it dawned on me once more how impulsively I'd acted coming here with him. I knew very little about him, about Norse Mythology, and about the Aesir gods. His webpage hadn't been more than a few sentences. I'd taken all of five minutes to search on my phone, gaining a very cursory understanding of who exactly I was dealing with here. I had assumed he was on the 'good' side because he was related to Odin and Thor, historically the 'good' side of the gods in Norse Mythology. In truth, I was dealing with a god that had hundreds of years compared to my meager twenty-six.

That doesn't actually mean he was good, though, or acted with my best interests in mind. He'd made some kind of deal with the goddess of Hell, a deal that involves starting Ragnarok, the end of his home city. If he could get power from that, why wouldn't he? It's what the royals did on Earth all the time.

And somehow, I was a piece in this game. Somehow, I was important to all of them, to 'him'. Fenrir. Whoever he was.

"Mag?" I asked, my voice soft and hushed as I followed him into the room.

"Hm?" He was looking for something in the closet by his bed.

I faced the mirror, looking at my reflection. The red and gold dress that seemed so fun earlier suddenly felt too decadent for me. I was an imposter. I wasn't meant to be here; something wasn't right about all of it.

Dumb, dumb idiot. I scolded myself for following a god on an intergalactic field trip and now being stuck here with no phone—not that there'd be reception if I had it—and no way to get home.

"Are you planning to have something to do with Ragnarok?" I asked, keeping my tone soft, non-judgmental as I asked. I did not want to appear as a threat. Maybe I could remain on his side long enough to get home and then run from him. The moment the words left my lips, I wished I'd remained silent.

He appeared behind me in the mirror, a sinister look on his face. I swallowed, staring at his reflection as he watched me with cold, evil eyes. The malicious intent blazed through his turquoise pools, the look scorching my skin. The man I'd been falling for was gone. A power hungry god stared back at me.

CHAPTER II

"I didn't want to do it this way, but I think it's for the best." In the mirror, he lifted a metal object that encircled my neck and clipped on in a mere moment.

"What the fuck? What is this, Mag?" I yelped, grabbing the golden collar he'd just snapped around my neck. I scrabbled at it with my fingers, tugging it and trying to unfasten it, but I couldn't find the clasp. Turning to face him, I searched his face for any amount of playfulness gone awry, or joking intent. I found only malice in his expression.

"I would say I was sorry to have to do this to you," he growled in a hair-raising tone. "If I cared anything about you,

Ana." He stood before me, a gold chain clenched in his hand leading to the metal encircling my neck. "Now, kneel."

My mouth flopped open, and I stared at him with disbelief. I couldn't keep down the laugh rising in my chest.

"Kneel? What the hell—" I scoffed.

The collar around my neck electrified, snapping my body rigid with the current, and I fell to the ground. I convulsed in front of him, eyes bugging from my head as the current made my muscles spasm, and screamed.

"This is what's going to break you," Mag snapped, leering over me with a frightening look on his face.

"A fucking electric dog collar?" I gasped when the electricity subsided. I lay coughing and panting, and he sent electricity through the metal tether again. I screamed, writhing in pain and clawing at the collar that seemed unbreakable. I checked again. Panicked. There was no clasp, nowhere to unfasten it from my neck.

"Something like that. Now kneel in front of me," he snarled, yanking the chain in his hand and making the collar dig painfully into the skin of my neck. Shakily, I started pushing myself up on my forearms, but I had no intention to kneel before him.

"Fuck you—"

He reached down, grabbing my hair with a fist and almost making me yelp in pain as he yanked me to my knees.

"That is the last thing you'll say without permission, do you understand?" His tone struck terror through me. "You belong to me from here on out. You'll do everything I tell you, or you'll be punished. I'm tired of your smart mouth; you're much prettier when you keep it shut. I'll shock you any time you do something I don't like, without hesitation. I'd recommend you don't try me."

I eyed him, wanting to believe this was just something sexy he was taking too far, but the lingering twitches in my muscles and the strands of hair breaking free from my head told a different story.

"Why?" I finally asked.

"Did you really think for one second"—he spat, a wicked grin on his face—"that I would want *you*? That a god like me would come down to Midgard and just choose you? I need you. Hel is right that you're the only one who can free that stupid mutt, Fenrir. I think I'll keep you to myself for a while though, just to piss him off." He circled me, eyeing me with pride as I kneeled where he left me.

I wanted to ask him for answers to the million questions racing through my mind, but the violent shock from the collar was still vibrating in me.

"You are more important to him than you know, and I believe once you free him, he'll want to drag you to Hell with him." Fear and terror struck through my chest like a bolt of lightning. Why? Who was this Fenrir?

"Why would you do this to me?" I whispered. Immediately, a responding shock through my whole body had me writhing on the ground before him once more. Tears streamed down my cheeks, my mascara running in black tear tracks down my face. He was laughing over me, looking entirely evil as he watched me try to catch my breath.

"Firstly, you're not asking any questions here. You only speak when spoken to—is that clear? Secondly, I don't give a damn about you other than your helping me and being a weapon I can use against him. I can do whatever I like with you. I don't care who you are or who you're Fated to; as long as that is around your fragile little neck, you belong to me." He pointed at the collar. "And as long as you belong to me, you'll do what you're told unless you'd like to lose your life. If that's not enough of a threat for you, I'll remind you that my sister slept with your best friend. What was her name, Kerri? We know where she lives and who she is. I'll kill her too. You both mean less than nothing to me."

Sweat started to bead on my forehead as I tried to comprehend his threats.

"I'm just going to tell the other Aesir. Someone will help me." My voice sounded pathetically timid. It was followed by another teeth-clenching shock that had me whimpering in pain.

"How many times until you learn?" he asked with amusement in his voice, watching me sobbing on the floor, twitching with residual shocks. He grinned, the malicious intent still sparkling in his eyes. "No one is coming to save you. The other Aesir don't care, and we're spinning the story that you're here willingly. Hel *sent* you to trick me. That's what we'll tell Odin. You *want* to be my little whore, the whore of the Aesir. You *want* their hands all over you. You *want* me to keep you kneeling next to me, ready to serve my every single need until you can get close enough to Fenrir to free him. Once you 'have us all fooled,' you'll sneak down to the prison and free him. It's a death penalty crime. Odin will have you killed for it." My stomach was turning now from the look in his eyes. He'd played me. Now I was out of my element, out of my realm. Alone. No one could rescue me.

"And don't worry, I'm going to help you keep quiet." I wanted to whimper in terror as he said those words. He wound the chain around his hand and dragged me to his feet. He crouched down, and before I could move, he struck like a viper. His hand wrapped around my throat, pinning me to the ground with his incredible strength. I yelped in surprise as his second hand closed around my throat, and he started squeezing. I struggled against him, feeling my face redden as my body demanded oxygen. I fought him with everything I had until the need for air made me weak. He let go then, and I sucked in air, coughing from the sudden change in airflow. While I was gasping on the ground, he aimed a quick jab at my throat, rendering my vocal cords completely useless. I lay on the ground silently sobbing, not even sure where to begin processing the pain, the betrayal, the confusion and fear in a world I entirely did not understand.

At that moment, a tremor shook the palace, and all of Asgard quaked. If I had been standing, it would have knocked me from my feet. Even Mag was set slightly off kilter, having to step back to maintain his balance and upright position over me. He waited for the quaking to end, and when it did, he looked at me with a wicked grin that made my tongue turn sour in my throat.

Without warning, he shocked me once more, making me open my mouth to scream. Nothing came out, all the cries of pain locked in my head. With the collar on, I had no way to defend myself from him, and with my voice gone, I had no way to beg for mercy or plead with anyone.

"Wallow for as long as you need." He sneered at me, rolling me under his foot as he inspected his work on my throat. He reached down, and just as he summoned items, he disintegrated the dress from my body, leaving me exposed on the ground. He then walked to the wall, attaching the chain to a ring bolted there as if I were a beast. "When I come back, we're going to the feast at Valhalla tonight."

I lay on the tile cursing myself for what felt like hours. How could I possibly be so stupid to trust a god? To think he had good intentions? I'd grown up hearing about Ted Bundy, how he used his good looks to his advantage to do horrible and terrible things. Here was a divine man doing the same thing and I'd been a fool. Easily fooled.

I tried to break free of the collar, to slip it off or find the clasp, but it felt completely unbroken. I couldn't find where the metal connected. I pulled against the ring in the wall, but it was firmly set into the stone. By the time Mag returned, I had only managed to pull the sheet from the bed off and wrap it around myself.

My throat ached and a sharp pain hit every time I opened my mouth and tried to scream for help, leaving me to make a tiny coughing noise and promptly give up. Just breathing was painful enough, and I wondered how long I would be mute.

"Get dressed," was all Mag said as he walked into the room. He summoned some clothing and threw it at me on the ground. I started to pull on the skimpy gold skirt with gold chains holding it together and dripping down my hips and curves. The top matched, chains and all. My skin was so exposed—I'd never worn something so revealing. It felt like I was barely wearing more than lingerie.

"Look at you," Mag said with mock pride as I stood before him. "Not so hard to break you, hm? Just take away your voice and all your bite is gone, wolf girl." I glared at him but didn't dare to take a swing. He would just take a better aimed one back at me.

"Let's go, pet." He took the chain easily from the ring in the wall. Anger seethed through me as I thought of how many times I'd pulled against that chain this afternoon. "Don't try anything out there. I'll shock you until your body gives out and your brain scrambles without killing you, got it? Do everything I tell you."

All I could do was nod and allow him to lead me down through the castle. Several servants glanced my way, but none maintained eye contact long enough for me to ask for help. We wound through the palace down toward what sounded like a huge party. I could hear music, people shouting and singing merrily, and the sound of cups and plates clinking.

The feasting hall was as beautiful as anything else in Asgard, open air balconies showing a grand view of Asgard City and the mountains beyond. Tables were laden with heaping mounds of food. Fresh produce was piled high, golden yellow apples the crown jewel of the hoard. Plates of meat steamed, dripping with fat, with potatoes and other root vegetables whipped together into a mash with herbs. Gallons of wine and mead sat on the table.

It was incredibly loud, and many of the Aesir around were men who grinned wickedly as Mag walked me toward a table near the front of the room. At the table already sat an enormous man with a white beard and a golden eye patch encrusted with precious gems—that must be Odin. Next to him was Frigg, the blonde goddess leaning toward Odin, watching him with loving interest as he spoke to her softly. Next to them were Thor, his hammer sitting on the table before him, and his blonde wife, Sif, Mag's mother. She looked bemused as her son came and took a seat next to Tora at the end of the table.

"Kneel beside the table," Mag hissed at me, and I obliged, placing my hands in my lap as I kneeled next to him. I tried not to cringe as several Aesir men watched me from the crowd.

"Who is that?" Frigg asked, jutting her chin toward me but making no motion to get up and help me.

"Some silly human I met in Midgard," he told her non-chalantly, petting my head with a hand. "She came up to me begging to serve the gods, wanting to come here at any cost just to have fun with the gods of Asgard." He purred the lies easily.

"It's true," Tora crooned. "He slept with her one night and the poor thing just begged him to bring her here. Said she could never go back after his *godly* cock. She came to be an Asgardian whore, isn't that right Anais?"

"Stop being disgusting," a passing goddess snapped at the two of them. She too had bright golden hair, and two massive lynx cats circled her feet as she walked, weaving between her legs. She glared at me with complete abhorrence, and all hope that she may help disintegrated as my dress had earlier.

"Lighten up, Freyja," Tora said as she grimaced at the two cats following close behind the goddess.

"We haven't had someone to have such fun with for a while, so I thought it'd be worth it to play along with her," Mag said, and his father, Thor, nodded with a wicked grin. So, the whole family lacked morals. Fantastic.

I kept completely still for nearly the whole meal. I begged silently for anyone to notice me, notice I wasn't here by choice, but they were all far too busy with their feasting and merriment, save for a few men whose eyes hungrily devoured the flesh my outfit had to offer. I prayed for the first time in years, silently in my head; I couldn't help it, not knowing where else to turn. I turned to my mother's god in my moment of weakness. Tora was aware of Mag's plan, involved herself, and I was truly alone.

"Nice toy." A man with only one hand approached the table, and Mag—who had moved me from the end of the table to kneel in between his wide-spread legs as he lounged in his chair after the meal—grinned with extra enthusiasm.

"Thanks Tyr." Mag stroked my hair some more. "You're welcome to play with it if you like." My breathing became quicker as Tyr reached out, stroking my hair with his hand.

"I think I'll take you up on that. If you don't mind, maybe she can visit our table over there. We'll get some music for her." He frowned slightly at my throat when I didn't respond enthusiastically. "What happened to her neck?"

"She likes to be choked, right pet?" Mag grinned, his hand sliding into place over my throat, making my body go rigid as he squeezed. "Ah ah ahhh." He clicked his tongue with a shake of his head when my fingers began clawing at his hand, trying to get him off my airway. My throat's stabbing pain returned in force before he finally let go and threw me at Tyr's feet. I gasped for air, pushing myself up on shaking arms as I coughed and sputtered.

"Hm, so she is a dirty Midgard whore then." Tyr chuckled. Gripping the metal collar, he lifted me into the air with just one arm. I clawed wildly as I began choking again, trying to kick out at him, but I had no momentum to land a blow.

"Come, whore. Entertain us." Tyr set me down and dragged me toward a table of men whose grins made my skin crawl. Someone snapped at the band and music began playing, sultry and rhythmic. Several men began to whoop with excitement.

Tyr sat in a chair and motioned for me to come sit on his lap. I hesitated, feeling frozen with so many eyes on me. Some had even been brave enough to reach out, running their hands over my ass through the thin gold fabric.

A severe yank on the chain had the collar snapping my head back as I lurched toward Tyr's lap. I was going to get whiplash from this collar get-up. Not to mention a cardiac event.

He had me straddle his thighs, with my chest in his face. I wanted to close my eyes, to whimper with fear and shame as he touched my body in front of all these strangers. No one made any move to help me—even the other women watched with mild bemusement. Tora was sneering at me from the head table. Mag sat next to her, his hand raised and ready to electrify my collar the moment I fought back.

I'd been passed around the table several times by the time Mag came to collect me. Each Aesir had their fill of running their fingers over my breasts, my stomach, even dipping them between my thighs.

"Are you crying?" Mag snapped at me, seeing the mascara streaking down my cheeks. I could only silently sob in response.

"She's been crying the last two rounds," Tora drawled, taking a seat on Tyr's lap. I hadn't realized she was watching me.

"It must be such a burden to please the gods," Tyr said mockingly to me, but he watched Tora eyeing me with malice.

"Stop crying. Now," Mag snapped at me, a wicked smile twisting his face as he knew I wouldn't be able to comply. When I let out a wet sniffle, he electrified the collar, making me seize and fall to the ground, writhing around. It must have looked rather funny, because all the gods at the table laughed, including Mag. When the electric current subsided, I lay twitching on the floor of the great hall, tears, snot, and drool dripping down my face.

"That's too fun. We really haven't had some good entertainment in a while," one of the gods purred, and everyone joined in agreement with him.

I lost count of the days somewhere around the two week mark. Mag hit me in the head several times during my stay and knocked me unconscious for unknown amounts of time, causing me to lose count of my days in Asgard. The weather never changed, so I had no indication if the seasons were changing.

I starved much of the time, living primarily on whatever the gods fed me from the table at dinner each night for fun. I had grown incredibly weak, not that I was particularly strong to begin with, and with the regular beatings, I was increasingly breakable.

Mag damaged my throat again as soon as it healed enough for me to whisper, insisting he did not want me to be able to tell anyone anything about what was happening. Not that it would have made a difference; they all enjoyed what they did to me. Even when my throat began to heal the second time, I kept quiet. Trauma kept me mute in hopes of escaping any further torment. I'd had terrible nightmares for weeks, my predicament carrying into my sleep as I relived abuse from Mag and his friends over and over each night.

The collar never came off my neck, and I'd developed a permanent mark from the metal digging into my flesh when they choked me with it. I slept on the floor of Mag's room each night, chained to the ring in the wall like an animal.

Several times my heart stopped from the electric current of the collar, and I'd officially died on the floor multiple times. But Mag brought me back each time with an electrical current in his fingers mimicking an AED. They made me dance in the feasting hall and at the parties after, gyrating and grinding my hips into their faces and laps while they laughed and made crude jokes. The worst electric shock had been when I bit Tyr's finger hard enough to make it bleed after he shoved it down my throat. Mag shocked me so hard I'd lost control of my bladder on the floor. He'd resuscitated me in a puddle of my own piss. That night in his room, he choked me so hard I passed out from asphyxiation.

Somewhere in there, Mag started forcing himself on me. He would degrade me the entire time, choke me with the collar, and threaten Kerri's life. Pinning me on his bed wasn't difficult—he was so strong, and I was weaker by the day. I tried to block it out, to close my eyes and pretend it wasn't happening, but it haunted my dreams. I made sure to keep quiet whenever he was around, no matter what was happening. If I sustained many more severe injuries to the throat, I would lose my voice permanently.

I was plagued with PTSD already. When I woke from the nightmares, it was always Mag over me, shaking me awake just to slap me and tell me to stop disturbing his time with whatever goddess was over for the night.

Each night, I prayed I would die, seeking salvation from whatever god might be listening in my head. I wasn't sure if I was going crazy, but sometimes I thought I sensed another presence inside my mind. So I prayed to the presence, begging to die in my sleep so I would be too far gone to bring back in the morning when Mag noticed.

I had never been so utterly alone in all my life. Not even the servants would look at me when they came to make Mag's bed in the morning and clean up his room. I'd reached out one day and grabbed a woman's arm to try to get her to help me. I desperately needed water and couldn't reach it from where I was chained. I hoped she might get some for me. She screamed and ran from the room. When Mag found out, he punished me severely with a mix of electric shocks and kicks to the ribs. He'd definitely broken one; I'd heard the crack, and the sharp stabbing pain still hadn't gone away weeks later. I prayed that it punctured a lung, but had no such luck.

Over time, the prospect of freeing Fenrir and being dragged to Hell became a welcome image. I was ready to go. Ready to end this suffering. Yet the thought of eternally living in the realm of torture made tears spring to my eyes. I wasn't the best person, but did I really deserve this end?

CHAPTER 12

B ecoming conscious in my dream, I recognized the snow-covered forest around me and leapt to my feet. I was in my forest. My wolf should be around here somewhere. I listened for the familiar howling calling me, but I heard nothing in the blizzard, only the groaning of the wind. Wandering, I searched for a familiar trail. The snow-heavy branches all looked the same. I shivered in my dream and in the room in Asgard. After the sun went down, it grew chilly in my skimpy clothing.

I walked through the forest on what felt like a small path overgrown with vines. Branches hung low from the trees. I ducked under their spider webs, leaving them frozen in place. The wind whipped today, flakes smacking the side of my face as they pounded sideways. Mist, thick and heavy, made it so I could barely see a few feet in front of me.

Snow was building quickly, making it harder to trudge through the winter landscape. The storm was picking up; it felt so real, even in sleep, that I swore I could see flakes sticking to my lashes.

"Anais?" someone called, their hopeful voice cutting through the wind and storm. It was a deep voice I didn't recognize. I froze, my eyes darting around the misty forest to locate the source. Was it another Aesir coming for me? I listened for any further noises or calls. Nothing. I began to pick my way through the forest again, listening for both the wolf's howl and the strange man wandering around.

"Anais!" the voice called louder this time, making my heart race. I picked up my pace through the woods. It sounded like he was searching for me but didn't know where I was.

I rushed through the forest until I heard a wolf howl and stopped dead. The sound came from the opposite direction I was headed, the same direction where the man was calling for me. I stood, debating if I should approach or not. On one hand, I couldn't resist seeing and getting comfort from my wolf. It was the only semblance of my normal life remaining, and I hadn't been able to sleep deeply enough to have this dream in the month I'd spent here. On the other hand, there was a man calling for me over there, and I wasn't ready to relive any more trauma before I woke up and started another day of my waking nightmare.

The wolf's howl lifted up louder, calling for me. I felt my feet moving toward it, running through the snow-covered forest. It took me longer to reach the howling than it did to run from the man's voice. I darted through the trees, climbing under fallen logs and through thickets covered in snow. The whole way back, I listened carefully and heard nothing but my wolf calling for me. I could hear the howling on the other side of a boulder and slowly crept forward to peer around it for my familiar four-legged friend.

Confused, my brows knit together. The clearing was empty. I listened for more howling, inching forward as I peered through the thick mist of the storm. It wasn't until he moved that I saw the man standing with his back to me, stopping me dead in my tracks. He was a huge, daunting shadow, taller than any person I had ever seen in real life. Dressed in all black, he was a looming figure with an athletic build and messy raven black hair whipping in the wind. His head moved side to side slightly, making me imagine he was scanning the woods. Looking for me, trying to lure me to him. He tipped his head back, put a hand against his mouth to amplify his voice, and howled.

My wolf howled—but it was this person. My wolf's howl was coming out of the man looking for me. The mournful howl came to an end, and he scanned the treeline once more. Before I could see his face, I was turning to run back into the forest. I opened my mouth to scream, but all that came out was the strangled choking noise that always came out these days.

"Anais!" the stranger behind me yelled, and I could hear him pursuing me in the snow. "Anais, wait!" he called, his voice deep and velvety. It was so enticing I nearly turned back to him—

"Wake the fuck up!" Mag kicked me in the already broken rib and I gasped awake. "You're being loud as fuck for someone who can barely do more than whisper. Do you want me to send you to Tyr's room for the night?" I shook my head, my soft whimper the only plea not to subject me to a night of sexual abuse at Tyr's single hand.

"Maybe you should; she's getting really annoying," drawled Erika. She was sprawled across Mag's bed, frowning at me. Since I'd arrived in Asgard, she'd been here several times, and I thought she might enjoy torturing me more than Mag did. She loved when he made me watch them have sex. She also loved to have him electrify my collar in my sleep just to watch me jolt awake screaming through my hoarse vocal chords. That was definitely why I hadn't dreamed of my wolf until now—I hadn't had restful sleep in weeks. I was so worn out, I felt I could fall back into a deep sleep at any moment.

Mag crouched next to where I lay on the ground. "She's right. I'm sick of looking at you. I think I'll have had enough of you by the end of the week." I couldn't imagine what he would need me for—to free the Fenrir guy for Ragnarok or something? I was so weak from being here, I couldn't remember everything he'd told me about his intentions. He didn't elaborate in front of Erika, and I thought maybe she wasn't in on the plan, that she just loved to torture me.

Mag grinned at me as if he could see the spark of hope deep inside me. "Erika knows of my plan for Asgard. She'll come with me. Now, don't make another noise or I'll call Tyr to come get you." He aimed another kick at me and I held in the grunt of pain that wanted to escape my lips. He walked back to Erika, who mumbled something to him about wanting to feed me to a giant snake, and Mag snorted. He grumbled something that made her squeal with laughter as she looked over at me.

I took as deep a breath as I could and then closed my eyes, willing myself to get back to my dream and find my wolf. Find out why my wolf's voice was coming from the man hunting me.

I was soon back in the forest with the blizzard swirling around me. I listened, and sure enough, I heard my wolf howling in the wind. I started toward where the noise, the wind picking up and making it even harder to see.

I heard crunching in the snow behind me and I whipped around to be face to face with my wolf as it came through the trees. It seemed relieved to find me, and it bounded forward before seeming to stop itself, waiting for me to close the distance.

"There you are," I said in my normal voice. My throat was not hurting, so I knew I wasn't speaking out in real life. I didn't want to be sent to Tyr's room under any circumstances; even in my dream I was aware of that fact. "I've been looking for you." I walked forward, reaching out to the animal. It met me halfway. I wrapped my arms around its ruff, crying into its fur as its head wrapped around my back, pressing me into its body comfortingly.

We sat together in the trees, hidden away in the storm. I heard no more from the man calling my name, no howling from anywhere else. My wolf was protecting me—from Mag, from the imposter wolf man, from the waking world beyond that was threatening to crush my soul entirely.

I didn't know the total time I'd spent in Asgard, convincing everyone that I was seducing Mag and the other Aesir rather than being coerced into every act on threat of bodily harm. No one knew any difference as they looked at me, as they ran their hands over every inch of me both at the table in the feasting hall and in private when Mag felt 'generous enough to lend me out.' I was Mag's plaything disguised as a human temptress, getting close to him and the Aesir to do whatever it was he was going to have me do.

I was noticeably thinner than when I'd arrived because of the meager diet of table scraps and constant stress. It didn't help that my damaged throat hurt like a dagger was driving into it every time a god felt generous enough to offer me a bite of food.

The day after the dream with my wolf, Mag had me sit on his lap, my legs entwining around his, my body completely pressed up against him, my lips on his neck. My fingers swept along his jawline, running through his golden beard.

"Tomorrow, you're going to help me set my plan in motion. Would you like to hear it?" he purred softly in my ear as I trailed kisses down his neck, his hands running ran over my waist. I was listening, terrified of what I was about to hear. His sinister chuckle struck fear right through me. Around the room, no one was paying attention to us—no one except for Tora at Mag's side. Her smile was malicious as she hung on every word. The rest of the Aesir were violently drunk, feasting and dancing, listening to loud music beyond where we sat.

"You're going beneath Asgard Palace. In the depths, there are prison cells holding hoards of beasts, enemies of Asgard who are ready to destroy everything and everyone you love, Anais." If I wasn't terrified of the electric shock, I might've shuddered. In my pleas to be free of this nightmare, I'd forgotten that ultimately, once I freed Fenrir, I would be dooming the world, including everyone I loved at home.

Frigg and Odin sat at the head of the room, not paying any mind to the plans their grandson was whispering to me. None of the other gods or goddesses paid any mind, busy with their nightly feasting festivities. Tyr was ripping chunks from a turkey leg at the table no more than forty feet from us, his eyes glued to the golden-haired goddess being circled by two lynx cats at the head of the room. She sat next to Thor, lazily twirling the end of her braid around her finger as she stared at nothing in particular.

"Allow me to give you a lesson in mythology, since I didn't give you enough time to research it before we left Midgard. You were so eager to follow me without any hesitation—for that I must thank you." He kissed my cheek teasingly before continuing.

"Loki, the God of Mischief, had three children with the giantess Angrboda. The first was a daughter Hel, Goddess of Helheim, the realm of torture and suffering on the edge of the frozen lands of Niflheim. Truly terrifying is what she is—she's half a rotting corpse. She has a city where she tortures the souls of anyone who does not make it to Valhalla. Since Valhalla is only for those warriors who die in battle, most end up in Hel's realm. I'm sure you will, too, when you die after Fenrir drags you to Helheim himself. The second child of Angrboda and Loki is Jormungandr. He is one of Loki's two children who received the God of Mischief's ability to shapeshift, but only into one form. Both of Loki's sons can shapeshift into a Divine Form. Jormungandr is the World Serpent, a snake so long it can wrap around the earth twice through the oceans. The third child is Fenrir, the great wolf." Mag's eyes flared at the name of the last son of Loki.

My thoughts caught on the word 'wolf,' trying to remember if he'd mentioned that before. I masked the frown threatening to cross my face. I hadn't realized that's why the wolves were so dangerous here—they were led by the brother of the devil.

"Odin began to have visions of Ragnarok about eleven hundred years ago. In his visions, he saw the half beautiful woman-half corpse of Hel, the massive serpent, and the wolf, Fenrir. He saw Hel lead her armies into Asgard as the serpent flooded Asgard and drowned Thor. Fenrir killed Odin himself, swallowed him and then the sun to doom Midgard." Mag's eyes fixed on the Allfather, who was speaking in a hushed tone to Frigg beside him. They reminded me of the statue I saw weeks ago in the Palace Plaza. I imagined everything around it burning at Ragnarok, the destruction of this beautiful city, of the beautiful room where we stood. They deserved every bit of it, these horrid gods and goddesses that were so gleeful to play with mortal lives just for fun. I wondered why Mag would want this, the death of his father, the unleashing of this beast on his home. For his home to be decimated by the trio from Hell.

"When the Allfather had these visions of Ragnarok, he knew these beasts were related to Loki. He banished the serpent to Midgard. He banished Hel to Helheim, to rule and to be the Goddess of Torture. He brought Fenrir here as a teenager to be raised in Asgard. I grew up with Fenrir for a time, when he lived here. He was raised by Tyr, and well, you saw what Fenrir did. He took Tyr's hand, all because Tyr made sure Fenrir was bound to keep him from getting more powerful."

"Are you on the edge of your seat yet?" His whisper had grown rather breathy with excitement, and his hand was circling higher on my leg, his thumb brushing over my sex through my thin panties, visible under tonight's skimpy black dress held up by delicate body chains. I wanted to cringe away from him, but he grabbed the metal collar encircling my neck and pulled me close so I couldn't escape his words.

"When you unleash him, all the siblings from the underworld will get together, reform in Helheim. Then they will come here, and they will destroy Odin and Asgard, unleashing all their revenge pent up after being bound and banished for so long. That's Ragnarok. They will destroy the Aesir. But Tora and I will survive, and as the only living heirs, we will assume the power of the Allfather. We will rebuild Asgard, and we will come back to destroy Loki's filthy children once and for all."

So it *was* a royal power play. He wanted the power of the Allfather. He was willing to free the being that would be instrumental in raining Hell upon the people of Asgard, Midgard, and all the other realms, whoever was unfortunate enough to live there. Odin, his grandfather, would be eaten by the enormous wolf. That would leave him and Tora to take the throne and rebuild Asgard. How they would survive Ragnarok

I did not know, and he did not offer details. I could not ask him any of the circling questions in my head.

"Tomorrow, you'll face the wolves who guard the entrance to where Fenrir the great wolf is bound. I want you to free him. You'll need the knife of Gleipnir, which is in the room where he's held. Break the glass and use the knife to cut him loose. Then bring him out the door to me." Against my will, my hands ran over his chest and neck as he continued whispering to me, continuing the charade that I was his temptress.

"After he takes you with him, I'll turn you over to Odin. Tell him that Hel sent you to tempt me, to trick us. She is the child of the trickster god, after all. The punishment for freeing such an enemy of Asgard as Fenrir is death. Once he's free, he can unleash Ragnarok, and then the plan is complete. I will rebuild Asgard and the trio will slink back off to Helheim. The deal was that if I helped free her brother, Hel would return to her own realm and let Tora and I rebuild Asgard in peace. We'll rebuild Midgard in time too, but with the fall of Asgard, Midgard will fall too." He purred, and chills went up my spine. Kerri, my family, my home. It was going to die, all because I had fallen for Mag. Allowed him to lure me here and trap me alone. I wanted to cry, to beat him with my fists and scream in fury.

I had let this man show me an ounce of attention, and that was all it took to pull me into the plot of a villain seeking power across realms. Kerri was going to kick my ass if she ever saw me again. Plus I had to deal with these wolves tomorrow, and it was dawning on me how likely it was that I would die by one of their jaws first. I was sure no Asgardian wolves or dogs of Odin's were anything like the wolves I fed at home at the sanctuary. Mag didn't seem to care if I lived or died, so if the wolves tore me to pieces, he likely wouldn't stop it. What about when I faced the wolf Fenrir himself and cut him free? Would he not snap me up as a snack on the way to Odin?

I wanted to scream as loud as I could. I wanted someone in the room to acknowledge me. To hear me. To see me. *Please notice me,* I begged everyone around me, reaching out to try to get the attention of anyone, anything I could reach with my mind.

I cried and swiped the tears from my cheeks before he saw them. I prayed, begging the Christian God I grew up with for help in my desperate time of need.

Mag stood, casually brushing me off his lap into his chair. My body straightened, fingers curling around the clawed armrests as I sat waiting for his next command. My leg stretched out from the slit in my deep crimson dress, and several gods nearby made sure to take a long mental picture. Mag was surveying the fallen night outside, the purple mountains beyond where palaces glinted in the hillside.

He turned, looking back into my eyes, a wicked grin stretching across his face. "Come, let's walk." He stretched out a hand and I obeyed his silent command. I rose from his chair, walking to him gracefully and placing my thin, mortal hand in his. He led me through the palace, deeper into the belly of the building. We descended a magnificent turquoise-and-white stone staircase into the depths, and rock walls rose on either side as we made our way down.

"This is where we will come tomorrow. Beyond this door are the wolves who guard his chamber, and then the wolf himself. Fenrir." I wanted to shiver at the name. I studied the towering door, intricately carved with a depiction of an enormous wolf surrounded by its pack.

My mother had told me enough times that my volunteering at the wolf sanctuary would end with the wolves getting me. She just got the location wrong; it would be Asgard where the wolves got to me.

Mag wrapped on the door, and the two wolves on the other side snarled and snapped, barking at the noise of his fist landing on the wooden door. Their deep growls rattled the heavy wood doors, and I wondered how large they were.

"Hey Fenrir. Do you know what I have?" He taunted the wall with a malevolent chuckle. There was no other reply than the two animals in the next room continuing their barrage of howling barks and snarls.

"Did you really think, *darling*, that for one second I would want you? Truly?" He turned on me, dragging a finger down the side of my face, studying me. "You are beautiful to be sure—you will be missed from the world when you die—but you're not *really* my type." He was talking loudly, and the beasts had quieted on the other side of the door.

"I knew everything about you before I even got there, Anais. Your boring life working with those stupid mutts. Your stupid little coffee shop with your drinks full of sugary shit. Your overbearing and insolent mother. I had to fit into your life flawlessly, so you wouldn't question anything I told you, anywhere I wanted to take you. I think I did well, don't you?" He gripped my chin with one hand to look over my terrified, fury-filled face. "We studied you for weeks, Tora and I. You were the perfect choice. The connection you have with wolves. Your gullibility. Your desire for fantasy to be real. It is, but not in the way you expected, hm? Turns out you really couldn't be a better choice to free the Prince of Hell." He chuckled, and I thought I could hear a deep rumbling from the other side of the door, shaking the walls.

"It's been so much fun to play with you, to bend you to my will and the will of the other Aesir. So easy to break you too, Anais. Just like the wolves you love so much, all it took was a collar and some domestication. Some training." He grinned as a snarl ripped from the other side of the door, sending my knees into a bout of unstoppable shivering. As much as I loved wolves, I only felt sheer terror when I heard the noise the monster wolf was making on the other side of the door. "And now every man in Asgard has had her mouth wrapped around their cock. Just know when you take her to Hell, she's already a dirty slut used by everyone before you." The growl on the other side of the door became deeper, and I stumbled slightly as the palace swayed with the vibrating noise.

Mag grinned, obviously taunting the wolf behind the doors. "Well, I'd send her in to you right now, but I have to enjoy one last night with her while you're … shall we say, incapacitated? Unable to defend her? Unable to do anything?" He reached out, grabbing me by the throat and sending me into a panic. I fought my instinct to claw against him, not wanting to risk permanent injury.

"I hope you're not disappointed." Mag sneered as he spoke to the door. "She's not exactly that pretty. Granted, she was prettier when I first brought her here, but that's the price of being broken. No matter. She won't live long, anyway."

Backing me against Fenrir's door, he took the opportunity of the deserted hallway to force himself on me, making me sob and cry in pain as he used me. I could hear a struggle on the other side of the door, muffled shouting, and the wolves continued their barrage on the door.

I prayed again to the Christian God, waiting for a response that never came. Feeling increasingly desperate and broken from myself, I turned to other gods, praying for anyone to save me. *Please, Jesus, Aphrodite, Buddha, Someone. Anyone. Please help me. Fuck, I'll even take the Goddess of Hell right about now.* No response came, just Mag's horrible huffing sounds in my ear. *Wolf God Fenrir...* I was giving up, the flame of fight dying out slowly inside me. I threw my last desperate bid at the beast on the other side of the door.

"I am here."

I jumped at the voice inside my head, a deep man's voice with a hint of an animalistic growl that made a shiver shoot down my spine. Mag's glare focused on me, narrowing his eyes as if he could tell something had changed. I swallowed and felt him finger the collar around my neck as a silent reminder of his power.

Fenrir? Please, help me, I can't go on like this... I had no idea how this was working, but I didn't have the time to question it. This had to be a hallucination, but the voice felt so real...

"You must help me, so I can help you."

I stilled as Mag resumed his thrusting, but a strange calm washed over me. I wasn't alone anymore. This Fenrir was here, even if he was supposedly going to drag me to literal Hell after this. It sounded like he had a plan, and that was good enough for now.

Tell me what to do. I could shake with relief that I didn't feel so alone.

"When he lets go and steps away, come through the doors. You'll be able to open them. Gerri and Freki are waiting for you on the other side. They won't hurt you."

Mag finished with a grunt and stepped back from me as his lips twisted into a satisfied smirk. "Oh, I'm sorry Ana, didn't you get off too?" He chuckled at his own joke when I smoothed my skirt, waiting for him to turn. I wasn't listening to his words anymore. Sweat beaded on my forehead when I thought he might force me ahead of him. But he didn't. As always, he turned his back on me, trusting that I could never hurt him and was too obedient to try to run away.

Lunging for the handle, I hauled the heavy wood door open and darted through. Two massive wolves, as large as Great Dane dogs, stood on the other side of the door, making my heart stop. I stared at the golden eyes of both wolves, one black and one white. Both beasts bared their teeth at Mag behind me through the open door.

"Get down!" the deep voice snarled at me.

I dropped to the ground, covering the back of my neck with my hands as both wolves leapt over me. Gasping, I looked back to see the wolves standing at the threshold, blocking Mag from following me.

"Calling her to you early, Fenrir?" Mag yelled, looking over my head with an evil smirk. "I wasn't going to send her to you until tomorrow, but I suppose you couldn't wait just a little longer?"

I pushed myself up, stumbling back from the snarling wolves. As I looked up, I saw a man, a human man, that Mag was directing his taunts toward in another part of the room. The stranger wasn't looking at Mag, though. He was locked on to me, unblinking, with pale golden eyes that were definitely not human. My head swung back and forth as I looked for the great black wolf I was supposed to free. There was no one other than the man, who was kneeling in front of a massive boulder that had to be the size of my apartment building. As I looked at him, I saw he was bound to the boulder with golden metal ribbons, just as Mag said Fenrir would be. He was gagged as well, unable to speak to me aloud.

"The knife, in the case on the wall. Hurry," the gagged man encouraged me.

Looking to my left, there was a glass case around a strange, golden knife. It looked unlike any blade I'd seen before, pure gold. I almost thought I heard a high-pitched ringing in my ears the longer I stared at it. I scrambled toward it, my bare feet padding on the chilly stone floor.

You're a human? I couldn't help my eyes sliding to him over my shoulder again. He was beautiful, to put it lightly. Somehow, the shadows and darkness that seemed to dance behind him were more striking than Mag and Tora's ethereal beauty. Long, shaggy black hair fell in front of his entrancing and unnerving yellow eyes. He was completely nude save for the metal bonds crisscrossing him. I was going to try to keep Kerri's taunting from my head and ignore that fact. Of course, growing up in the church I went to, I'd learned nudity was something to be ashamed of, to be shy about.

"At the moment," he responded evenly.

I thought you were supposed to be a wolf. My brows knit together.

"Questions later." He raised his eyebrow at me with urgency. One of the wolves behind me cried out in pain and I smelled

burning fur, making me hurry to the glass case. My fingers ran along the edges, looking for a latch or some way to open it.

"You have to break it. Be as careful as you can … please." His inflection alluded to the knife being precious, or delicate. I turned to look at the golden-eyed stranger, who was watching me with concern, before scanning around the room. There was nothing with which to break the glass; the room empty except for the man and the wolves. Turning back to the problem at hand, I didn't see any way for me to break it other than with my elbow.

It took several hits before the glass finally shattered, splintering into dangerous daggers that barraged my arm and shoulder. A particularly nasty shard cut deep into my arm until I felt a frighteningly cold tingle in my fingers. I cried out in pain, but my scream was cut off by my recovering throat. I could feel the glass digging deep into my flesh and blood starting to drip down my side.

"Don't look." He sounded commanding in my head, and with a trembling lip, I nodded, keeping my eyes level instead of looking down. Taking the strange knife in my fingers, I listened as the ringing in my ears got louder. Sickening vibrations reminded me all too much of the collar still around my neck as they pulsed through me from the hilt now in my grip. Looking it over, I saw no damage, remembering him mentioning it was delicate.

I heard a loud yelp, and my attention was drawn to where Mag was in the doorway, struggling with the wolves. One was on the ground writhing and crying out with pain.

"Hurry, he's going to kill Gerri and then Freki. You need to free me, now." Fenrir made a muffled shouting noise to try to get

my attention, snapping me out of being frozen watching the two animals fight the lightning god.

As I turned to walk back his direction, I found myself staring into those unnerving eyes again. Mesmerized by him and horrified by his predicament, I couldn't break myself away. I dropped to my knees in front of him. My lips pursed as my gaze met his pleading, desperate look. He was staring at me like I held all the oxygen left in the world, and he was begging me for one final breath. He scanned me, taking in the crimson and gold outfit I wore, lingering on my collar. Fury flashed in his expression, but his eyes returned to the pleading expression immediately when he gazed at my face again. I reached out, gently running a finger along his jet black hair, which made his eyes flutter momentarily. He shuddered, the sigh of someone who hadn't been touched so gently in ages.

"There's no time for this now. Get my arm loose first. Hurry."

I started cutting the strange gold metal away from him, the sickening vibration getting stronger as metal ground through metal. I waited for the blade to shock me the way my collar did, but it never came.

Blood was starting to slick everything, and I was becoming increasingly panicked at the lack of feeling in the fingers on my injured arm. I gasped for air as I continued sawing. The sickening buzzing from the blade in my hand made me lean to the side and heave up what little food I'd gotten at dinner.

"Try to stay calm. Breathe." His voice lost the desperate edge it had a moment before and instead sounded as though he were trying to soothe me.

My eyes flicked to him at the more gentle tone in his voice. Finally, the metal snapped away, and I started on the next binding. Seconds later his arm was free, and I was preparing to start on one of the bands around his chest.

I'd lost track of the fight behind me. I listened as I frantically sawed through the next bond but didn't hear any fighting, just heavy breaths.

"Anais." Mag made a disappointed clicking noise with his mouth. I chanced a glance over my shoulder to see him stopped at the door, shaking his head. Only one wolf remained, pacing between us protectively. "Did you forget that you're still mine? Give me one reason not to kill her right now in front of you, Fenrir. Just to see the look on your face." The next moment, I was riddled with electricity, bringing me to the floor. After-shocks left me convulsing next to Fenrir, the knife still in my hand.

I choked in pain on the ground while Fenrir struggled to free the rest of his arm where I failed to remove the bindings. He was almost free, but I hadn't managed to remove all the ribbons. When Mag released his electric hold on me I lay panting on the stone, watching as Fenrir wiggled free of another tether.

"Enjoying that, Fenrir?" Mag smirked as he made a show of lifting his fingers, snapping them together milliseconds before I squealed in pain again and writhed on the ground, trying futilely to get the collar off. When the electric shocks stopped, I lay twitching, watching as Fenrir strained against his bonds, several snapping as he continued to wrench and tug his arm desperately against them.

Mag laughed, snapping his fingers again and again, making me yelp and twist. I worried my heart may explode from the shocks. Tears wet my face, and when the last electric bolt zipped through me I lay gasping, feeling as though I couldn't get air into my lungs.

Now free of the bindings on his arm and chest, Fenrir reached down to grab at the collar around my neck. I squeaked in fear, feeling his fingers wrap around the metal before it snapped easily in his grasp. Pulling the broken collar from my neck, he discarded it as I lay panting on the cool stone ground. He snatched the knife from my hand, and I watched with glazed eyes as he slid the blade between his cheek and the gag in his mouth, sawing for just a moment before the band of metal fell away. He immediately turned and started freeing his other arm.

It's gone... He can't hurt me anymore. I lifted a shaky hand to my neck, feeling my bare skin and the wounds where the metal had rubbed my skin raw. To be free of it after more than a month had tears brimming, and I couldn't help letting out a choked sob as they began leaking down my cheeks. The relief mixed with intense pain.

"I am going to fucking kill you, Mag!" Fenrir roared, making the room quake. He was freeing himself far faster than I could, throwing the metal ribbons from himself and rising to stand as he cursed Mag. The knife fell with a clang to the ground beside me. Slowly and with only my good arm, I started pushing myself up to my knees, wrapping my good hand over the blade once more and then rising to my feet.

"Well, Geri is dead, Odin will assume the girl did it when she entered, and if you're still here, you'll both be sentenced to execution. Besides, she's losing blood. I don't think you have the time to kill me right now, Fenrir." I could see Mag's evil sneer from the corner of my eye. "Ana, this was fun. Maybe we'll do it again before Odin executes you, hm?" He winked as I glared at him. "I'll be seeing you," he offered before turning and walking away.

By the time I looked back to the wolf-man, he was standing tall over me, black pants wrapped around his legs. This... This was a GOD. He had to be at least as tall as Shaquille O'Neal. He was staring down at me, the corner of his mouth curving up as I stared back at him. I used the back of my good hand to brush away the tears.

"You are funny, hjarta." He tipped his head, his eyes narrowing on my arm with a flash of panic. *"And you are injured. Let's go."*

His mention of my injury made me acutely aware of the feeling of glass burrowing into my flesh. The smaller shards that peppered me burned, and blood worked its way out around the glass with every heartbeat. My head started to spin.

"Don't look," he reminded me, reaching out toward me. His voice was slightly softer again, although still commanding.

"Don't touch me," I hissed, taking a step back and tightening my grip on the blade handle.

"I can carry you. We have to go through a seam." He took another step forward and extended his hand.

"I said don't touch me!" I growled, lifting the end of the knife toward him, prepared to try to defend myself. The vibration made me want to retch again, but I swallowed and forced myself to remain facing Fenrir.

"Okay, okay," he conceded, showing me his palms in surrender and backing up a half step. He was studying me, continually returning to where my arm steadily dripped blood onto the floor next to me. If I didn't know better, I'd think he was a vampire the way he looked at me and that blood.

"What about those?" I pointed with my knife to the gold ribbons that looked like they were tattooed into his skin around each wrist and his neck.

"I don't think they restrict my power." He didn't take his eyes from me to even glance at the gold on himself.

"How can you talk in my head?" The knife was shaking in my hand, and a small groan passed my gritted teeth.

"Anais." He said my name slowly, as if he were savoring the first time it rolled off his tongue. "I need to get you through the seam. You're badly wounded; we don't have time for questions right now."

My vision was starting to go double, and the light headedness was making me feel like I was watching the scene from outside my own body. "You're going to take me to Hell," I accused, backing away on wobbling legs. I stumbled, looking down at the blood on the ground around me, panting with terror as black seeped into my vision from every angle. The blade slid from my fingers as dizziness collided with darkness in full force.

"Yes I am." He reached down and scooped my limp form into one arm, my head falling against his chest. I looked up into faintly glowing golden orbs just before my eyes rolled back into my head, giving in to the darkness.

CHAPTER 13

I ntense pain and loud voices dragged me unceremoniously from unconsciousness.

"She's bleeding too much!" a voice boomed above me.

"She is, but I'll stop it. Sit there and I'll get her something for the pain." I could hear a woman's voice and shuffling noises around us. "I'm going to summon some IV fluids and an anesthetic from Midgard. She's going to be okay, Fen—"

"We should take her to Midgard now, their healers know more than you do," the deep growling voice snapped. I opened my eyes to a slit, the dim light of the room blinding. My eyes felt like they were moving in slow motion as I turned a fractional amount to see I was leaning my heavy head against a man's bare chest. My breath blew across his dark chest hair, and his heartbeat thundered in my ear.

"Don't be stupid. Do you really think Odin hasn't already sent Aesir there?" the woman responded. "We know enough to save her right now and help her recover."

"What if we took her somewhere else on Midgard? Another country?" The man's voice was tinged with panic.

"And how will that be better for her, Fen? Waking up in another country, where she doesn't speak the language, with *you*? And Aesir after you both? Absolutely not." The woman's voice was becoming accusatory, and suddenly my body felt too overwhelmed with pain to listen to their argument anymore.

I squeezed my eyelids shut again and a whimper escaped my throat as sharp, searing pain burned through my arm. It hurt, everything hurt, and it was all I could think about.

"I know, I know, *hjarta*," a deep, silky voice said somewhere above me, and I opened my eyes to slits again to look up at him. He was carrying me, his arms hooked under my back and knees, cradling my limp body close to his broad chest. He glanced down at me, his dark hair falling in front of his eyes. "I'm going to make it stop soon," he promised before looking back up to where I assumed the woman was standing.

I moaned, trying to force my eyes open from a too-long blink, and gasped at the pain coursing through me. Trying to look down at my arm, all I could see was a bloody mess of glass protruding from my ripped flesh.

"Oh God..." I made a terrified whimpering noise followed by a choked sob. His arms tightened around me. Adjusting his grip, he sat down, pulling me ever closer and settling me on his lap. He gently cradled my shoulders, holding me in a sitting position.

"It's okay. You're going to be okay," he reassured me, lifting an arm to stroke my hair. "I'll try to heal you the right way first, but I won't let you die. I promise."

I wasn't listening to his words. Adrenaline surged through me the moment his other arm slackened. Mangled arm be damned—I was going to get away from this monster from Hell and try to go home. Using my good arm and my legs, I shoved hard against his chest and fell to the floor.

"Agh!" I cried out when I hit the ground, the glass burying deeper in my shoulder. My entire body ached with protest at my sharp movements.

"Anais!" Fenrir roared, reaching for me on the ground. I flinched, not from pain this time but the fact that he already knew my name and seemed so comfortable saying it.

"N-no! D-don't t-touch me!" I gasped, trying to yell. My voice came out too choppy and raspy to be considered anything more than a broken whimper. I pushed myself out of his reach and to a standing position. Squinting around the room to get my bearings, cradling my injured limb to my chest, I stood slouched over and shaking as my arm dripped a steady flow of blood onto the floor.

My gaze darted around as my body strained to keep me upright and conscious. There were three people in the room: the giant Fenrir, the man I remembered as the lieutenant from the forest, and a tall, wispy woman with long white hair and glacial blue eyes who must be Hel. All three were staring at me with concerned expressions, and I stared back at them, equally as bewildered. I would not go down without a fight this time.

I wouldn't just automatically submit and let them walk all over me. If they killed me for it, so be it, but I was going to fight, to try to escape.

"We just want to help." The man with short brown hair and amber eyes put a hand up toward me in a 'stop' motion. What was his name again? Jerry? I tried but couldn't remember, my memory blinded by pain.

We all stood frozen. I looked down, seeing I was spattered with blood and still wearing the crimson dress, which my blood was blending into all too well. Red ran down my arm, was hand printed across my body and smeared across my legs. It was a complete mess, and it was going to make me sick if I looked any longer.

I heaved breath in and out of my lungs and frantically sized up the door behind Fenrir. It seemed to be the only exit available, but I would have to dodge him and the other man. Not so easy on my unsteady legs.

"Don't try it," Fenrir hissed in frustration, shaking his head at me. "Just sit down and let us help you."

"Let m-me go! I w-want to go h-home!" I cried through my raspy throat. I stumbled towards the door a few steps, and Fenrir moved in front of me to block my escape route. "I s-said don't touch me!" I hissed when he reached for me again. But I was unsteady now, overcome with a wave of dizziness. I tumbled sideways in my efforts to escape. Fenrir caught me, stopping my head from hitting the corner of a table, and he lifted me gently. I batted at his hands but quickly became too weak, my body going limp in his arms once again as I blinked away the black spots in my vision. I was going to die here, with strangers, in fucking Hell.

"You're going to be okay," Fenrir murmured to me, ever so gently tucking my hair behind my ear. His tone was reassuring, but his voice was tinged with terror when he next spoke. "Hellia! Help me!" he snarled as he gathered me in his arms. He sounded panicked, but consciousness was escaping me again and my eyes were rolling back in my head. The voices in the room fell away, sounding quiet and muffled. The lights became fuzzy as things started to move in slow motion around me. I faintly felt the prick of a needle in my arm before deep, dreamless sleep overcame me.

"She's dead weight!" someone yelled loud enough to shake the cabin and jar me from sleep. I blinked and found myself groggy as I looked around the unfamiliar room. A chandelier swung slightly above me, and my back hurt from laying on a hard surface. Fog clouded my brain and forced my eyelids closed, my head falling back again with a wooden thud. I faintly heard the distant rumbling of male voices, but the sharp ache in my arm was enough to distract me and lure me back to sleep.

The same voice jarred my eyes open once more, and I looked around to see where the noise was coming from.

"You need to focus and not be playing savior with pretty mortal girls!" I caught a glimpse of a man, tall but nowhere near the height of the wolf-man.

Now Fenrir was yelling, his tone argumentative. "I'll save whoever I damn want, Jorm! Especially the woman who cut me free!"

"She's just a tool. You used her to get free and now she's worthless. Discard her!"

"I will never, *ever*, 'discard' her. Get out of my house!" The walls shook again.

I saw a flash of bright red hair fly out the door before it slammed, shaking the house. The heavy weights on my eyelids won, and my head dropped back on the hard, uncomfortable surface where I was laying with a thud.

I blinked slowly, my eyelids feeling heavy, and dizziness made my vision swim. I couldn't move, couldn't feel anything. Waiting for a long moment, the dizziness subsided long enough to gather my bearings slightly. I was laying in a different place now, the surface under me soft, and I was facing a big arm chair where the werewolf god was sitting, pouring over a thick book. My blinks were long and slow, and I scanned the other books sitting next to the chair. All were in English, so I could read them, and as I read the titles slowly in my head, I saw they were all medical textbooks—surgical procedures, human health, and critical care of surgery patients. The effort of reading the titles alone was exhausting. In his hands was one about infectious human diseases. He skimmed the page quickly before flipping to the next, reading inhumanly fast, or so I thought. I wasn't sure if I was hallucinating the whole thing.

My blinks became longer, and I watched his dark eyebrows crease as he skimmed the page. I watched with heavy lids as his lips moved, murmuring something unintelligible to himself before flipping to the next page. My eyelids were closed before the next page turn.

"How is she?" Fenrir's gruff voice had me blinking slowly awake, nausea overtaking me immediately, but I still couldn't move. I focused on inhaling and exhaling the air from my lungs.

"She's recovering, slower because she's mortal, but it's only been a couple days and it looks good to me," Hel said, her back to me.

I became increasingly aware of my painfully cracked lips and my parched throat. Eyeing the wooden cup of water on the table, a rag laying next to it, a whispered grunt escaped me. I tried to move any part of my weighted body toward it, immediately drawing Fenrir's attention.

"You need water," he said, crouching next to the couch and bringing the cup to my lips. He very gently tipped a miniature mouthful down my throat before pulling back, waiting for me to swallow. It was cool and helped soothe my stomach slightly, so I tried to lean forward for more. He brought it back to my lips, tipping another swallow down my throat.

"Not too quickly," he warned in a soft voice. I only found myself able to get down a few more sips before I was panting from the effort and my eyes were falling closed. "That's good," I heard him breathe a sigh. "That's good, right?" I assumed his question was directed toward his sister. I didn't hear her reply.

This time when my vision adjusted to the dark firelight of the room, I found him sitting in the arm chair, forearms braced on his knees, dark hair hanging across his face down into his eyes.

"You're awake." He gave me a small smile that looked relieved.

I groaned, closing my eyes to go back to sleep. Turning my head away from the firelight, I was sure I could easily catch sleep again in the next few moments.

"No, no, you need to try to eat something." He gently took my chin and turned my head back toward him.

"I can't—" I wheezed. "D-don't touch me…" He let go of my chin immediately.

"Here, water first." I opened my eyes when I felt the rim of the cup against my lips again. I swallowed two sips before he replaced the cup with a tiny bite of fluffy bread that melted on my tongue.

"Good." He sighed after I'd swallowed several small bites. "Now have a drink of this." He held another cup to my lips, and I tasted a very rich, meaty broth on my tongue. The flavor wasn't recognizable, but it was strong, gamey, and after just a small amount I was pulling back.

"You can't drink anymore?" he asked, frowning at the cup and then at me. "Come, try again." He lifted it to my lips but I turned my head away, closing my eyes and settling back to rest.

I jumped awake, my eyes darting around the room. It was daylight outside, making the cabin brighter than the last time I was conscious. I was fully awake this time, feeling having returned to my whole body. Holding in a low moan, I turned my head to see my bandaged shoulder, becoming painfully aware of the ache there and the stitches in my skin under the bandage.

I turned toward the pair of amber eyes watching me from the kitchen. The lieutenant, who seemed to pause in the middle of approaching me with fresh gauze in hand, watched me with a concerned and fascinated expression.

I gasped, scrambling up, swinging my foot over the side of the couch. Woozy didn't even begin to describe the way my head was still swimming from the drugs and blood loss. Even the day after they removed the glass from my shoulder, I was dehydrated and unsure of what they were giving me when I was unconscious.

"Do not"—the brown haired man reached a hand out toward me like he was taming a velociraptor—"try to run." He gave a small shake of his head, not breaking eye contact with me. "Don't do it." He kept his voice low as he raised an eyebrow at me.

I started to hyperventilate as he took another step closer, my hand reaching up to smack my neck and ensure the collar was really and truly gone. This man couldn't shock me, couldn't punish me for disobeying unless he got his hands on me. I was free.

"I'm Jerrick. You remember me, right?" His voice was kind and warm, oddly comforting. But he was still a man, still getting closer, still reaching out toward me.

"Don't touch me," I snapped, scooting to the edge of the couch opposite of him.

"Yeah, you said that." He sighed, running a hand through his short brown floppy hair. "I'm sorry, but I have to finish wrapping that." He pointed to my arm. I slowly looked down, shivering with the fear of seeing the mangled mess again. Instead I saw only white bandages halfway wrapped and some dark stitches pulling my red skin together tightly.

"No." I slid both legs off the table when he took his next step.

"Can Hellia do it?" He was trying to accommodate me, but all I wanted was to run for the door. It could be no more than seven meters to the door from here. I would have the upper hand, being closer. I could probably just make it out the door. Maybe I could scream for help.

"Anais," Jerrick's tone was warning, but I bolted anyway.

I threw the door open to a blizzard. Wind whipped snow into my face and chilled my skin. Trees moaned in the force of nature outside, and thick clouds rolled between sheets of frozen water. I didn't take a moment to think it through, didn't take stock of how my body felt before forcing myself into the frozen tundra, barefoot and wearing some sort of pajamas.

I took another step into the shin-deep drifts beyond the threshold of the door, stumbling and inadvertently putting out my injured arm to catch myself. Before I could hit the ground, a strong arm caught me, breaking my fall and saving my arm from terrible pain.

"Where do you think you're going?" The looming figure of Fenrir towered over me. "It's too cold, and you're too small and weak. You'll die in minutes." He scooped me up easily and carried me back inside the cabin.

"Put me down!" I screamed, thrashing in his arms. My fighting did little to dissuade him. "Get off me, you giant motherfucker!" He didn't set me down once the door slammed behind us, just continued through a large doorway into a bedroom. I struggled in his arms as he sat down on the bed, still keeping a tight hold on me.

"Do not run like that again," he demanded. "You won't survive out there."

"Maybe I don't want to survive Hell!" I yelped, trying to escape from him, feeling panic rise as I took in the bed and his grip on me. I started clawing at him, digging my nails into his skin with no result.

"I'm not going to hurt you. We will talk about everything later, but you need to rest." He looked down at me with some exasperation. "Please."

"I told you not to touch me!" I renewed my struggle, thrashing against him and trying to get a decent hold to push myself away from him again. "Get your hands off me!" I was starting to sweat from him touching me so much, from being restrained by someone so much larger and stronger than me. So much larger and stronger than Mag, even.

"Let me go!" I shouted over and over, panic gripping me

"I'm never letting you go," he growled, a dangerous edge in his tone. "You keep trying to run, and I'm scared I'm going to find you frozen to death outside the door tomorrow morning if I take my eyes off of you for another second." He muttered something under his breath about Jerrick being useless that I didn't quite catch.

I continued my efforts to get away with no results. I twisted this way and that, pinched and stretched my new stitches, kicked and clawed at him, but nothing worked.

"I swear to the gods, I'll keep hold of you until you give up and sleep in my arms." His threat finally made me pause, panting from the effort of all the movement. I lay limp in his arms, feeling his chest against my back.

"Here, I have something to help her rest." The woman's voice was back. "Let me see her good arm." I looked up to see the white-haired woman smiling with a sympathetic look at me, a syringe in her hand.

"No!" I yelped, trying to struggle away from where he now held my good arm still for his sister. "Okay, okay, I'll be good, I won't run. Okay? Please, please don't do this," I begged them. Fenrir cleared his throat uncomfortably as Hel plunged the needle into my arm and pressed the chilly liquid into my veins.

"I'm sorry. We're not trying to scare you." Hel's voice was soft and filled with what sounded like kindness as she removed the needle from me and sat down on the bed near Fenrir's leg. I glared at her, not trusting a word. "We don't want you running and getting hurt. It's eternal winter out there. You'll get killed, and we can't have that; you just got here."

The drugs forced my body to relax back against Fenrir's chest, and he adjusted his arms to gently hug me to him, my head lolling back on his shoulder. I didn't fall asleep immediately this time, and as my eyes slowly closed, I felt him brushing my hair as he heaved a sigh behind me. I begged my body to let me pass out before any abuse started; I couldn't handle anything more. Darkness seeped into my vision and consumed everything.

"I've got you now. No one is going to hurt you here. Anyone who tries to hurt you? I'll kill them. No one who has hurt you will survive me." He was whispering in my ear as I slid away, "You're safe, Anais."

CHAPTER 14

S oft daylight warmed the insides of my eyelids, gently shaking me from sleep. My lashes fluttered as my eyesight adjusted to the soft grey light streaming in from several windows around me. Brows furrowed, I looked around, trying to assess where I was. I lay in an enormous bed placed on an elevated part of the room, one step leading down to where I could see a kitchen with a table on the left, a living room with huge chairs and a couch to the right. The tall windows placed around the room showed thick snow covering pine trees, with a creek running through snow drifts on one side.

A dull ache in my arm took my attention from my surroundings, and I looked down to see a bloodied bandage wrapped around my shoulder. I slowly tried to squeeze my fingers and found I could only partially do it right now. My hand still felt on pins and needles. My clothes were missing, replaced with a silky black tank top and comfortable matching pants.

I glanced around the room, looking for any sign of Fenrir, but saw none. Pushing myself up on my uninjured arm, I swung my legs over the side of the bed to stand. I reached up to my head and felt two thick braids of my hair running across the top and down my shoulders. Chilly air pricked my skin, and I wrapped my good arm around myself as I shuffled into the main room. Thick curtains hung between the bed and the rest of the room, pulled back and secured with black ropes.

In the main room there was a large hearth, a fire crackling with life in the center and warming the room. The furniture was a mixture of black leather and wood pieces, all worn from use. Blankets draped over the couch and chairs, and the pile of books about human health were still sitting in the living room. Shuddering, I surveyed the rest of the sitting area, searching for a good escape route, which was still looking to be the main heavy door across from the bed space.

"How are you feeling?"

I hadn't noticed the woman sitting at the corner of the table until she spoke. Though her voice was soft, I jumped at the noise, whipping around. Hel remained seated at the table, several books and documents spread across the table top before her.

She was tall, even sitting, and slender with pasty skin, her long white hair partially pulled back in a bun while the rest hung down over her shoulders loose, with parts braided and secured by silver beads the same Odin's had been. Her eyes were pale blue, reminding me of the ice that covered the lake where we skated in the winter. Everything about her was winter embodied—there was no rosiness to her cheeks. Her brows and lashes matched her snowy hair color, and she did not glow with godly life the way Tora, Mag, or Odin had. No, it almost seemed as though shadows followed her, just a step behind her. She sat in silence, waiting for my response and regarding me with a calm expression as I warily sized her up.

"Fine," I finally said, wrapping my other, deadened arm across my chest defensively. I didn't say any more, waiting for her to introduce herself. We remained in the uncomfortable silence for several minutes, looking at each other, and my gaze darted around the room to see if there was a reasonable means to escape. Beyond all the windows continued the harsh snowstorm, and wind moaned against the sides of the house.

"Where am I?" I finally dared to ask. She sat back, crossing her arms on the table. She motioned for me to sit across from her, and I slowly took the seat, never letting my attention fully leave her.

"My name is Hellia. We're in Niflheim," she said. My blood instantly chilled at the name. My mouth dried, and I shrank away from her in my chair. Hel. This was the Goddess of Death and the underworld. Disguising herself with a nice name to try to fool me just like Tora and Mag.

Her face remained stoic, but the look in her eyes softened toward me. Everything about her contrasted the dark wood room, only lit from the windows and the fire. I swept my eyes over her again, looking for any sign of her being a corpse, of decay or rotting flesh as Mag had described her to me. I saw none, and while she had nearly no color to her skin, she looked healthy with full lips and cheeks, her hair was thick and shiny rather than brittle and dead as I had expected it to be.

"Why did you bring me here?" I studied the pages before her, maps and documents that looked fragile with tattered edges.

"My brother brought you." She made no move to cover the pages but watched me carefully.

"So you are the goddess Hel." It wasn't a question.

She nodded a confirmation. "I am."

"Why did Fenrir bring me then? Does he want me as a prisoner too, or what?" I asked, glancing around for the large dark figure as if he might suddenly appear in the room.

"You saved him." She shrugged with a cool attitude. I glared at her, wanting more of an explanation. I didn't trust these gods anymore; they toyed with mortals for fun. He was probably keeping me as a toy and would turn me over to Odin any moment. Or she might.

"How does he talk to me in my head?" I asked skeptically.

She looked somewhat dumbstruck by the question, taking a moment to consider. "I'll let him answer that."

I narrowed my eyes on her, frustrated with the lack of an answer.

As if she knew my thoughts, Hellia straightened in her chair, readying for a deep conversation before adding, "I know your name, but it would be more comfortable if you told me."

I glared, squinting at her. I was not telling anyone anything.

She cleared her throat and clasped her hands on the table in front of her. "He brought you here to help you heal. You did an amazing thing for us, freeing him—"

"So you both can destroy my world? Everyone I love?" I cut her off with a hiss.

She offered a sympathetic smile. "I see Mag and Tora told you plenty about us."

"Yes. They filled me in on the crime I committed, and the mythology has been circulating on my planet for some time." My mouth was so dry, I began to search the dark, black counters of the kitchen for a glass and where I could get some water, but I made no move to rise.

Hellia stood—she could be no taller than Kerri—and moved off to the counter, a goblet appearing in her hand. She filled it at a tap on the wall over the basin sink.

Turning, she placed it on the table in front of me. I made no move to accept it, worried about poison or more drugs that would make me lose my senses around these strangers.

But my parched lips begged for the cool liquid to wet them, needing it desperately after all the blood loss. I reached out, snatching the cup, looking down into the water inside. If they wanted to kill me, they would have already done it when that asshole was holding me down. I drank deeply from the goblet of crisp, cool water. Hellia watched me in silence, her hands clasped before her once more.

"We have no plans to destroy the Earth," she said, making me snort in disbelief, sending ripples across the top of the water in the cup.

"Isn't that Fenrir's fate?" I growled.

"It was, in the original prophecy for his life from Odin. But the Norns, the weavers of the tapestry of Fate, never said that. Only that Fenrir will kill Odin at Ragnarok." I stared at her, trying to understand. I looked her over again, this beautiful icy woman that sat before me, blinking slowly and not making any sudden movements.

"Don't you want him to eat the sun and destroy the Earth?" I asked. She shook her head, her finger tracing the wood grain of the table.

"No, I want peace. I want to rule Helheim so my people can thrive. Everyone thinks I am this terrifying, horrid goddess, and I never wanted to be that. I still must be that toward the other gods so they do not know, but I want my realm to be joyous and welcoming. I don't want people to live in fear here." A sudden warmth rose in her face, but it wasn't rosy cheeks. It was genuine kindness for her people.

Genuine. That had no meaning anymore. These people had thousands of years to perfect their acting, their tricks on mortal minds, their lies.

"I thought you were supposed to be a corpse. Also, Fenrir was supposed to be a massive wolf. I expected him to be a wolf chained down there."

She smiled fully, the expression warming her cold features considerably as the skin around her piercing eyes crinkled. "Yes, I suppose you would think that. We do have our … Divine Forms. However, we often prefer our human forms. It's easier to communicate and to fit into smaller spaces like this cabin. For Fenrir at least. We all inherited our father Loki's shapeshifting ability." She sighed, her fingers brushing against her cheek, as if she might suddenly peel away the mask hiding the decayed flesh below.

"Why didn't he just let me die there? Why is he trying to keep me here?" Her smile faded, and she looked me in the eye, sending a shiver down my back.

"You saved Fen. He wouldn't leave you after all you've done for us. He brought you here to recover and hide you from Odin and Mag so you won't be harmed. Fen just wants to protect you." She spoke the nickname of her brother with fondness and obvious love.

"How long has it been?" I asked, looking out the window again at the snow. The storm was now raging, and heavy flakes fell thick on the ground.

She followed my gaze. The soft light from the window illuminated her face in the dark space. "You've been here for two days."

"Can I go home?" My voice broke, suddenly wishing more than anything Kerri was here, yelling at me for my stupidity and complaining about the scar that would be left from the arm wound.

Hellia turned away from the window, fixing her gaze to mine. "No. Not yet. I'm sorry." My heart sank at her words, and tears pricked my eyes. Crushing was the only way to describe the feeling taking over my chest.

I was stuck here, in this strange frozen world, with no way home. I was stuck with the literal devil herself, and a monster wolf. I had a price on my head from gods with enormous power. I was completely powerless here, weak and fully at their mercy.

A noise tore me from my thoughts, and Hellia moved to sit in the chair next to me. She gently picked up my hand, cradling it between her ice cold ones. I yanked it from her grasp, pulling my feet up on the chair and curling into a ball to protect myself.

"Anais," she said, and I realized she was right. I hated that she used my name without me having told it to her.

Without moving, I slid my eyes to her, glaring at her from under my brows. Her face suddenly looked concerned and sympathetic as I curled tighter, trying to keep her out. She sighed, lifting her hand as if she might brush it over the braids in my hair but then thinking better of it. She slowly lowered it to the table again. The human emotions crossing her face shook me, her stoic and unphased attitude disappearing into a worried brow.

"I don't blame you for not trusting me," she said softly, brushing her own hair back behind an ear. "Tora and Mag told you a terrible lie and put you in a horrible position, but I need you to know how your actions saved my brother's life. He can live free now, here with me, with his family." I didn't move, my body locked in place in the chair.

She heaved a sigh and sat back, skimming the papers strewn across the table. "Fen is out right now. He'll be back in a bit."

"I don't care where he is. Tell him to stay away from me," I snapped at her.

"He's not going to hurt you. None of us are." Her voice was soft despite my hostility.

"That's what the last ones made me think too," I hissed, turning away from her and glaring out the window. She didn't say anything more for a moment, the sound of our breathing and the wind moaning outside filling the room.

"If you have any more questions, I am happy to answer," she ventured, but I made no move to interact with her again. My despair grew in my chest, swallowing me whole. I was literally in Hell.

After a long silence, Hellia went back to the other side of the table and began pouring over the documents in front of her again. I watched her for some time. She would read some runes and lean over to a large map, marking it with a sleek black pen. Finally, I rose without a word to her. Her eyes flickered up, but she made no motion to stop me as I walked back to the bed and climbed under the blankets.

I lay staring at the wall and pulled the blankets up over my head. Secure that I was away from her sight, the tears began falling down my cheeks. I heard footsteps and the swish of the big curtains falling over the doorway, giving me privacy from the larger room. I cried myself to sleep under the covers.

CHAPTER 15

"**A**re you awake?" Fenrir's voice was flat as he pulled back the curtain to enter the bedroom where I'd been laying for days. Over a week at this point. I wasn't entirely sure exactly how many days it had been since Hellia and I spoke, but I watched the sun light the sky and then the world darken again without moving from bed, without eating, without showering or moving more than rolling to my other side. Fenrir came to talk to me many times, but I ignored him.

I didn't respond to him now, continuing to watch snowflakes pelt the window outside. I heard him walking toward my side. Flicking my eyes to him I saw he was wearing a tight black outfit that showed off his muscular build. He was much more cleaned up now, his hair was cut shorter but still shaggy enough to be tied back. It was partially pulled back today, some pieces in front still hanging in front of his eyes. His beard was trimmed to be no more than five o'clock shadow, and the gold tattoo bands around his neck and wrists flashed in the dreary winter daylight. I didn't allow myself to linger enough to appreciate any of it, returning my gaze to the trees bending in the howling wind outside.

"I brought you some food. Come eat." It was more of a demand than a request. He came back to the bedroom often, several times a day, trying to coax me to eat and bringing magic tea that stayed hot for hours. I had a collection of undrunk mugs on the bedside table. Not having felt hunger in days, I continued staring out the window without a word. Today I missed home, just like I did every day, and it was enough to make me weighted with sadness. Hellia said I couldn't go home, and with everything else that already happened, it crushed me. So here I was, laying in bed, crushed. Like road kill.

"Anais, get up." Fenrir's voice was becoming exasperated. "You've been staring out the window for days, you won't take care of yourself, you won't eat, or drink, or move—and it's starting to make me angry."

I didn't move, wondering why he was angry about it while I gazed out the window. I let the thoughts and pain of missing my life at home, the nightmares of what happened in Asgard, and the fear of what would happen in my future overwhelm me, day after day.

"You need to take a shower and have something to eat. I'm not going to allow you to starve to death, do you understand me?" He was leaning down, hands on his knees, his face getting closer by the moment.

I glared up at him, huffing before I rolled over, turning my back on him and yanking the blankets up to my face.

"Please don't make me force food down your throat." His growl sounded borderline menacing, but I was somewhat immune to threats now. I was scared of him, but my depression was stronger than my fear. It weighed me down, coaxing me back to sleep.

"Just throw me out in the snow so I can freeze to death in peace," I snapped. Closing my eyes, I burrowed my head against the pillow to block him out.

"That's not going to happen." He wrenched the blankets off of me.

"Hey!" I barked, my skin prickling with the change in temperature, even in the warm cabin.

"Get. Up. Now," he growled, leaning over me so I could see his flashing eyes and disappointed scowl.

"Or what?" I spat.

He didn't respond, just sighed heavily, standing upright while running a hand through his now-trimmed hair. He seemed to debate with himself internally before he grabbed me and threw me over his shoulder in one fluid movement. I didn't have time to process what happened before blood was rushing to my head. My hair fell in a greasy curtain around my face. I hadn't let Hellia braid it for me again; I wouldn't let anyone touch me.

"Put me down!" I yelped, scrabbling at his back. The floor felt very far away from up here, and though I felt secure in his hold, I also didn't trust him not to let go and send me face first into the floorboards.

He just growled, stalking to the bathroom and setting me down in the shower. Without a word, he cranked the water on and let it blast me. I stood getting soaked in my pajamas, my mouth falling open in shock as the water pummeled me.

"You ASSHOLE!" I screamed.

He glared right back, folding his arms across his chest. I had to be a sight—soaked in black silk pajamas, standing under the shower water, glaring at him with balled fists and shaking with both rage and fear. Mostly rage.

"If you're not going to take care of yourself, then you force me to do it for you." He shrugged.

"I don't *want* you to take care of me!" I hadn't moved. Water soaked my hair completely and was now dripping down my nose and chest. I avoided it up until now, but I did have to admit—at least to myself—that the shower felt somewhat nice.

"Then take care of yourself! Gods, Anais." He waited for me to move, but I stood unmoving, the crushing thoughts about my predicament barreling into my head again. I just blinked away the water collecting on my lashes and tried not to look at him. He rolled his eyes before striding toward me, tugging up his sleeves. My breath hitched as he reached for me, and I backed away a step.

"Stay still," he ordered.

"Don't touch me!" I jumped away when he reached for me again.

"I have to so I can wash your hair." He gripped my good arm firmly but not painfully, tugging me toward him. I froze in his grip, trying to focus on breathing as he used a bar of soap that smelled oddly like the lavender shampoo I regularly used at home to lather his hands. He carefully scrubbed the lather into my hair at my scalp.

My stomach dropped, and I was quaking under his touch, but he continued anyway. I stood motionless, my shoulders hunched and tense, ready to fight against him at a moment's notice. Unbothered, he continued to brush his fingers through my hair, gently detangling any knots he found. I couldn't decide if I liked it or hated it. It was both; I hated that he was touching me at all, and yet it felt … good, gentle and kind.

"Can I trust you to finish washing yourself? Or do you need me to do it?" He rinsed his hands in the stream of warm water and then brushed one along the back of my neck, making me go rigid.

"I'll do it, just go away." I swatted his hand off me.

"Good," he huffed. Leaving the shower, he walked toward the door. "When you're done, there's fresh clothes for you on the bed. Then come eat."

I rolled my eyes, not even able to think of food.

He turned when I didn't respond out loud, raising an eyebrow at me. "*Hjarta*, I will hold you down and have Hellia force feed you until you've had a proper meal. If you don't want that to happen, I suggest you come eat of your own volition." He left the room then, slamming the door behind him.

Dressed in the dry clothes he left for me, I made my way out to the living space. Hellia was there, and she looked up with a friendly looking smile from where she sat at the table again. Fenrir lingered in the kitchen behind her, leaning against the counter, and we fixed each other with a glare as I walked in.

I sat at the table, feeling my damp hair draping down my back. I felt the prickle of being watched and broke my glare at Fenrir to look at Hellia, who was staring at my wet hair.

"Can I braid that for you?" she asked, her voice tentative and hopeful.

"Sure, I guess." I leaned back in the chair, slumping down and crossing my arms.

Before I could change my mind, she was behind me, gently combing through my wet waves. Her fingers were even more delicate than Fenrir's, parting my hair and twisting it deftly. She was careful not to brush my skin with her ice-cold fingers, which I appreciated. If I wasn't being glared down by Team Jacob over there, I could probably fall asleep to the feeling.

Without a word, Fenrir pushed a bowl of steaming soup in front of me, accompanied by a piece of warm bread with butter melting into the fluffy center. My eyes flicked back up to him, narrowing when we made contact, and he raised an eyebrow at me, daring me to argue.

"It's really good," Hellia chimed from behind me. "Jerrick made it yesterday; roasted red pepper is his favorite, and he made extra to send for you. He's not a bad chef, you know?"

Fenrir didn't move, waiting to watch me eat. As I stared him down, I noticed he had a small braid in his own hair, woven into his hairstyle. Evidence of his sister, I supposed. I sighed, feeling Hellia tie off my braid and sit in the chair next to me.

She looked up at her brother. "Quit staring at her like that. Gods, Fen. I wouldn't want to eat with you hovering like that either." She made a dismissive motion, shooing him back to the kitchen.

She held out her hand, and I watched as dark shadows writhed in her hand rather than Mag or Tora's shimmering golden heat waves. The shadows produced a plate full of different sweet pastries, which she set on the table before picking one up and biting into it. Somehow, seeing that she was eating too encouraged me.

Taking a sip at a spoonful of the soup, I had to admit once again Fenrir was right. The small mouthful gave me renewed life as it warmed my stomach. I could feel him watching me as I kept taking spoonfuls, struggling to keep myself from gulping the whole bowl.

The door banged open and Jerrick came in, letting in a gust of chilly air. I shivered, my skin rising in visible bumps.

"Hey guys, guess what the forecast is today?" he asked jokingly.

"Shut the damn door," Fen snarled.

"Okay, jeez, hello to you too." Jerrick slammed the door behind him before shaking his head, spraying cold droplets everywhere, a few landing on my arm. "Dick," he mumbled under his breath, throwing a quick glare in Fenrir's direction before spotting me at the table and brightening with a beaming smile. "Hey Princess, what's up?"

I scrunched my nose at the nickname, and Hellia scowled at him while Fenrir narrowed his eyes on the new arrival. Had I been acting like a princess?

"How is the arm today?" Jerrick asked as he threw himself into the chair across from Hellia and me, completely oblivious—or acting like he was—to his companions' glares.

"It's fine," I mumbled. "Thank you for the food."

He nodded proudly before looking around. His smile faded when he made eye contact with the scowling siblings. "The fuck is going on here today? Have these two been pissy all afternoon?"

"He has," I nodded toward Fenrir.

Jerrick turned in his chair to look at his friend. "What's got your tail in a twist?"

Fenrir glared at him, rolling his eyes and subtly tipping his head toward me. Good. Maybe if I was a big enough pain in the ass, he'd take me home.

I thought I saw Fenrir give a subtle shake of his head, but he didn't say anything as he turned to the sink, getting a cup from the cabinet and filling it with water at the faucet. He set it on the table in front of me, a silent demand to drink.

Jerrick turned back toward me, making a comedic face once he was turned fully away from Fenrir, and Hellia snickered. Fenrir took the seat across from me, next to the lieutenant, fixing him with a glare.

"Bad news." Jerrick turned serious, leaning forward on the table as he addressed Hellia, who was now sitting up and listening at full attention. "I just got a message from Ylfa that the Aesir have been hanging around the gate at the Niflheim–Helheim border. We need to start planning to head home, or else they're going to find us out here, Hellia. Sure, we have wards over Kaldr, but it's not as safe as Helheim. I want to get all three of you back there as soon as possible."

"Why me?" I was stirring the soup rather than eating it now, feeling full after only half a bowl and some bites of bread. Fenrir was watching, his attention flicking between the bowl and my face. I refused to make eye contact with him, knowing he wanted to pressure me to eat more.

"It's not safe for you out here. You're the two they're hunting." He pointed between Fenrir and me. "As the security detail of this party, I'm ordering us to start the return hike in the next couple days."

"*Security detail.* Okay, Mr. Mall Cop," I whispered, rolling my eyes.

Hellia laughed out loud next to me. "Like those security guards for the modern markets, the ones with the little tiny motor cars?"

"Golf carts," I corrected her, and she renewed her laughing while Jerrick had a look of offense on his face.

"I'll get him a little security outfit and badge when we get to the castle," she joked to me, almost making me smile. "Maybe I'll make you security guard of the month too."

"I resent this," Jerrick said with indignation. "I have been your lieutenant for centuries, Hellia, and you're allowing—nay, *encouraging*—the newest member of this pack to reduce me to no more than a sentry for human merchandise." He shook his head at her but grinned as Hellia was laughing even harder now. "I do want one of these golf cart motor cars, though."

"I think you should be demoted to court jester," Fenrir growled softly, but he was smirking now too.

Jerrick turned on him with outrage brimming in his expression. "Listen, you don't know what it's been like getting bullied by her and Ylfa every day and Jorm not helping one damn bit. And now they have another one on their team"—Jerrick motioned toward me—"so I swear to the gods, dude, you better be on my fucking side, because you and I are outnumbered." Jerrick pinned him with an exaggerated glare.

"I'll think about it. Their team seems a lot better," Fenrir mused with a lazy eye roll.

"You prick!" Jerrick was up, putting Fenrir in a headlock, and Fenrir in turn was pushing against him playfully, laughing as Jerrick grumbled insults. Even though it was playful, I found myself flinching back from the quick, violent movements.

"Quit acting like pups," Hellia snapped, making them still. Both turned to her with guilty expressions. She placed her elbows on the table, slowly clasping her fingers. It was very obvious this situation had happened before, that the three had known each other since childhood and Hellia was the voice of reason.

Jerrick let go of Fenrir, sitting back in his chair and looking guiltily at me. "Sorry," Jerrick mumbled, and Fenrir dipped his head apologetically toward both of us.

"We'll go in a couple days. For tonight and tomorrow, let's add an extra patrol in the afternoon and two in the night." Hellia continued with business.

Both men nodded, and they continued their discussion of the trek to Helheim and the dangers the Aesir presented. My crushing thoughts returned, weighing on my shoulders, making me sink into the chair.

"So." Hellia turned to me after a long while of sitting at the table. "I had an idea. I wanted to see if you'd help me test it?"

I slowly nodded my agreement, sitting up slightly and wondering what was about to happen. We'd been sitting long
enough that I was getting tired, and my stomach was starting
to gurgle in an ask for more food. I sat up further, curiosity
rousing me from where I'd been slouched.

"Take my hand." She offered it to me. "You know about
summoning, right?" I nodded, remembering Mag and Tora
telling me about it on the way to Asgard. I'd just seen her use
shadows to summon the plate of brownies minutes ago.

"Great. So picture your favorite meal, wherever it would be
on Midgard right now. Picture it clearly in your mind. Imagine
picking it up, how it feels in your hand, how it smells and
tastes."

I looked at the three of them wordlessly. They all watched
me back, just as silent.

"Please, humor me." Hellia took my hand with one of hers
and I flinched at her icy touch. "Sorry," she muttered but didn't
let go. She held her other hand out flat in front of her. I closed
my eyes, imagining my favorite pizza from home. I pictured it
sitting before me, steaming in the cardboard box as it sat in the
to-go window of the shop in Vernon.

"Is it working?" I opened my eyes and looked at her empty
hand.

"Mmm, no. Not quite. Try it again."

We tried several more times to no avail.

"Let me give it a go." I swallowed as Fenrir offered a hand out
to me across the table. My heart thudded twice in the space of
one beat as I reached out. In slow motion, our fingers met. His
hand wrapped around mine, which felt tiny in his grasp. My
stomach twisted uncomfortably. I took a deep breath, trying to

shove down the tingling feelings and the butterflies threatening to flap their broken, mangled wings in my chest.

No. No more gods. No more romance. No more butterflies. No more heart palpitations. Stop it, I scolded myself for the feelings attempting to bloom inside me.

Closing my eyes once more, I focused on the pizza: the heat of the melted cheese coming through the bottom of the cardboard box, the steam rising from the vents, the crispy crust, the sound of the oil popping on top.

The scent curled around my nostrils and my eyes sprang open, seeing the large flat box sitting in Fenrir's hand just above the table. Straight from the pizza shop in Vernon.

"Alright!" Jerrick pulled the box to the table and opened it, grabbing a slice of the pizza and dangling it into his mouth. "So good," he mumbled around a mouthful.

"Do it again," I told Fenrir, and I reached out, grabbing his hand and closing my eyes. This time, I imagined a case of soda at the grocery store: the glass bottles clinking together, the fizz and pop of the carbonation, the hiss of the lid as it was opened. Fenrir grinned, holding it in his hand as I thought of the sweet fruit flavors.

Feeling much bolder now, I imagined a smooth bottle of my favorite tequila, the heavy cool glass bottle in my hand. It appeared in Fenrir's hand, and in one swift movement I'd snatched it, unscrewed the top, and lifted the bottle to my lips, swallowing several mouthfuls. It was enough to get me buzzed in the next few minutes, scalding my throat on its way down.

"Whoa-kay." Jerrick wrestled the bottle from my grasp. "You're recovering," he told me with an accusing finger point-ed at me. Fenrir took the bottle from him, inspecting it with a frown.

"That's part of recovering on Midgard," I argued, reaching for the bottle again. The tall brute held it out of reach.

"Pretty sure it's not," Jerrick argued back, grabbing the bottle from his friend and taking a hearty swig himself before putting it on the table between the two men's arms. I sat back down in my chair, pouting but vowing to get my hands back on that bottle and drink myself under the table tonight.

"For the record"—Hellia's voice was barely more than a whisper, and she leaned in toward me when the two men were distracted—"I'd do the same thing." She winked as she summoned an airplane-sized bottle of tequila and passed it to me under the table.

By the end of the night, I was afraid to stand for fear of keeling over and giving away to the two men across the table how plastered I really was. The room was spinning slowly around us like a carousel, and my heavy-lidded eyes watched the wall lazily as it twirled around.

I couldn't look to my left because Hellia knew exactly how drunk I was, having been my supplier all evening. It was a bonding experience, and by the evening, I had warmed up to her considerably, feeling like she was maybe even a friend. Each time I so much as glanced in her direction, a smirk threatened my lips, so I remained focused on the spinning room around us. She'd given me several airplane shots mixed into soda. I would have thought the werewolves would smell it, but with the tequila already open and sitting on the table, temptingly I might add, they seemed none the wiser to my dosed drinks.

We finished the pizza and stayed at the table as the three talked about something more with strategy; I stopped paying attention. I had only really picked at a slice of pizza, much more interested in downing the drinks Hellia kept refilling. I could feel Fenrir's quizzical look trying to figure out what was wrong with me, but I was too drunk to care. I absently twirled a lock of my hair around one of my fingers and swayed slightly.

"I think humans need to go to bed," Jerrick told Hellia, nodding to where I was slumping in my seat next to her.

"I'm fine—" I hiccuped loudly and clapped a hand over my mouth. My eyes were barely open; I could tell I had the glazed look that screamed '*I'm wasted*' all over my face.

"What the—" Jerrick started, eyes narrowing on me.

"Hellia," Fenrir snapped, glaring at his sister. Hellia looked toward the ceiling, avoiding eye contact.

"She needed a drink." She shrugged to the ceiling. "Who am I to deny a girl a drink when she needs one?"

"She's definitely had more than a drink," Fenrir growled, his eyes boring into her.

"Thanks, camp-tain obvious," I slurred at him. Jerrick was grinning ear-to-ear on Fenrir's other side, shaking his head before clapping him on the shoulder. Next to me, Hellia's eyes darted to Jerrick, and then both of them were shaking with laughter as Fenrir glared daggers at them. I didn't care if they were laughing at me, and I almost wanted to laugh with them just for the sake of remembering how to move my face that way.

"I'm glad you both think this is funny," he snapped at them as they failed to stifle their snickers. He stood from the table, clearing away the trash but mistakenly leaving the tequila bottle unattended. I snatched it quickly, tipping it to my lips.

"Come on Fen, she's not so fragile—" Jerrick was saying.

Fenrir wrenched the bottle from my hands. "That's *enough*," he snarled, his voice stern and deep. When I might normally have been afraid, I just looked at Jerrick and rolled my eyes, making the lieutenant chuckle. I didn't need him to tell me what was enough or not.

"She needs rest. You two go find somewhere else to be." Fenrir dismissed his companions, clearing the rest of the table and taking the tequila with him to lock away. I reached out, grabbing Hellia's icy hand before she could get up.

"Thank you," I mouthed to her.

She winked at me before getting up and heading for the door with Jerrick, who was making some kind of signal to Fenrir that I could not discern. Apparently Fenrir couldn't discern it either, because he just cocked an eyebrow and fixed them with a frown until they both shuffled out the door and it thudded closed behind them.

I was busy watching the fire crackling in the hearth across the room when I noticed him out of the corner of my eye. I turned, squinting through my tilting vision to see him clearly. He was leaning against the counter, his shoulders no longer hunched and tense but relaxed as he crossed his arms in front of his broad chest. His expression was soft, all annoyances dissipated, a hint of a smile on his full lips as he watched me in the chair.

"You're done being grouchy?" I mused.

"You're sassy normally, aren't you?" He sighed, his arms unfolding so he could push against the counter behind him.

"Psht, who? Me?" I huffed, brushing him off. I was loving the false sense of confidence the booze was giving me. He crossed the distance between us in no more than three steps, leaning on the back of my chair as he looked down at me. Normally, his massive frame hovering over me might be intimidating, but in my current state it was somewhat comforting.

"It's cute," he said, his voice softer with a deep rumble to it I hadn't heard before.

"Cute?!" I sputtered, looking up at him as he leaned over me. I glared at him, sizing him up with a look, and he smiled.

"Yeah. Cute." His fangs caught the light of the fire.

I huffed again, trying to stand up but tangling my drunken legs in Hellia's chair. He caught me by my good arm and kept me from falling flat on my face. He guided me back toward the bed. I flopped down on top of the covers, my eyelids immediately starting to fall closed.

"Fenrir," I demanded softly, my eyes still closed.

"Yes, *hjarta*?"

"Why do you care about me so much? And what does that *hjarta* thing mean?" I yawned, still feeling as though the world was spinning as I curled up and settled my head on the pillow.

He paused at the bedside, and I felt his fingertips gently brush my hair back from my face, leaving blissful tingles in their wake. I wished he would stand there and brush my hair until I fell asleep.

"You'll understand later. Just rest now, Anais."

CHAPTER 16

I paused at the mirror in the bathroom after removing my pajamas, taking in the image of my body. I looked gaunt and lifeless from the weeks of this ongoing nightmare. The curves of my body were more slight than I ever remembered seeing before. My hair had grown longer but lost any shine I'd managed to maintain in the human world. Under my eyes were deep purple half moons, hinting at the nights I'd stayed awake staring out the window. I looked fragile, broken and stitched back together, like a goddamn frankenstein.

My hair dried in long waves, and I combed my fingers through to detangle any knots. There were fresh clothes in the armoire, a shirt and pajama pants that reminded me of home. I wished I could wear my favorite oversized t-shirt with wolves on it from the gas station and my plaid pj pants, and smoke my weed pen while I baked cookies with Netflix in the background. I would give anything to be home right now.

Sighing after I dressed, I paused before the curtain. I could hear a rhythmic rumbling noise beyond the curtain, but no voices. I poked my head out of the curtain. Fenrir lay snoring on the couch, his open mouth showing his elongated canine teeth that looked like vampire fangs. They seemed much less dangerous right now—he almost looked a little bit cute. I rolled my eyes at his bare, shirtless chest. At least he wore his usual leather-armored pants.

I slowly crept out, using silent footsteps to cross the room. Putting my toes and the ball of my foot on the ground first, I shifted my weight to my heel before lifting my other foot and moving forward. I approached him without making a sound, not a twitch of the wolf-man's ears. Looking down at him, I took the moment to study him while his unnerving eyes were not boring into my soul.

He was arguably the most devastatingly handsome man I had ever seen, even more so than Mag's classic beauty. He was missing the ethereal godly beauty of the other Aesir I'd seen in Asgard; instead, that ethereal quality was replaced by shadows. I admired his beautiful dark lashes, his chiseled face with a strong jaw, the short dark facial hair framing his lips. His face had life where Hellia's lacked it, his skin flush with coursing blood and a heartbeat. Whereas she was dead, he was very much alive.

'I'm never letting you go.' His words felt less menacing now, during the day, him sleeping with his mouth open like a dumb

idiot. They were still haunting me though; he'd made clear he thought I was his to possess.

He was so tall, fitting on the couch because it appeared specially made to accommodate someone of his size. I looked over the length of his body, and—only because he was asleep—I allowed myself to linger and admire his broad chest and lean, muscular abdomen. White scars caught my eye in the shape of claw marks across one side of his abdomen and one shoulder. As I studied his face closer, I saw faint matching white scars across parts of his nose, cheek, and lip. The scars on his torso were much more visible, and I was surprised I hadn't noticed them when I cut him free before. Then again, a lot had been going on in that moment, and I had more important things going on than looking over this man's body.

There would be no admiring or showing any interest in any conscious gods. Not after Mag. Fucker.

Fenrir snored loudly, making me jump with surprise. He stirred but didn't wake, his head flopping to the side. His eyes remained closed but his mouth open, a small puddle of drool started to pool at the corner of his pillow. For a god, he certainly didn't seem that tough right now.

I carefully snuck away to the kitchen, finding bread, peanut butter, and jelly easily in the cabinets around the kitchen. Wondering if they actually ate this or if it was left for me, I dug around in the drawers and cabinets to find a knife and plate.

I made myself a sandwich, listening to the wind moaning against the cabin as snow swirled against the windows. I silently made my way back to the living room and sat in the chair across from Fenrir, wrapping myself in a large blanket and eating my sandwich in peace. I pulled down the neckline of my pajamas, letting the itchy healing wound breathe. It was the most relaxed and peaceful I'd felt in weeks. This living nightmare had been going on and on, and I was exhausted both physically and mentally. I was beginning to recover. Though we were in Hell, I had to admit the amenities were nice—five star comfort on the bed, and that rain shower was pretty nice too. I'd still give anything to go home though. One star for grouchy ass werewolf service.

"Ah … mmmph…" Fenrir's sleep mumbling drew my attention from the window back to the large sleeping form just a few meters away. He groaned in his sleep and stretched his limbs before settling back on the couch, a bit more fitful this time. He twitched and murmured random noises, which I had to admit I did find mildly entertaining as I finished off the first half of my sandwich and began stuffing the next in my mouth.

"No!" he yelped, his entire body jolting as his eyes snapped open, roving the room wildly until he found me looking at him. I was staring, my sandwich halfway shoved in my mouth as I watched him with concern and curiosity. He closed his eyes again and breathed deeply a few times before looking back at me. We stared at each other in silence as I chewed and observed him.

"I was dreaming."

"I didn't ask." I inspected the last quarter of my sandwich in my hand, debating if I wanted to go make another one or not. I was starving after the days in bed healing without eating much of anything. Although, now that he was awake, I didn't really feel much like turning my back on him again, even just long enough to make a sandwich.

Across from me, he pushed himself up on his elbows, looking at the food in my hand and then out at the gathering blizzard outside.

"Is that all you've eaten today?" He nodded to the remnants of the sandwich in my hand, which I was now scarfing down hungrily. I slowly nodded, the peanut butter sticking my tongue to the roof of my mouth so I was temporarily mute.

"You need more. Is there anything I can get you?" He sat up, and I wished he was still sleeping. It had been so peaceful, and he'd been such nice company when he was drooling and incoherent.

I shook my head, wistfully imagining making breakfast burritos after one of the sleepovers where we'd made a drinking game out of the Twilight Saga and got completely wasted, not waking until after noon the next day.

"Come on, Anais. You need something more. He starved you in Asgard; you need to eat." His voice was still stern but took on a pleading tone.

I frowned at him, not understanding how he knew that information. "I'll make another sandwich in a second," I assured him halfheartedly, which he accepted with a disapproving snort. The sound reminded me of the wolf in my dreams. I stifled my smile at the thought. We sat for a moment of silence, but it wasn't necessarily tense. I dragged my eyes away from him to the window, watching the snow pound down.

He got up after a while, walking off somewhere in the cabin as I spaced out. I was completely checked out and torturing myself, thinking of home. Before I left, I had been fighting with my mom, and then I'd disappeared. She probably thought I was dead. Kerri would never forgive me for letting myself be taken, if I ever saw her again. She probably went looking for my phone and found it on the passenger seat of that car, parked outside the dark, uninhabited cabin. She might've gone looking for me in the woods. I definitely scared her badly, and I didn't know how to get a message to her to assure her I was alright—save for where I was.

My thoughts were abruptly interrupted as Fenrir came back to the living room and put another plate with a second sandwich in my hands, taking the first empty plate from me and putting it on the table.

"I'm not—"

"Eat it." He gave me a look that told me no nonsense was about to be had before he added, "Please."

My stomach growled loudly at the sight of more food, betraying me to the entire room. I sunk my teeth in, devouring half in just a few bites. Fenrir smirked with pride before laying back down on the couch and biting into his own sandwich.

"Gods, what is that stuff?" He inspected the sandwich. "Do you eat this all the time? Hellia said humans eat it a lot on Midgard."

So, it was Hellia who was leaving food for me. I covered my mouth with a hand, hoping it looked like I was being polite while chewing. Really, I was covering the threat of a smile on my lips at the thought of this demon prince experiencing peanut butter for the first time.

"I ate it a lot as a kid, at school for lunch."

We munched in silence, my sandwich was gone in seconds. I debated licking the crumbs from the plate but thought better of it. I didn't need to look that desperate in front of him.

"Where is everybody?" I asked, looking around for signs of Hellia or Jerrick around.

"They're working," he mumbled as he shoved the last bite of food into his mouth and brushed his hands together.

"You're not?"

His gaze fell on me, and I tried not to shiver.

"I'm protecting you." He shrugged as he broke eye contact, as if it explained everything.

I snorted through my nose. "You fell asleep on the job," I said.

A grin split wide across his face and he chuckled softly, stretching all his limbs on the couch once more. I averted my eyes from the scene, not sure I could keep the blush from climbing my neck to my cheeks. Whether it was from his rippling muscles or that smile, I wasn't sure.

"Your stitches should be ready to come out today if you want." He nodded toward where my stitched skin was exposed. "I'll remove them for you." His tone was firm again.

"I'll do it myself in a minute," I said as I set my plate on the side table.

He was already up, crossing to the bathroom in just a few steps. I heard him shuffling things around inside and I couldn't help my eyes darting around the room looking for an escape. I didn't think I could tolerate him touching me or being so close again. Trying to judge how far it would be to the front door, I weighed the odds that Team Jacob could track me through the snow outside.

I shrank in my chair as he came back out, trying to make myself as small as possible. He didn't seem to notice as he sat down on the edge of the coffee table, unspooling some bandages. His eyes met mine once more, and as he took me in, I realized how I must look incredibly pathetic, quivering against the back of this giant chair. I wanted to be brave, to show no fear, to tell him confidently to 'fuck off.' But while my brain thought one way, my body was reacting another.

"Please. I just want to help." His harsh tone had dropped and was softer, becoming oddly comforting. Coaxing even. He frowned as, without thinking, I reached for my neck, feeling for the electric shock collar that was no longer there. I still expected to be suddenly riddled with electricity for not complying.

I slowly and with some effort pulled the shirt over my head, leaving me in just a soft sports bra. I clutched the shirt to my chest, trying to cover as much as I could while leaving what was necessary exposed.

Fenrir's face remained calm, non reactive, as he leaned in to inspect the wounds on my shoulder. It took all the control I possessed not to show the shivers that skittered across my back as his breath drifted over my bare skin. He was so close to me, his concentration completely focused on my injury. We sat in tense silence as he looked over the wound and gently used a pair of nail scissors to snip the stitches. His fingers were delicate on me again when he pulled the stitches free, as though he were touching the most breakable object he'd ever laid a finger on.

The jagged, healing flesh looked horrific. I couldn't stand to keep my eyes on the scarred flesh very long, dropping my gaze. Through my peripheral vision, I could see Fenrir watching me, his expression soft as he carefully wrapped a fresh bandage under my armpit and around the healing flesh, hiding the scar from view.

"Thank you," he growled softly, the words coming out barely more than a whisper.

"For what?" My voice in comparison sounded snappy, defensive.

"For freeing me," he said, his voice still hushed.

"I didn't want to." I lowered my voice but retained the snap in my inflection.

"I know," he murmured.

We sat in silence once more, but unlike earlier, this silence was tense. The room was thick with more unsaid words, two heartbeats, and both of our breathing.

When he finished wrapping the stitches, he brushed his fingertips along the edges of the bandage. Every time his fingers met my bare skin, they sent the most intense, pleasurable tingles I'd ever felt. It took everything not to gasp when his fingers brushed across my collar bone. Gently, he ran a finger over my throat, over where the collar had been. Goose pimples rose across all my skin, and I breathed faster as I sat up straight under his touch, swallowing, waiting for his hand to clamp down and constrict my airway.

"Anais, I..." His voice trailed off. My wide eyes darted to his, silently begging him not to close his huge hand around my throat. He moved his hand away from my neck, but I stayed rigid as he caressed my cheek, brushing over it with a thumb. I squinted at him. What game was he playing? Who did he think he was, that he could just touch me like this? Was I his prisoner? Why was he looking at me like that?

We sat, frozen for a moment. Our eyes glued to each other's faces, he leaned in a fraction of an inch. My tongue darted out, wetting my lips, and his attention locked onto the movement.

As his gaze raised back to meet mine, I swallowed. His eyes had lost all their unnerving quality. Instead, it had been replaced with another expression, reminding me of his eyes when I first entered the room to free him in Asgard—the begging, pleading look. It was one I'd never seen anyone wear before … but I wanted someone to look at me like that forever. I imagined it was the face of a man dying of thirst in the desert and seeing an oasis. He was centimeters away now, his expression thirsty, and he was still leaning in. I could feel his soft breath across my face and see his fangs through his parted lips.

"What?" I snapped, leaning away from him. He was getting too close for comfort and bringing back images of the Aesir now. He winced, backing up from me a bit. The expression remained on his face as he sat up. "Why are you looking at me like that?" I didn't understand how I both wanted him and hated him. How could I be remotely attracted to anyone after what I'd gone through?

A loud thudding and voice from outside announced someone's arrival. His hand dropped away from me, and I yanked my shirt back on.

"Careful," he growled, and I thought maybe he winced as he watched my stitches stretch with the effort of my harsh movements. The door burst open and cold blasted me. I was grateful for a good cover for my still-pimpled skin. I thought he was about to kiss me.

"Hey-yo! What's going on here?" Jerrick paused after coming in the door, looking between both of us with raised eyebrows.

"Move!" Hellia shoved him further inside so she could come in behind him. She slammed the door shut on the winter outside. "You're going to let all the hot air out, dumbass."

"I get the sense these two were about to keep things plenty hot on their own, Hel." I turned my face toward the corner, flustered and overwhelmed with everything that just happened in the span of three minutes.

"Leave them alone, Jerrick." Hellia's tone was warning.

"Excuse me miss, is this mutt bothering you?" I turned back to Jerrick winking at me and gripping Fenrir's shoulder playfully.

"Yeah, actually," I replied dryly.

Fenrir stood, towering over me and Jerrick as he moved off to the kitchen. Jerrick snorted at him, obviously not pleased with the lack of reaction to his taunts.

"I'm leaving for patrol. Are you coming with me?" Jerrick jutted his chin toward Fenrir.

"I want to go," I interrupted.

All three of their heads turned toward me, silence sucking the air from the room.

"You can't—" Jerrick started, looking shocked.

"Yes, she can." Fenrir cut him off with a pointed look at the incredulous lieutenant. His eyes returned to me, scanning me up and down. "But you're not wearing that. You'll freeze."

"What?" Jerrick sputtered. "She's injured! And she's mortal, and—"

"She wants to go, so she'll go. I'll bring her back if I need to." Shadows curled around Fenrir's exposed upper body, clothing him in black leather I could only compare to armor. "She's safest with me anyway." I couldn't help but hear the note of pride in the undertone of those words, even if it didn't show at all on his face.

"Do you want me to go with you?" Hellia's voice was quiet and directed toward me.

I shook my head. "I'll be okay."

"Put these on," Fenrir said as he handed me a stack of thick winter clothes.

I walked back to the bedroom, letting the curtain sweep behind me to block where I was changing.

"Are you sure this is a good idea? She's so small…" I heard Jerrick whispering on the other side of the curtain.

"She wants to see what's out there, and she needs to get ready to trek to Helheim. She's going to be out in the cold then; she might as well get used to it a day ahead of time." Fenrir's tone was final. Hellia made a noise of agreement with her brother.

I pulled on the warm, fleece-lined leggings and thick sweater. Grabbing the wool socks, I sat on the edge of the bed, listening as they continued talking.

"Be careful, okay?" Hellia said.

"I won't let her get hurt," Fenrir growled softly.

"I know you won't … but try not to scare her off too?" Her voice was so quiet, I almost missed that last sentence.

They fell silent again when I re-entered the room. Fenrir held out boots for me to put on, and when I stood again, he wrapped a navy cloak around my shoulders. A cloak? Where the hell was I?

"Have fun. Be back in an hour for dinner." Hellia waved us off, plopping herself down on one end of the couch and summoning a book.

I followed Jerrick out into the snow, staying on the little worn path made of boot marks and paw prints, reminding me I had yet to see the men's wolf forms.

"This town is called Kaldr. We've been coming here since we were kids," Jerrick said over his shoulder as we joined a larger trail and several more cabins came into view.

"That's Hellia." Jerrick pointed to a cabin set deeper in the trees, barely visible between thick branches of evergreens. "That's me." Another cabin closer to the trail, each window lit with a candle in a dish. Warm and inviting, just like him.

"Jorm, Fen's older brother. He's not here right now." The cabin Jerrick was referencing sat against several large rocks. Trees grew from the top of the boulders, and the roots draped down onto the roof of the cabin. Dark windows hinted at a foreboding emptiness, as though his house disapproved of me just as much as he did.

"That's who you were fighting with the night you brought me here, with red hair." I looked up at Fen, who just nodded silently.

"He's a shit head, so don't take anything he said that night to heart." Jerrick turned away, continuing down the trail. I wasn't sure if he was talking to me or Fenrir with that comment, but I didn't ask him to clarify.

"This is the village," Jerrick said as we walked toward several buildings. They lined a trail leading down to the water and a couple docks with boats tied up. Ahead, I could see and smell a catch of fish being hauled out of the boats onto the dock and shore. A much larger lodge stood in the middle of the smaller structures, elaborately designed with wood carvings on the sides. Its gently curving roof stood out against the sharp peaks around the fjord behind it.

"That's the long house," Fenrir said from my side, watching me take in structure. "A long time ago they used to house families, but we've always just used it as a community building. Everyone in Kaldr has private residences because Jerrick—"

"Did nothing wrong, *ever*!" The amber-eyed lieutenant snapped from ahead of us, turning to glare at a chuckling Fenrir.

"Good morning, Fenrir! Jerrick!" a woman bundled against the cold called to them. Her silvery hair flashed under the edge of her hood as she walked toward us.

"Good morning, Revna." Fenrir dipped his head respectfully.

Something was oddly familiar about her, I couldn't quite place what it was.

"Hello, who are you?" She smiled kindly.

"I'm Anais, it's nice to meet you."

"Oh, such a beautiful name." She smiled knowingly at Fenrir. "Thank you for freeing this one, by the way." She motioned toward Fenrir standing behind my shoulder. "I don't know what he did to deserve you freeing him, but it certainly has been wonderful to see him back around the village. The wolves couldn't be more pleased about it." She motioned toward a cabin behind us, where several normal-sized grey wolves were laying around and two young adolescent wolves were playing, paws battering at one another.

I turned back to her, squinting and trying again to place why she seemed so familiar.

"I didn't deserve it," Fenrir murmured, and I felt his eyes on the back of my head.

"Of course you did, dear." She tipped her head, giving him a tight-lipped, sad smile.

I chanced a glance over my shoulder, catching him staring. We locked gazes for a long moment before we both looked away.

"Well, don't let these two keep you out in the cold too long. They're built for this and you're not, dear." She nodded a good-bye and shuffled off toward the cabin, where the wolves stood with tails wagging like domesticated dogs as she approached.

"C'mon, we need to check the borders of the wards for Aesir and then get back. Hellia's summoning Mrs. Lutvega's meatloaf for dinner tonight," Jerrick gloated with a victorious arm movement.

"There, do you see? Damn it. That's too close. We need to leave tomorrow morning." Jerrick pointed at several footprints quickly being buried by the falling snow.

"Fuck," Fen growled, kneeling.

"What are we looking at?" I asked, just seeing footprints in the snow but nothing else out of order.

"We've put protective shields around Kaldr," Jerrick said. "Hellia made them, they mess with the psyche. Any intruders feel a sudden sense of dread once they encounter the barrier that's so overwhelming they immediately turn back for fear of immediate death. This set of prints is a little far inside the barrier for my liking. They should have turned back at least eight meters ago. I suspect the enchantment is weakened."

"At least it turned them back. Now we know it works." Fenrir sighed, looking over the nearly covered footprints.

"We already knew it worked, the question is for how much longer? What happens when it doesn't work anymore? Helheim is safer right now. We know they won't come there with certainty." Jerrick folded his arms across his chest, waiting for Fenrir to respond.

"Why won't they go to Helheim?" I asked.

Jerrick turned back to me. "Because they think they can't get out once they come in. It's not true, but it's been a rumor that's persisted and we've supported for more than a thousand years. If they find out they can come and go as they please, we'll be under attack immediately. We have wards against anyone who doesn't belong, some shields like this one and others Hellia's created, but Odin's Aesir are strong enough to break those wards if they really try. Hellia can kill them all if she needs to, but it will be a huge strain on resources and she will be extremely weak if she uses the full extent of her power."

"We'll go tomorrow morning, early." Fenrir began leading us back toward his cabin. "Since Helheim is on the same plain as Niflheim, we'll have to do it the old way and cross Niflheim to the gate between realms. I'm afraid if we use the seams, the Aesir will use Heimdall to track me."

The thought of hiking across the mountains around us was daunting, but the thought of visiting Helheim was becoming less and less terrifying. The village of Kaldr was not anything like I would expect for the vacation home of the Queen of Hell and her brothers. This small, comfortable village felt welcoming and warm. I almost wished I could come back sometime under better circumstances. Almost.

CHAPTER 17

"Anais," someone whispered close to my head, gently brushing the hair on my face behind my ear. "Anais," he called again, only slightly louder but still keeping his deep, growling voice below a whisper. I felt the hand move from my face to my hand, which was resting on the pillow by my head, his thumb swiping over the back of my hand.

My eyes cracked open, feeling confused and disoriented at the early hour. It wasn't time to be up—it was still dark outside, and I didn't hear anyone else awake and ready to leave. When I looked up, Fenrir was leaning over me, his gold eyes glowing faintly in the dark room and his hand still over mine. It took me a moment to register, and his thumb swiped gently over the back of my hand again.

"Wha?" I jumped up, suddenly awake and scrambling back from him. He grimaced as he watched me dart away and yank my hand from his grasp. "What? What's happening?" I asked. I pressed a hand to my chest, feeling my heart hammering beneath my palm.

"I'm sorry," he said, his voice soft. "I didn't mean to scare you." He frowned as I glared at him.

"What do you want?" I growled, yanking the blankets up around myself to cover my exposed skin. Looking down at the silk camisole and pants I was wearing—the pajamas provided to me—I was thankful it was dark so he couldn't really see my face. I would never wear something this revealing around strangers. "What time is it?"

"It's very early," he whispered back, keeping his voice and tone gentle despite my hostility. In the dim light of the room, I could see him offering me a tentative smile. It made me curious, and some of my immediate defensiveness dissipated. I loosened my grip on the covers, letting them fall back down. "I wanted to show you something," he said.

"Show me what?" I asked.

"It's a surprise," he said with a grin. I raised an eyebrow at him while he summoned a set of clothes for me and left them at the foot of the bed.

"The last time I got a surprise, it was that collar around my neck," I said quietly to his back as he started for the door. He stopped, running a hand through his hair.

"I promise it's not anything like that." His hand dropped to flex at his side as he spoke. "I think... I think you'll like it. I hope you'll like it." He walked out to the living space, letting the curtain fall behind him.

I fumbled through the dark room, pulling on the thick leggings, boots, and oversized warm sweater. Tugging the hat on my head, I trudged out to the living room, squinting at the dark night outside. The fire was the only light in the room, and when I looked at him, the firelight illuminating the curve of his muscles, and casting shadows on his face, I had to remind myself he was the Prince of Hell. I was supposed to be scared of him.

"Here," he said as he approached me, and I stiffened while he wrapped a thick, heavy, velvety cloak around my shoulders, fastening it at my neck.

"Are you warm enough?" he asked, his brows drawing low with concern as he looked me up and down.

"I'm fine," I said. It was plenty warm in the cabin. I wouldn't really know until I faced the weather, but even if I was cold, I was so determined not to show any weakness I wouldn't have told him anyway. "What could you possibly have to show me at"—I tore my gaze from him to look at the clock hanging on the wall—"1:35 in the morning?"

"Walk with me." He nodded for me to stick with him as he walked toward the front door. "I think we might have a short window of clear sky tonight."

I frowned, trying to figure out why he would wake me for clear sky in the middle of the night; surely not to go stargazing? He held the door for me, then trailed behind.

"We're going for a hike?" I asked as he let me lead down the trail from the cabin, the same one we'd walked on patrol hours ago. It looked different in the dark, more menacing.

What little light came from Kaldr reflected off the grey clouds and the white snow, making it slightly less than pitch black. Shadows from the looming trees blocked much of the light from reaching the forest floor.

"Yes," was all he said in reply. "Are you warm enough?" he asked again, and even though I couldn't see his face, I could hear the concern lacing his tone. I felt a chill under the cloak, but I was sure with the walking I would warm back up.

"Yeah, I'm fine. Which way?" I asked when I came to the main trail.

"Down that way." He nodded down a dark trail leading away from the well-lit path that led to Kaldr. I could feel him walking close to my back, shortening his strides to stay behind my pace. With his long legs, he could easily lap me. I wished he'd be in front to lead and so wasn't behind my back where I couldn't see him.

I paused, and he stopped behind me. Light from the lanterns lining the main trail shone through the darkness, flickering against the menacing trees. I could see Jerrick's house ahead, the candles in each window glowing in the dark. The trail Fenrir motioned to was dark, leading away from all the buildings and light. Glancing warily at him over my shoulder, I met his questioning look in the dark. "You're not gonna kill me in the forest, are you?"

"No!" He sounded abjectly horrified that I would even suggest it. I could see from the light of the closest lantern that he looked bewildered by my question.

"Hm," was all I said before setting off down the trail. "I can't see," I said as I frowned, trying to pick my way through the dark, stumbling through the difficult snow. Worried I would have to catch myself on my one good arm, I started reaching toward the darkness to find a tree trunk to steady myself on.

"Here." His hand tentatively took mine in the dark, leading me down the path. "Is it alright?" he asked, his voice sounding soft and almost tinged with hope, which I wasn't sure if I'd hear if I was busy glaring at him in daylight.

It was more than alright. Tingles were crawling up my arm from where we touched, and it took everything to keep from automatically entwining my fingers between his. "It's fine. Whatever." I huffed, but my faux deception was broken moments later when I slipped in the snow, my hand tightening on his as I struggled to remain upright.

"You're okay," he reassured me, and I felt his other hand on my waist, making sure I stayed upright. He was sure-footed in the snow, even after being locked up for so long. I had to admit I was jealous.

"Thanks," I mumbled, resisting the urge to brush him away from embarrassment for simply touching me. His hand dropped from my waist, but he didn't let go of my hand. We walked for a short while further down the trail.

"You said there was going to be a clear sky? That seems rare here." My foot slipped again, and I grit my teeth as my bad arm automatically came to hold on to him. I hated that I was clinging to him in the dark.

"It is." He held my hand a little tighter, and as my fingers desperately dug into his arm to keep me on my feet, I was sure I felt him purposefully flexing under my grasp. "I haven't seen it in 800 years."

"You were locked up for a long time," I said, and in the dim light, he nodded. "What did you miss most?" My curiosity about him was overriding the desire to keep him out.

"My family." I could hear the sadness in his voice. "I missed a lot here." He sighed heavily, and I realized his fingers had found their way between mine, our palms pressed together. It seemed so innocent, to hold hands, for what was supposed to be a horrible world-destroying werewolf god. "I missed having people around, especially them. What do you miss? From your home?"

"Oh." I blinked. I hadn't planned on sharing any information with him, but here he was, being honest with me when we were alone together. "Um, well... I guess I miss my family too. My best friend, she's like my sister. And my boss at work, she's kind of like my family too."

"Do you still have your parents?" he asked. My stomach soured at the thought of my mother trying to control me. It was only because she worried, but still, it was difficult to deal with.

"They're alive, but we don't always get along. I kind of popped off at my mom before I went to Asgard," I admitted. It wasn't my finest moment.

"What does that mean?" he asked, sounding seriously confused. "Popped off?"

"We argued," I corrected myself so he could understand. "She's angry with me, and I was angry with her."

"Are you still angry?" he asked.

"No, not really." I sighed. "A lot has happened since then. I just want to go home and talk to her. Apologize and see if we can fix things up between us."

"I wish I could take you home, but it's dangerous right now." He sighed, and I hoped he didn't see me swipe at my eye clumsily with my recovering hand.

"What about your parents?" I asked.

"My mother was executed when Odin sentenced us all. And my father is Loki." He paused in the forest. I could hear running water and felt we must be near a creek of some kind. "He's still locked up in Asgard."

"I know a little about him… Well, what the humans on Earth say about him. But so far the mythology hasn't done me very well." I stumbled slightly as the ground tilted downward.

"I'm going to pick you up," was all the warning he gave me before he swooped me into his arms.

"Ack!" I yelped, my hands jolting around his neck, holding myself close for fear of falling into the freezing darkness.

"I've got you, it's alright," he reassured me before stepping across the creek. I could faintly see where the snow broke and assumed the water ran in a creek bed there.

"Yeah, I feel that," I growled, battling internally between my urge to push out of his arms so I could walk on my own and the desire to lean into the alluring scent of the sweat on his neck. Who was he to grab me up and damn near throw me over his shoulder like a caveman? Who was I to be kind of enjoying it?

"You know, regular-sized people don't really like being picked up and carried around at will by giant gods. I would think you might have more manners at your age." I had to admit it was flattering, though, to be carried like I weighed nothing. On Earth, I was considered average height, and no guy I knew could pick me up and carry me without a fair amount of effort. I was curvy and midsized. But next to him, here in his arms, I looked as tiny as a rabbit in the jaws of a wolf.

"Oh, I don't know that's true." I could hear the smirk in his voice. "The wolf has always put me more on the wild, uncivilized paths in life. I think Hellia would tell you none of us have any manners except her."

"Please put me down," I insisted after we'd crossed the creek.

"Of course." He set me delicately on my feet, ensuring I was steady before sliding his hand back in mine, immediately entwining our fingers without hesitation. Almost as though he were hoping to hold my hand again, rather than simply holding on to guide me.

I followed him wordlessly as the trees thinned, and we came to a small snowfield with a clear view of the sky. Clouds drifted lazily by, but the snowfall, which had been ever present when I watched out the window the past few weeks, was missing.

"Here." He stretched out a hand and a blanket appeared, spread across the snow with pillows creating a place to lay back. Reluctantly, I let go of his hand, and he guided me toward the blanket nest he'd set up.

"Are we stargazing?" I asked, sitting down and looking toward the clouds above. When he didn't respond, I paused, watching him in the dim light as he scanned the treeline. "What are you looking for? Is Mag going to come get us here?" My head was on a swivel, trying to find what he might deem a threat. "Is there something dangerous here?"

"No." He immediately sat down next to me. "I was just double checking. I want to make sure you're safe… You prayed to me, and you entrusted me with your life. I take that privilege seriously." He fixed me with a solemn stare.

"You're very intent on me trusting you," I observed as he lay back, his head on one of the pillows.

"If you're fearful for your life, you can't rest properly, and you might do something dangerous. Like try to run off in the snow wearing barely any clothing again." I could feel his pointed look through the darkness.

"Well, could you really blame me?" I asked.

He looked at me for a moment more. "No. I couldn't. You had every right to be frightened. I'm… Well, I imagine I'm pretty frightening, especially to someone like you." He sighed, laying back so he was looking at the sky. The clouds still had not cleared, but I slowly lay back next to him, so we were side by side.

"What do you mean, someone like me?" I asked.

"Just … mortal, and human. Small." He glanced over at me. "I'm supposed to be a God of Death and Destruction, who gains power from suffering." He swallowed, his eyes taking me in, and I tried to keep my skin pricking from the intimacy in the moment. "And you're the opposite of me, so good, kind-hearted, and light. You're … pure."

I screwed up my nose at that. "I've had sex. I'm not pure." I looked toward the clearing clouds. Was I really having a purity talk with a God of Hell?

"I meant pure as in morally good. No darkness. You don't … hurt people. Or kill them." He sounded matter of fact with a small bite of resentment in his voice. It was amazing to me how expressive his voice was when I couldn't see his stony face. Or maybe he was being more vulnerable since we were one on one. I couldn't tell, but either way, I appreciated that it made him seem more like a human and less like a grouchy deity.

"Well, yeah, killing people is wrong. And I wouldn't want to hurt anyone purposefully," I said.

"Not always," Fenrir said, and I heard him shrug against the blanket.

"I don't see a situation where killing someone would be right." I frowned as the first star peeked through the thinning clouds. "Or that I would want to."

"Even Mag?" he asked.

I swallowed hard. "That's not really fair…"

"What he did isn't fair. I'll kill him for you." He snorted.

I opened my mouth to protest, to tell him that killing and violence was never the answer, just as the sky above us burst into color. Ribbons of green and blue light danced across the clear sky, bending and dipping, turning purple and magenta against the dark night sky.

"The Northern Lights?" I asked instead. "You brought me to see the Northern Lights?"

"Well, it's an aurora. Not the same one the humans on Midgard see. We called it the Dancing Sky when I was younger." His smile was audible.

"It's beautiful," I breathed.

"That is why I wanted to show it to you," he whispered. His head was turned toward me but I couldn't tear myself from the beautiful lights above to look at him. I would have to trust him to protect me, from whatever was in the forest and himself.

I wasn't sure how long we lay like that as I watched the colorful show. At one point his hand brushed mine, and I couldn't help myself. I caught his hand, holding it as he immediately laced his fingers between mine. It was new yet somehow felt like we'd done this a hundred times.

I didn't know why I kept hold of him, why holding hands felt so comforting when he was essentially a stranger. Although, I supposed I was starting to trust him, since I'd prayed to him and he'd responded. That never happened with a god before. And I needed someone. I was tired of dealing with all of this completely alone. He was grumpy and growly during the day, but at least he wasn't killing me or holding me prisoner at the end of a leash. He'd taken me to see this beautiful aurora in the middle of the night.

The show above was over too soon. The ribbons of light grew smaller until they disappeared completely, dissolving back into the dark night sky. By the time the clouds rolled in above us, I hadn't realized how cold I'd gotten. Between laying on the ground and not moving in the freezing temperatures, I was shivering uncontrollably. I felt Fenrir's hand slide from mine, moving up my arm, feeling my chilled skin.

"You're cold." His tone was concerned.

"I'm f-fine," I gasped, sitting up.

"You're cold," he growled back, muttering a curse under his breath. "This is my fault."

"It's okay," I said, but I could hear my teeth chattering.

"Come." He tugged my hand gently as snowflakes started pouring from the sky, bringing a deeper cold as the wind picked up.

I slipped again, feeling his arm catch me before I went down. "Thanks," I muttered.

"Please, let me carry you," he said. He didn't give me a chance to argue, sweeping under my legs and lifting me easily into his arms. Taking off at a healthy pace, we were halfway back to the cabin in just a few moments. "I understand you dislike it, but it will be faster."

"I really could walk—" I protested even as I admired his long-legged strides and how he knew where to go even in the pitch-black forest.

"It's dark and you're cold," he said, muttering another curse under his breath. "I'm sorry, *hjarta*. This wasn't the best plan." He adjusted me in his arms, pulling me even tighter to his chest.

"I liked it," I protested. "It was pretty, and worth it." He snorted at my words, marching back toward the cabin and throwing open the door. He settled me on the rug in front of the fire. I couldn't help my hands snapping out to warm by the fire, and I shivered again as I realized I was chilled to the bone. Goosebumps raised on my skin, and my whole body shook so hard, I couldn't force myself to stop.

Fenrir unclasped the cloak around my shoulders and dragged a blanket made of furs around me, cloaking me in warmth.

"Th-thanks," I chattered, my continued shaking making him grimace as he sat next to me on the floor.

"Here." He pressed a hot cup of tea into my outstretched hands. "Drink this, it will help ... I think." He nudged me to drink it, only satisfied when my lips met the rim to take a sip. "Sorry to interrupt your sleep the night before we leave," he mumbled.

"I already said it was worth it." A smile tugged at my lips, but I quickly hid it behind the rim of the cup.

He offered me a somewhat bashful smile. "I heard you."

"Can I ask you something?" My body was coming back to life now that I was sitting before the flames.

"Anything." He scratched his neck, and even by the firelight I could see his cheeks reddening slightly.

"If you're a God of Death and Destruction, and you get your powers from suffering … why do you want me to live? Why do you want me to feel better and rest and *not* suffer?" I fixed him with a curious look.

He was silent for a long moment, just staring at me, before he started laughing. His fangs caught the firelight in a distracting way, accentuating his frighteningly beautiful features. The way his dark hair fell over his face down to his shoulders. His smooth voice rumbling with his laugh.

"What's funny?" I asked, my voice completely unamused as I refused to acknowledge any flicker of interest in him.

"Just… You don't know me yet." He smiled, finishing with a chuckle. "I would never hurt you."

"You don't hurt women and children?" I ventured.

"Oh no, I do. If it were up to me, I'd kill anyone and everyone. Hellia is the benevolent sibling in our trio." His stony sincerity made an entirely different kind of shiver—the kind that had nothing to do with cold—shoot up my spine. His sharp cheekbones and jaw, the fangs in his grin, turned menacing, and his eyes flashed dangerously. "I personally rather enjoy suffering, killing … feeling others' pain at my fingertips. Of course, not my family, but pretty much anyone else I don't care. If someone around me is suffering, I won't stop it, won't help them. I'll probably prolong it if I can, just to relish in the feeling. I've never minded someone being injured, bleeding before me … but then there's *you*." His eyes narrowed on me as he emphasized his last word.

"Me?" I asked, my voice entirely breathless for another time this night. "What makes me different?" My heart pounded in my ears as I leaned forward. I was somehow completely disgusted and intrigued by him, by his way of thinking and what he was telling me.

His head tilted as he observed me in a way that was entirely animalistic, reminding me of the predator inside him, the one I hadn't seen yet. The one so dangerous the Allfather locked him up for years. After his admission that he enjoyed causing people pain and suffering mercilessly, I should be wetting my pants in terror.

"You"—he scanned me suspiciously, but with a softness too—"who makes me worry for your life and comfort. Someone I actually worry about... Besides my family, I've never worried about anyone else before. You, whose suffering I don't want to prolong or draw strength from and instead want to protect from all of that. Even from myself."

"Why?" I asked, remembering what he said earlier about killing Mag for me. It horrified me, but I couldn't deny my curiosity and the tiny flame of excitement it stoked.

"You're different." He shrugged as I sipped my tea. "You're special ... and you're mine." He said it with such softness and tenderness, but I couldn't get past the word. I choked, trying not to snort tea through my nose. When I regained my composure, I swallowed and fixed him with a glare.

"I am not *yours*. I don't belong to anyone. I am my own person," I snarled. I found myself recoiling from him. "You said no collars and leashes here."

"I haven't—" he protested, but I cut him off.

"Calling me *yours?*" I hissed at him, putting the tea on the floor. "Like I'm some piece of property that was just passed from Mag to you. Thanks for letting me know how you really feel. Disgusting." I pushed myself to my feet, shoving the blanket off my shoulders and stalking toward the bedroom.

"I'm sorry—I didn't mean—" he protested, a bewildered look coming to his face as he scrambled to his feet.

"Oh, I know what you meant," I snarled over him. "You thought you'd show me some pretty lights, promise not to put a real collar on me, then jump me with your possessive 'you're mine' bullshit, and I'd just fall in line as your sex slave now?" I glared at him, stopping him from following me.

"No, please allow me to explain—"

"I don't care what else you meant." I narrowed my eyes at him. "I'm not interested in your explanations. I'm not yours, I don't belong to you, I am not your property."

He opened his mouth but closed it again under my cold look. He nodded, and I turned to the bedroom, letting the curtain swish behind me without another word.

CHAPTER 18

"You've ridden a horse before, right?" Hellia asked as we stood in the foggy morning forest. Both of us wore dark wool cloaks. My hood was pulled up in an attempt to keep my ears and the back of my neck warm. The wind hadn't picked up yet today, but it was still below freezing.

"A long time ago, when I was a little girl." I regularly glanced at the woods nervously. I expected to see a terrible hulking werewolf Fenrir come crawling toward us any moment, ready to claim me as his and drag me off into the woods, but I had seen no sign of the wolves yet. It wasn't that I would mind if his wolf form was truly half human, half animal, because he was human so often. And his human form was … well, gorgeous. But the prospect of seeing that movie type of werewolf in real life made my skin crawl. The disjointed limbs, awkward body positioning, and general monster-ness were not something I wanted to witness that man become.

"You'll catch on quickly, I'm sure," She gave me a dismissive wave. "It's faster than a horse overall. Also, it's going to be cold for the next two nights when we're high in the peaks. If you feel ill, you have to let us know. We'll need to go on foot for a few days; Fen will be too obvious as a wolf, and I'm sure Odin has sent his search parties down here by now. He won't send them into Helheim, but we're in Niflheim right now, so we're fair game. We'll start coming down from the mountain range in a couple days, cross the valley, and then one final peak before we're home."

It wasn't my home—in fact, we were going to the center, the palace of Hell. The capital of the dead. Helheim.

A crunching noise caught my attention, and I looked up to see a grey and brown wolf as tall as a draft horse come around the corner. I stumbled back from the shock of seeing the massive beast. It looked just like any full bred, healthy grey wolf; it was just … enormous.

"Here, come say hi. It's still Jerrick, now he just can't talk and be an ass." He snorted as Hellia held a hand out, then pressed his nose against her palm. Relief swept me seeing his wolf form. No grotesque horror show here, just a massive fucking wolf.

Go Team Jacob. I chuckled under my breath to myself, thinking of the animated wolves.

I eased toward him, reaching out with a hand to stroke the soft fur on his head. A wolf this large had only been a thing of dreams, and yet here it was real. He was huge, and I couldn't imagine how the other one could be even larger. I was beginning to understand why Mag was so afraid of Tyr's bitten-off hand.

Hearing the obvious snap of a twig behind me, I turned and froze as I locked eyes with the massive black wolf. *My* wolf. Instinctively, I reached down and pinched my arm using my sharp nails.

"Ow," I whispered, staring at the indentation from my nails in my skin before checking to see if my wolf was still there. It wasn't a dream. I was wide awake, but yet my wolf was right here in front of me. He lowered his head, his tail swishing slightly behind him. For a moment, I wondered if I was hallucinating.

I slowly approached the wolf for the first time in real life. Did he know he was in my dreams? I scrambled to remember when the dreams started. I had started seeing the wolf regularly when I was in my late teens, right before I left the church. I'd had several sleepwalking incidents and dreamed of the wolf almost every night for a year. I thought it was my brain fabricating a replacement for my Christian faith to cope. The dreams grew less frequent in later years, averaging once every two weeks or so. I'd missed them when they'd gone, not sure how to get them back.

Standing before me, he was nearly the same as the dream, only much larger and with gold banding. His fur was jet black, thick and shaggy. The eyes were the same yellow as his human form. Part of me wanted to walk to him, to put my hand on his ruff as I'd done a hundred times. Part of me wanted to run, terrified.

I swallowed, thinking of how large his teeth must be. He was bigger than a bear. If a regular German Shepherd could do major damage to a human, bringing them down on police forces, then he was a super weapon.

I swallowed hard, my hands beginning to shake. The wolf flattened its ears and slowly lay down on the ground. He put his head between his paws, and his tail swept back and forth across the icy snow behind him. He looked sort of dog-like, making his gold eyes larger like a begging dog. He was almost cute.

He snorted, making me want to smile at the familiar gesture, but I kept it from my face. My eyes wandered to the gold cuffs wrapped around his legs, snout, and neck. The wolf in my dream never had those.

"He's alright. I promise he's still the same Fen. Just less sassy," Hellia encouraged, smiling fondly at the giant canid.

I walked a few steps toward him, reaching out a hand. He lifted his head, his ears twitching back up, and slowly rose to his feet to close the distance between us. Gently, he pressed his head against my outstretched hand. My heart thudded rapidly and blood was rushing by my ears as I softly scratched the giant predator on the head. I had to be dreaming.

This was so fucking weird. I was petting a wolf ... but also petting an annoying man. I felt like I didn't think this through when my magical creatures obsession started in high school.

"Alright, time to mount up," Hellia said with a clap of her hands. Jerrick barked, bouncing around gleefully. "Zip it, you mutt!" She climbed gracefully onto his back as if he were a horse, settling behind the wolf's shoulders. I slowly moved to

Fenrir's side, and he crouched slightly as I clumsily scrambled up on his shoulders.

I brushed my fingers over the coarse fur on his neck. He bent his head back to gently prod my leg with his nose, ensuring I was in place before straightening. He was so tall I would have to duck to avoid the branches on our way out as we went under the dense trees.

Hellia and Jerrick led the way out past the edge of town. The people of the village were not surprised by the wolves. A few even waved us off. This was their safe place, the one place Odin and his goons wouldn't think to look. Fenrir's home. It's really a lovely little place—he's lucky to call it home. A tiny voice in the back of my mind wondered if I would ever make it back here again.

We set out, climbing an increasingly steep trail up into the peaks. The trees quickly dissipated, falling behind us as we climbed higher into the rocks and snow. As the trail narrowed and became more angled, I found myself leaning forward, hugging Fenrir's ruff to ensure I didn't fall off and roll down the steep incline. He was sure-footed on the mountain trail, and he occasionally reached back, tapping my leg with his snout as if to tell me it was safe, and he wouldn't let me fall. Then again, maybe I was assigning words he wasn't saying. Maybe he was actually marking his property, just like the other night when he said he was never letting me go.

We gained altitude quickly, Hellia and Jerrick always several feet in front of us. I looked down at the fjord and at the small village nestled in the tree line. Kaldr soon disappeared over the ridge of craggy rocks, and we left the village behind, continuing deeper into the mountains. Up here there was no foliage, no wildlife; it was a barren and frozen rocky wasteland. Nothing blocked the howling wind here, and while it was not as severe an incline, I still had to lean down close to Fenrir's body so the wind wouldn't knock me from his back. Conveniently, laying close to his body kept me warm, too.

We continued on a trail I couldn't see for miles, the two wolves following a long, ancient way they knew by heart. To me, everything looked the same; snow and sharp mountain peaks in every direction.

I mindlessly brushed Fenrir's ruff, combing my fingers through his thick hair over and over for the entire day's journey. Of all the times I walked in the forest with my wolf, I'd never ridden on its back this way.

We crossed several peaks that first day, finally stopping at the wide mouth of a cave. Hellia dismounted and began setting up a fire in the middle of the cave, more for my benefit, I thought, than anyone else's. Taking a seat by the crackling flames, I held my chilled fingers out to warm them. I turned and watched the two beasts securing the cave and sniffing around the edge of the snow.

"What happens to their clothes?" I asked Hellia, and she laughed.

"I haven't thought about that in ages. We can summon and create any material good with our power, including clothes—unless an object is enchanted, like the knife you used to cut Fen free. When they 'wolf-out' or whatever you want to call it, their clothing shreds right off and returns to the magic fibers of the world from which it came." I nodded, not understanding one bit of how that worked.

I noticed she was standing out toward the cold while I huddled close to the fire.

"You don't need heat?" I guessed, and she nodded.

"Gods don't need it, and those who are dead don't need it. Only humans have physical needs for survival. It's been a long time since I traveled with a human." She smiled at me.

I inadvertently shivered, then grimaced. Of course I would be the weak link here. That's why Fenrir's brother Jorm hated me. I was helpless out here. Dead weight.

"Speaking of, here, eat up." She handed me a cup of soup she'd pulled from thin air. I sipped carefully and gratefully at the hot liquid, noting that Fenrir was watching me, ensuring I was eating.

The wolves joined us in the cave, both blocking us from the cold, even though I now knew Helia did not need it. "They'll keep watch, just lay down and rest," she told me, handing me a blanket she'd summoned. Suddenly feeling self conscious about how tired I was, I lay down next to the fire, resting my head on my arm. I heard Fenrir settle against the wall behind me and rolled to look back at the massive wolf. He lifted his head as I turned, watching me with golden eyes.

A chill wind swept a dusting of snow inside, and I shielded my face from the icy blast. I glanced over at Hellia, who was leaning on Jerrick's fur-covered shoulder, talking to him while the wolf snorted and let out a bark that almost sounded like laughter. I wondered what was between them, if anything. Their relationship was obviously centuries old, hundreds of lifetimes for me. I looked back at the huge animal behind me, his massive tail thudding on the ground twice. Scrambling to my feet, I walked back to him and noted his tail twitching several more times as I approached. He laid his ears back as I sat and leaned into him. He was warm, and it was much more comfortable than the cold, hard ground just feet away.

"This doesn't mean that I'm *'yours'*, okay?" I fixed him with a glare, but he just settled his head, leaning against my leg. The smell of him was the same as his human form: piney and earthy but also slightly sweet, a wildflower scent. He swept his tail across my legs, blocking any more cold that blew in from the outside. I was gone in seconds.

The dawn light woke me, and it took a minute to orient myself. Blinking the sleep from my eyes, I found myself staring into Fenrir's eyes as watched me wake. I blushed, wondering if he had the same thought processes as a wolf as he did as a human. When I reached out, he pressed his muzzle against my hand. I stroked the fur on his head and gently scratched behind his ear. His eyes closed at my touch, and a low growl, like a purr, rumbled from him.

"Good morning!" Hellia's voice was chipper, and the sun showed on the snowy peaks today, bathing the world in blinding light. Snow clouds gathered around some peaks in the distance. I snatched my hand back from the wolf, not wanting to be caught in a tender moment with the monstrous creature.

"I have breakfast for you." She walked around the fire and handed me a warm mug of coffee, the heat from the tin cup burning my fingers. Fenrir rose as I sat up to sip the drink. He gingerly turned in the cave and walked out from behind me, pausing for a moment to sniff my head. Hellia and I locked eyes as he did, and while I raised her a questioning eyebrow, she grinned, stifling a laugh.

"He worries about you," Hellia commented as he moved off to join Jerrick in sniffing around and loping through the rocks and ice, securing the perimeter outside the cave.

"Why?" I asked, watching after him. He still hadn't answered the question himself yet, and I had a feeling he was hiding something. He was withholding some knowledge, and I was set on figuring out what it was.

"Well, you're a human here, so he worries about keeping you alive. Heat, food, blood. The things humans need." She poured herself a cup of coffee and sat next to me. "I think it's more than just that, though." Her voice dropped, not wanting them to overhear.

"What do you mean?" I blew gently on the coffee, watching the ripples travel across the top and bounce back again after hitting the rim.

"He stayed by your side for a week after he brought you here. He worried when you didn't eat, and I made sure to get an IV from Midgard for you. Every time you screamed in your sleep, he was there. Every time I changed your bandage, he wanted to know how you were. You are the one who rescued him, the unrescuable. He is loyal—all the wolves are. I would say you have a guard dog for life." She sipped her coffee as we watched the two beasts. "Don't let him scare you."

Jerrick dropped on his front legs, tail wagging in the air in a play bow. Fenrir leapt at him, knocking him to the ground. They wrestled, paws battering at each other playfully. It was just like the wolves at the sanctuary. My heart panged, missing my home, my family, at the sanctuary. Gladis, Lexus, Romeo.

"What's he like, usually?" My curiosity was piqued now.

"Before he left?" She sighed, her eyes unfocused as she traveled somewhere thousands of years away in memory. "He was always smart and loved to read, even as a pup. Strong, and always tall. Fiercely loyal. He and Jorm used to gang up anyone who looked at me in a way they considered 'wrong.' He was funny, and silly, especially with Jerrick. They were thick as thieves growing up. I still think they're best friends. But he's haunted now, I can tell. He's quieter than he used to be. He won't talk about it yet. Sometimes you can see in his eyes, he just … goes somewhere else. I know he's happy to be home, though, and I can't thank you enough for your sacrifice to make that happen." She looked at me again, opening her mouth to say something more but then thinking better of it and sipping her coffee instead.

We spent two more days traveling through the snow, staying in caves as campsites, with me using Fenrir for warmth in the freezing nights. I had yet to see the trail we were actually following, just endless snow-covered rock.

Finally, it was time to descend the peaks to the valley floor. Hellia explained that we would need to cross the valley in human form to blend in better with the people in Niflheim.

We were going to be using a more well-traveled path, with a better chance to run into trouble.

The sun was blindingly bright on the snow as we trekked down the mountain. We were at a much higher elevation than the mountains at home in Vernon, and the deep snow made for slow going down the mountain on human legs.

I walked between Hellia and Fenrir, Jerrick leading the group at the front. Fenrir was back in his leather-scaled armor with the many blades hanging all over. Today, he had a forest green hood pulled up, shading his face. His eyes glowed faintly in the shadows.

"This is going to take forever on foot," I groaned as I slipped in the snow, then swatted away Fenrir's hands when he tried to help steady me.

"It won't be so bad when we get down to the main trail, promise." Jerrick smiled at me over his shoulder.

"How long will we be on foot? Will you be wolves again before we get there?" I asked. The past days had felt surreal; *they* were surreal.

"Ready for me to shut up already, sweetheart?" Jerrick said with a smirk and a flirtatious wink.

"I'm ready for you to shut up already," Hellia said, interjecting before I could respond.

"Yes, please stop talking," Fenrir growled at him from behind me.

"I wasn't asking either of you," he said with a huff.

I looked at the brown-haired leader of our party for a long moment before bursting into laughter. Real, shoulders shaking, lungs wheezing, belly aching laughter for the first time in nearly two months. The smile stretching across my lips felt foreign but welcome. My cheeks ached as I swiped a finger at a tear threatening to leak from my eye. I knew it wasn't particularly funny, but with my broken brain, I was just happy to be laughing.

The tall brunette was smiling brightly, fangs showing in his proud smile. I tried to calm my breathing back to normal, but in the excitement, I gave myself hiccups. The smile was stuck on my lips, making the muscles in my face burn.

I glanced toward our companions. Hellia shared my same wide smile, looking relieved and happy to see me finally showing some ease. Fenrir grimaced at me, and I saw him shoot a severe glare at Jerrick. The smile faded from my lips as Hellia gave her brother a frown and a sharp elbow to the ribs. He frowned at her, trying to understand what she was silently telling him.

We trekked further and further down the mountain in silence. The snow became steadily less thick on the ground, but the sky had clouded with ominous, grey, low-hanging clouds that promised another blizzard.

"Here." Hellia burst forward on a path carved through the snow and woods, obviously a worn trail. "This will lead us through the valley and toward the gate to Helheim."

I took a deep breath. The trail cutting through the forest looked daunting, and yet a flicker of excitement sparked in me. I set out through the snow after my new companions.

CHAPTER 19

"I have to use the bathroom." I was near stamping my foot at him.

"Okay, so do it," Fenrir said.

"Not here! I want privacy!" I grit my teeth angrily.

"I said no to going off the trail and out of my sight. It's too dangerous here. There could be Aesir anywhere," he growled, folding his arms across his chest and waiting for me, apparently, to drop trow in the middle of the trail. We hadn't passed many people, and it was empty now, but I craved privacy all the same.

"You are insufferable. Let her pee in private." Hellia waved him away and nodded for me to step off the trail into the woods.

Before he could argue with Hellia or I anymore, I leapt off the path and walked into the brush, looking for a private place to catch my breath for a moment. To collect my thoughts alone. I figured if I kept quiet and didn't make any noise, no one would find me or know where I was.

I crept through the bushes, finding a sheltered spot to relieve myself before starting to pick my way back to my group. I was about to call out for Hellia when I felt a hand clamp around my arm with bruising force. My yelp was smothered by a hand over my mouth, and I made to wrench my arm away but the hand gripped me tighter, cutting off my cry into a small whimper. I turned to see an Aesir holding me and another coming to join him.

"We've been looking for you, girl," the one who held me hissed in my ear.

"Odin wants you dead," the other added, brushing the back of his hand against my cheek. I flinched away from his touch, trying to determine how to get myself out of this mess. He stroked my hair back from my face, surveying me with a wicked grin. My heart was thundering in my chest as terror colder than the icy winter around us surged through my veins.

"There's no reason we can't have some fun with her first. I remember you—Magni's whore, right? She's a pretty little mortal thing. Did he ever let you borrow her?" The Aesir holding me gave a wicked smile laced with malicious intent. "I'll hold her for you, then you can for me." He shoved me to the ground in front of his companion, and I squealed as I tried to fight back. The effort was futile. Once on the ground, he pressed a knee into each of my shoulders, pinning me. No matter how I twisted my body, I couldn't move beneath him. I kicked out at the second man, who was laughing with excitement at my thrashing.

"She is much more feisty than I remember!" he chortled, his hand pulling the waistband of my pants down, exposing my panties and bare ass to the freezing snow. I took a breath to scream, but the one pinning me slammed his hand over my mouth again. I screamed against his hand anyway, the sound muffled, and writhed in fear as the other man continued to pull down my pants.

"I'll give you only one chance to get your filthy hands off her before I eat them the way I ate Tyr's." The deep voice, dark and silky as night, chilled my bones. All three of our heads snapped to where the foreboding figure stood in all black, his form sharp and dangerous against the dim grey-and-white winter. Knives glinted against his chest, and his eyes glittered dangerously under his hood. The man near my legs stood, leaving my pants pulled halfway down. The man over me stood too, but he placed a boot on my chest before I could rise or roll away. His strength kept me firmly on my back under him. I tried to push myself from under his foot, but his singular limb was a dozen times stronger than all of me. I squirmed like a fish out of water.

In the seconds that took, Fenrir had shifted to his Divine Form. The massive wolf slammed into the men, sending them flying and crashing into the trees. I gasped for precious air when the heavy weight lifted from my chest. The wolf's yellow eyes never left the two men, now several meters away, as he towered with me between his legs. He let out a roar that sounded more like a lion, or maybe a tyrannosaur, than a wolf. The noise made the trees tremble and the foliage quake around us. Terrified shivers overtook my body, and my shaking hands pulled my pants back up before I rolled and pushed up into a sitting position. My hair obscured my vision, falling loose from the bun Hellia had twisted it into that morning.

Slowly, on shaking legs, both Aesir men stood and faced the wolf baring his teeth at them. The god who'd placed his boot on my chest reached for the sword on his back, but Fenrir was faster. His vicious teeth clamped around the man's neck, and blood spurted like a punctured water balloon over both of them. He screamed as Fenrir shook him violently, breaking the man's neck in one motion. Oh my God... Fenrir just killed him. Over me. He took an *immortal life*, simply because this person captured me in the woods.

My brain couldn't comprehend the carnage before me, nor that I was the reason behind it. People were dying over me, even if they were the villains in my story. This went against everything I had been taught, every moral. It went against the notion of forgiveness drilled into me, and I couldn't help my mind wandering to thoughts of what Jesus Christ would think at the end of my life of gods killing other gods over me. If he was even real.

The scream of terror rising from my lungs caught in my throat, and I remained frozen on the ground, staring at the dead Aesir's blank, sightless eyes, watching the blood slow its flow from his neck. Moments ago, that man wanted to attack me, hold me down for his friend to abuse me. I should be grateful for being saved. I was grateful. And also terrified.

Fenrir shifted back to his human form, clothing forming so fast from the shadows around him that I saw only his muscled chest splattered with blood for a moment shorter than a breath before he was clothed and hooded once more. It took two steps for him to cross the space to where the second Aesir man cowered on the ground, and by the time I blinked, Fenrir was clutching the man's throat. He lifted the Aesir into the air, crushing his windpipe the same way Mag used to do to me. The scene was horrifying, and it had me scrambling back from the two terrifying gods.

"How many more of you are there in this area?" Fenrir snarled in the man's face. The Aesir sputtered and coughed, clawing in vain at Fenrir's hand around his throat.

He loosened his grip long enough for the man to choke out, "A whole squadron."

"Where," Fenrir demanded, slamming the man's head back against a tree, causing him to groan. A flurry of snow fell around them from the branches above.

"Like I would tell you." He moaned as red blood began streaming down the side of his face and then quickly stopped as he healed.

"Where?" Fen snarled, in one fluid movement unhooking a silver knife from his cross belt and stabbing it up into the man's stomach. I gasped, terror coursing through my veins as I watched Fenrir murder the next Aesir. I had never seen anyone die, much less be murdered violently in front of my very eyes. A squeak of fear slipped past my lips as I continued pushing myself away from the horrifying scene.

"Over the hill! Over the hill!" the man shrieked as Fenrir twisted the knife in his gut with a sickening squelch. I shuddered.

"Go." Fenrir shoved the man toward the hill beyond, removing the knife from his abdomen with a tearing motion that made me want to be sick. "Tell them to leave. And tell them that anyone who places a finger on her will die, slowly and painfully, in Helheim. For my entertainment."

The Aesir wrapped his arms over his bleeding torso, bent over double with pain as he stumbled. His wounds were not healing this time, and he'd die of them; no doubt the knife twisting and removal had ruptured vital organs. I suspected Fenrir's knife was enchanted or otherwise special, which prevented the Aesir from healing himself. His blood dripped on the snow, leaving an easily visible trail where he scrambled away.

I shook uncontrollably on the ground, staring at all the red blood splattering the crisp snow. The lacerated body of the dead Aesir lay no more than ten meters from me. I couldn't help but take a long mental picture of the teeth marks in his neck and the tearing damage those fangs did. I couldn't believe I just watched that. Fenrir was a monster—a monster who saved me, but still a monster nonetheless.

Panting in horror, I scrambled further back, toward the cover of low-hanging pine branches. Fenrir watched the wheezing, stumbling man disappear over the hill. I couldn't hold back the tears streaming down my face, couldn't tear myself from where the dead man and the blood pooling around him. I'd never seen a dead body before. Never witnessed a violent, gruesome death or murder with my own eyes. Certainly never been friends with a murderer. Panic gripping my throat, I turned and fled into the trees behind me. I only made it a few steps before the snow caught my foot and I tripped into a drift face first.

Hands slid under my arms and lifted me to my feet in one swift movement. I wrenched myself from him and staggered back. His hood was pulled down now so I could see his face, concern plaguing his eyes as they swept over me from head to toe.

"Are you hurt?" He walked around me in a quick circle, scanning every angle.

"Y-you murdered them," I gasped.

"Anais—" he said.

"The way you just killed him…" I looked at the broken, mangled body laying beyond his shoulder. Tattered clothes lay in ribbons around the deceased. "He was a person, with thoughts and feelings. Probably a family. It's like you don't care that you just killed him…" I couldn't understand his lack of remorse and, at the same time, the very real concern for me brimming in his expression.

"I *don't* care that I killed him." His voice was colder than the forest around us. He watched the tears falling down my cheeks, looking a bit confused, as though he didn't understand why I was crying. I wasn't even sure why I was crying, overwhelmed by the conflicting feelings of horror and relief. "He was going to hurt you. I'll kill anyone who even thinks they might hurt you." That truth crashed over me like an icy wave, sending fear bolting through me like a strike of lightning. Murderer. Killer. Life taker. On *my* behalf.

"You could have just scared them off, threatened them. Non-lethal injuries. You didn't need to actually be so violent, did you? To take their *life*?" My voice trembled with my emotions. I cringed again, my eyes drifting again to the bloody mess on the canvas of the woods.

"You don't have to understand. But I kill people who touch what's mine." He was laser focused on me.

"*Yours?*" I couldn't keep any of the shock from my voice.

"Mine." He snarled, the predator flashing in his eyes as it lurked under the surface. Protective. Possessive. The dangerous beast in his eyes had me swallowing, trying to decide if I wanted to spar with him or just shut up and be thankful I was saved at all.

"I am not your property," I said, hissing the words under my breath. "I told you that before. I don't belong to you. I'm not yours."

His growing grin was wicked, but there was something else in his eyes, something I couldn't quite identify. Something that made me want to take off through the woods and run from him. I wondered what he would do if he caught me. Would he kill me too?

His lips parted, tongue swiping across his lip and down a fang as he stood towering above me. I couldn't help but follow the movement. He was sizing me up like prey, and I felt the predator in him nipping at my heels, urging my feet to flee across the forest floor. My heart thundered in my chest; surely he could hear every beat from where he stood.

The snowflakes had doubled in size now, falling thick and fast. They soaked my clothes as I stood facing off with Fenrir. The shock of the whole situation had not dampened, and I was feeling nearly light-headed from the fear fusing with relief, and the tiniest, miniscule amount of flattery that I didn't want to admit to myself yet.

My prey instinct snapped and I turned, running as fast as I could into the forest behind me. I could hear him following, still in human form as we crashed through the forest. He was hot on my heels, and I squealed as one of his arms hooked around me, lifting me off my feet. I struggled in the air for a moment, but he didn't set me down until I stopped flailing. When I gave up my thrashing, he gripped my wrist firmly, spinning me against his chest so I was eye level with his defined pectoral muscles.

"I like it when you run from me." The guttural growl rumbled through his entire chest, and I saw a flash of fang on his lips. My heart hammered, trying to break free of my ribcage and keep running from the dangerous predator lurking inside him. At the same time, I felt a familiar tingle race through me from where he held me to the warm pulse between my legs signaling desire.

Was I truly scared of him? Yes. Was something thrilling about the fear I felt of him? Absolutely. Was I ready to deal with any of that? Hell no.

"You make it easy when you're being terrifying. Are you going to kill me, too?" I hissed back at him, struggling to back away. He held me fast to him. He opened his mouth to spring a retort, but we were cut off.

"As much fun as it would be to watch you two fuck in the forest, there are people waiting to get going." Jerrick's tone was dry, and Hellia snickered behind him with her back turned to us.

Heat flushed my cheeks at the thought, and the tingles radiating from his touch intensified. I hated that it did. I hated feeling any kind of excitement about him after what happened to me in Asgard.

"I'm not fucking him anywhere. Ever," I spat, finally ripping free of his grip, but only because he let me. Another pulse between my legs begged to differ. Fenrir smirked and inhaled deeply through parted lips. I wished he would stop looking at me like that; it made me feel conflicted. His eyes narrowed with a teasing expression, making the butterflies in my chest shake the dust from their wings.

I flipped my middle finger at him before storming through the underbrush to where Jerrick and Hellia stood a few meters from the main trail.

He killed those men, violently and viciously—but he did it to protect me.

CHAPTER 20

"We need to stop here," Hellia demanded as soon as we came across the first town along the trail. "We can't go any further today. I'm sure Anais is tired, it's freezing, and as much as we need to be anonymous moving through here, I think we can afford to stay in town." She was right—the snow had been pounding heavily all day since the Aesir attacked me, and despite my thick winter cloak, I was chilled to the bone and my clothes were soaking wet. Their clothes were soaked also, but they showed no discomfort. My hair clung to my neck and face, having mostly fallen out of the neatly twisted bun after the scuffle in the woods. Melted snow dripped down my back and chest beneath my clothes, ensuring I was thoroughly frozen.

Jerrick snorted, taking in the little tavern on the block of grey stone houses. The town looked nearly unpopulated. Few people wandered the main row of houses and shops. Most of the windows were dark, and it lacked the warmth that had been somehow present in Kaldr.

"They're going to be able to tell she's human if she speaks, or if they look at her too closely. They'll want to cash in Odin's bounty." The lieutenant eyed me with uncertainty.

"She'll be fine," Fen answered him, his gravelly voice seeming to soothe Jerrick the way Jerrick's voice had a calming effect on everyone else. Jerrick obviously trusted him implicitly and was more than glad, more than relieved, to have him back.

"True," the lieutenant conceded. "You'll huff and puff and blow the house down if anyone touches a hair on her head." He earned a snicker from Hellia and an eye roll from Fenrir.

I was too tired to take much more arguing out in the cold, shivers wracking my body completely. My knees knocked together like a cartoon character under my cloak. Fenrir glanced down, frowning as I chewed my frozen lip and tried to warm my fingers under my armpits. I reminded myself not to look at him.

"Once we're in, we'll split up for the night, you boys and us girls." Helia laid out the plan.

"No," Fen argued immediately.

"What do you mean, no?" Hellia sounded irritated.

"I mean I'm not leaving her alone in there," Fenrir growled.

"She's not going to be alone—she'll be with me," Hellia huffed. "You two can make bunk beds and gossip, do whatever the hell it is you two do together." She pointed between the two men.

"Yeah, I want to sleep in Hellia's room," I chimed in. There was no way I was sleeping in the same room as a violent murderer. Fenrir's head whipped in my direction, fangs flashing in the dim light and making the hair stand up on the back of my neck. I wasn't sure if it was from terror or some kind of excitement. Maybe both. "I don't share my room with *murderers*," I said pointedly at him.

He groaned, his eyes closing. He leaned his head into his hands, fingertips massaging his temples. I tried not to focus on how oddly erotic I found the movement and sound; the pulse between my legs jumped to attention for the second time today.

"For the hundredth time, I don't *care* if you don't like it that I killed them, Anais," he said.

"Alright, alright, let's just see what's going on when we get in there." Jerrick stepped in between everyone, raising an eyebrow at Fenrir. "It's getting late, we need to get in rooms, and she needs to eat and sleep so we can leave early tomorrow."

"Fine," Fenrir conceded. He turned to me. "Don't look at anyone but us." I nodded, the seriousness of his tone making me nervously cast about the little street. He took my chin between his thumb and forefinger, firmly making me look into his eyes. "Don't look anyone in the eye when we're in there. Don't let anyone see your full face, and don't speak under any circumstance until you're inside the bedroom. Even then, whisper only."

I nodded, keeping silent.

To my surprise, the tavern was bustling, a crowd gathered to eat and drink. Music drifted from a back corner where a lovely woman with rosy cheeks played a large harp. I expected it to be terrifying, but it was just like a renaissance faire combined with every tavern I'd seen on TV. It was friendly, noisy, and something smelled delicious and rich. It was still cold inside though, freezing, as if there was not actually a fire in the fireplace and all the bodies in the room were made of ice. From my viewpoint, I could mostly see pants and heavy boots on the floor. All the people in the tavern were men, except for a barmaid, the harp lady, Hellia, and me. I heard some whispers around us and nearly crashed into Fen's back as he stopped suddenly in front of me.

The chorus of voices behind me became louder. Chuckles, low whistles, and other vulgar noises made the hair on the back of my neck stand up. Fen reached for my arm, dragging me by my wrist in front of him and pulling me close to his body, keeping my back pressed against his hard chest with his hands on my shoulders. I glanced at the heavy weight on my shoulders. He wore black gloves to hide the gold cuffs at his wrists. It was very on brand for him, all black clothing all the time.

"We don't allow whores here," the owner sneered as Jerrick approached the innkeeper's desk. Hellia's eyes flared but she held her tongue. I couldn't help but roll my eyes under my hood. The audacity.

"Funny as you are, my friend," Jerrick's crooned, smooth and deadly, "we need two rooms for the night for us and our wives. You see, we're Hell Hounds, but we've both taken the

weekend away with our ladies before the Great Fenrir returns
for Ragnarok. We need two rooms for tonight."

The innkeep snorted, looking over Jerrick's shoulder at Fen
and I.

"Somehow, I doubt that's what's going on here ... but if
you're Hell Hounds ... then fine." His eyes moved back to
Jerrick, taking in his armor and smelling the forest on him.
His bow and quiver were slung across his back, and he had
the blades strapped every which way around him. "Thank
you for serving the Queen." The innkeeper's voice was low,
begrudgingly thanking the lieutenant. "I only have two rooms,
the ones there." He pointed to two doors overlooking the
main hall. Shit. Everyone in the tavern would watch us go in.
Even worse, they'd probably be able to hear anything above a
whisper clear as day. I'd need to be extra quiet.

"Thank you," Jerrick said, placing a currency of gold pieces
I had never seen on the counter. Before I could get a good look
at the coins, Fenrir took hold of my wrist again and herded me
in front of him as he bee-lined for the stairs. Jerrick and Hellia
right on our heels, we all made our way up to the rooms. I
could feel all eyes in the tavern watching us and hear murmurs
and low laughs reverberating around the room. Fenrir made
for the far door, pushing me inside the room and following me
in. I turned and stared, wide eyed, as he locked the door and
drew his finger down the entrance, making some kind of seal
that would break if the door opened.

He looked at me, lifted a gloved hand, and pressed his finger
to his lips. I nodded, looking around the room. The single large
bed would fit Fenrir, but it took most of the room. Next to it
stood a tiny dresser, then a door to an even smaller bathroom

stall. Fen looked enormous in the room, and I shrank, feeling like a mouse in comparison. The room was tiny, not even enough space for me to sleep on the floor. I rolled my eyes, thinking it was just like the books I loved reading at home, but it wasn't as fun as I imagined.

Fen removed his cloak and took mine to hang by the door. I shivered, hugging my sweater tighter around me, and wondered if I should try to survive the night in these frozen wet clothes.

"Just take them off," Fen hissed in a whisper.

I felt the heat rushing to my cheeks as I turned away from him. I shimmied the soaked, fleece-lined leggings off my stinging legs. My thighs were red with the cold. I tossed away my socks and pulled the sweater over my head. Casting a nervous glance over my shoulder, I saw he was removing his own soaked clothing. His shaggy hair fell down to muscular, flexing shoulders, and then further to where his waist tapered above his pants. With a fluttering in my chest that I was determined to ignore, I averted my eyes and dove for the bed. I threw myself between the icy sheets and immediately regretted it. My body was completely wracked with shivers.

How was I going to survive in this unheated room? Did he remember I'd need heat to survive? Surely a real fire would alert everyone in the tavern that a human is here, if they hadn't already figured out who I am and just been too afraid of my guard dog to try approaching me for a closer look. I was going to die of hypothermia. What happened then? Would I be undead here? Could I go home?

My thoughts whirled like a tornado as I pulled my body in as tight as possible. I pressed my hands to my thighs, trying to retain any warmth that was left in me. I felt the sheets move behind me as Fenrir slid into bed. He extinguished the small bedside lantern, and my eyes took a moment to adjust to the dark. The small window above the bed let in a sliver of moonlight to illuminate the bed ever so slightly. I stared into the dark corner I faced, trying to calm my body as shivers ravaged me. I was so cold, it felt like being in the forest the night Mag had brought me to the hospital. When I'd been lost in the woods, *like an idiot*, and woken up in a hospital. A deeper shiver washed over me at the memory, and I reached down to wrap my hands around my toes. Curled in the fetal position, I lay trembling in the frozen bed.

A warm arm wrapped around my waist and pulled me across the bed effortlessly. I melted into his broad chest, his warmth like the best heated blanket ever. His chest hair tickled my back, and I could feel his defined muscles everywhere we touched. It was enough to make me forget all the blood this afternoon.

"This is why you needed to be with me, *hjarta*. You'd freeze to death with Hellia," he whispered to me, his hot breath stinging my cold ear. I pressed back against him harder, as if that would make warmth seep into my body faster. His hands ran over my arms and thighs to warm them. A soft purr rumbled in his chest, making my breath stutter. I wondered if he thought I couldn't hear it over my chattering teeth.

"I could have stayed with Jerrick," I whispered as quietly as I could. His fingers paused, digging into my chilled skin slightly, making my heart beat faster for just a moment.

"Would you like me to switch with him? I'm sure he'll be happy to come and keep you company." My breath hitched, and I couldn't find words for a moment. No. I didn't want Jerrick.

"No," I said. I lay in silence, allowing my body to receive the needed warmth.

I tried to convince myself it was just like sleeping next to the wolf in the woods, he was just human tonight. It was no different. It meant nothing. Completely smashed against him, I could feel every movement of his body and his heart beating against my back. I tried to convince myself it meant nothing more than survival.

He wrapped around me, his cheek resting against my head. Warmth radiated from him, and as we lay there, I became very aware that my undergarments were just as wet as the rest of the clothes I'd already stripped off. The strap of my bra between my body and his leaked a few drops of icy water.

"You can take them off too, if you want," Fen said with a purr in my ear, making a different kind of heat sting the apples of my cheeks.

"No chance," I told him flatly, careful to keep my voice barely a whisper.

"It's going to be uncomfortable." I felt his fingers gently brush the wet strap that was already starting to bite into my skin as it dried. "And I can't imagine it's good for human skin to stay in cold, damp clothes of any kind. I'll get you some pajamas if you want."

I wanted to argue with him and demand to know why he didn't offer them from the start, but I was too overwhelmed trying to fight the need to rip the wet clothes from my body and then curl up next to my personal heater and pass out. We lay in silence for a moment, his hand brushing over the fabric. The cold underwear was becoming uncomfortable too.

I looked back at him over my shoulder. My eyes had adjusted to the dark room now, and I could see him in the moonlight. His strong jaw was illuminated in the dim light, and his eyes glowed faintly. He raised an eyebrow at me before I rolled my eyes.

"Fine. But no peeking, seriously. Can you help me get that?" I nodded to the clasp on my back. It seemed entirely too soon to be getting naked in bed with this man, but the cold clothing was even worse than the shame in my thoughts.

His fingers gently ran over the clasp, unhooking it for me so I could peel it off. I held the sheet over myself so he couldn't see, but he looked away and rolled a bit to give me room as he handed me a silky pajama set that wasn't particularly warm. At least it would cover me while I had to lay next to him. I shimmied them on, throwing my soaked underwear across the room into my pile of wet clothes.

"Better?" he asked, turning back toward me after I settled back down.

"Mhm." I nodded, shifting so my front could face his hot body and warm up. My eyes flicked up to see him watching me, head propped up on an elbow. "What?" I growled, making sure to keep my voice quiet still.

"Your lips are still blue," he commented, making me blanch and bite my frozen lip self-consciously.

"I'm sure I'll warm up soon enough," I hissed, but I couldn't take my eyes off him. Off his lips in the dim light of the room. I wanted to reach out and touch him, but I wasn't sure if I should.

"Let me help, if it's okay with you." He leaned in slowly, giving me enough time to reject him. I thought about it but kept still until his lips were hovering above mine, brushing mine softly. I could feel myself trembling, but I wasn't sure why. "You're in control," he whispered, his hot breath stinging my frozen lips. "Okay?" All I could do was nod, seeing the pleading, begging look in his expression.

His lips burned as he pressed them to mine. My heart started playing hopscotch in my chest, and I found myself wrapping my arms around his neck, pulling him closer. The tingles returned, following his hands as they ran along my body. It was more addictive than any drug I'd ever tried, any sugary treat I'd ever eaten, any bad habit I'd ever picked up. I couldn't get enough of him.

"Anais," he groaned softly into my mouth, making the hair on the back of my neck stand up. His hand slowly swiped up my side, his thumb brushing over my pebbled nipple through the silk pajamas. He kissed down my neck, pausing at the hollow where my neck met my shoulder.

I'd watched him be so violent earlier today, and here he was placing delicate kisses on my skin as though I might crack and fall apart at his every touch. His lips had consumed mine once more, and I was struggling for breath between the intense, increasingly desperate kisses.

But what if he was just using me? The same way Mag did, for some ulterior purpose? I couldn't stop the intrusive thoughts from making me snap rigid under his touch. Flashbacks of Mag barged into my head, and panic swelled in my chest.

"Stop," I breathed, gulping air. His hands paused their movement instantly, his mouth pulling back from mine. His breath still came quick and ragged as he watched me, the pleading look having returned. His tongue swiped out across his lips, savoring the taste of my mouth on his.

"N-no more." My voice trembled. I was afraid of what he might do if I said no. Mag would have forced me to keep going.

"Okay," he said. With a deep, satisfied sigh, he settled down against his pillow again, watching me and stroking my hair. I traced the gold lines on his face, mesmerized by those liquid-gold eyes glowing faintly in the night. After a while, he pulled me closer, higher, so he could tuck his head under my chin, resting on my chest and listening to my heart.

"Is this okay?" he whispered.

"Yes." I was glad for the darkness, so he couldn't see my flushed cheeks. My arms wrapped around his neck. I gently hugged his head, ruffling his hair and placing a delicate kiss on his head. He took a shaky breath, startling me a little bit.

"No one has touched me like that for a long time," he murmured. My heart shattered as my mind flashed back to him chained and unable to move. I wanted to ask him everything, to know what had happened all the years he was chained. I couldn't speak though, couldn't ask every question I wanted to, couldn't have anyone outside overhear my voice. It didn't matter right now, anyway. I kept stroking his hair and planting gentle kisses on his head until we fell asleep completely entwined, the smell of him everywhere.

The next morning, my eyes fluttered open to a gentle touch on my hair and soft light coming in the window. He sat on the edge of the bed, dressed in his usual armor and arsenal. "Good morning," he said in a deep, rumbling whisper. I pushed up to my elbows, pulling the warm blanket with me. He stood and gently patted a pile of new clothes for me with his fingertips.

I nodded, and he turned to face the corner, leaning on the wall as he waited. He was so tall, the top of his head nearly met the ceiling, which must be about eight feet high in this little inn room. I unwillingly let go of the warm blankets, wishing so badly that I could talk to him right now instead of this intense silence. I pulled on the black tunic and some darker brown pants. Surprisingly, they fit well on my curves, but I was concerned for my blessed chest since the tunic was rather loose and there was no bra. I turned to Fen and opened my mouth, not really sure what I was going to even say. He must have heard the movement, seen me out of the corner of his eye, because he turned and showed me—*a corset?* I stared at the brown leather piece.

He smiled softly and nodded for me to spin around. I obliged, pulling my hair to the top of my head, arms raised as he reached it around me. He gently put the corset in place, and I let go of my hair with one hand to adjust my breasts into it. He stopped me. My breath caught as he took my wrist and brought it back to my head. I kept my hands there and tried to remember how to breathe again while he adjusted my left breast, then my right in the corset. His touch was so gentle, the complete opposite of everything I knew of him as a dark, world-destroying being. Once everything was situated, he pulled the corset tight in the back—not tight enough it hurt, but I felt much more secure than my regular bra. He leaned over my shoulder and looked into my eyes, silently asking if it was where I wanted it. I gave a little nod, my heart picking up its pace as I stared at his lips, remembering them from last night. My eyes met his as I felt him tie the corset off low on my back. I let go of my hair as I turned to face him, letting it fall around my face. He gently reached toward my face, tucking a wave of it back behind my ear. His eyes dropped to stare at my lips while his fingers lingered on my neck. The feeling made my skin erupt into goose pimples just as it had days ago.

A double thud on the door shook us both. "Jerrick." Fenrir scowled at the door and stepped away. He wrapped the purple cloak, completely dry and warm, around me again and pulled the hood up to shade my eyes. Taking his own black one, he pulled it on and flipped up the hood to shade his eyes as well.

As he turned away from me, I looked back at the bed we'd been laying in just minutes ago, where we'd cuddled intimately and I'd felt so incredibly safe. It was a shame we'd be back to cave-dwelling tonight, but it was probably for the best until we had separate rooms again in Helheim.

CHAPTER 21

W e traveled two more days before we approached Helheim City. I saw it in the distance during a brief break
in the fog and snow, the lights shining at the bottom of a fjord.
Standing a few meters from the shelter, I watched the lights
flicker and sparkle under the stars. It seemed so bright for a city
of dead people, the city of torture. The Kingdom of Hell.

"I'm sure it looks just like home." Fenrir offered a small smile
as he came to stand at my shoulder, watching the lights.

"What do you know of my home?" I asked, pulling my
arms tighter around myself. Since our kiss at the inn, we hadn't
talked about it, hadn't had any time alone. Now, Hellia and

Jerrick had gone to bed, but I was having trouble sleeping—and it appeared he was as well.

"Not much anymore, I'm afraid. I haven't been to Midgard in a long time." He was looking down at the city, but I could feel him watching me from the corner of his vision.

"You'll know soon enough, I suppose. And I'll learn about your city." I nodded to the lights and turned to go back into the cave.

I supposed I would know soon what the city of the dead was like. I imagined how cold it was at the inn. The city must be the same way. Would it be a terrifying place? The complete opposite of Asgard?

I looked at Hellia sleeping against Jerrick, who was already snoring on the other side of the room. I thought of the inn the other day and things we'd left unspoken since. The kisses, the intimate cuddling, what had he meant by it all? Maybe he was just excited to share a bed with any woman he wasn't related to. He did say he hadn't been touched in a long time; maybe it didn't matter by who. Biting my lip, I turned back toward him.

The picture of him from behind, standing in the snowy landscape and looking out in the distance, brought back a faint memory of a dream. When I'd been in Asgard, I'd dreamt of a man calling my name; if the wolf was him, then the man calling for me must've been him.

With a shake of my head to clear the thoughts, I stepped back out of the cave and marched to where he stood. He looked down, surprised and somewhat bewildered at my change in attitude.

"I don't know what that was the other day," I said, fixing a hand on my hip, the other pointing at him accusingly. He listened intently, curiosity at my words growing in his expression. "But I am not interested in keeping any more gods' beds warm or ... or being used, for touching or anything else. I know you haven't been able to do whatever you want, and I'm the first woman you've seen that you're not related to, but I am not playing." I huffed, folding my arms across my chest as I waited for him to respond.

"I know." His voice was gentle and quiet. It only made me feel more confused, and therefore more furious.

"So stop kissing me!" I blushed deep crimson. "And the other things." My mind flashed to the feeling of his thumb on my nipple. I watched the corner of his mouth twitch up, as if he were thinking of it too.

"Anais." My name on his lips had a shiver skittering down my spine that had nothing to do with the freezing wind. His small smirk had dropped, his face serious once more. "I am not playing a game either. Please do not mistake my affections for anything other than what they are."

I swallowed at his words, daring myself to look back up into his intense stare. "So, then tell me what they are. You've been dodging my questions for long enough." I scuffed my foot in the snow awkwardly.

"I mean to say that I like you, Anais. You saving me was part of that, but it's not the only thing." His eyes swept my face, his hand reaching up to brush my cheek. His expression turned sad when I instinctively cringed away from the sudden close contact. "But I also know that Mag hurt you. I don't want to push you too fast." His voice dropped quieter as his eyes followed the patterns my boot was making in the snow. "I don't want you to be scared of me."

I bit my lip. I couldn't say that he didn't scare me; admittedly, he did. "I can worry about what is too fast and not for myself, thank you very much."

His expression turned guilty, and I waited for him to say more but he didn't. After a long moment of awkward silence, I took a few steps toward the cave mouth again.

"I'm going to bed." I paused, looking over my shoulder to where he was absently staring out at the forest. His expression was contemplative, as though he was fighting an internal battle. "You know, Fen…"

His eyes flicked to mine instantly, widening so slightly I wasn't sure if I was imaging it.

"What happened at the inn… It wasn't too much. If you wanted to know if I liked it before I told you to stop… I did." I scanned him warily, taking the moment to be in awe of him. Tall, handsome, and powerful, yet so gentle with me, always soft and delicate when it came to me. As if he truly was afraid he'd scare me off like a fawn in the forest.

He looked at me for a moment, his expression softening significantly. "I did want to know, thank you." He dipped his head. His dark hair fell down over his eyes, partially obscuring them.

"I just … need to go slow." I felt embarrassed admitting it out loud.

He nodded, his eyes never breaking from mine. "As slowly as you need, *hjarta*."

We stared at each other in silence for a moment, my heart-beat thumping in my ears. I momentarily wondered if I made a mistake encouraging him, but I couldn't pretend I wasn't attracted to him. I felt empowered after the inn, after he'd stopped when I'd said to. And I felt empowered now that he'd acknowledged what happened with Mag and was trying to be restrained to allow me to heal.

I turned away, walking back to the cave and sitting in front of the fire. He stayed outside for a long while, and eventually I grew tired waiting for him. Laying down, I rested my head on my arm, letting my eyes drift closed as I listened to the fire crackle. A cold gust blew in from the mouth of the cave, and I curled into myself to block the chill that hit my back. I was suddenly so sleepy, barely still awake when I heard his footsteps behind me.

"Oh, *hjarta*. I'm sorry, I lost track of the time. I should've gone to bed earlier." I heard him whispering to himself with a quiet tsk-ing noise. Gently, he replaced my arm with his own to cushion my head. I was too tired to argue, to even open my eyes as he pulled me close to him, cuddling me against his warm body. Not that I'd have argued anyway; his body heat was a blessing in this frozen world. If I was fully awake, I might've been embarrassed to be cuddling with him in human form, but for now I was too exhausted to double check that Hellia and Jerrick were still asleep and not witnessing this intimate moment.

With his free hand, he brushed back my hair, and I could feel him looking at me, feel his soft breath as he studied my face.

"What do I have to do to get you to believe me, hm?" he asked softly, obviously not expecting an answer, thinking I couldn't hear him. He gently tucked my hair behind my ear and I felt his presence even closer, his lips brushing my eyebrow. He placed a kiss on my forehead before tucking my head under his chin. My nose was against him; he smelled uniquely him, sweat and forest mixed with a subtle pine scent. I snuggled closer to him inadvertently, allowing myself to give into some deep part of me that wanted desperately to relax under his protection.

"I smell those *fucking* cats," Jerrick announced, his head whipping side to side as a low vibrated from him.

We just entered the clearing where a massive stone arch with a silver gate loomed tall as the trees. The gate was menacing, sharp points and barbs glinting in the designs. Matching stone walls stretched either direction, cutting through the forest to divide the realms. Beyond was invisible, the fog and snow too thick to see into the realm of Helheim.

"I smell Tyr," Fenrir whispered with a growl, his eyes scanning the gate ahead of us and the trees to either side.

"Tyr?" I whispered to no one in particular, my heart jumping into my throat. I checked over both shoulders as though my one-handed abuser might be lurking right behind me. I took a step closer to Fen's side, and he immediately put an arm around me, pushing me in front of him.

"That's right, you little Asgard traitor—did you miss me? I missed that tight pussy of yours." Tyr appeared from the trees near the arch. I shuddered at the evil smirk and wink he gave me when my terrified eyes made contact with his. On the other side of the arch, Tora appeared with two of Freyja's giant lynx cats. All four of the Asgardians stepped into the path, blocking the gate.

A vicious snarl ripped from Fenrir's throat above me, and I worried my legs might buckle with the fear of the sound. His grip on my shoulders tightened, and I bit my lip to keep from whimpering with the pain in my newly mended arm and the fear of facing these gods.

"You *disgust* me, Tyr," Hellia drawled, strolling casually past us. "And I don't even know why you're here, Tora. You no longer have anything I want, so you're of no use to me."

One of the cats hissed at her, taking a few prowling steps toward my white-haired friend. The cat's claws flashed against the snow, and the feline bared its fangs at her. Hellia did not show any fear of the animals; in fact, she looked bored.

"Jerrick, kill." She pointed lazily toward both felines.

The wolf burst forth, barreling into the cats and becoming a ball of teeth and claws. It was mere moments before both lynx lay slain in the snow. The wolf was barely panting, his muzzle streaked with blood and gore as he bared his teeth toward Tyr. Tora had the good sense to look somewhat horrified and take several steps back from the snarling wolf.

"I'm the God of War; I'm not scared of you." Tyr laughed at the lieutenant.

"You should be scared of *me*," Fen snarled. He flicked a hand at Jerrick to join my side, then nudged me against him in a silent order to stay with the wolf. He stalked forward to approach Hellia's side a few meters ahead of us.

"I had her, you know," Tyr sneered at him, his eyes flickering to me over Fen's shoulder. "She cried a lot."

There were no more words, only the black wolf bursting forth and tackling the god to the ground. I buried my face in Jerrick's shoulder fur, not interested in seeing what was happening. I still hadn't bleached my mind successfully since his last bloody battle, and I wasn't ready to watch another murder. Even if Tyr did most definitely deserve it.

Tyr put up a fight from what I heard, but when I peeked through my fingers, I saw Hellia intervene with her power to make the god fall to the ground, screaming in pain and clutching his head the same way Tora had done weeks ago.

Slowly I looked around, and I squeaked with terror at the gore spread across the snow, feeling my breakfast threatening to make a reappearance. I slammed my eyes closed again, trying to focus on breathing and smelling anything but the iron scent of blood.

"Jerrick, take him back to the palace." Fen was human once more, and I swallowed thickly, looking him over. Blood spattered his face, making *him* look like the God of War.

Jerrick left my side and trotted forward, sinking his fangs into the shoulder of the downed god and dragging him along roughly, provoking cries of pain from Tyr.

"You didn't kill him," I whispered. "And where is Tora?"

"That coward ran the second I looked her way," Hellia chortled, nodding towards the woods. "She's taking the bifrost back to Asgard. I'll kill her another day. Someone needs to report to Odin that Tyr isn't coming back."

"You didn't kill him?" It came out more like a question this time as I watched Jerrick drag Tyr through the gate that was now open.

"I want it to be long and painful for him." He put an arm around my shoulders, guiding me toward the gate and scanning the trees over my head for any further threats. "He deserves to suffer. I'm going to make sure he does."

Passing through the gate was like having a large bucket of water dumped on my head. Hellia explained it was her wards washing us all of any hexes or evil intents that might have followed us. Jerrick was long gone with Tyr now, the blood trail the only indication the lieutenant was ahead of us. Now that we were through the gate and firmly in the realm of Helheim, I could see the city faintly glowing with warm lights through the fog ahead.

"I don't want to go through town yet," Fen growled to Hellia. She nodded, leading us off the main path into the trees on a much narrower trail.

"Why can't we go through town?" I asked, keeping my ears pricked for any noises of torture coming from the city's direction. What was he keeping from me there?

"I'm not ready yet. I just want to get home." Fen shook his head and suddenly looked oddly weary in my eyes. He hadn't been home for hundreds of years, we'd been traveling for days, and I was not making things easy. Of course he was desperate to get home with as little fanfare as possible.

Through the trees, an enormous castle loomed, somehow familiar. I again flashed back to the times in my dreams when I'd seen this very same castle far in the distance. This was where he was leading me in the dreams the whole time, but why here and not Asgard? The castle was made of grey stone, set on an outcropping of a cliff higher than the rest of the city skyline. We climbed a steep trail to the side, but I could see a wide bridge lit with flickering street lamps leading from huge doors to the city below. Each window of the massive building was lit with a flickering candle, just like Jerrick's cabin in Kaldr. When I bent my head back to see the roof I noticed a tower, higher than any other, disappearing into the low-hanging clouds.

"Wow," I breathed, taking in the gothic structure. It didn't look particularly Nordic in design like the long house and cabins in Kaldr. The castle was much more like the famous Notre Dame cathedral in Paris. Elaborate designs were made into the stone, and gargoyles resembling dragons leered down at me from every edge. "It's very European style," I observed to Hellia, who was looking up at the castle next to me.

"It is." Pride radiated from her. "I created it in the sixteenth century; it was very in style then." She walked toward a large, sheltered part of the building where a door led inside. "You'll find that Helheim City is a collection of different eras and styles. Mostly I like to keep it traditional in style, but there are a few modern influences."

"So, it looked different when you lived here before?" I looked up at Fen over my shoulder.

"Yes, it was much smaller and Nordic in style. But Hellia has walked me here in dreams many times, so I am familiar." He held the door for me to follow Hellia inside the dark castle.

We entered directly into a large kitchen, a fire crackling in the hearth making the room stifling hot as dancing flames reflected off copper kettles and pots hanging from the ceiling. A wood table sat in the center of the room, surrounded by chairs and benches, and countertops with cutting boards and vases of utensils rimmed the room. An archway opened into a greenhouse full of plants. Beyond the windows of the green house, the winter raged on.

I followed Hellia to a swinging door that opened into a grand hall beyond. The temperature dropped when we left the kitchen, matching the cold outside, but I was the only one who seemed bothered by seeing my breath hang in clouds around me indoors.

We were now standing in front of enormous doors that I knew led to the bridge connecting the palace to the city. The doors were large enough for elephants to easily pass through, and everything in the castle was supersized the same way Asgard was. It made Fen look normal in stature. I felt tiny. On Earth, I always thought of myself as fairly tall at five-foot-six, but I was nothing compared to the giants I now associated myself with.

"I can't wait to sleep in my own bed." Hellia stretched, a smile on her face as she looked around the palace. Wishing I could sleep in my own bed, my eyes dropped to the ground, staring at the toe of my boot on the cold stone floor. Suddenly, the days of travel, the riding, and the constant cold were all catching up with me. My eyelids felt like they had small weights attached, wanting to drag them closed.

"You look tired." Fen's voice was soft. He lifted a hand to touch my hair, but when my eyes widened to full alert once more, he dropped it to his side. I watched his fingers flex slightly at his side, as if he was still thinking about touching me but fighting an internal battle.

"I have a bedroom for you," Hellia smiled, motioning me to follow her. "It's this way." She led me up the stairs and down a hallway not far from the main steps. Even though there were minimal turns, I could tell the castle was a place to get easily lost. Halls led down a dozen different directions, the same plush navy carpet running down each one.

"This is yours. That's Fen's." She pointed at a door further down the hall from this one. "I'm on the other side, and Jerrick is too. If you need anything, just yell; wolf ears can hear you pretty much anywhere in the castle." Behind me, Fen nodded before departing for his own room.

Pushing open the door we were standing in front of, she led me through into a beautiful bedroom draped in indigo and navy fabrics. A real fire warmed the room from a hearth beside massive windows showing snow outside. A bookshelf stood tall against the wall by the window, the old leather-bound covers and yellowing pages giving the room a familiar book smell.

"I tried to make it as much like home as possible, but if there is anything you're missing, just let someone know." Hellia's voice sounded apprehensive as I looked around the gorgeous room. "You're also welcome to explore wherever you like. I'll have the staff keep real fires to try to warm this place up for you."

"Thank you." I nodded, looking around the room. The light was starting to dim outside, indicating it would be night soon. Hellia returned the nod and dipped her head, slipping out the door. For the first time in weeks, I was truly alone.

CHAPTER 22

When I fell asleep, a memory dragged me back to Tyr's room in Asgard. The giant Aesir leered over me, pinning me to the bed. His breath smelled like dinner and mead, and the touch of his hand pricked me like needles.

"No!" I screamed, trying to claw at him and fight my way free. He just laughed, his single hand pinning me down to the bed with incredible strength. "No no no!" I could feel the metal around my neck, feel his unwelcome touch, feel the sweat slicking my skin making the sheets stick to me uncomfortably.

"Get off me! Get away from me!" I screamed. "Help! Please someone help!"

There was nothing I could do, nothing I could say to make him stop. I continued screaming and trying to wriggle away, but it was futile, and my dream state kept me locked beneath him. I tried to order myself awake but couldn't get my body to respond.

"Ah Anais, come now, be a good whore." My head whipped to the side, meeting Mag's turquoise pools. He stalked around where Tyr was assaulting me. "Hm, I should have had you perform publicly. You are a sight."

"Fuck you! You're not even real!" I thrashed violently.

"Oh, I'm very real, Anais." I went still and rigid.

Tyr continued on as if he wasn't listening to the conversation I was having with the golden-haired god.

"You didn't think Fenrir was the only one who could dream walk, did you?" Mag was by my head now, and I was still pinned, unable to remove myself from the situation as I looked up at him.

"I hate you," I spat.

"Such strong language, darling. What would your mother think of you hating me? Or the pastor? I think they would want you to forgive me, Anais. I think that's what your God wants, what he demands, right?" He mockingly pouted at me.

"I'll never forgive you," I snapped.

"What will your Christian God think of that?" He shook his head with a disapproving click of his tongue.

"I told you I don't believe in that God," I snarled.

"Still? After I've shown you that we exist?" He reached out, fisting my hair and forcing me to look up at him when I tried to look away.

"He might exist, but I still don't accept him as my God anymore."

"Hmm," he mused, "so who is your God? Is it Fenrir? Even after he dragged you to Hell?" His taunting tone boasted with mockery.

"He saved me from you sick fucks." I tried to kick at Tyr to get him off me but was still locked in place, paralyzed. I was starting to become frantic to get out of here, to wake, to get out from under the crushing weight of the memory and the conversation with Mag.

"I'll take that as a yes. Well, you're going to have to get away from him, Anais. That's what I'm here to tell you. If you don't turn yourself in to Odin soon, he's going to come for you and all your new friends in Hell. He's going to hurt people to get to you—is that what you want? You want your new lieutenant friend to die for you?" He pouted at me again, reaching out to catch a stray tear on my cheek with his finger tip.

"No, don't hurt anyone." My tone turned pleading. "Please, they didn't do anything."

"What about your friend Kerri?"

"No!" I sobbed. "Leave her alone, please. Take me instead."

Mag snorted before he said, "That's the point, Ana *darling*. Turn yourself in, and people will stop dying. Stay out there, and who knows how many lives will be lost in your honor."

"Please," I begged. "Please don't kill anyone over me. I'm just a human, what do you want with me anyway?"

"It's all up to you. Turn yourself in." Mag took in the scene of me under Tyr, and a cruel laugh filled the air. "You know, I really should have come to watch more often…"

Fen, I need Fen to wake me up, to get me out of here. "Fen!"
I screamed this time. "Help!"

"Oh Ana, darling, he can't do anything to me here inside
your head." Mag's smile was wicked as he leaned over me. "Already calling him by nicknames, hm? That didn't take long."

"Anais." I heard Fen calling my name distantly. "Anais, wake
up *hjarta*."

I tried, attempting to force myself awake. Tyr's laughter
rang in my ears, and I thrashed, trying to fight off this attacker
in my sleep. I couldn't get my body to wake my brain, to pull
me from the dream.

"Running to hide behind your scary dog?" Mag taunted.

"Fen, help me," I whimpered, my voice breaking into a sob.

"Shit." Fen growled, his voice still muffled and far. "Anais,
I'm going to touch you so I can wake you up. I'm sorry."

I felt a hand on my shoulder gently shaking me. My eyes
snapped open, and I heard a cry escape my throat as I finally
jumped awake. My hands flew out, grabbing on to Fen's bare
arm and pulling myself to him, clinging to him as though I
expected Mag and Tyr to follow me from my dream into the
waking world. Clawing myself closer, I practically climbed
him, wild eyes darting around the room. My nails bit into his
skin. The sheets were scrambled around me, sticking to my
skin; I kicked them away as I scrambled up Fen's body where
he sat on the edge of the bed.

I wrapped my arms around his neck, hugging myself closer
as I waited for a threat to emerge from the shadows.

"It was just a dream. It wasn't real this time," Fen whispered,
wrapping his arms around my back, crushing me against his
chest. The pressure was comforting, as was knowing he was

looking over my back, protecting me. "You're okay. No one's going to hurt you," he soothed, cradling my head with one hand.

But it was real, and Mag made a very real threat. I took a shaky breath and buried my face into his neck, closing my eyes as I smelled the familiar forest and pine smell of him. We sat in silence, my ragged breaths beginning to slow and my heart thundering.

"How did you know to come wake me?" I finally croaked.

"You called for me." He squeezed me impossibly tighter. "I will always come when you call."

A scuffling noise from the door had my head on a swivel, and I shrank into him, feeling myself trembling when I didn't mean to.

"It's Jerrick and Hellia." His voice was soft and comforting. He rubbed circles on my back, helping to calm my breathing. "Everyone heard you screaming. They're just worried."

There was a soft knock at the door, and Fen looked down at me, allowing me to answer.

"Come in," I said, my voice sounding meek in the room.

The door pushed open, and Hellia poked her head into the room. "Are you okay?" she whispered just loud enough to hear. "We heard you scream."

"Yeah, nightmare. I'm sorry I woke you." I spoke softly as I slid from Fen's lap, feeling his hand linger on me for just a moment before letting go. Part of me wanted to tug him back, feeling safer when he was touching me. Part of me was disgusted his sister saw him holding me in his lap.

"Oh, it's okay, I was up anyway." She smiled, and I noticed she looked particularly tired. "Um, I'm starving? Want to come eat in the kitchen? I want food from Midgard."

"Sure." I pushed myself out of the bed.

"Meet us down there," Hellia said as she flashed a smile and then disappeared, letting the door fall shut—but not before I saw Jerrick's concerned face behind her.

"I'll wait for you in the hall," Fen stood and started for the door. I leapt forward.

"Wait," I gasped as my fingers found his warm forearm, feeling the soft hair on his arm under my grip. My cheeks started to heat with a blush. "Um, I'll just grab a robe and some slippers. I'll come with you."

Sensing my need not to be alone, he nodded and didn't pull his arm from my grasp. I reluctantly let go, quickly sliding a robe over my shoulders and slippers on my feet. "Ready?" he asked, holding the door open to the hallway.

"Yes." I walked past him, catching the scent of his sweat with a whisper of pine and almost pausing to bury my nose against him again.

We walked silently downstairs to the kitchen, finding Hellia and Jerrick already sitting with coffee. Fen directed me to a seat at the table next to him, close to the fire so I would be warm.

"Can you and Fen get us something to eat from home? Something fun." Hellia scooted a cup of coffee across the table to me and I took it, grateful to wrap my fingers around the warm ceramic. "It's decaf, so you can go back to sleep."

Fen offered his hand to me, and I took it. An odd craving hit, one for donuts. I imagined a box of them, the classic ones that reminded me of Homer Simpson. Pink frosting with colorful sprinkles. I loved that strawberry-flavored icing when it melted on my tongue. Shadows reached through the realms, pulling the fibers of the world around us to leave the perfect box of them in his hand.

"What are they?" Fen asked.

Hellia reached over him to pluck one out of the box. "Delicious." She shoved it in her mouth as she sat next to Jerrick. "This is exactly what I wanted, thank you Anais."

"It's a donut." A smile twitched the corner of my mouth again at the thought that this man was about to try pink donuts for the first time ever. "It's like … a really spongy cake, with strawberry frosting."

I watched as he bit into one, his eyebrows furrowing. "It's very sweet." He studied it in his hand with a skeptical look on his face. A smile spread across his face, but his lips twisted as though it were too much for him as he searched my eyes. "This is what you like?"

"Sometimes. Not all the time, but it's good for breakfast." I shrugged, a smile threatening my lips.

"It's all sugar," Jerrick snorted as he shoved two in his mouth at once. "It's *not* good for breakfast. It has no protein."

"Some of us just like donuts and coffee for breakfast, Jer. Just because you hork down a pig and half every morning doesn't mean everyone else wants to." Hellia gave him a pointed look as she lifted her coffee to her lips.

"Not to mention it's disgusting to watch." A new voice that was as light and melodic as a windchime sounded in the room. I turned toward the door, seeing the most ethereal woman I'd ever laid eyes on walking toward us. Dressed in a sea-foam-colored dressing gown, she had long, pin-straight blonde hair that fell past her shoulders and elongated ears with sharp tips.

She slid into Jerrick's lap, looking as tiny against him as I imagined I did next to Fenrir.

"Why are you up, Talin? I said to stay and sleep when I left." Jerrick frowned, wrapping an arm around her as she leaned against his chest. She yawned at the mention of sleep, and I turned away to yawn too, catching Fen watching me with a little smile.

"Yeah, but then the screaming startled me again, and then I felt like I was missing out on something." She looked down at the donuts, tipping her head to one side with curiosity before taking the coffee out of Jerrick's hand and sipping it. He didn't seem to mind.

"I'm sorry," I said softly. She looked at me for the first time with wide, surprised warm brown eyes, as if she hadn't expected me to be here.

"Oh! No! Anais, I am so sorry, it's completely fine." She looked abjectly horrified. "I didn't mean to say it disturbed me terribly or anything, I just was worried. You sounded really scared... Nightmares?"

"Yes. Asgard," I mumbled, feeling embarrassed with all the eyes watching me, knowing they all heard my terror not more than half an hour ago. A fresh wave of shivers swept through me at the memory of the dream and Mag's threats.

She nodded, sympathy in her expression. "I'm Talin, by the way. Master Archer for the Hell Hounds. I'm a light elf, from the Alfheim realm."

"Anais, human from Earth." I offered her a small smile and she returned the gesture before finishing Jerrick's coffee. Her eyes flicked to my side with a curious look, and I suddenly became aware of Fen staring at me, chin propped up on his hand, elbow on the table. He seemed completely entranced, unaware of anyone else sitting around him.

"What?" I asked him. "Fen? What are you staring at me for?"

He jolted when I said his name. "Nothing, just thinking. Sorry."

We sat for a while in the kitchen, chatting and eating the donuts. Talin fell asleep against Jerrick's chest, and he excused them, carrying her tiny form from the room. Hellia sighed and stated she had to go back to her study for work, leaving Fen and I alone in the kitchen light.

"Are you tired?" he asked.

"Not particularly," I said, my eyes flickering up to his.

"I want to show you something." He stood, and I followed him from the kitchen. The castle was dark and quiet. I heard none of our companions, only our footsteps as he led me up the stairs and toward our rooms. Midway down the hallway, I paused in front of a painting I'd not noticed before. The figure in the middle was Hellia, her beautiful creamy white skin, the icy blue eye and snowy hair—but half her body was corpse-like. Dead grey skin hung from her bones and her beautiful blue eye was missing from the socket, leaving a gaping black hole in her face where it should have been. With no lips to cover them, her teeth were bare and exposed. Her white hair remained but looked brittle and dry. She wore a black dress embroidered with gold, and on the side with my friend, the dress was beautiful and well fitted, but on the dead side of her it was tattered, shredded, and weary.

My blood ran cold as I stared, horrified, at the painting and wrapped my arms around myself, staring into her one beautiful eye and the dark empty socket. Behind her stood the enormous black wolf, her human hand resting on his back, fingers curled in his fur. His eyes had the same unnerving quality in paint as they did in real life, and the same gold thread from Hellia's dress wove around his legs and muzzle. On the other side of the painting where her body was a corpse was the World Serpent, massive horns growing from its head and a sharp serpent tongue hanging from a mouth between long, slender fangs.

Across from this painting was another of equal size. Three cloaked women worked at a spinning wheel, like the one Aurora touched in Sleeping Beauty. The wheel was enormous, taller than the three women, two of whom stood while the third sat on the ground between them. All were beautiful and fair skinned, with blonde hair falling down to their waists. The two women standing handled a golden thread between them, and the third spooled it. The oldest looking woman, standing on the left, had a raven sitting upon her shoulder. In one hand, she held a pair of golden blades that looked like scissors. Two of their gazes were soft and ethereal, but the one who held the twin blades had a sinister expression that sent a chill down my spine. I looked back to the painting of Hellia, realizing the sinister glare was pointed directly at her across the hall. Purely coincidence, I was sure.

I studied the depiction of Hellia again and suppressed a shudder at her decaying flesh. She stood with her bare feet on a pile of bones and human skulls. She looked nowhere near this terrifying in real life. If I had just seen this painting, I too would have thought the three were plotting for world destruction.

"Does she really look like that? In her Divine Form?" I asked barely above a whisper, looking up at Fen with widened eyes. He took a deep breath, looking into her clear blue eye before nodding subtly.

"Hellia looks how she wants to look, but yes, this is what her Divine Form looks like. She uses some of her power to constantly cover this side of her face." He turned back to the painting, looking at the giant reptilian beast to the right.

"The World Serpent. That's Jorm, right?" He nodded and looked over the painting with a sigh.

"A long time ago, Odin foresaw Ragnorok coming, the end of Asgard. He claimed in the visions he saw Asgard fall to a great wolf, a giant serpent, and a woman who was half human and half corpse. We were a secret from Asgard for a long time, living here with our mother. After Odin's visions, he sent Thor after us, knowing we were the children of the trickster god, Loki. He banished Jorm to Midgard and Hellia with our home to Helheim. I lived with Tyr in Asgard for many years before I was bound. I was prideful." His voice sounded strained, full of regret as he recited the story. "My strength was unmatched, and many of the Aesir wanted to test me. There was not a chain that could hold me—I could break any restraint just by flexing. I was getting bigger and bigger, more powerful by the year. It scared them, and I was a young, prideful idiot." He spat the words out, now looking into the eyes of the wolf behind Hel. "They invited me to play games of strength out on an island. They showed me a golden ribbon, said none could break it. I was skeptical, but I allowed them to convince me, to pander to my pride." He shook his head, looking at the gold cuffs on his wrists.

"I told them they could put them on if I could hold one of their hands in my jaws for insurance. Tyr obliged. Once they put the chains on, I was trapped. The more I struggled against them, the tighter they became."

"What happened to Tyr's hand?" I asked, though I knew very well what had happened. Not only had Mag mentioned it on Midgard, but I'd seen it first hand in Asgard.

"I bit it off." He grinned now, a wicked grin that made my hair stand up on my arms. His fangs glinted in the soft candlelight. "Just like I'll take his other hand and bring it to you. For what he did to you." He looked truly evil at that moment, and I could understand how Odin's visions would be terrifying. But from what I could tell, the trio's only real crime was being born.

"They dragged me back to Asgard, forced me out of my Divine Form and secured me to that boulder where you found me." He shook his head, and I saw a shudder run through his body at the memories. "They can be cruel, the Aesir of Asgard, but you already know that," was all he said, ending the story.

I wondered what exactly that meant, what cruelty he endured for his time. It was hard to believe that he was just left alone down there for 800 years, and I was sure the Aesir would have their fun with a captive just as Mag had done with me. We stood in silence for several more moments taking in the tapestry. I looked at the gold on his wrists and neck shimmering in the flickering light, then turned to look at the gold thread held in the hands of the women in the painting behind us once more.

"The Norns," he said grimly, turning to face the painting of the three women. "They are the weavers of the Tapestry of Fate under the tree of life, Yggdrasil. I need to visit them soon." I looked at each of their faces. He studied them for a minute more before he spoke.

"Come." It was a simple word, but he said it with such a gentle tone I was following him down the hallway once again.

He led me to a door in the same hallway as our rooms. He pushed it open, revealing a tall, winding staircase leading up. He started to climb, and internally I panicked at how out of breath I was about to be in front of him. By the top of the stairs, I was panting and trying to be cool about how much I was struggling. I saw a small smile playing on his lips, but he didn't make any comments.

An open doorway led into a completely circular room surrounded with tall glass windows opening in every direction. It was a moment of clarity, the night sky peeking through the clouds above, and a fog settled over the glowing lights of Helheim City far below.

"This is my favorite room in the castle," he said softly, watching as I approached the window to look out at the city. "Hellia showed it to me in dreams when she built it."

"This view, it's incredible." I gazed out for a moment longer before turning to look at the interior of the room. A large daybed stood across the room, and two armchairs were set near us. Books, heavy leather-bound scripts with yellowing pages, were stacked all around the room in piles, sprawling across the bed and floor. "Were you reading?" I asked, glancing at the half-empty bookcase near the door.

"Yeah, I was, until I heard you." He picked up the books on the bed and chairs, stacking them in a pile on the ground before motioning for me to sit wherever I liked. Nervous he might take it as an invitation, but suddenly exhausted and unable to keep my eyes open much longer, I lay down on the daybed.

"What were you reading about?" I asked with a yawn as the moons disappeared behind the clouds again and plunged the room back into darkness.

"Just things I missed while I was away, some of Hellia's Midgard stuff. She's obsessed with human culture, in case you couldn't tell. She always stays up to date on what's going on with the people through the ages." He lay down next to me, close but not touching, the same way he'd done when we saw the dancing sky.

"How old are you, anyway?" I asked. He looked like he could be no older than his early thirties. Compared to Thor and Odin, he looked much younger, closer to Mag's age. On the spectrum of gods, he must be younger.

"I don't really keep track of that anymore. I don't know what date my birthday is"—he growled with a shrug—"and I don't really care."

"Okay, well, do you have an estimate?" I didn't think it was unreasonable to be curious.

"Maybe a millennium and half," he said and frowned, thinking.

"Fuck!" I gasped, slapping my hands over my mouth. "Are you serious?" I mumbled to him around my hand.

"Yes?" His eyebrows were dropping low over his eyes.

"Wow… Ahem. Wow, wow, wow." I was just staring at him. An estimated 1500 years old. My twenty-six years were comparatively a blip in his timeline.

"What's wrong?" he asked, a defensive tone coming to his voice.

"You're old. Like *really* old." I bit my tongue.

"And?" He raised just one of those dark eyebrows at me. I could barely see it in the low light of the room.

"And just…" I stared at him. "I've never seen a living fossil before." He snorted, rolling his eyes, but I could see he was smiling.

"What are you learning about humans that you've missed?" I asked, settling into the bed and closing my eyes.

"Well… I was just reading about these cellular telephones," he said, his brow furrowing. "But I don't understand how the concept of the telephone fits with human cells… Does it work through your blood or something?"

"What?" I asked, genuinely confused as I tried to understand what he was asking. "Cellular telephones…" I said slowly as comprehension came to me. "Oh, no, cellular can mean something else. A cell phone is a little device we carry around to be able to speak with one another, and text."

He propped himself up on his elbows, fixing me with a confused look.

"Is it a parchment? What is text?" he asked, brimming with curiosity. "Like you can write books or letters to one another?"

The realization dawned on me that catching him up to the twenty-first century was going to be a task; there were so many things that were different now, and I was sure some of it was going to blow his mind. Airplanes, photographs, and movies.

There were so many larger things than pink donuts he was about to discover and try for the first time. The thought made me laugh. It was a full-bodied laugh that shook my shoulders and made my face hurt from smiling. After not laughing for so long, it was so loud, and I covered my mouth with a hand to stifle it.

"Please," he whispered, making me look into his begging eyes. "Don't cover your smile. It's beautiful, and your laugh…" He reached out, pulling my hand down before gently tucking my hair behind my ear, making me tingle a bit at his touch. "I would like to listen to it forever…"

I fixed him with a look. I couldn't decide what game he was trying to play with little comments like that.

"What? Have I upset you?" He frowned, gently stroking his fingers over my hair behind my ear again. The tingles from his touch didn't fade.

"No." I scrunched up my nose at him. "I just don't know how to take it when you say things like that."

"Like what?" he asked, refocusing on studying my face, as if he were memorizing every centimeter of it.

"When you make comments about not mistaking your affections or listening to my laugh forever… We barely know each other. We haven't even gone on a date yet; how can you know you want to listen to my laugh forever? That I'm the person for you?"

He smiled softly, the moon peeking from the clouds and illuminating the room once again. The light lit his eyes, making them shine brightly, the yellow striking. "How can you not be?"

We lay for a while more, talking about Midgard, about cell-phones and texting, until I fell asleep next to him after making him promise to wake me the moment I started screaming again. He promised, and I fell asleep to him stroking my hair gently.

CHAPTER 23

I woke in the morning, the diffused light from the suns flooding the room and the landscape before me. Fog had rolled in and blanketed the city below. I shielded my eyes and looked beside me at the empty bed. He was gone. My stomach twisted, and my heart began racing immediately. Cold sweat dripped from my forehead as Irealized I was alone.

What was happening? Why did I have this reaction to him being gone? It didn't make sense, the intense connection I already felt for him. We'd known each other what, a month? I was not a needy or clingy person in relationships, and this wasn't even a relationship, it was just the situation we found ourselves in since we saved each other's lives. That was all it is. He just hadn't been able to date anyone for hundreds of years, just wanted someone to cuddle up with at night.

I scrambled to my feet from the messy bed, pulling my winter cloak on to shield myself from the cold of the castle, and put on the slippers I'd left at the door last night. The winding stairs seemed much longer in the day as I ran down them, nearly tripping twice. Finally, I reached the corridor where our rooms were, my heart racing faster than it should be. I didn't meet or hear anyone, and when I knocked at Fen's door, no one answered.

I turned to the empty hall, remembering Hellia telling me he could hear me anywhere in the castle. My voice sounded small in the echoing massive hallway. "Fen?" I listened for him, hearing only faint voices and noise from the dining room where everyone was surely having breakfast. "Fen?" I called again, clearing my throat, my voice stronger but with a tinge of desperation coming through. I had to find him. The air was being pulled from the room the longer I was without him. It felt like a panic attack, and I hadn't had one of those since highschool—

"Yes?" he answered, coming up the stairs into view. I sucked in air at the sight of him. "Are you alright?" He was dressed in all black; the deep thin v-neck showed the top of his chest, and a long hoodless jacket with a partial collar framed the gold on his neck. His brows were drawn together, concerned as he swept me over.

"I—You were gone. I just—" I stammered and shook my head, suddenly feeling silly for pulling him away from whatever he had been doing, all because he wasn't there when I woke up.

We're both adults. He had things to attend to other than making sure I didn't wake up alone when I overslept. I was twenty-six years old dammit, enough with this. His expression shifted from concern to understanding, as if he was having a realization as he took me in. His eyebrow slowly raised up his forehead. I must look ridiculous with my bed head and pajamas under a cloak, calling for him in the middle of the hallway.

"I'm sorry I worried you," he said. His voice was soft, tender, and he crossed the distance to me with ease. He stopped short of touching me, and I was grateful, as my skin was hot with embarrassment. At the same time, I craved his touch.

"You didn't worry me, I—It was just—" Flustered, feeling like he could read my thoughts like subtitles on my forehead, I meant to make for my room and get away from whatever all these feelings were. But my legs didn't move. I stayed by him, the pressure in my chest relieving at his closeness.

His pine scent was enticing, and the V of his shirt made me want to reach my fingers out to the gold shimmering around his neck. It felt as though all would be well again if I could just reach out and touch him. The intense feelings would dissipate even more than they were. My eyes flickered up to his. He watched with interest and knowing.

I opened my mouth to demand to know what it was he knew, but he spoke first.

"I won't leave without telling you again, I promise. Go get dressed. I'll be waiting out here and you can come to breakfast." He gently nudged me toward my room while I continued staring at him, trying to piece the puzzle of what he knew together. The door closed behind me, and I tried to process what was happening while I stumbled to the armoire for fresh clothes. My head felt like it was in the clouds, the thick grey clouds outside my window that were heavy with snow.

When I returned to the hall, looking far more put together wearing a full outfit and having run a brush through my hair, Fen was waiting as he'd promised. He offered his hand to me but I hesitated.

"I'm not needy, you know. I'm not clingy." I held his gaze, withdrawing my hand.

"I know," he said.

His response shocked me. "I, um. I-I'm not sure what that was this morning, but it was not how I normally am." I stumbled over the words.

"I know," he repeated, offering his hand again.

I stared at him, dumbfounded. It was obvious he wasn't being truthful with what he knew. I was reminded that his father is the God of Mischief, in addition to all the other things I knew about him. But he had said he would never do anything bad to me, never harm me. I thought I believed him.

I took his hand, letting him lead me down the main staircase. Several workers around the palace watched us pass with wide eyes, turning and whispering, some women even giggling. I took a moment to look back at them as well, these people who were in Hell. They were all young and beautiful, looking rather full of life as they gossiped in Fenrir's wake.

"Hellia struggled for a long time to make Helheim and Niflheim a matriarchy under her rule. Obviously Midgard and Asgard are still firmly patriarchal, but Hellia fought many battles to stand on equal ground with them. Some were bloody, others were political, and ultimately she won." Fen's voice beamed with pride for his sister. "Jerrick is the only man who holds power in her armies. She's highly respected, as are all those who work for her."

"What about the innkeeper? He called us whores, and only men were inside the bar."

"It's an ongoing battle in Niflheim." He gave a tight smile. "Also, Jerrick is definitely going to kick that guy's ass next time we go through there. Probably Hellia will chew him out too. They only didn't because we were trying to stay anonymous."

I watched a group of staff walk by, smiling and talking animatedly. Everyone seemed comfortable and at ease. Some threw interested sidelong glances at Fen, but no one approached us.

"I am still learning names," Fen admitted in a hushed voice as he escorted me into the dining room. Jerrick was there, wolfing down a plate of breakfast sausages so quickly I wasn't sure if he was breathing.

"Welcome back," Jerrick mumbled around a mouthful. He motioned to a seat that Fen pulled out for me. There was a spread of food on the table, fruit and pastries, eggs, sausages and bacon, and steaming pots of coffee and tea. Hellia was sitting at the head of the table, her feet kicked up across the corner, reading what looked like a newspaper.

"Good morning!" She lowered the paper, looking over it at me with a chipper smile. She looked so beautiful and perfect it was unreal, like a doll. "I'm glad you're joining us this morning." She lifted the paper once more, fully invested in the story she was reading in a foreign language.

"Chew your food, Jerrick; you're going to choke some-day." A woman with dark skin walked into the room from the kitchen door. Her tight curls were pulled up into a high ponytail that hung down her back, with long tendrils floating around her face. She was completely dressed in scaled black leather armor similar to the men's, and a lethal set of pink knives glinted from where they were strapped to her thighs. Her face wore a disgusted expression as she paused to watch Jerrick inhale the sausages, oil dripping from his lips.

"You're nasty, you know that?" she asked him as he wiped his chin with a napkin.

"Anais, this is Ylfa." Fen introduced me to the woman. "Ylfa leads our armies with Jerrick; they're both lieutenants. She's a wolf as well, and she leads and organizes packs of Hell Hounds."

"Unless Jerrick chokes on his bacon—then it's just me." She finally tore her repulsed look away from where he was tearing at three bacon strips at once. She nodded to me.

"I'm training with you today," Jerrick argued, reaching across her for the coffee. "I need all the strength I can get before I become your punching bag." This made her grin, showing fangs just as sharp as both men's, as if she were already imagining it in her head.

"Can I watch?" I blurted out, surprising myself at my eager tone. Even Hellia lowered the newspaper again, watching us for a moment.

"Yeah," Ylfa responded, grinning at Jerrick with playful malice in her brown eyes. "You can watch me beat him to a pulp any day." Jerrick shoved her playfully with one hand. "Are you coming too?" she asked Fen, who paused shoveling eggs into his mouth to shrug. It was disgusting how both men ate like wild animals.

"What is *wrong* with you two?" Ylfa's expression, the nauseated look she was now fixing on Fen, told me she was thinking the same thing. "There will be more food later. You're not going to starve to death between now and lunch." She clicked her tongue at them in disgust before turning back to me. "Sorry you have to endure this breakfast table with us. You'd think they would pretend to have some manners the first morning you're here." She rolled her eyes.

Hellia looked at all of us expectantly, ready to change the subject. "I was thinking about having a ball, to honor Fen coming home and just generally enjoy high spirits with our people. It'll be fun."

"Party girl." Jerrick rolled his eyes with a smirk. "Any excuse to use the ballroom and get drunk."

She looked at him incredulously. "Says the man who drinks himself under the table every time and spends every night off at Cobra dance club downtown!"

"I never said I was a perfect being," he said. Jerrick laughed and dodged a pasty she threw at him.

"Manners, please!" Ylfa snapped at them. I never thought I would see the Queen of Hell look guilty for starting a food fight. "We have a guest, one I would say Fenrir is trying to impress, so quit acting like a pair of pups."

"Oh, I really don't mind." I smiled a little and glanced up at Fen. "It's nice, your family. I'm sure after more than a thousand years you can't take things too seriously."

"Exactly, *Ylfa*, stop taking everything so seriously," Hellia said mockingly, tossing a pastry at her. She caught it with one hand, squeezing it as she grimaced at the queen. Jam squished between her fingers, and I thought maybe she had claws at the tips of her fingers that were puncturing the delicate dough.

"Someone has to keep all of you in line," she grumbled, letting the pastry fall to the table and then wiping her hand on a napkin.

"You weren't around in Kaldr." Hellia shook her head at the woman lieutenant. "She already knows they're a bunch of unmannered ruffians. Fen included."

"Fen the most." Jerrick laughed at his friend, who rolled his eyes.

"Ylfa, I appreciate you worrying about the first impression my family makes on Anais"—Fen nodded to her—"but unfortunately, my sister is right, and they have already made their irreparable first impressions."

"Hm." Ylfa pursed her lips in a way that suddenly reminded me of my mom.

I couldn't help but smile as I looked around the table at these interesting people all being so comfortable with one another, even with me there. I looked sideways, glancing up at Fen, who was watching me. He smiled back, stretching his arm across the back of my chair. I blushed, feeling a tingle of excitement as he leaned in closer to me.

"I'd like to go see the city later today. Would you join me?" he asked as the others continued talking around the table.

"Just us?" I asked.

"Yes. Please think of it as my first attempt to court you," he said with a smile.

This had me snorting through my nose. "Court? My god. You know it's 2023, right? Usually guys say things like 'hang out' or something now." But I loved it, the difference. That he didn't just want to 'hang out' with me.

"Are you saying I'm old?" he asked, a teasing tone in his voice.

"You *are* old," I giggled, starting to cover my mouth again but then stopping when I looked into his eyes and remembered last night. "Are you sure you won't need a walker for going around town?"

"See, Ylfa?" Jerrick interjected loudly. "Anais doesn't have manners either. She doesn't respect her elders."

"Are *you* calling me old?" Fen snapped at Jerrick, his tone sharp in contrast with how he spoke to me moments before.

"She called you old." Jerrick pointed at me.

"She's allowed to say whatever she wants. You, not so much." Fen's eyes narrowed and Jerrick swallowed his mouthful of food and lowered his head submissively.

"Understood," Jerrick said apologetically.

Fen snorted through his nose, before looking down at me with a tender smile.

CHAPTER 24

"Does it look okay?" I asked Hellia, tugging nervously at the hem of the thick knit sweater. She'd helped me get a nice soft sweater, a pair of jeans, and a pair of winter boots from my own time period. I also pulled a knit hat low on my head, making sure my ears would be covered in the snow. Looking in the mirror, it felt odd to suddenly be wearing my regular clothes again after months of wearing clothes from the realms.

"It looks cute. This is what you would wear on Midgard?" she asked curiously, tying off the small braid she'd been weaving into my hair.

"Yeah. Is it too 2023? Maybe I should wear one of your dresses…" I glanced over at the cloak hanging from the armoire. It felt more normal to wear clothes from their realm rather than my own now. "The dresses are prettier…"

"No," Hellia said and shook her head. "He'll like this. He would want you to wear your own clothes and be comfortable." I nodded, looking in the mirror. A flash caught my eye, and I glanced down to find a bead at the end of the braid. It was a wolf. Glancing up at Hellia, she shrugged with a smile playing around her lips. "I thought it was cute. I hope it's okay."

I nodded again and swept it back into my hair, letting it blend in to be a hidden secret. "Doesn't he think it's weird?" I asked her as I sat on the edge of the bed to lace the cute winter snow boots. "That he's like … over 1500 years old, and he wants to date me? I'm a twenty-six year old from Canada. I am nowhere near as interesting as goddesses… I'm a child compared to him, an infant, not to mention mortal, and—" I was starting to psych myself out.

"Just stop. He doesn't care about those things, he just likes you." Hellia patted my shoulder when I stood again. "Go be yourself and let him get to know you. Give the old man a chance."

That made me snort. "And don't let him scare me?" I repeated her own words from the trail.

"Scare *him*," she said, and she winked, making me laugh again.

"Okay." I shrugged on my jacket, an oversized winter jacket with hockey patches like I might wear from home. Nothing was specifically mine, since Fen was the only one who could summon things I pictured in my mind and Hellia had summoned these for me. Having been around Earth many times, she knew enough of what I asked for to get close enough to what I might normally wear.

"Okay." She smiled at me, holding open the door to her bedroom. "Have fun."

I walked down the hall out to the stairs, feeling completely comfortable for the first time in a long time. Late afternoon light came through the windows, filtered by the clouds as always. Hearing hushed murmurs, I quieted my footsteps, peeking around the corner of the stairs to look down the main entrance hall.

Fen was standing with Jerrick, talking in voices too low for me to hear what they were saying. The lieutenant reached out, straightening something on the front of Fen's shirt and saying something that had him taking a deep breath before nodding. Jerrick smiled brightly before the lieutenant's eyes found mine. I felt my cheeks tingle with being caught and slowly stepped from the shadows into the light at the top of the stairs.

Jerrick smiled encouragingly at me before whispering a final word to Fen. He turned to look up at me as I descended toward the main entrance way.

I had to admit that—after the weeks of silk pajamas, corsets, and cloaks—it felt odd to be wearing something that would be so normal at home. It was comfortable, but I felt like I now stood out like a sore thumb. Nervously, I reached up to tug at the hat on my head.

"Hi," I said. My quiet voice betrayed my nerves as I approached the bottom of the stairs. He didn't take his eyes from me, that infamous pleading look returning to his expression as he took me in.

"You look lovely," he murmured, almost more to himself. He cleared his throat.

"Thank you," I said as I allowed myself to look him over. He was dressed in all black, as usual, with a particularly soft-looking sweater that suddenly made cuddling very appealing. His hair only was partially pulled back with pieces still dropping into his eyes and around his face. "You look nice too." Suddenly, I was impatient for the cold blast of air from outside to cool my hot face.

He cleared his throat again before he said, "Thank you. Are you ready?"

I nodded, walking under his arm as he held one of the front doors open for me. It was snowing heavily, but the wind was mercifully absent. Thick flakes floated lazily through the air, reminding me of one time when I was a kid and we had snow like this for Christmas. Kerri, my sister, and I had played together all day after opening presents, making snowmen and forts in the front yard.

Outside the castle, the snow magically melted off the path toward the city. The lights blinked through the snow ahead. Flakes landed in my hair, and I blinked them from my lashes as I looked up at Fen. My stomach dropped when his lips twitched up in a smile, and I took a deep breath, allowing myself a moment of feeling the familiar excitement of a first date bubble up.

"So, where are we going?" I asked, looking around at the grey stone bridge, the small drifts of snow on the railings, and the tops of the trees as we passed over a ravine.

"I thought we should see the city, then find something to eat when you're cold." He was slowing his steps so I didn't need to jog to keep up with him, which I appreciated.

"You've not been in the city, right?" I asked as we approached the end of the bridge leading into the streets of Helheim City.

"No. I've walked here in some dreams, but when I was younger, it was just a little town, not much bigger than Kaldr." He was glancing at the road ahead, but his eyes mainly remained on me. His gaze made my stomach do flips and prickle the back of my neck.

"Wow…" I took in the street as we stepped onto beautiful cobblestone. Here, the cobblestone walkways remained clear of the snow, street lights flickered even during the day, and flower beds in front of some buildings contained winter berries and little yellow flowers. The buildings were only a couple stories high, a mix of shops and restaurants along the bottom with residential spaces along the top. They were not as tall as the buildings of Asgard, adding to the cozy feeling of the town.

People milled about the streets, everyone seemingly in a cheery mood. They started noticing us, greeting us with polite nods and whispered hellos. I found myself shrinking into his side, slightly wary even though everyone around was kind and posed no threat. My fingers twitched, and I wanted to reach out for his hand but shoved mine in my pockets instead.

I had so many questions but, after a few more greetings, I was afraid of being rude. I glanced up, catching Fen's eye, and he leaned down to hear me better with a questioning look.

"Are they dead?" I whispered to him, subtly nodding toward the people around us.

He smiled. "Some are, yes. They can't leave the realm. Others are alive, a mix of Hell Hounds, gods, and other beings that live here or in Niflheim. Only spirits of those who believe in the Norse Gods come here. When the dead spirits pass through Yggdrasil and the Norns send them here, they come through a processing area where they're able to choose where they want to live. Their human body is revitalized to their youth preference, so they are compatible to live here."

I nodded, looking around at all the people who looked content and unrushed as they milled around the street. Several restaurants had patios where people sat overlooking passersby, sharing drinks and food.

"They can eat if they're dead?" I blurted, then slapped a hand over my mouth, looking at him with a guilty expression.

"You can ask questions, you know. No one will be offended." He grinned at my embarrassment, his fangs flashing. "Yes, they can eat. They don't need it for survival the way Hell Hounds like Jerrick or humans like you do, but they enjoy it. Some enjoy cooking and running restaurants. Everyone does what they want here."

"It's a beautiful city," I said as we walked down the street and turned on to another that looked equally as cozy and stunning.

"Hellia did a wonderful job," he agreed, looking around the new street before he came back to me. "You can look at anything you want too," he said when I glanced into the windows. I'd never gotten out in Asgard after the first day, so I was curious to look around.

We paused at the still-lit window of a jewelry store. One side of the display had all silver pieces, and the other was entirely gold. The side with gold had many bracelets and necklaces resembling Fen's golden bonds on his skin, thick bands of gold intended to be tight to the skin. On both sides, there were pendants, beads, and bracelets with wolves and serpents.

"Your people really love you," I murmured as I studied the beautiful works of art.

"They do. Well, they love Hellia. They trust her, and they should; she's a strong leader who would burn everything for them. I would too. I would do anything to protect them—and you." The last bit was whispered so quietly, I wasn't sure it was meant for me to hear.

"They are lucky to have your family." I admired the gold bands, but in the reflection of the storefront window, I saw him grimacing. "Do you not like it?" I whispered, and he shook his head.

"Gold reminds me of the prideful idiot I used to be, the one who was caught and bound. It reminds me too much of Asgard." He glanced down toward his wrist, where the black sweater covered the bands on his wrists.

"May I?" I offered a hand to him, and he immediately offered his in return. I gently pulled up his sleeve to examine the gold. It looked tattooed into his skin. When I ran my fingers over it, there was no edge. It was part of him.

"Do you think it's from Odin?" I asked, trying not to feel too giddy when his skin rose into goosebumps at my touch. I knew he didn't get cold.

"It must be…" He frowned at the shining bracelet. "But I don't feel it putting a damper on any of my power." I glanced up to see his cheeks flushing slightly as I traced my fingers over the gold. "I'm not sure what they're for or why they're permanently on me. They're not the chains that held me." I let go of him reluctantly, letting his hand fall back to his side.

We wandered through town, looking at the storefronts of seamstresses, jewelers, blacksmiths, craft makers, bakers, and everything in between. There were so many roads, I hoped he was keeping track of where we came from. The snowflakes stayed soft and thick all day, and I was starting to feel the cold in my bones.

"Here, let's stop and get you something to eat and drink." Fen ushered me into a restaurant overlooking the fjord below. He directed me to a pair of stools by the window and sat me down. Only moments later, a young waitress brought sweet coffees and warm apple pie to the counter.

"This is not what I expected," I said when she left. "I thought Hell would be ... well ... hot, for one." I looked out over the snowy fjord landscape, the water meeting the snow-covered banks of the shoreline.

"You are Christian. That is understandable," he said, offering me a fork and scooting the plate of pie closer to me.

"I'm not." I shook my head, thinking of my mom and our argument, and how Fen was the only one who responded when I'd asked the gods for help. "When I was growing up, my family was Evangelical Christian, but I stopped believing in it a long time ago. I was fighting with her about it right before I left Earth."

"When did you stop believing in God?" he asked. His soft tone made me feel safe to answer the question without judgment.

"Maybe seven or eight years ago, when I graduated high school. When I moved out, I got the Sunday shift at the wolf sanctuary where I work, or well … worked, and then my family moved away. I never went back to church." I sipped the coffee and looked into his eyes.

"Well, I am glad Helheim breaks your expectations then. I have a feeling that, if you were to actually see Lucifer's domain, your expectations would be broken again." He huffed a laugh.

"Lucifer? You mean Christian Hell actually exists?" My eyes rounded and my face blanched at the thought that I would go there if I died. My mom had baptized me, after all. I wouldn't come here.

"Of course. There are thousands of realms. There are larger politics at play, with some alliances between the other underworld realms and Hellia. I have been to Lucifer's realm. It is beautiful but far too hot for me." He smiled, leaning forward and putting his chin in his hand as he looked down at me. "Tell me about this wolf sanctuary where you work."

"Oh, it's just a little place on the edge of town." I blushed, a pang of sadness hitting me as I thought of Gladis and the animals. "I've just always really loved wolves since I was a little girl, and that was the only place I could really go to be around them. My mom also never let me have a dog, so the sanctuary wolves became my dogs."

I went on to tell him more about home and the sanctuary. He listened intently, hanging on every word, his eyes never leaving me for longer than a few seconds. He kept asking questions, wanting details, memorizing names, paying particular attention to Kerri's after I mentioned it several times.

"I think we will lose the light soon. Are you ready to start walking back?" he asked. I nodded. Thanking the waitress, we walked into the street, the cold coming back in full force. I shivered under my jacket.

"There's a sea otter there," Fen said, nodding toward the view of the water between the buildings.

"Where?!" I couldn't help my excitement, bouncing up to my tiptoes and placing my hands on his arm to steady myself as I searched the shoreline. "I don't see it." I frowned, balancing to try to see at his eyeline. He chuckled, lowering his head to my level and gently using a thumb and forefinger to turn my head.

"There, against the rocks," he said softly, his breath tickling my ear.

"I see it," I murmured back, entranced as I always was with animal watching. "Oh, it's so cute!" I squeezed his arm with excitement. He smiled, was beaming actually, and didn't move under my touch. I sank back down on my heels, not letting go of his arm as I watched the fuzzy brown creature swim along the shore, pawing a clam on its belly. The softness of Fen's sweater made me want to rub against him and purr like a cat. Everything about this place was like a Christmas dream, and I was resisting the urge to give in and let myself be swept up into this crazy Hallmark movie moment.

I began to drop my hands from him, but he caught one of them and intertwined our fingers. His eyes questioned if the action was okay, and in response, I leaned into his arm, gently squeezing his hand.

The sun had gone down, and street lamps illuminated the falling snow and the walkways. The streets were familiar now, and the castle in view ahead. He looked out over the darkened street with warm lights sparkling in each window of the residences. "They're using real flames," he mused, taking in the candles winking throughout the street before looking at me.

"What does that mean?" I asked.

"They're doing it to welcome you. You are the only one who needs real flames here to survive. They're trying to show support for you." He grinned.

My face flushed, and I looked out over the brightly lit town. The city was beautiful, even in the eternal winter. I admired the amazing palace rising against the high walls of the fjord, wreathed with trees and sharp rocks on either side. The whole castle glowed with light against the dark winter night, more candles burning in the windows than before.

"I can't imagine how good it must feel to be able to walk around outside. How did it feel to stand up after ... how long was it?" I asked as we reached the bridge to the castle. He chuckled, sounding somehow both relieved and sad.

"Something like eight hundred years. It felt amazing." He smiled. "I can't tell you how grateful I am that you came when I called for you."

"Well, you know, you were the only one who answered me when I prayed for help." I squeezed his hand. "How did you do that, by the way? Talk in my head?"

"I, um." He sounded startled, like he wasn't sure how to answer the question. "You called for me ... so I answered."

I frowned, feeling like there was more to the story than that, but he was purposefully being vague. I wasn't sure if it was the right time to press the issue or not.

"I think they probably heard your old man knees crack on Earth when you stood up," I teased to change the subject, seeing he was uncomfortable.

"Excuse me?" He faked outrage, nudging me playfully. "You're feeling well enough to make so many jokes now, are you?"

"Well, you keep kissing me, so I'm pretty sure you're not going to kill me for a verbal assault on the elderly." I held eye contact with him as he opened the door for me, walking into the main hall of the castle. It was dim, only lit by the candles in the windows and wall sconces.

"Correct," he growled, and I heard the door shut behind us. The hall was empty, no sign of anyone. Quiet from every direction. "I would like to kiss you now, Anais."

My stomach flipped again as I looked up at him. "I'll allow it." My eyes darted to his lips. It was absolutely comical how far he needed to lean down, but I wasn't laughing. I was fully focused on how his warm lips touching mine burned like an insane fire, and how I was happy to go up in smoke. I wrapped my arms around his neck, pulling myself closer as his tongue slid against my bottom lip. Opening my mouth to him, I allowed him to explore me and equally explored him with my tongue and hands. My fingers found his hair, brushing the long strands. When my tongue slid down one of his fangs, he gave a low growl.

I was so focused on the kiss, I almost missed the scuffling noise. I started, but his arms tightened around me protectively, allowing me to relax into him slightly. "It's my sister and that idiot I call my best friend," Fen breathed against my lips before kissing me again. There was a muffled shout and feet thundering down Hellia and Jerrick's hallway, but neither of us paid much mind, too wrapped up in our goodnight kiss.

CHAPTER 25

Hours after he kissed me, I couldn't stop thinking about his lips. Darkness of the early morning hours mixed with a thick fog that rolled in after we returned to the castle. I lay in bed in my pajamas, wishing I had something to read. I'd paced circles around the room, taken a bath, and lay with my eyes closed in the hopes of slipping into sleep. Between the coffee on the date and the enormous amount of sleep I'd got during my recovery, I felt wide awake at the early hour.

I rolled over, looking out over the few tops of trees that peeked through the fog. Quickly, they disappeared back into the thick clouds continuously rolling through.

"NO!"

Fen's shout was so loud it made me jump nearly a foot from the bed. I wasn't sure if I'd heard him inside my head or out loud. My stomach dropped uncomfortably and my tongue soured in my throat, a seed of dread planting itself in my chest. His voice sounded panicked, and it gave me the same feeling I'd had when he spoke to me in my head in Asgard. I needed to go find him immediately. Swinging my legs over the bed, I got up, not bothering with slippers or a robe. The seed of dread blossomed into subdued panic coming from where Fen's voice called out.

An unseen force tugged on my feet, urging me to leave my room hastily. I was practically running the moment I was moving. I wasn't sure how I knew where to go, or even where I was going in the first place. The force driving my feet didn't lead me far, just down the hall to Fen's door. I knocked. No one answered, so I knocked again. Slowly, I set my fingers on the handle and gave the heavy door a push. It swung open to his bedroom, and I slid inside.

"Fen?" I asked quietly, scanning the room to find it empty. The firelight from the hearth illuminated the room enough for me to see his still-made bed and empty chairs with books strewn about. Intense fear panged through me again, squeezing my chest, tugging my feet toward the bathroom door. I paused, knocking again and pressing my ear to the door. Nothing on the other side.

"Fen?" I whispered again, slowly pushing open the door to meet a room full of burning steam. I squinted, trying to see through the thick clouds, and took a few steps into the soaking wet inferno. My hair was already damp from the moisture in the air, starting to cling to the skin of my neck as I walked deeper.

I looked for the familiar dark figure, having trouble seeing in the steamy room. I expected him to be standing at the sink counter or in the shower. Instead I found him sitting on the ground with his back against the wall, his head drooping between his knees. He was without a scrap of clothing, and his wet hair was plastered to him as though he'd just got out of the water.

I could see him shaking visibly, and he didn't acknowledge my presence at all. It was unlike him, since normally he heard and smelled me before he saw me. As large as he was, he looked small and broken in the moment. His commanding presence, normally ever-present, was missing, leaving him shivering in terror on the bathroom floor.

"Are you okay?" I tried to keep my voice soft but he jumped at the sound anyway. His eyes were wild and unfocused, fighting an internal battle.

"Anais," he panted. He was looking at me, but he wasn't seeing me. As if I wasn't really there, and he was looking through me.

"What happened?" I sank to my knees next to him. As I looked him over for what was wrong, I saw fabric tangled around his arm. He watched with rounded eyes as I took his hand gently and unwound the delicate fabric from him. It must've gotten tangled around him when he was getting out of the shower or something. Glancing up, I saw the curtain across the room pulled down, the rod on the floor and the fabric torn from where he'd obviously struggled with it.

"I… I…" He stumbled on his words, staring at the piece of fabric and me, his cheeks turning red with embarrassment. "I don't know why…" He was still shivering, his eyes wet with tears, not just the residual water from the shower.

I frowned. "Because it reminds you of being tied down." I discarded the fabric a safe distance away from us before shuffling closer, still on my knees next to him. "You were kept prisoner for hundreds of years. Anyone would have a bad reaction to that." I reached out to gently place a hand on the back of his neck. I pulled his head to me, leading him to rest his temple against my shoulder. He reached his arms around me, squeezing me closer as he buried his face into my neck, his body giving a violent shake. It took me a moment before I realized he was sobbing into me. His arms were tight to the point where it should have been uncomfortable, yet something in my soul told me he needed this, and knowing that somehow made it okay. The way he was so shaken had tears pricking at my own eyes. He was holding on to me like he was terrified I may disappear in a cloud of smoke.

"It's okay," I soothed, brushing his hair gently. My voice wobbled slightly as I continued to reassure him. "It's okay. Everything is okay."

We sat like that for a long while, until he calmed to breathing normally and the steam cleared from the room. Slowly, he sat back up, lifting his head from my shoulder. I curled closer to his side, gently brushing my fingers over his arm in an attempt to keep him grounded in the moment with me.

"I'm terrified that I'll wake up one day and find this was all a dream." His voice was quiet as he scrubbed at his face with a hand. "I felt it pull on my arm, so I twisted to get away, and it got worse ... and then I started thinking this was all a dream. That I was waking up back in Asgard, and this was just the only chain I felt at the moment. I couldn't breathe, and then I could feel the chains on my chest again..."

"You had a panic attack." I brushed my fingers through his drying hair. "It's okay. You're safe now."

He looked down at me for a moment before giving a small, half-hearted laugh. "I think I'm supposed to be the one saying that to you."

"Oh stop," I said and clicked my tongue at him. "You've been saying that to me since day one. You be the damsel and I'll be the knight in shining armor for a moment. It's okay, you're safe now, *baby girl*." I brushed his hair behind his ear again for extra emphasis of my teasing tone, making him give a more full-bodied laugh.

"I can't describe how embarrassed I am that this was all because of that flimsy curtain." He glared at the rod lying on the ground.

"There's nothing to be embarrassed about. I think I'd freak out too if something suddenly wrapped around my neck." My hand went to where I knew my skin was scarred from the collar Mag kept on me. He watched the movement with a sad expression. "It's early, and you look exhausted. Come. I'll put you to bed." I stood and took his arm, gently tugging him. "I'd carry you the way you do to me, but you're too big."

He chuckled softly, allowing me to help him up. I was reminded, when he was towering over me again, that he was fully nude. Unable to help myself, I glanced down and swallowed the gasp that wanted to escape my throat as my eyes darted back to his. He was a giant, and every proportion of him matched accordingly. My cheeks immediately burned as I took several steps back from him.

His usual playful smirk was back now. "Don't get bashful on me now, *hjarta*." He folded his arms across his chest but didn't make any attempt to cover himself. I grew a sudden, newfound interest in the counter next to me while my heart felt like it was sprinting circles in my chest. "What about saving me? Being my knight in shining armor?"

"Yeah, well, what do you do when the damsel is always naked?" I snipped. "I'm trying to be respectful."

"I don't care if you look—"

"Okay yeah, well I care, so put some pants on. 'God cares,' as my mom would say." I moved my eyes to the ceiling, admiring the vaulted height.

"Anais."

"Fen." My tone was slightly exasperated now, and I raked a hand through my damp hair.

"Anais, *look* at me."

My name and the return in his commanding tone had my eyes meeting his once again.

"Everything I am belongs to you. I don't give a damn what the Christian God thinks of anything we do or don't do. He's not here, he can't see us. I don't ever want you to feel shame for looking at me. I give you every permission," he said.

I bit my lip at his words, staring into his confident gaze for a long moment before my traitorous eyes slowly scanned down. To say he was well endowed was an understatement; he was greatly endowed, on a godly level. I couldn't help myself from focusing on the trail of dark hair low on his abdomen. He had a defined V shape at his hips, and powerful thighs.

Everything about him was like a greek statue come to life, and just … massive. My mind started to wander toward thoughts of touching him and the prospect that I could probably fit two hands on him… Was he getting hard from me looking at him?

"Anais." His voice snapped me from my thoughts, and I suddenly became very aware of my face and the way my eyes had widened to the size of dinner plates.

"Er… Well, um, thanks?" I said, flustered as our eyes met again and he laughed. "I'm glad you're laughing again, but seriously. Pants. Now please."

Shadows enveloped his legs immediately, and in the blink of an eye he was wearing dark, comfortable pants.

"Thank you." I cleared my throat, mentally trying to shake off the image of him that still had my mind reeling. "Now, it's early in the morning and you look exhausted." He followed me when I beckoned for him.

"Please don't go," he begged softly when I tugged back the covers for him to get in his own bed. "I want you to stay, please. I know you don't have nightmares when we sleep next to one another, and I don't either."

"Okay," I relented, sliding into the bed and resting my back against his headboard. "Come, lay here with your head on my lap."

He needed no further invitation, laying next to me and resting his head on my thighs. I gently stroked his hair, watching his eyes close. I gave him a head massage, gently scratching my nails over his neck and down his shoulders. His skin rose in goosebumps, and a shiver of pleasure twitched across his shoulders.

"When I was tied up down there, Odin's wolves—Geri and Freki—they only let Odin pass with his friends. He used to come down and play darts with Tyr and Mag and some other friends every third Saturday of the month. That's how I knew what day of the week and what month it was when I was down there."

"What do you mean, play darts?" I was almost afraid to ask, but I had to know.

"I was the dart board…" His voice was quiet, and I knew he was telling me things he hadn't told anyone yet, not even Hellia.

My fingers squeezed in his hair, imagining him tied to the rock while Mag pelted him with sharp darts.

"They never poisoned them or used silver, so that I'd heal. But they still hurt … especially when they left them in until the next month. And I really hated when they got me in the eye." He sighed, rubbing his eye with the back of his hand.

Tears were stinging my own eyes now, and I bit my lip to keep quiet as he continued. I stroked his hair, trying to keep myself calm. Rage and anger bubbled under my grief for him. I hated Mag more with every passing second, and I hadn't thought that was possible.

"I really thought I was going to be down there forever, Anais. I thought I was never going to get out." When his voice cracked, a tear slid down my face. I brushed it away quickly.

"Well, you're free now." I sighed.

"Am I?" he whispered. "If getting tangled in the fucking curtain in my bathroom can bring me down like that? If you hadn't come in there, I'd still be on the ground." He sounded embarrassed, ashamed.

"I'll make you a deal," I said with a soft purr. He listened intently. "As long as you wake me from the nightmares, I promise to always come untangle you and make sure you're free."

"Deal." He threw an arm across my lap, pulling me close and sighing heavily as he closed his eyes. "Thank you."

I sat, still stroking his hair while he slept deeply. I watched the morning sunlight break through the clouds outside. His room was dark, all black and dark colors on the walls, and the fabrics absorbed so much of the precious daylight that came in from the beautiful large windows. I frowned at the gloom, thinking he needed more color.

Books were scattered everywhere, just like the circular room he showed me the night before, and I smiled at the thought that he liked reading so much. I noted one was carefully placed over the arm of a chair and tried to imagine him sitting there, reading. The thought had my skin heating with how attractive it was.

After a while, the action of stroking his hair started to make me feel sleepy. I laid my head back against the headboard, closing my eyes and letting myself drift off listening to the crackle of the fire and Fen's gentle snoring.

CHAPTER 26

I drifted in and out of sleep. The fog was thick and diffused the light, bathing the room in grey. The wind moaned outside the windows, and thick snowflakes smacked against the panes.

A thudding on Fen's door startled me fully awake. He jumped too, his hand on my leg tightening to squeeze my thigh as he regained consciousness.

"Fen?" Hellia yelled from the hallway. He turned his head, looking toward the door with confusion. "Fen!" It sounded urgent when she wrapped the door again.

"Stay," he whispered to me, pressing a kiss to my thigh where he'd been resting his head. It was so fast I barely had time to blush about it. He immediately leapt from bed, crossing to the door in a matter of paces. Annoyance radiated from him as he threw the door open. I could see the scowl on his face from just his profile.

"We have to go to the Helheim training camp," Hellia murmured to him, and I saw her eyes flick to me. They widened only momentarily before returning to her brother's face. "I'm sorry to interrupt," she said, then she dropped her voice even more, out of my hearing range. I watched the muscles in Fen's back tense at her words.

"We'll be there in five minutes," he growled, starting to close the door and turn back toward his room.

"Maybe Anais should stay—" Hellia said.

"Absolutely not," he snarled, catching the door before it closed all the way. "I won't leave her alone here, unprotected. She stays with me. Always."

"Of course." Hellia didn't argue any more, her voice barely coming through as the door shut in her face.

"What's happened?" I asked, scooting myself out of bed and getting ready to run down the hall to replace my pajamas.

"There was an attack from Odin's men last night, in a town where one of our Hell Hound training camps are." He held a hand out, offering clothes that appeared from shadows in his outstretched palm.

"Oh no," I whispered. My stomach dropped and anxiety raced through me like I'd been struck by lightning. Mag was making good on his threats to hurt people to force me to give myself over. I took the clothes and scrambled to pull them on over my pajamas. Panic was sloshing in my stomach. He said he'd hurt Kerri.

Fen's head snapped to me, and he regarded me with demanding curiosity that I didn't meet. I was still unsure if he could hear my thoughts or not; he'd been ambiguous when I'd asked but ultimately said that he couldn't. I had a feeling he was lying. I flicked an eyebrow up at him, and he turned away.

"Anais," he said, stopping me before we left. He turned serious, all business, as cradled my chin and tipped my head up to where he was leaning down. "You will stay by me today. You will not leave my sight. Got it?"

"Yes," I said, scrunching my nose at his order.

"Repeat it," he growled in that scary voice. I didn't cower.

"Really, Fen?" I snapped.

"Repeat. It. So I know you're listening to me." He glared at me, neither of us giving in to the other until finally I realized we weren't leaving until I did.

"Fine," I huffed. "I will stay right next to you all day and *never ever* leave your side, my knight in shining armor, my personal bodyguard." I rolled my eyes. "Happy?"

"Very," he growled and let go, waiting for me to walk out the door in front of him.

Hellia and Ylfa were waiting for us at the bottom of the stairs, both dressed in black leather armor and training clothes.

"Let's go." Hellia nodded to me, heading out the main castle doors into the whipping wind and sleet. As we stepped out, Fen and Ylfa shifted. Both flew into their wolf form so fast I didn't actually see them change. Ylfa was interesting, slightly smaller than Jerrick with a rusty-color coat. She still had the shaggy fur that protected against the cold, but her stature was slightly different from the men's—her legs were longer, everything was slightly leaner, and her tail was shorter. I tried not to stare, not wanting her to feel uncomfortable.

Scrambling up Fen's shoulders, not nearly as graceful as Hellia leapt onto Ylfa's back, we turned down a trail that led to the woods rather than town. It was a well-worn trail, and it didn't take long for the castle to disappear into the trees behind us.

Then we were coming to a group of buildings and canvas tents surrounded by a stone wall. Wolves Ylfa and Jerrick's sizes were everywhere, mixed with people and elves with bows slung across their shoulders. Some people, I supposed Hell Hounds in human form, were sparring in a ring, others lifting weights and talking.

I clambered down from Fen's shoulders and he shifted back to his human form. As always, he was taller and bigger than everyone else around, and some began gawking. Several men whispered to each other, obviously giddy to see Fenrir. Several wolves lowered their heads and wagged nervously in his presence. He came to my side, placing a hand on my back to escort me wherever it was we were going.

"What are they training for?" I asked, looking around. I watched as three wolves in varying shades of grey and brown—wearing leather armor pieces that covered their heads, necks, and shoulders—walked in with mounted riders sitting in saddles on their backs. Each of the riders had a bow slung across their back and a quiver attached to the saddle at their side.

"This is the main HellHound training center in Helheim. They train archers, foot soldiers, HellHounds to work together to fight Odin's armies here. This is where Jerrick and Ylfa come each day, and where Talin lives," Fen said.

"When she's not in my castle," Hellia threw into the conversation with a grin and joking tone. Fen glared at her and she shrugged. "She pretty much lives in Jerrick's room half the time. I don't care, I'm just telling the truth."

Ylfa was called away to several wolves and archers, telling us she would see us later. We followed Hellia toward a particularly large canvas tent, ducking the flap into a round room with a sprawling table in the center. A map was spread out on it, and around the room, chests with supplies were stacked against the fabric walls.

"Wow, full house today," Jerrick said, walking in through an opening connecting to another room across the tent from us. "Did you really bring Anais?" He raised an eyebrow at Fen. In turn, the dark-haired man glared at his lieutenant, who raised his other eyebrow and said no more. When Jerrick turned, I caught a glint of something in his ear.

"What is that?!" Hellia yelped, grabbing both sides of Jerrick's head to yank him down so she could inspect the new gold rings that pierced his ear.

"Talin did it," he boasted with pride. "Elven-made jewelry leaves permanent piercings." He had several gold hoops on the crest of his ears and one in each earlobe. Even I had to admit the look suited him well.

"I want her to do mine!" Hellia demanded, looking around for the small elf.

"Can we focus please?" Fen snarled next to us. "We're here for a reason. We were told one of the Niflheim camps got attacked." He was looking around like he expected to be attacked now, here. "How many are down?"

I looked up at him with widening, guilty eyes. I knew they were coming for me, and I didn't want anyone else to get hurt on my behalf. Mag had warned me. I'd tried to ignore it, but now it was happening. Attacks were being made, and who knew how many were injured, or even worse, dead. On my behalf. He glanced down at me and placed a gentle hand on my shoulder, squeezing as though he was reassuring me.

"Yes," Jerrick turned serious, standing at his full height. "Last night, the Aesir attacked Eski."

"There's nothing there," Hellia said as she frowned. "What did they want?"

"Information." Jerrick shook his head. "They took two prisoners and injured four more. Talin and I were patrolling close by. If we hadn't been, it would be much worse."

"Is she hurt?" Hellia asked.

"Not terribly," the light elf's voice chimed from behind us. She walked to his side and folded her arms across her chest. Her midriff was exposed, showing some fresh bandages wrapped around her abdomen. She showed no pain, bumping Jerrick with her hip playfully. "Can't get rid of me that easily, flea bag," she teased him, making him grin at her.

"What happened?" Hellia fixed a serious look on Talin now. Talin, in turn, dropped her arms, putting them behind her back and standing up straight in front of the queen.

"This morning at approximately 0300 hours, a group of five Aesir attacked Eski. They attacked without warning or provocation. From our understanding, they did know you were not in Eski. Their goal was to get information on Anais and Fenrir's whereabouts and the weaknesses of Helheim City. They injured four officers in my squadron and took two as prisoners, Elyse and Wyll."

My gut twisted at her words. People were taken prisoner over me… They were going to die for me. Real people, elves or wolves, with names and families.

"And you?" Hellia asked, narrowing her eyes on the bandages.

"Silver arrow to the lower abdomen. I'll recover fully in a couple days." She relaxed slightly. "I took down three of them and sent the last two scurrying home to Odin with an arrow to the shoulder." At her words, Hellia's mouth twitched up ever so slightly.

"Good" was all Hellia said.

"Can you save them?" I finally found my voice. "Wyll and Elyse, can you help them?"

"They are trained. They won't give any information to the Aesir," Fen said confidently behind me. "You're safe here, Anais."

I was shaking my head now. "But the Aesir will kill them both if they don't give the information up, won't they?" I watched Talin's expression sadden as she dropped her gaze to the ground. These two people were part of her squadron. She knew them, and she knew they would die, if they weren't dead already.

"Yes," Fen stated.

"I don't want them to die over me, over something I did! Please, you have to help them, Fen." I turned my pleading eyes on him. He tensed, his eyes flitting to his sister and friends behind me.

"Anais, they are protecting you. Protecting Helheim. That is more than worthy to die for." He rubbed at his temple with his fingers.

"How can you even say that?!" I yelped. "I'm just one person. I can't expect people to die for me!"

Our three friends watched the argument in silence; all they were missing was a bucket of movie theater popcorn. Hellia was doing little to keep the bemused expression from her face as she watched her brother argue with me.

"Everyone here will die for you if I tell them to," Fen growled, his tone commanding dominance of the conversation.

"You can't do that, Fen. I don't want anyone to get hurt on my account! And Odin will keep coming after all of you, over and over, until I give myself up." My lip was trembling slightly.

"He will *kill* you, Anais. Absolutely not—" Fen started.

"She's right. We could save a lot of effort and our own people if we give her over now," a new, yet familiar, voice added to the conversation. "In fact, we could use her as a trap to get all of Asgard in one place for their slaughter." The tall snake shapeshifter, Jormungandr, watched me disdainfully with his greenish-yellow serpentine eyes. "If Fen wasn't so busy playing Beauty and the Beast with her, she could be a useful tool."

"You slithering son of a—" Jerrick started.

"If you so much as breathe wrong, I'll tear out your throat—" Fen snapped at the same time.

Both men took a step toward him, Fen blocking me with his body, but Jorm stayed completely calm, merely looking between them with boredom. His long red hair was braided in intricate patterns, falling past his shoulders. He flicked his forked tongue over a row of sharpened teeth, four fangs glinting in the top row.

"Boys, please." Hellia snapped her fingers, gaining everyone's attention. "We are not giving Anais to Odin," she stated, looking pointedly at Fen, who turned back to Jorm. A low rumble trembled the ground under my feet. "We are not ripping throats out or insulting my mother. We are not fighting between us, got it? We are a family. No. Fighting."

All three men looked at her with varying amounts of guilt expressed on their faces, Fen with the least, still putting himself between Jorm and myself.

The redhead looked down at me again and curled his lip. "Really though, brother, what is it about *this* mortal girl? She fell for Mag, how smart can she be?"

My cheeks flushed hot with embarrassment. Fen snarled, grabbing the front of his brother's armor hauling the man to his tiptoes, so he was barely touching the ground.

"Stop!" My voice had Fen's head and confused eyes turning to me. "He's right. I did do that."

Fen shook his head, "It's not fair. You haven't known Mag for hundreds of years—"

I shook my head, and he fell quiet. "I let a strange man take me to a different fucking *realm*, Fen. My best friend on Earth probably thinks he kidnapped and murdered me." I nodded toward Jorm. "She most definitely would agree with you that it was a stupid decision to trust him. And it was."

Fen looked conflicted, frowning at me and then glaring at Jorm. He still had a fistful of his brother's armored jacket in hand, and I tried not to notice too much how the veins in his hand were rippling as his hand flexed.

"He tricked you, Anais," Jerrick was snapping at me now. "Jorm doesn't understand everything that's happening here. He needs to shut his mouth before I shut it for him."

Jorm smirked at Jerrick. "Stop trying to defend her and make her feel better for being so useless. Let us use her for a trap; at least then she'll be worth something."

Fen lashed out toward his brother, but suddenly a wall of shadow drove between the three men, forcing them apart. The shadows writhed in the air, blocking each man's view of the other for a moment, before the walls bled to the ground and the shadows disappeared around the room.

"No *fucking* fighting," Hellia barked, pinning all three with a glare when they turned to her. "Don't make me tell you again. And you"—she pointed at Jorm, fixing him with a truly terrifying glare—"shut up about Anais. She's my new friend, she is smart and kind, and you'll keep your mouth shut if you don't want me to banish you back to Midgard."

She reached out, grabbing my wrist and pulling me along with her and Talin, turning her back on the men. I heard a growl behind us and looked over my shoulder to see the three men hadn't moved, all glaring at one another. Reluctantly, Fen disengaged and followed me when I was just about to disappear from view, Jerrick at his side moments later.

"Hellia, people can't die for me," I murmured to her.

"They don't. They die for Helheim." It was Talin who answered. "Just as the Aesir will die for Asgard. Not for any individual, but for the good of the city—or what Odin deems the good of the city. We all understand. It is the way it is, Anais."

I shook my head, chewing my lip. I glanced over to see Fen and Jerrick involved in a deep, intense conversation just a few paces behind us. Which was good, because I didn't want him overhearing.

"Mag walked in my dreams, the night I had the nightmare. The nightmare was ... about Tyr ... but Mag was there, and he spoke to me." I shuffled uncomfortably, glancing at the men to make sure they were still talking and not paying our conversation any mind.

Hellia's eyes saddened. "Oh, that explains why you couldn't wake up. He had you trapped there until outside interference woke you." I didn't want to ask how she knew I couldn't seem to wake myself from that dream. I wondered how many times she was held prisoner in sleep. Or how many she'd held someone prisoner.

"He threatened you and your people, and my friends and family at home." I hushed my voice even further until it was barely more than a whisper. "He said if I don't give myself to the Aesir, he's going to keep coming after you. Keep attacking your people. Whether they're dying for Helheim or whatever, I can't allow that to continue when I know I could stop it."

Talin and Hellia were both shaking their heads immediately. "No," Hellia said, continuing to use a hushed voice herself. "It's a trap. He wants you there to lure Fen to come kill Odin and kick off Ragnarok."

"But my best friend Kerri..." My voice was starting to break. "She's in danger. He said he'd kill her. She slept with Tora, they know where to find her and how to get her."

"Don't worry, I will send some guards of my own down to Midgard to guard her, okay? And she won't even know they're there. I would bring her here, but I think that would frighten her unless you were there, and it's just too dangerous to send you to Midgard right now."

"Just, whatever you do," Talin looked at me, nervously, "don't leave Fen, okay? Always stay with him until we can get this figured out."

"I don't need him to defend me," I started to argue, and both women shook their heads.

"I'm all for women being empowered without men," Hellia said, her eyes serious and hinting at the centuries of battles she'd fought to prove herself. "But this is very dangerous, and he is the most powerful god in the Norse realms, not to mention one of the most powerful across all the realms. Talin is right, you need to stay with him. It's for your safety."

"I can't just be chained to his side for the rest of my life!" I argued. Sure, we'd just had a nice date and some moments, but this was starting to feel like I was being set up, forced to be with him. My hand slid to my neck, rubbing at where the collar had sat for weeks. "I want to go home, back to my family and my friends. I'm *done* being attached to these men against my will, dragged around at their side like a dog on a leash."

Hellia's eyes flicked over my shoulder for just a moment, and Talin stared at the ground.

"I understand," Hellia's voice was gentle. "You can't go home, not yet, not until we resolve these issues with Asgard. But think of him as your bodyguard. You do as you like and he'll follow you."

"That doesn't help. I am not his property to guard! And that doesn't stop the fact that more people will be hurt on my behalf, more of your Hell Hounds and friends," I argued, looking at Talin. She dropped her eyes to the ground again.

"I'm sorry Anais, but right now we need to focus on protecting you. I order it." Hellia grimaced, looking over my shoulder with a nod. Talin nodded her head.

I felt Fen's presence at my back, knowing it was him who Hellia was looking at. Hopelessness swelled in me, and I felt held prisoner. I looked around desperately, but everyone's steely gaze was hardened toward me. Firm with their decision to protect me first. Except one. Green eyes framed by ginger brows across the room watched me with curiosity and skepticism.

Fen and I walked in silence along the trail back to the palace on foot. I was furious, feeling alone once more in my fight to try to save people. Blaming myself, I chastised myself for ever trusting the gods of Hell would do the right thing. Fen was following me after I'd insisted on walking back to the castle on my own two legs. We approached the castle doors, and he held it for me so I could enter.

"Would you like to go upstairs?" he asked.

"No," I snapped. "I'm going to my room. I want to be alone." I took off up the stairs and down the hall without looking back. He didn't follow me this time.

CHAPTER 27

Waiting until darkness fell outside, long past dinner—which I'd skipped—I snuck down to the kitchen to find something to eat. No one was in the warm room filled with copper kettles and the smell of real fire. I looked around, trying to see what was available for me to make and eat. It wasn't like my kitchen at home, and I had no idea how to use any of the appliances to cook. I grew increasingly frustrated as I shuffled through the pantry, muttering angrily to myself about being silly for thinking they might have Pop Tarts.

"My brother forgot to feed his pet tonight?" The voice behind me startled me. I hadn't heard anyone come in while I was rifling through the pantry. When I jumped, I smacked my head on one of the pantry shelves. I backed out, rubbing my head as I turned to face Jorm, who stood with his arms crossed and a sneer on his face.

"I skipped dinner. And I'm not his pet." It felt futile to argue it—everyone could see the metaphorical leash that chained me to Fen. I still had to, though. To try to fight for my independence.

"You're angry with him for not saving Wyll and Elyse." He stated it, watching me with a bemused look. "For letting them go to Asgard as prisoners for execution since they will not release any information."

"No one should be dying over me." I shook my head, my heart panging with grief for the two lives that would be lost in keeping me safe. I stared at the red-haired man for a moment. "Do you really think if you turned me in, it would stop people getting hurt?"

"I think it would cut to the chase. Instead of Aesir attacking Niflheim and starting to test the borders of Helheim, we could use you to start Ragnarok. My brother needs to stop avoiding this war, pretending he doesn't want it. Pretending for you like he isn't who he really is."

"Who is he, then?" I asked.

He paused, thinking for a moment. "Let me show you." Nodding for me to follow, he led me from the kitchen into the main foyer and down a small alcove to the side of the stairs. "Has he told you how he gains power yet, Anais?" he asked as we approached a large statue of a pair of ravens sitting in a tree. He reached forward, stroking one of the raven's heads. Stepping back, we watched as the statue twisted and sank into the ground, leaving a winding stone staircase down into the bowels of the castle.

"Yes," I said. "Death and suffering."

I fell silent as I followed Jorm down the steps. I wondered what more I was about to learn about this man who wanted so desperately to get closer to me.

"He's a death god, as we all are from the underworlds. Lucifer, Hades, Anubis, King Yan, Shinigami—there are hundreds across realms who draw power from death. Life and death are great powers." He led me down into a corridor that felt like it was underground beneath the castle.

"But he also said suffering?" I looked around at the dark walls, thinking how creepy it looked compared to the castle upstairs. He led me down another hall and toward a set of stairs.

"Yes, especially if he's inflicting it." He turned, giving me a pointed look. I felt my face drain of color, and I swallowed as I followed him down the flight of stairs to what could only be described as a literal dungeon.

"What is this place?" I asked in a whisper. Around us were barred cells, some with shadowy figures cowering in the back as we passed. Whimpers and sobs filled the air, and the iron scent of blood permeated my nose.

"The realm of torture. I know Hellia and Fen have been trying to pretend Helheim is this magical fantasy land, but the truth is they both are death gods. Yes, above the castle it's a wonderful city, but both of them derive their power from down here, the death and suffering. This is where the wicked are sent by the Norns after their passing."

He led me further down, past more and more cells full of beings cowering in terror. Some were people, some were unrecognizable to me. I heard only gasps of horror and cries of fear as I passed.

"He said he would never hurt me," I whispered, more reminding myself than anything else.

"True. He likely won't." Jorm turned down a hallway lined with doors. "But what about hurting people for you? Earlier it seems you were skeptical of that."

My heart raced. That was my whole point, I didn't want anyone to hurt on my behalf. Jorm pushed open a door, leading me into a room that looked straight from a horror movie. I scanned the tools of torture lining the walls in horror, the weapons glinting in the firelight, the old splatterings of blood now crusted on the walls. As I made my way into the room my eyes met a familiar pair, watching me with terror from across the room.

"I"m sorry! I'm sorry! I'll never do it again I swear to Odin! I'll never touch her again! Please tell him to stop!" Tyr was barely recognizable where he lay on the ground. He was missing his other hand now, and the entirety of his handless arm was gone too. His chest was ripped open, his lungs visible as they rapidly inhaled and exhaled in his ribcage. Normally gods healed at an incredible rate, but he was barely healing at all. Blood leaked all over the ground, and at the sight of his exposed organs, I couldn't help turning and retching into the corner of the room.

Looking up and wiping my mouth with my sweater sleeve, I turned a pleading look onto Jorm. "This is too much, this is—" I wretched again, shaking as my body expelled mostly stomach acid.

"This is my brother. This is what he does. He and Hellia have been putting on a nice front for you, but you should see the reality." He leaned down next to Tyr. "Although, Tyr, you deserved this long before the girl." He clicked his tongue at the sobbing man.

"What do you think of my brother now?" Jorm asked, rising once again to his full height as he turned toward me.

"He's a monster…" I whispered. I was shaking, my legs threatening to give out under me.

"Jorm, what are you doing?" Fen snarled from behind me. I whirled, knocking sideways against the wall. I fell on my ass, gasping for air. He was covered in blood, looking like an absolute nightmare, something from a horror movie as he held Tyr's disembodied hand in his own.

"Oh my God!" I screamed when I saw the hand, scrambling back and jumping away from Tyr's blood on the ground. "Oh my God, oh my God," I started muttering in panic, covering my eyes with my hands.

"She deserves to know the truth," Jorm said. I peeked through my fingers as he continued, "You insist on hiding it from her. Pretending you're some good guy to impress her."

"I'm not pretending—she knows. But she shouldn't have to endure seeing it," Fen hissed, kneeling next to me on one knee. "Anais." His voice was calm. "I will never hide from you what or who I am."

"Please, you have been—" Jorm said.

"Jorm, leave right now before you join Tyr on the floor," Fen snapped, making me flinch. We both waited until his footsteps left the room.

"He said you did this for me." I glanced at Tyr's hand, horrified.

"I did," he said with a note of confusion. "He hurt you."

"That doesn't make it okay to hurt someone back!" I yelled. "I can't believe I have to teach morality to a god."

He growled, reaching out and grabbing my jaw, pinching my cheeks hard enough to make my lips pout as he turned my head to make me look at him. "You and I have a different definition of morality, *hjarta*."

"I don't want you to hurt people for me." Tears were pouring down my cheeks now. "That's not how I was raised. It's not okay."

"Well, you're going to start learning other ways," he said with finality.

"Absolutely not. I do not have to be okay with you killing people if you want to be my boyfriend." I huffed. He let go of me, brushing my hair back behind my ear even when I tried to cringe away from his bloodstained hand.

His smile made me deepen my scowl. "I am your 'boyfriend'? What does this word mean?"

"You are *not* my boyfriend. I don't date violent murderers." I glared at him.

"You went on a date with me after I murdered the Aesir." He said it matter of factly. My face flamed with the realization of the truth. "You kissed me at the inn the night after I did it. I think you could be open to learning a new moral code."

"Okay, if I accept you are a vicious killer … if I agree to go to Christian Hell for dating you, can I live upstairs and pretend I don't know about all this until then?" I squeezed my eyes shut, trying to picture living upstairs and ignoring the bloody massacres going on down here every day.

He tipped his head at me, confused. "Why would you go to Lucifer's realm?"

"My mom baptized me as an infant; my soul is committed to the Christian God." I started to get up from the cold ground.

He was shaking his head, remaining kneeling so we were nearly at eye level.

"That is not how it works. It is dependent on the individual and what they believe the time they pass to the afterlife realms." He watched me. "It's about the god you have the most connection with."

I stared at him as he took my hand in his, bringing my knuckles to his lips to place a delicate kiss on me. "We have a new religion now, *hjarta*. The Christian God cannot have you. You prayed to me, you came to me, and I intend to make you mine, forever."

My heart was threatening to break free of my chest, pounding loudly in my ears. I sat stunned, too stunned to pull my hand from him, not even sure what to respond to this new information.

"You said you'd never hurt me... How am I supposed to believe that when this is what you do to people who upset you? I upset you all the time." I wiped at my face with the sleeve of my sweater.

The corner of his mouth quirked up. "Anais, more than the fact I would not live with myself if I ever injured you, intentionally or unintentionally, Hellia would not let me take another breath for such a crime." He looked at Tyr for a moment before offering the severed hand toward me. "I was going to wrap it in a box for you. I wanted to give it to you as a courting gift."

"That's disgusting," I shrank away from the hand as he chuckled. "No, thank you."

"You're so polite, it's funny," he purred, rising to stand now.

I was becoming increasingly aware of the repeated squelching noises with every breath Tyr took, and I started to feel ill again.

"When I get Mag, I want you to deliver his death blow," Fen said solemnly.

"What?!" I squeaked, his sudden comment taking me by surprise.

"I want you to kill him. You can do it—"

"Listen, Prince of Hell, regular good people like me don't enjoy killing people. It's not like a fun activity we do on the weekends. It's actually pretty traumatizing, so you can stop fantasizing about this, because it's not coming to fruition." I pointed my finger at him.

"We'll see," he gave me a wolfish grin.

CHAPTER 28

"Take the knife." Jerrick waited for me to wrap my fingers around the handle. "Don't be afraid to really cut me with it, okay? You can't hurt me with it; it's not real silver."

I nodded, trying to soothe my thudding heart. I squared off with him, waiting for him to move toward me the way we discussed before starting practice. He'd outlined ahead of time that he would act like he was attacking but touch me only very gently for now. I gripped the knife tighter to keep my fingers from shaking visibly. Never in a million years would I imagine I would actually be stabbing someone. Hurting someone that way was unthinkable. It was one thing to read about the heroine doing it in a book and another to be out here, mentally preparing myself to *stab* someone.

We were out on the training balcony beneath my bedroom window. Below us, the forest stretched to the edge of the fjord walls. Snow swirled in the air but melted as it hit the stone of the balcony, leaving a space free of drifts for training. Jerrick offered to train me in self defense this morning at the breakfast table, and I'd agreed begrudgingly with the encouragement of Ylfa and Hellia. Fen was absent, Hellia telling me he was called out to a Hell Hounds training camp for something early in the morning. I was grateful after my arguments with him yesterday and last night.

I felt Jerrick's presence at my back, and he wrapped a muscular arm across the front of my chest as if he were attacking me in slow motion. Admittedly, I was feeling better about contact from men generally, and Jerrick was more than simply good looking. He was very tall, not taller than Fenrir but taller than Mag and most other men I'd encountered in my life. He smelled like the woods the same way Fen did, but with an undertone of something warm and sweet like vanilla. His hold on me was extremely light, barely touching me, thankfully not sending me into more of a panic.

"In the thigh, remember?" Jerrick prompted me, and I flipped the knife in my hand, pausing for several breaths before driving the blade backward down into his thigh. The feeling of the knife hitting flesh was so strange, and yet it made me feel powerful. I drove the knife into his flesh, torn between excitement and abhorrence at the feeling of the blade sinking into the muscle.

"Good," Jerrick said as he made me rip the knife from his body with a sickening wet noise. I watched the wound heal almost immediately when the knife was removed. That ability would make it incredibly difficult to defeat any immortal being.

"We're using a steel blade today, that's why I'm healing, but we'll get you an elven silver blade in Helheim." He took a step back, repositioning himself behind me again.

I nodded, taking in the information and trying to pay attention to every advantage he gave me. If I was ever going to have a chance at defending myself from Mag or any other Aesir, I needed to listen carefully to the werewolf lieutenant.

We practiced several more times, him teaching me different ways to stab and twist myself away. After a while, he started changing patterns and springing surprises on me, letting me try to keep him off of me or take slashes at him. Then he would pause and instruct me how I could better use my weapon and body to do more damage or get out another way. It hadn't gotten easier to stab him, even though I knew he healed rapidly. It went against everything I'd learned when I was younger in the church.

"I'm going to start touching you now, okay? I'm going to get more physical, but I promise I won't hurt you. I want you to understand what it really feels like, so we can build your muscle memory for if it really happens. Just tell me if we need to stop." He looked at me with an earnest expression.

Taking a deep breath, I nodded. The next attack was half speed, but he firmly planted a hand on my arm, which sent a shock through my body. Memories of the Aesir somehow mixed with the straight up facts that a very handsome, funny, kind man was touching me. It was confusing, and exciting, and different from Fen. I tried to ignore the pricks on my skin as we continued our training, but somehow kept finding myself distracted by the lieutenant.

After several different attacks and instructions, we began to work on different levels, practicing as if I were surprised on the ground or crouching. One such time, he took me to the ground, and I couldn't help getting flustered at the overt lewdness of it all. He was between my legs, my knees bracketing his hips. My cheeks turned red as I lay face to collar bone with him.

"From here, you can get a potentially deadly shot on someone's kidney, okay?" He didn't seem at all bothered by the situation, fully focused on teaching me. "So place the knife"—he guided my hand and aimed it toward his lower back—"right there. Stab, hard as you can, then you're going to twist to detach the kidney and send the person into shock."

"I can't," I whimpered, letting my hand with the knife fall away. It was too much, it was too violent, and it was starting to get to me. I was overwhelmed with the mix of feelings coursing through me, and a few images of Asgard threatened to make an appearance in my mind.

"Yes, you can," he said, encouraging me and repositioning my hand with the knife aimed at his back.

I took a deep breath, gathering my strength, and then plunged the knife in. I wanted to be sick at the feeling, but again a thrill ran through me as my blade sank into him.

He sucked in a sharp breath through his teeth. "Yep. Just like that, then you'd twist." I pulled the knife from him again, and he raised up a few centimeters to show me how to position the knife at his belly. "If you can't get your arm around back, you can also gut someone—"

"What *the fuck* are you doing?" Fen snarled.

He was storming out onto the balcony, a downright murderous look on his face. His attention was firmly locked on Jerrick, whose eyes grew round as he scrambled back from me, staying low to the ground. Fen was bristling as he loomed over the lieutenant. Jerrick kept his eyes turned down, shaking his head slightly as he muttered several curse words under his breath.

The scene reminded me of the wolves at home when a more powerful wolf required a less powerful one to submit and show their stomach as an act of surrender.

"Self defense training, that's all. I was just teaching her to go for the kidneys, and I was going to teach her how to get someone in the belly. I wasn't trying to do anything, *anything*. I swear." Jerrick showed his palms in surrender and made no move to get up. Fen's eyes were blazing as he stared down at his friend, and I watched his hand flex menacingly as he stood over the lieutenant.

Fen turned, glaring down at where I had risen to my feet now. "Are you okay?"

"I'm fine. He was just teaching me where to stab. It's not a big deal, Fen." I stepped toward Jerrick to help him from the ground, but Fen's flashing, dangerous look stopped me.

"He shouldn't be on top of you like that," Fen snarled, turning back to Jerrick, who hadn't moved.

"He didn't mean anything by it… He's trying to help me," I protested. "It was useful! Now I know how to defend myself from someone who's on top of me. All my nightmares are of someone on top of me like that…"

Jerrick was starting to visibly sweat under the daggers being glared at him. "I wasn't trying anything. You know I wouldn't. Fen"—Jerrick didn't flinch when Fen narrowed his eyes on him, just raised his exposed palms a tad higher—"I know, remember? I know, and I would never…"

"Know what?" I asked, looking between the two men. I was starting to fear for Jerrick's life, just a little bit. It appeared Jerrick, too, was just slightly fearful of the rage boiling under his friend's eyes.

Neither answered me, Fen continuing to stare down at the lieutenant who made cautious, flitting eye contact with him.

"Know *what*?" I repeated. "Someone tell me."

Fen's eyes slid to me, and we stared at each other as I waited for him to answer. His expression softened ever so slightly before he seemed to remember the situation. His expression hardened again as he looked down at the lieutenant, flat on his back below Fen.

"I'll be the one to train her from now on," he growled before stepping away. "Get out of here."

Jerrick scrambled to his feet, dipping his head to Fen and walking out the doors, leaving us alone on the balcony.

"Slightly jealous, are you?" I asked, folding my arms across my chest as I watched the wolf-man glare at his friend's back until he disappeared from sight. "You didn't need to be like that with him."

"He shouldn't be touching you like that," he snarled before turning to me.

"So you are a jealous type." I couldn't help the small smirk growing on my face. I could admit it felt a little good to be the subject of his desire so much that he wouldn't even let his best friend train me.

He rolled his eyes at me, the scowl deepening. "Just reset yourself," he growled, bending down to pick up the knife and hand it to me.

"What?" The blood drained away from my face now as I hesitantly took the knife.

"We're continuing training." He looked down at the knife in my hand as shadows wrapped around him, melting away his casual attire and leaving him bare chested with black athletic pants.

My mind flashed back to the position Jerrick just had me in, and the thought of that being a shirtless Fen instead was too much. With the thoughts that already crossed my mind today, I wasn't sure I would be able to train with him. My body already buzzed with anticipation of his touch. I didn't need to add him crawling around between my legs.

"I've had enough for today," I said as I sheathed the knife on my hip.

"Reset. Now, Anais," he snarled, his tone not leaving any room for an argument.

I huffed, taking the knife in hand once again. Standing, facing him, my chest starting to heave slightly as I waited for him to move toward me.

"I won't hurt you." His voice softened, but only very slight-ly.

"I don't promise the same." I gripped the knife harder in my already white knuckles.

His mouth twitched up. "Good."

He was so fast, I didn't have time to prepare myself the way I had with Jerrick.

I yelped in surprise when he took me to the ground in less than two seconds, hovering over me in much the same way Jerrick had. Even though he had thrown me on my back in less time than it took for me to gasp a breath of air, he still cradled my head with a hand on the way down, ensuring I didn't get hurt as I fell to the floor.

"Show me what you learned," he growled, pinning me beneath him.

Heat flushed through my cheeks, down my neck and heading in a direct shot between my legs. I wanted to snap my knees together, but with Fen in between them, it was impossible. His breath was blowing across my face, his gold banding glinting in the daylight and distracting me, making me stare at the pulse thrumming in his neck. Trying to regain control over myself, I raised the knife to his back, pressing the tip against where I guessed his kidney would be based on what Jerrick just taught me.

"Go on," he encouraged, looking down at me. I could feel my cheeks burning.

"I-I don't actually want to hurt you..." I kept my hand poised with the tip of the knife against his back.

"You can't," he said, still not moving.

"But the darts—" I remembered what he'd said about feeling the dart needles in his skin for months at a time.

"This is different. I want you to be able to defend yourself, even against me. Now stab me." His tone was harsh, and the undertone of a growl had shivers skittering down my spine.

I swallowed before raising the knife again and plunging it into his side. It was probably too high to hit his kidney this time, since we were face to face and he was so much taller than me. He didn't make any noise, merely grimacing slightly as the blade sank into his flesh. I drove it in until my hand at the hilt met his warm flesh.

"Now twist," he instructed, and I couldn't help but notice the way his eyes dropped to where I was now chewing on my lip anxiously. His own tongue darted across his lip as he looked down on me.

"What?" I didn't ask because I didn't hear him but because he was so close. I was completely distracted by his piney scent mixed with salty sweat; it was so intoxicating, and it made the space between my legs pulse in a grotesquely needy way I was too ashamed to acknowledge fully.

"Twist the knife," he repeated, waiting for me to comply.

Slowly I twisted my wrist to dig the blade into him, scrunching up my face at the noise it made.

"Good." His voice was breathy, and his expression could only be described as barely restrained carnal desire. "Now take it out." He waited for me to remove the blade. I felt some blood drip from his closing wound onto me and the urge to lick his bodily fluids from my hand was suddenly overwhelming. What was wrong with me? This was disgusting!

"What Jerrick was about to show you," he continued, covering my bloodied hand with his own and moving it so the tip of the blade pressed against his abdomen, "is that if you can get your hands underneath someone, you can get to their vital organs here."

I wasn't listening anymore, scanning across the muscles flexing in his abdomen beneath the tip of the knife. Soft hairs covered his muscled chest, and near the knife, I caught sight of that little trail of hair from his navel. The image from the bathroom popped into my head, making my breath quicken.

"Anais? Are you listening to me?" My eyes snapped back up to his, and a blush burned my cheeks at being caught not paying attention.

"Yes," I said, flustered and obviously lying.

"What did I say?"

"Um..." I bit my lip, trying not to allow myself to get distracted by the way the daylight was illuminating his shoulders and biceps. "You said to twist the knife." The way his dark hair was falling in front of his eyes now had my attention.

"That was minutes ago." He didn't sound particularly disappointed in me, and I thought I caught a flash of a fanged smile on his lips. "I said to stab upward under the rib cage to try to pierce a lung."

"Okay," I breathed, slowly dragging the tip of the knife over his skin, pretending to try the motion.

"Do it," he ordered.

I paused, fear and instinct telling me not to brutally ram the blade into him. Reminding myself that he was a god and would heal almost instantly, I stabbed the knife into him, shoving the blade as hard as I could under his ribs to reach a lung.

"Good girl," he breathed again, closing his eyes as he took a deep breath through his nose. The way his lips parted was so erotic I could barely focus on getting oxygen in my own lungs. The words leaving his lips were orgasmic, and my shivering had less to do with nerves and more to do with how turned on I was.

He reopened his eyes, and I quickly added an additional thanks to the powers that be for the fact that women didn't have the same issue of particularly visible arousal that men did. If I had a boner right now, it would be stabbing him harder than this knife.

I slowly slid the knife from him, tossing it to the ground next to me. The wound healed almost instantly, but he didn't move. I allowed myself to get used to having a man over me again. Hooking one of my legs around him, arching my back ever so slightly, I used my leg to pull myself closer to him.

"Jerrick didn't get this close to me…" I whispered, reaching a hand up to brush back his shaggy hair by his eyes before giving a playful tug.

He growled, a low rumbling noise at the lieutenant's name. "He'd better not get as close as he did again, if he values his life."

"My, my," I mused with a small tsk-ing noise, sounding more cool, collected, and confident than I had in months. "Do you ever think to ask what I want?"

"I don't think you want *him*." He leaned closer to my face, my fingers still holding his hair, pulling his face down toward me. I couldn't help focusing on his fangs. They really did make him look part vampire, and some deep part of me, the part that wanted to lick his blood from my fingers, wanted to bare my neck to him so he could bite me like one.

"Well, what do *you* know?" I teased. "Maybe I want you both?"

I couldn't believe it came out of my own mouth, and my cheeks immediately flamed with the thoughts of being in bed with both men, being pinned between them, both of their mouths on me. It wasn't something I'd ever thought of for myself, to be with more than one partner. Years ago, when I was a Christian, I believed having such thoughts at all was a sin. Surprisingly, I was okay with it now, even if it was a sin. The mental images my brain now flooded with had my whole body warming with a mix of embarrassment and desire. He stared deep into my eyes as his lip twitched up in a snarl. The intense eye contact continued as he tried to decide if I was joking. Hell, I was still deciding if that was a joke.

I couldn't help myself bursting out laughing at his serious face. "I'm fucking with you, wolf-man." I started to wiggle myself free from beneath him, already planning to go out to the pool deck and soak my sore muscles in the hot water.

"So, does that mean you admit to wanting me? Do you want me to be your boyfriend?" He purred the questions. His voice was somehow deadly and playful as he pushed my shoulder back to the ground. I was still pinned beneath him, but it felt less like training now and more like barely restraining whatever hormones demanded we get closer.

"Don't make me stab you again," I threatened, reaching for the knife. He caught my wrist and pinned it on the ground, firm but gentle enough that, if I really started struggling, I could get away from him. While being restrained made my heart jump with nerves, I also found it making me desperate to touch him, to continue being touched by him.

"I think you're starting to like putting that knife in me a little too much." He leaned down so his lips brushed mine as he spoke.

I gave in to the need for him and leaned up to press my lips against his.

My free hand found its way to his hair, pulling him closer as his arms slid under my shoulders. My leg on his hip tightened, using him to leverage myself closer as I kissed down his jaw to his neck. I sank my flat teeth into him, making him gasp.

"Oh Gods, Anais, don't do that…" he murmured. I could feel him twitching through his pants as I tangled my legs around him. His voice was begging for me to keep doing that.

I listened to the devil on my shoulder that bid me to bite him again, harder. I wanted to draw blood, to leave a visible mark on him. Some part of me wanted to claim him as mine, just as much as I wanted him to claim me.

"Anais." His desperate tone was filled with both pleasure and the strain of whatever control he was trying to maintain. I couldn't tell if he was begging me to stop or keep going, or both.

I lapped my tongue over the healing flesh before biting again, deep enough that a drop of sweet, hot blood touched my lips. I closed my lips around the tiny puncture wound my teeth left, trying to lap more blood as it started healing right away.

"Anais, stop!" he barked, yanking away from me before I got another taste. He was holding me an arm's length away now, watching me with wide eyes as we both sat, panting. He was shaking, his arms quivering as though it was a great effort to hold himself away from me despite his divine strength.

Something in me wanted to hiss at him and try to lap at the blood on his neck leaking from his quickly healing—almost healed—neck wound, but I didn't want to appear completely feral, even if I felt that way.

"I'm sorry," I whispered, my cheeks flushed with embarrassment. Why did I do that? What came over me? I was too old to not be able to stop myself. But I thought he liked it... He sounded like he liked it...

"We're done." He stood. "No more training today."

"I'm sorry, Fen, really, I didn't mean—" I pushed myself up, brushing myself off self-consciously.

He slid a hand into my hair and made a fist to firmly pull my head back, forcing me to look up at him. It was such an unusual way for him to touch me, rough compared to usual but still gentle enough that I wasn't scared by him.

"I didn't stop you because I didn't like it," he growled. "I stopped you because I liked it too much. You're not ready for what that does to me yet. I can't lose control, and you... You make me want to throw caution to the wind, *hjarta*." He watched my throat move as I swallowed, taking in his words. "Now, go inside before you wreck the rest of my self control."

CHAPTER 29

"D on't forget the ball tonight," Hellia reminded us at the breakfast table the next morning.

"Did Fen ask you to the ball?" Jerrick teased. I aimed a kick for his shins that he dodged with a dramatic flare.

"I was actually going to ask you." Fen smiled with over-exaggerated flirtation, batting his eyelashes at the lieutenant.

"Well, paint me polka dotted, I had no idea. I'm wearing blue, so make sure you match appropriately please. I hope you got me a nice corsage." He crossed his arms, leaning back in his chair until Ylfa made a motion as if to push him backward.

Scowling, he gave a flamboyant huff before his face broke into a grin.

Hellia rolled her eyes, smirking at me as she started to lift the newspaper once more before she paused. "Anais, you're welcome to pick a dress from my collection."

"I already got her one," Fen said.

I looked at Fen, shocked.

"You don't have to wear it, though. You can pick one of hers," he said quickly, his eyes rounding slightly at the expression I was wearing on my face.

My eyes flicked between them, and I nodded to Hellia. "I'll take a look."

"Come on. We'll leave these two lovers together." She stood, eyeing the men, who feigned innocence by staring at the table before they made eye contact and both started snickering.

I followed her from the room, glancing back to see Fen leaned back in his chair and watching me leave. Blush seared my cheeks, feeling him staring at me. Jerrick murmured something to him and Fen suddenly moved, swinging his arm across the table and stabbing a fork into the wood where Jerrick's hand was moments before. Jerrick roared with laughter and the two started bickering as Hellia led me out to the hall.

"They better not damage my table, stupid idiots." Hellia snorted.

"Are they always like that?" I asked.

"Always."

Her room was enormous, a window the length of an entire wall looking out over the city and fjord. She walked back toward a huge bathing area with a pool looking out over the incredible view and a closet the size of my room downstairs.

"Those are all the dresses. Feel free to try anything you like." She flopped down on a couch in the middle of the room. "There's a changing room down on the other end." She pointed.

"You've worn *all* of these?" I stared at the enormous collection, feeling like I was in a movie set closet.

"At least three or four times each. Perks of being twelve hundred years old." She shrugged.

I browsed for a while, looking through the stacks of dresses in every style, every fabric, every color, and every fashion era. I tried a black dress first, but it was too glam for this event. Hellia agreed it was too dark, so I moved on to the singular red one. I wasn't planning to try it on, but I couldn't help pausing to look at the deep crimson gown. It had Asgard written all over it, and I wonder where she had worn it before.

"Red isn't really your color. Or our color. That's from an old event; I need to get rid of it," she said, her face looking sour. She took it from the rack and threw it in the corner.

"Maybe this one?" She handed me a deep purple gown that was absolutely stunning. I took it, feeling the fabric. She helped me with the fluffy skirt and I admired it in the mirror.

"I love it." I ran my fingers over the amethyst tulle skirt.

"Take it. Can I do your hair later?" she asked, pausing as she reached out for my head.

"I'd love that." I smiled gratefully.

She grinned and started twisting my hair back, thinking of hairstyles as she looked in the mirror.

"How often do you have parties like this here?" I asked.

"Not very, but I enjoy them. I like inviting everyone here to the palace. It makes it feel warmer, more alive, even if it's not really." She started rifling through jewelry. "I also grew up in a house full of men, save for my mother. Ylfa was in training camp across Niflheim at that time, and there were only a few other girls in my training pack. It's nice to have another woman around who puts us on equal ground with those buffoons."

She sent me on my way with the dress and the promise that she would see me later for hair and makeup.

I could hear the bustle of people and music floating to my room from the main hall. Laughter, music, and cheery voices—it was so strange to hear those sounds in the realm of the dead. But it sounded like what Hellia said, warmth. Life. The sounds were so alive down there, so cheerful.

Walking to the mirror, I looked over the emerald green dress that had been left in the armoire for me; smooth and silky material fell in a gorgeous skirt, the top was a strappy tank-top style that showed off my freshly healed scar. The skirt flared slightly, covering my legs entirely, and I had to admit I felt sexy as I swished the skirt back and forth. Underneath were matching emerald slippers. It was simple but incredibly elegant, even with my jagged healing skin.

I'd wanted to stick with the dress I'd borrowed from Hellia, but after seeing what Fenrir picked, I couldn't resist putting it on. The emerald color made my eyes stand out and matched my skin tone perfectly. Plus a secret, very deep part of me I couldn't fully acknowledge couldn't wait to see his face when he saw it.

A knock at the door jerked me back to the room and away from the magical dress in the mirror.

"You look stunning." Hellia's voice was soft as the door snicked shut behind her.

"It's the one he picked," I said, looking slightly guilty, but she smiled broadly, dissipating all the nerves about my choice.

"It's a good pick, it looks amazing on you."

I nodded as I looked at myself in the mirror, trying to imagine hulking, dark Fenrir picking such a lovely dress. I couldn't picture it. Hellia pulled out a chair and had me sit before her while she brushed through my hair.

"I used to braid Fen's and Jorm's hair when they were little," she purred, stroking a brush through my long locks down my back. "When they would sit still, that is." She began twisting the hair around my face back so it was out of my eyes but still hung long down my back in loose curls and waves. I tried to imagine Fen when they were little, but that was just as difficult if not more than imagining him picking the dress.

She kept her eyes averted from the mirror as she worked, pulling back a large swath of hair partway through a metal ring adorned with gold metal leaves and foliage. Attached with a chain to the ring was a matching golden pin. She stuck the pin through the hair that was partway through the ring, securing it on the back of my head. I looked like a princess from a fairytale.

"Does he expect me to dance with him tonight?" I asked, watching her closely. Her face did not change as she inspected my hair before her eyes met mine in the mirror. Mag had made me dance, after he imprisoned me. I wasn't sure I was keen to do it again.

"I think he expects you to do whatever you want to do." Her voice was gentle, kind. I realized as I looked at her that she was warm despite her frigid appearance. She dearly loved her family, and that brought warmth to her face. "I actually think he might prefer if you wanted to hide out here all night; he's not the one for big parties. Jerrick, on the other hand…" She laughed to herself, shaking her head. "Jerrick is probably already drunk off his ass doing a jig somewhere."

"Jerrick didn't mention Talin before we came here," I frowned, wondering about the pair. "How long have they been together?"

"Well, they've been on and off for decades, but they've never been Fated," she said, adjusting the hair falling down my shoulder before reaching for the makeup on the counter.

"Fated? What does that mean?" I asked.

She paused, her eyes wide as she looked at me. She released a breath through clenched teeth.

"What? Should I know that or something?" I felt embarrassed.

"No, no, why would you?" she asked. Slowly, she returned to dabbing a brush in the blush palette. "Fated means it has been written in your Fate that you will fall in love with a specific person."

"Like, a Fated Mates trope in a book?" I wondered if she even read fantasy romance books the way I did. I blushed slightly as I thought about my embarrassing collection of fantasy romance books at home. I glanced down at my arm, where a tattoo of an open book was inked with three mountains growing from the pages, their peaks stretching toward three stairs.

"Exactly, like the universe decided it when you were born." She moved to my eyebrows, using a dark pencil to shape them. "When someone in Norse realms is Fated, it's woven into the tapestry of Fate by the Norns at the tree of life, Yggdrasil. We told you that gods lived long enough for their Fate to change, right? Your Fate is ongoing, your whole life. We have to check if they change every hundred years or so. Well, you don't have to, but I like to check on mine and my brothers'. Sometimes a Fated bond will develop before the pair meet, sometimes after—it's all dependent on the individuals."

She paused, looking at my tattoo also. "It's beautiful. What does it mean?"

I blushed deeply. "It's from one of my favorite book series. It's like a romantic fantasy..." I mumbled. Of course she didn't read those kinds of books, she's the Queen of Hell. She's got so many more important things to read.

"I love those kinds of stories," she said brightly. "Could you and Fen get me this one?" she asked, pointing to the tattoo.

"For sure, I'll get you all the books. There are a bunch."

"That would be great, thanks!" She sighed with a content smile as she brushed down a few fly away hairs on my head.

"Do you know anyone who has been Fated?" She paused, looking me over after her handiwork.

"Yes. It's not really mine to talk about though."

I lowered my eyes feeling a bit awkward asking. "Sorry, I didn't mean—"

"You didn't do anything wrong. It's just not mine to discuss." She offered one of her most winning smiles that showed how truly stunning she was in her human form. It instantly relieved the feeling that I'd pried too much.

"Do the Norns have my Fate?" I changed the subject.

"Yes, they do."

"Will you take me to see them?"

"Fen will, soon I hope. One of them is an asshole and I hate her, so I don't go visit them often." She winked at me in the mirror.

I just nodded. He probably would want to know if his Fate changed over the last several hundred years that he was locked away. Although, I was sure Hellia had filled him in, if she was keeping such close tabs on everyone in her family.

She clasped a delicate gold chain with a tiny moon pendant around my neck. Everything about the piece fit with the outfit.

"Thank you, Hellia." I looked beautiful, and I turned my head to try to admire the metal hair pin she had put on the back of my hair.

"You're welcome. I'll see you down there." She dipped her head and left me in the room alone.

With a deep breath, I set my shoulders back, and my heart hammered in my chest. The castle had gotten warmer the past few days. Hellia had more real fires lit throughout, and I didn't need the heavy winter cloaks indoors anymore. The door handle felt heavy, leaden in my hand as I hauled it open and stepped into the hallway.

CHAPTER 30

The dress danced around my legs, the silky-soft fabric ruffling as I walked down the hallway from my room. In that moment, alone in the hallway, fully in my right mind and in control, I couldn't keep the joyful smile from my face at the sound of the beautiful dress swishing.

Stopping to look up and down the hall and seeing I was alone, I twirled in the dress, letting the green fabric flare out around me. Only after allowing myself a moment more did I scold myself to stop spinning in the dress like a silly girl.

I paused at the corner, leaning around to look down the staircase at the crowd below. It was a full house, people everywhere dressed in finery of all colors. Hellia said this would be open to the whole of Helheim, and it appeared all of Helheim came. The area at the front doors was completely full, the crowd pouring into a ballroom I had yet to see. There were so many people, all calm and having fun, laughing, eating, drinking, dancing. A hand pressed against the wall next to my head, and I turned to see Fen leaning over me to peer around the corner.

He looked down at me, his eyes sweeping over the dress. A small smirk curved the corners of his lips as he devoured the sight of me in the garment he'd picked.

"You wore it," he purred.

"I didn't find anything I liked in Hellia's closet." A lie.

"You look like a dream."

Heat rose in my cheeks at the compliment. "Funny, when I've been stuck in a nightmare."

He just offered me a small smile before looking back out over the crowd of laughing, cheery people below. The music was floating from the ballroom. A giant, cavernous room with windows looking out over Helheim and the fjord on the ground level, it sat opposite the dining room and was anything but a nightmare just then. Nightmares happened behind closed eyes and were set in Asgard. And I wasn't trapped anymore. I shouldn't have said that.

"Do you feel like going down? You don't have to."

I paused at his words, realizing I felt an emotion rippling off of him. Anxiety. He was dressed in all black per usual, his gold revealed by rolled-up sleeves and a V-neck. Tonight he also wore a brooch on his outfit lapel, the design matching the florals on the ring in my hair. Among the arrangements was an emerald gemstone that matched the color of my dress perfectly. A dash of pink raced across my cheeks when I saw it flash. I wondered if he didn't want to go down there, if the crowd made him nervous or if maybe I did. It was hard to think I, or anything, could make this murderous wolf-man nervous.

"For a little while," I decided, watching all the people enjoying their evening below. He nodded, offered a hand—which I took—and then led me toward the stairs. As I was preparing to step down to the first step, a roar of cheering and applause startled me. I froze and looked out over the people cheering for Fenrir. I broke my hand from his and stepped back to let him have his moment, but he turned to me, confused.

"It's for you," he murmured, somehow audible through the loud applause that grew as Fen took my hand once more and pulled me to the front of the steps. I stood completely still, stunned by the noise and attention of all these people, all of his people. Dazed, I looked down at my hand, still in his as he kneeled before me. Why was he doing that? It looked like he was about to propose or something. There were so many people watching me, I couldn't breathe...

Jerrick was wobbling up the stairs, leaning heavily on the railing. He came to Fen's side and kneeled before me as well.

"Are you drunk already?" Fen hissed under his breath with a throaty chuckle.

"No, who would do that?" Jerrick hiccuped loudly, and a few girls at the front of the crowd giggled as he swayed with a smug grin at Fenrir.

Ylfa was here now, shoving Jerrick off kilter on his knee so he nearly tumbled sideways into Fen. She was dressed in a magnificent canary yellow dress, the color making her seem as though she was glowing. It clung to her generous curves, and the satin fabric shined brightly as summer in the dark hall. "Dumb, drunk idiot." She snorted, gathering her dress to kneel beside Jerrick in front of me. Jorm was on the other end, trying his very best not to look down the row at any of us, having not acknowledged anyone upon his arrival.

"Why are you all doing that?" I hissed, about to rip my hand from Fen's. My heart was pounding so loudly I was sure everyone in the room could hear it, even over the noise of the crowd. My blood roared in my ears, and I felt like I was starting to gasp for breath, darkness creeping into the edges of my vision. He gently pulled my hand so I was standing next to him.

"Hellia." Fen nodded to the hallway we had come from, where Hellia was now walking in the shadows, nearly about to be in the light of the party.

"Oh," I gasped, remembering she was a queen. I began to hike up the dress so I could kneel alongside him. I wobbled, still feeling a bit lightheaded.

"No, you stand," he whispered, stopping me and taking my hand. He placed it on his shoulder as I stood next to him. He was so tall, his shoulder was still at chest height for me. "You're alright," he assured me gently, soothing my thudding heart, coaxing it to slow toward a regular pace.

I waited nervously as Hellia came toward us. When she came into the light, I could see she was wearing a light cherry-blossom-pink dress that matched her light features so well she looked like a fairy of wintery spring. She wore a dark obsidian crown, contrasting the soft pink of her dress. She paused before Jorm. He took her hand, bringing it to his forehead. Too soft for anyone else to hear, she said something to him before he let go and she moved to Ylfa. Ylfa took her hand, repeating the ritual, and then Hellia moved to Jerrick, who suddenly looked stone cold sober as he took her hand.

On Fen, she paused after he let go of her hand. She whispered something to him that was long, and we all waited before he nodded to her. She smiled fondly before looking at me. I lifted my hand, prepared to greet her the same way the others had.

"I don't expect you to do that; you owe no allegiance to me." She whispered, "Can I hug you, though? For saving my brother?" Blushing at this special treatment, I nodded and pulled her in for a deep hug. She was freezing cold, like hugging a huge ice sculpture. She squeezed me tightly and whispered in my ear with icy breath before letting go. "Thank you."

The crowd exploded with cheers and people jumped with excitement. It reminded me of a high school prom. Hellia let go, giving my shoulders an extra squeeze. She smiled at me with gratitude before turning to the crowd and descending halfway down the stairs, pausing to address the people before her.

"Thank you all for joining us to celebrate my brother's return. Please enjoy everything, and take with you as much food as you like when you leave tonight. If you catch my brother drinking, make sure it's a double in celebration. If you catch my lieutenant drinking"—she turned to look at Jerrick, who gave her a double thumbs up and a cheesy smile—"then gods help us all." Everyone laughed, and Jerrick rolled his eyes sarcastically. "Let's party!" She ended with a laugh, and everyone cheered as she descended the rest of the way into the crowd to begin meeting eager party-goers.

Fen rose, and I let my hand fall from his shoulder as he towered over me once more. He offered his hand to me and I took it, following him down the grand staircase into the crowd. They parted for us as we walked side by side through to the ballroom. Though the castle itself was dark and ominous, the ballroom was warm and full of life. Real fires burned on the candles in all the chandeliers, and music filled the air as people joined together on a dancefloor. The smell of food wafted from the other side of the room, making my mouth water.

Jerrick came by at the same moment someone stopped Fen to talk. The Lieutenant began tugging me from Fen's hold. I saw Fen cast a sideways glance, taking note of where I was going and who I was going with before he let go of me reluctantly. Jerrick handed me a glass to fill from one of the literal *fountains* of wine decorating the wall, one with red, one with white. Choosing red, I filled my glass and turned back to the party.

I glanced at Jerrick by my side. He was making glaring eye contact with someone across the room. Jorm leaned against the wall in the shadows, watching us with his serpentine eyes. Jerrick raised an eyebrow and jutted his chin toward the World Serpent, inviting him over. Jorm's eyes flicked toward me for only a fraction of a second before he slunk off.

"Don't mind him," Jerrick said as he rolled his eyes, turning back to refill his wine. "He's got a stick up his ass, but I promise he'll warm up, as much as his cold-blooded heart will allow."

I nodded, taking a deep drink of my wine without considering that the alcohol of the gods might be different from what I was used to. The effects hit me immediately, making me feel as though I'd had a couple drinks after just one sip. I took another deep drink, watching the lights become fragments and the colors grow more vivid around me.

"So," Jerrick turned to me with a smug look. "You're wearing the dress Fen picked? It's beautiful on you."

My face flushed as I looked down at the beautiful green fabric clothing me. I brushed my fingers over the skirt, loving the silken feeling of the fabric under my fingers.

"He has good taste," I murmured.

"He does." Jerrick smiled at me before tipping back the rest of his wine.

"I'm sorry you got in trouble yesterday," I mumbled, taking another drink against my better judgment. If I kept up at this pace, I wouldn't make it through the evening. "I know you were just helping me, and he doesn't have any right to be that way with you—or anyone."

He shook his head. "I was out of line. I got carried away with your training, and it is I who should be apologizing to you."

I opened my mouth to argue more, but suddenly I felt Fen's hand on my back, and Talin slid along Jerrick's side like a cat. She was wearing a beautiful robin's-egg colored dress and stiletto heels, but she was still no match for Jerrick's height.

When I looked up at Fen over my shoulder, I felt the alcohol making my head heavy, the room starting to spin. "What is this stuff?" I asked, my words slurring as I looked down into the red liquid.

"Wine from Olympus. Hellia likes it imported." Jerrick grinned, pulling Talin close and leaning down to murmur something in her ear that had her chiming laugh ringing all around us.

"It's stronger than your human liquor," Fen warned me. "Be careful, *hjarta*."

"Too late for that." I giggled, taking a small sip. I was already drunk.

Fen chuckled, making me blush. "Dance with me?" He held his hand out for me to join Jerrick and Talin on the dance floor.

Feeling brave and warmed by the alcohol, I took his hand and let him pull me on to the dance floor. Sweeping me into his arms, he pressed our palms together, fingers intertwining on one hand. I could feel others' eyes on us, watching as he began leading me around the ballroom.

"Why are they staring at me?" I whispered. It felt as though all eyes in the room were on us now, everyone pausing their conversation to turn their attention to where he expertly twirled me so my dress flared out.

"Because you're stunning, my *hjarta*."

He twirled me again and then caught me before I lost my balance. I had to hold back that giddy smile from when I was in the hallway earlier; it was threatening to return to my lips in front of all these people. Looking up into his eyes—almost having to crane my neck to do so—the rest of the room melted away, and it was only us in the hall.

"*Your* hjarta?" I repeated his words. "I've told you I'm not your property. You don't own me." My accusing voice was soft, and my heart was hammering in my chest.

"I know," he purred back. "I want to be yours as much as you are mine."

Several hours into the party, the room was still spinning around me, encouraged by the wine and several rounds of dancing. I stumbled, distracted by the lights and Fen's eyes. He caught me and lifted me off my feet for a moment before setting me back down. A drunken giggle escaped my lips and his eyes widened to the size of dinner plates at me as he grinned at me, making me giggle more. It felt good to laugh just a little; I hadn't for so long. I covered my laugh with my hand, thinking how loud it sounded again. Fen reached out, gently pulling my hand down, away from my face.

"Don't, *hjarta*," he reminded me. His hold on my wrist was gentle, but I didn't try to break free. He was leaning in, smiling back at me, and was going to kiss me in front of all these people—

"I'm taking her. You don't deserve her," Jerrick slurred, nearly crashing into Fen. Fen frowned, making sure he was upright before stepping back. Moment ruined.

"You're right, I don't deserve her." He winked at me, making me smile with a blush, tucking my hair behind my ear.

Jerrick whisked me away toward the table of food and more wine, both of us reaching for some cheese-and-ham-filled pastries along with another glass of wine. Fen watched us go and then disappeared into the crowd. Except he never really disappeared; he was too tall to ever truly be out of sight.

"So you and Talin?" I asked Jerrick as I looked at the beautiful light elf chatting with her friends, who all looked incredibly similar to her. I was thankful they were all wearing different dresses and hairstyles.

"Yeah?" he asked around the pastry stuffed in his mouth.

"What's the deal?" I prodded.

"You're being nosey." He narrowed his eyes on me.

"You're nosey all the time. It's only fair." I shrugged as he barked a laugh.

"That is fair," he agreed, drinking deeply from yet another glass. This time it was filled with a deep brown liquid over ice. "I just haven't met anyone yet that makes me feel something different yet. I have fun, but Fe—my friend who's been Fated... He said he felt something change when he met his Fated, so I guess I'm waiting for that, if I ever get the chance for it." He took another swig from his glass. "I like Talin though, she's beautiful and intelligent. I wouldn't mind if we ended up Fated." He filled another glass, and I questioned how much of the extra strong booze he could drink compared to me.

"What about you, though?" He turned on me.

"What about me?" I stepped back defensively.

"Did you have a boyfriend at home?" He flicked an eyebrow up at me.

I stared out the dark windows for a moment, remembering Dan. It felt like ages ago, in my apartment in Canada. On Earth. Dan was never really my boyfriend. Mag had been at the time, but definitely not anymore.

"No. Just my best friend, Kerri."

"What're they like?" he asked as he gulped several mouthfuls of wine.

"She..." I trailed off, thinking of my red-haired firecracker of a friend. "She would hate you. You would love annoying her." He laughed loudly, and I couldn't help the smile on my face.

"I really miss her," I added softly, and Jerrick nodded, his brow furrowed with sympathy.

"I can't wait to meet her someday," he offered back, his voice hushed too. He was giving me hope. I didn't know if I could stomach it.

"Nice to see you all, and meet you Anais. Be good, kids." Mrs. Lutvega, a beautiful silver-haired elf with long, sharp ears like Talin's and smile wrinkles around her eyes, pulled the door of the kitchen open to excuse herself. That left Jerrick and Talin—who were near straddling one another the moment Mrs. Lutvega left the room—Hellia, Ylfa, Fen, and I sitting at the table, with me closest to the fire. We'd come in here after the ballroom cleared out, scrounging for leftover snacks and wine.

"Jer, take it upstairs," Ylfa snapped.

"Fine," he said when he managed to disentangle his tongue from Talin long enough to respond. She slid from his lap, her fluid movements emphasizing her small frame in comparison with his. "We'll see you all when we emerge from this party recovery coma." He escorted her out with a hand on her back.

"What does a light elf–wolf baby even look like?" Ylfa threw a look at Hellia.

She just shrugged. "Beats me. Maybe one day we'll find out."

I tuned out as they kept talking, my eyelids getting heavier and heavier, and slowly I found myself falling asleep in the brief periods when my eyes closed for a too-long blink. The pull of sleep was too strong, and my feet ached from dancing. The kitchen was just so warm, comfortable, and Fen was right here; sleep was all too enticing.

The next thing I knew, I was sleepily blinking in the kitchen. The seats across from me were vacant and slanted sideways. I slowly lifted my head and realized I'd fallen asleep leaning on Fen's arm.

"Oh, I'm sorry," I mumbled as I sat upright, trying to blink back the urge to crawl into his lap and curl up to fall back asleep.

"Don't be, *hjarta*." His voice was gentle, and I wondered how long he'd been sitting with me sleeping on him.

He made a move as if to stand, and I found myself reaching out to hold his arm down, keeping him seated next to me. Turning to me with a raised questioning brow, he settled back on the seat.

"I wanted to say thank you, for tonight." My voice was small, and he leaned in, hanging on my every word. "I shouldn't have said it was a nightmare earlier..." I still felt a pang of guilt from my comment. I pushed my legs under myself so I was kneeling on my seat, allowing me to gain the necessary height to be eye to eye with him. "It's not, and tonight wasn't, and... And you're not either, Fen."

He swallowed, watching me getting closer, not moving as I braced myself and leaned in toward his face. I placed my lips gently against his cheek, and in the mere seconds I was in contact with his skin, it went from its usually comfortable warmth to burning hot. Even in my drunken stupor, I took notice of the red flush spreading across his cheeks. I did have to admit I loved the effect I could have on him.

I couldn't help myself; a grin broke out on my face at the blushing giant next to me. He smiled in return, lifting his arm from my grasp to brush his fingers along my jaw, gazing intently into my eyes. I wasn't sure how long we sat like that, mesmerized by one another and studying each other's faces. He sat still as I ran my fingers over every inch of him, my fingertips tracing his jaw and nose, the stubble on his face, the curve of where his neck met his shoulder.

Being the drunken mess I was, there was no way for me to hide my ogling, and he seemed oddly pleased with it. His hands found my wrist as I touched him, following where I led for a long while before slowly dragging my hand down to his chest, letting it rest over his heart. My eyes flicked up to his as I felt his heart beating under my palm, and the pleading, longing look returned to his eyes.

CHAPTER 31

A day later, I'd recovered enough from the party to stumble my way down to lunch. Or brunch, by the smells of coffee and pastry wafting from the kitchen. The castle was silent, and I was sure I'd be the only one there until I walked in to find Hellia at her usual place, sitting at the head of the table reading her paper, her feet kicked up across the corner of the table. Fen was already there too, drinking coffee and looking at a page of Hellia's paper. He looked up the moment I walked in, rising to stand and pull out the chair next to him as an invitation.

"It's quiet," I observed as I took in Jerrick and Ylfa's empty chairs across from us. Hellia lowered her newspaper, looking pleased to see me. Her eyes flicked to Fen's momentarily, and I wondered how long they'd been awake down here together. Wondered what they'd talked about, if he told her about anything that happened between us. He pushed my chair in before taking his seat next to me.

"Ylfa is out at the Hell Hounds camp today, and Jerrick and Talin have been missing since the ball," she filled me in as Fen poured a cup of coffee for me. I couldn't help the red creeping up my neck as I noticed he also added exactly my preferred amount of milk and sugar to it before handing it to me.

"Thanks," I mumbled, taking the cup with both hands.

After the kitchen the other night, he carried me upstairs in my dress and dropped me off at my door. I drunkenly demanded he kiss me goodnight, and he obliged eagerly before sending me off to bed. I thought about that kiss, dreamed about that kiss in between nightmares of Asgard the entire time I slept. The more I tried to resist what drew me to him, the more he pulled me in. I spent hours reliving the way his hands fit on my waist, pulling me closer; the way he needed to lean down to kiss me, his tongue on my lips and in my mouth; how he always seemed like he could never get enough, like he was always desperate for more of me. It was addictive. I wanted to invite him in to stay the night, but I just couldn't bring myself to voice the words.

My eyes slid to him now, trying to get my heart to beat normally again after the memory flashed through my head. His hair was messy, falling into his eyes. He wore a long sleeve black shirt, and somehow, covering his muscular arms made him all the more drool-worthy. My gaze swept down to his hand resting on the table, the veins criss crossing his knuckles under his skin, and the memory of that hand touching me made my skin prickle. *His sister is right there, for God's sake. Get a hold of yourself, woman,* I scolded myself.

I saw his head turn fractionally, and I forced my eyes back to the coffee in my hands. I could feel him looking at me, as if he was aware I was just checking him out. It made my cheeks burn hotter, and I scrambled for something to talk about.

"The ball was fun," I commented, putting my lips on the rim of my cup to sip the hot drink. Hopefully, I could blame my reddened cheeks on the steam from the cup.

"It was." Hellia smiled happily before returning to her paper. "I love throwing parties; we'll have to do some more after all this Odin business is sorted."

"Hellia used to go to Midgard in the 18th century for parties like that all the time. Ylfa and Jerrick could barely keep her in the castle long enough to give directives," Fen teased, but she didn't look at all ashamed with her grin.

"It was so fun. I love ballroom dancing." She reached for a plate of sandwiches across from her.

"What was it like?" I couldn't help my curiosity.

"Amazing—the dresses, the colors, the music. I loved going to the Chateau de Versailles too, in France. It was so amazing when they had parties there, but the politics and inhumanity of humans ruined it most of the time. I wanted to bring the woman I was with, and Ylfa, but so many times the humans wanted to turn them away for the color of their skin and the fact that we were together as two women." She shook her head.

"I hypnotized so many people just to get them over those facts. The way humans treat each other is truly abhorrent."

"Kebechet is an Egyptian Goddess, the daughter of Anubis," Fen added.

"I didn't realize you had a girlfriend, Hellia. My best friend on Earth also has a girlfriend." I wasn't entirely sure, since Kerri said she was talking with Janine again before I left, but that was a month ago.

If Hellia could blush, I imagined she would be now. "Um, well… I've had girlfriends, and boyfriends too." She put a hand to her bloodless cheek.

Fen's eyebrow raised with curiosity, as if this was new information.

"I dated Bahlam for a while," she admitted. Her eyes flickered from his to mine, to the table, and then back to mine.

"Of the Xibalba?" he asked, sounding somewhat incredulous. "That's the Mayan underworld," he added to me before nodding for her to continue.

She bit her lip and nodded. "It's over now, though. I haven't seen him in several hundred years. I haven't seen Kebe in … maybe ten."

"Why?" I asked, and I immediately regretted prying when she already looked nervous. Her shoulders dropped away from her ears, and her eyes flicking back toward Fen.

"Bahl and I disagree on ruling, and I wasn't into his style, so I left. But Anais, you should see his realm someday. The jungle and the mist—it's incredible." She brightened at the memories.

"What about Kebechet?" Fen asked sternly.

Hellia swallowed hard. "Kebe... I just, I don't know... Kebe and I had a fight. It was a stupid fight." She looked at her plate, at the sandwich with only a few bites from it.

"Why don't you talk to her?" I asked, my heart panging at her sad expression. Hellia must've missed her last night at the party. Although, I also thought a decade must feel like nothing more than a week or so to immortals.

"I don't know. I haven't been ... strong enough to do it." Her words had my stomach twisting for her again.

"You're plenty strong, Hel. You can do anything you want to, or don't want to. And you have us behind you always." Her brother gave her a reassuring smile. "We love you."

She smiled gratefully. "Thank you."

The meal conversation was light from there on. I watched the snow beat against the window in the late morning light. It was blizzarding today, perfect for a cozy day in the bath. After a while, Hellia excused herself for work, and Fen left the hall when I did, following me from the room toward the stairs.

"What are your plans today, *hjarta*?" he asked me.

"I was just planning to be lazy around here, unless you had something in mind?" I looked up at him with large doe eyes. It was getting harder and harder to conceal my attraction to him.

"I was thinking about reading in the room upstairs, actually. I wanted to see if you would join me." The thought of him reading had my heart skipping beats. I loved reading, and I'd never met a man who liked it too. A reading *date*? I pinched myself on my arm to make sure I wasn't dreaming right now.

"I'd love to, but you'll have to get me a book... I can't read yours and Hellia's. I've tried, but I can't read whatever those symbols are." I shrugged at him.

"Of course." He immediately looked guilty. "I'll get you anything you want. I'm sorry I haven't offered before now. You need only ask for anything you want, Anais. You know that, right?"

"It's okay, really. But I will take you up on that offer when we get there. I want a book, my pajamas, a butterscotch latte, and what is the castle's drug policy?" I flashed a devilish grin at him.

He was fixing me with a bemused smirk when something unseen caught his attention.

"Wait." A look of concentration creased his brow before his face broke into a mischievous grin. "Do you hear that?"

"Hear what?" I frowned, straining my ears. I heard some muffled noises I couldn't quite distinguish. "What is that?"

He just chuckled. "Follow me."

I concentrated on the noises, trying to make out what I was hearing as he led me down a corridor of the castle I wasn't very familiar with but knew led to Hellia's room. Keeping quiet, we snuck around a corner into an empty hall. The noises were getting louder now but were still too muffled to distinguish. He smiled at me, mischief flaring in his eyes as he leaned his head against a door and listened to what was happening on the other side. Lifting a finger to his lips, he gestured for me to join him, leaning my head against the door to listen in.

"Fucking gods," Jerrick moaned loudly on the other side of the door. Now that we were closer, I could hear the noise of furniture—a bed, I imagined—moving, squeaking, and thudding against a wall. I could hear another person panting and humming as the sexual noises continued. Covering my mouth with a hand to remind myself to be quiet, I looked up into Fen's eyes, seeing his shoulders shaking with silent laughter. I had to swallow my own giggle as we stared at each other, listening.

"That's right." Talin's familiar voice was an unusually deeper sultry version. "You like getting fucked like this, don't you?"

"Yes," Jerrick whimpered.

Fen's eyes flared and his fangs poked out, driving into his bottom lip to keep quiet.

Talin said something too quiet for me to hear, but it made Fen put a hand to his mouth and squeeze his eyes shut with the effort of remaining silent. I could hear both panting on the other side of the door, and by the sounds the furniture was making, someone was moving rhythmically.

"Fucccckk," Jerrick hissed.

"Mmhm," Talin purred. "Yes, come with my cock in you, baby."

I slapped my other hand over my mouth to stifle the squeak that rose in my throat as I finally understood exactly what we were listening to. She was fucking him with a strap-on dildo! What did Kerri tell me that was called? Pegging?! I could tell I was blushing visibly now, trying not to make a sound as I thought about the tiny, slim elf and tall, athletic werewolf together.

"Uhh, Taaah-huh," he groaned, obviously overcome with ecstasy. It was my turn to bite my lip, not because I was about to laugh, but because I was suddenly feeling a pulsing between my legs. When my eyes next met Fen's, I swallowed, crossing my legs as casually as possible to try to dissuade the physical desire that grew as we listened to Jerrick and Talin's pleasure.

I dropped my gaze, embarrassed. But when I did, I noticed he was getting turned on too. I gasped, and his finger hooked under my chin, tilting my head back up to look into his eyes. The image of him standing naked in front of me the other day flashed in my head, and I licked my lips inadvertently. He growled, a low rumbling noise, as his eyes followed the movement of my tongue.

"Did you hear something at the door?" Talin asked.

"I actually did, hold on." We heard Jerrick getting up from the bed,

"Oh shit," Fen whispered, grabbing my arm and pulling me down the hall just as the door swung open. Jerrick stuck his head out, looking the opposite direction as we rounded the corner. Fen pulled me against him, and I clapped my hand back over my mouth, holding my breath, pressing myself as flat as I could against his chest as we listened to Jerrick step into the hall and take several deep inhales of air.

"Fen," he growled at the empty hall. "I know you're there. I can fucking smell you, dude."

"Maybe he wants to join us," Talin chimed from the bedroom.

Fen's eyes grew round, and he looked down at me, red creeping up his neck and across his entire face. He clamped a hand over his mouth as his shoulders shook with stifled laughter.

"Is that true?" Jerrick asked the hallway, teasingly. "Don't be shy, buddy. Talin and I already talked about it. We're cool."

A small snort and choking noise escaped me at Fen's bewildered expression.

"You too, Anais," Jerrick called down the hall, mockingly. "I can smell that you're into it from here." My face must be as bright as a neon light now.

"He can smell WHAT?!" I hissed at Fen.

Fen's hand slammed over my lips, pulling my head against his chest. He was biting his lip to keep from laughing, cradling me close to his body. It set me aflame all over again. Immediately, I started plotting how to kill both of these evil men later.

"Jer, come back," Talin's voice chimed, and we listened to his feet turning on the hall carpet, moving back toward his bedroom. He muttered a curse word under his breath as he must've made eye contact with her.

"Gods, Talin, you can't wait ten seconds before being an absolute fre—" The door slammed loudly in the hallway, muffling his words to be indistinguishable again.

My eyes darted up to Fen's. As we made eye contact and his hand dropped away from my mouth, we both burst into loud cackling laughter. I wanted to lean into him, to feel his arms around me, but he stood upright, grabbed my hand, and led me from the hall in the opposite direction toward our rooms.

"He sounded a little too excited about the prospect of you joining him." I giggled, following as he led me up a winding stairwell.

"Stupid idiot is always making jokes like that," he muttered with a shake of his head.

"Do you think he wants you to fuck him, or he wants to watch Talin fuck you?" I teased as we climbed.

"It doesn't matter, because neither will be happening." He was starting to get flustered at my teasing for once. I couldn't help being proud of making him be the awkward one rather than me.

"Jerrick sounded like he really enjoyed it," I commented. "You don't know, maybe Talin's really good at that."

He screwed up his face, looking skeptically at me. "I don't care if she's any good. I really don't want her—or him—to fuck me." We both burst out laughing again at his words.

"You don't know you like it until you try it." I wiped away a tear from all the laughing. He pushed open the door to the room, revealing the white-out conditions beyond the windows, completely blocking any view other than the falling snow.

"Well, I don't want to try that with those two right now." He scrunched his nose at the thought, holding the door for me to walk in first.

"Talin sounded like she wants both of you." I giggled, and the pulse between my legs reminded me of my thoughts of the same thing.

"I don't think you're one to talk." He flicked an eyebrow up at me.

"Can he really smell … *that* well?"

"What?" he asked, flopping down on the bed. "You mean, can he smell your arousal?"

My cheeks immediately burned as I sat next to him, drawing my legs up princess style as I sat next to him. I reached out and stroked his hair, willing my face to cool.

"Yeah, like, could he smell if I was turned on?" I chewed my lip.

"Yes." He rolled over on all fours and put an arm around me, pulling me toward him. My hands went out against his chest as I squeaked in surprise. The salacious look in his eyes had my core pulsing again and my body buzzing where his hand was now firmly planted on my back. "I can smell it too," he rumbled in my ear, and he took a deep inhale through his nose, his lips parted.

I swallowed and tried to remain calm as my fingers brushed over his muscular shoulders through his shirt.

"Oh? Like… Like right now you can?" My voice wavered with excitement slightly, and his grin was getting wider.

"Right now, in the hall downstairs, when we were training the other day…"

We slammed into each other's lips at the same time, moaning with pleasure as the pressure in my chest both started to relieve and intensify. Our kiss was harsh, desperate, and my hands went to his neck, pulling him in deeper.

"Take this off," I panted, plucking at his shirt. It was gone in a shadow the next instant. "Now"—I was giddy with tension at my next instruction but forced my voice to be cool and smooth—"take this off." I plucked at my own sweater this time. He looked at me for a moment, confirming it was what I wanted before his hand slid under the edge, making me shiver with anticipation. I still wore my leggings, and he was wearing his usual dark pants.

Instead of disintegrating the sweater, he let me get used to his hand on my ribs and hips before slowly sliding it up over my head to reveal my bra. My skin pricked as the warm sweater was removed, but his warm hands on me were a welcome replacement. Even more welcome were the kisses he was now placing along my collarbone.

"And take that one off," I instructed, my voice barely more than a whisper when his lips met my bra strap. He lifted an eyebrow at me but didn't question. Sliding the straps down my shoulders first, he leaned back up to kiss my lips while he undid the clasp and slid the garment down my arms.

He tossed it away, throwing it somewhere behind us before kissing down my chin and neck. My breath was becoming uncatchable now, my chest heaving as he took one of my breasts in his hand. His fangs scraped my skin, careful not to knick me, sending shivers racing up my spine. When he sucked one of my nipples into his mouth with a happy hum, I let my eyes flutter closed, leaning my head back to enjoy the feeling of his touch.

He was rumbling with a noise like a purr as he switched to the other side, making me gasp in response. My fingers found their way to his hair, squeezing his neck, my nails biting into his skin. Everything about us was slow, pleasurable, and left me ready for more of him. When I opened my eyes again, his were closed. He was enjoying the moment just as much as I was.

I moaned softly at the sight of him. His eyes were heavy with lust when he opened them and looked at me, a trail of saliva dripping from his mouth to my nipple, my breast still in his hand. His tongue swiped across his lips as he crawled up to kiss me deeply, his fingers dipping between my thighs. He seemed to know just where to put his expert fingers to set me on fire. The first stroke through my pants had me flaming instantly. The second stroke built me up at an insanely rapid pace, and the third stroke had me at climax already.

"I—ohhh!" I whimpered as I toppled over the edge. "Fffah-hhkk." I couldn't form a coherent word as I arched my back under his touch, my eyes rolling in my head as I ground against his fingers. There was a moment of silence. I couldn't see straight, but I could hear my own ragged breath mingling with his.

"Did you just—"

"Oh my God!" I squeaked, my daze lifting. I grabbed one of the many throw pillows to bury my flushed face in, hiding me from his view. I felt him tug the corner of the pillow up, ducking under to look at me. He had a proud smirk on his face.

"Through your pants and everything?" He was practically glowing.

"Shut uuup," I groaned, trying to claw the pillow back down to cover the renewed blush burning my cheeks.

"I can't believe you're that into me." The pride radiating from him was palpable. Even under the pillow.

"Shut up!" I barked, "That's not what it is!" That's exactly what it was.

"What is it then?" he purred, just as confident as ever, tugging at the pillow I wasn't letting go of.

"I just haven't, you know, haven't been touched like that in months, and I'm just really sensitive," I babbled as I peeked at him over the pillow. He was still wearing the smug expression, completely pleased with himself, and he snorted a laugh when our eyes met again.

"Stop!" I aimed a playful kick at him.

"I'm not doing anything!" he barked.

"You're laughing at me," I pouted.

"I'm not, I swear." He chuckled. "I just like that you like me. And you're cute when you try to deny it."

"Ugh!" I aimed another kick at him and he dodged. When he sprang back up, he tackled me sideways, rolling so I was sitting on his hips. His erection pressed against my slit, renewing my desire. His cheeks flushed as I gently ground against him, making him twitch eagerly.

"We can still fuck, if you want," I whispered as I licked my lips, feeling a lusty haze descending on me. I was feeling empowered in whatever relationship we had so far, and he was right—I couldn't deny how much I wanted him anymore. My brows knit together as I watched his smile falter with my words, interrupting the desire welling in me. I immediately stopped the movement against him.

"I don't want to just '*fuck*', Anais." He turned serious, seeming slightly upset by my words. He pushed himself up on his elbows, fixing me with an intense stare. "I don't know how to make it more clear than to say it: I am falling in love with you."

"*Love?*" I whispered. "You're falling in *love* with me?" My stomach lurched.

"Since the moment I met you." He took my hand in one of his, bringing it to his lips. "Since the moment you bled, without question, to make sure I was free."

I wasn't sure what to make of this, wasn't sure if he expected me to respond.

"So, you don't want to fuck because—" I voiced my thoughts slowly as my brain worked through the fact he just said he *loved* me.

"Because I want to worship you properly the first time. The way you deserve to be worshiped, *hjarta*. But I can't do that until we go visit the Norns." He was starting to sound slightly exasperated by the last sentence. He kissed down my wrist, his fangs scraping my skin gently. I wasn't sure if the impatience in his voice was from talking with me or agitation at having to see the Norns. All I did know was something inside me was begging for him to bite me with those fangs and suck my blood like a vampire.

"Why do we have to see the Norns?" I frowned.

"I haven't been in eight hundred years... I need to make sure, uh, nothing about my Fate has changed." He needed to go have a check-up at the love doctor first?

"You think you're Fated to someone?" My eyebrows slid up my forehead.

"I don't know." He looked away, his expression almost seeming guilty. "I just want to know, want *you* to know, before we erm, *fuck*." He cleared his throat, his eyes not meeting mine again. I slid off of him to the side, suddenly feeling self conscious.

My frown deepened. "Oh... Okay."

"We'll go tomorrow afternoon, just us." He brushed my hair back behind my ear. My stomach started turning as my mind flashed through the Aesir Goddesses who he could be Fated to. What if it was Erika? Or Tora? Would fate be that cruel?

"Hey." His voice drew me back to the present. "Don't worry. It's not going to be anything bad."

"I wasn't worrying," I huffed.

"Your eyebrows do this little crease thing when you start to worry about something—"

"What?!" I squawked. "How would you even know that?"

"Anais, I've been around you for a while now, and I've seen you worry over plenty of things." He was chuckling and stroking his fingers through my dark waves. "What are you worrying about, hm?"

I couldn't tell him I was worried that he would be Fated to someone, that just when I'd started trusting this guy, maybe even starting to fall for him, he would be taken away. Yet it was the way my life had worked so far; when things start to feel too good to be true, life takes a nosedive and breaks my heart into a bajillion pieces. It happened before. When I thought I'd found my community at church, it turned out Pastor Bryan was a bigot and raped my best friend. When I thought I'd found a guy who really liked me, he turned out to be a power hungry god who abused me. Now the guy I had just started trusting was possibly going to be taken from me.

He was right. It's better to know now before I like him too much and it hurts even more.

"Nothing," I muttered. *Liar*, I said to myself internally.

"Liar," he echoed, fixing me with narrowing eyes.

I was shocked when he repeated my thoughts out loud.

"What if you're fated to one of the Aesir goddesses? That would be awful…" My voice trailed. Surely he'd already thought about that.

"That won't happen. Don't worry about that." He smiled with a flirty wink, trying to be reassuring as he caressed my cheek. He sounded overly confident, and skepticism crept into my mind. "How do you know about being Fated, anyway?"

"Hellia told me."

His smile disappeared. "What did she tell you?"

"Just that the Norns weave it into the tapestry of Fate. And that no one gets to pick who they're Fated to, so how do you know it won't be an Aesir? What if it's Tora? It has to be a divine being, doesn't it?"

I was physically drawing away from him now, worried if I kept touching his bare skin, I'd develop feelings too strong for him, and it would break me entirely if it turned out he was Fated to someone.

"Tora would've tortured me with that information in Asgard if it was her. So unless we've been Fated in the last month, and she and Mag are being especially quiet for some reason rather than use that information as ammunition, I don't think so." His logic was sound and soothed my anxiety.

"That's true."

We sat in silence for another minute, him watching me, me watching the snow outside the windows. I felt like he was on the edge of telling me the secret, the one he'd been keeping the whole time. Suddenly, I felt too fragile to receive it.

His arms encircled my shoulders, slowly and carefully wrapping around me, pulling me against his chest. My bare skin touching him was too much, but I couldn't help leaning into him. With one hand, he rubbed my shoulder gently before sliding down to entwine his fingers with mine. He held his other hand out flat in front of me, ready to summon anything.

"Whatever you want, *hjarta*," he whispered. He leaned down to kiss me on the head and down to my cheek.

CHAPTER 32

"Do we have to take a seam? There's no way to hike there?" I already dreaded the feeling of traveling in the seams of the bifrost. I hated the compressed feeling, like I couldn't breathe as we descended into a freefall between realms. I wanted any other way out.

"Don't worry, it gets better each time you do it." Fen gave me a reassuring smile as I followed him and Jerrick. We'd just arrived at the gate to Niflheim, so Fen and I could take a seam to Yggdrasil. "I won't let you go," he promised.

His reassurance soothed my hammering heart.

"Fen, come here." Hellia called him to the side, giving me a tight-lipped smile before pulling him a few more meters out of my hearing range.

"Here's a silver knife." Jerrick handed the blade to me, wrapping my fingers around it. "It will severely injure anyone you stab with it. It won't kill a god unless you get a critical shot, but it will injure anyone severely. Anyone you meet out there is going to be stronger than you. This is really dangerous; you need to stay with Fen in case he has to bring you back here. No matter what, okay?" I nodded, swallowing hard and feeling sweat form on my palms as I waited.

"You're an idiot!" Hellia's conversation with Fen was getting heated, and she crossed her arms as she yelled at him in anger. She shook her head and glared at her brother, who was glaring right back at her, his jaw tensing.

I looked at Jerrick. "What is that about?"

"He's an idiot." Jerrick shrugged with a smirk. "Can't argue with her on that."

"I told you to do this before now! This is going to end badly!" Hellia continued shouting at Fen. He rolled his eyes at her and spun away, storming back towards us. She glared daggers at his back, obviously furious. *Great, he's going to be in a bad mood,* I thought. *This will be so much fun.*

"No matter what happens today, you stay by me." Fen's voice had turned back to that commanding voice that let everyone know he was in charge.

"Should I have Jerrick get a leash?" I teased, making Jerrick chuckle as he and a still-scowling Hellia watched us prepare to leave. Fen growled like the animal inside him, the dangerous rumbling noise making my heart jerk in my chest as he grasped my jaw with one hand to force me to look at him.

"I'm serious, *hjarta*. If Heimdall gives us over to Odin's men, they won't hesitate to take you to Asgard. To hurt you again. Tell me you'll stay by me. Even if the Norns say things you don't like, even if you still think sacrificing yourself is the answer, it's not. Stay by me. Tell me."

"I will. I will stay by you," I repeated.

He snorted with satisfaction, and I raised an eyebrow at him.

"We'll see you later tonight." Jerrick nodded to us as he watched Fen sweep an arm under my feet and pick me up. Normally I might have argued to walk through myself, but the seams still frightened me, and I had to admit I'd rather he held me than risk letting go and getting stuck in there by myself. I wrapped my arms around his neck, taking one last look at my friends. Hellia had a terrified expression on her face, worry brimming in her eyes as she watched. Jerrick, too, looked uncomfortable, but he had the strong face of a warrior plastered over it. Sweat prickled on my back, and I looked at Fen, wondering why everyone seemed so distressed.

"Hold on," he said.

I pulled myself tighter to him, burying my face against his neck. Before we even stepped through the portal, my stomach dropped at the thought that I might lose this man in a matter of the next hour.

When Fen stepped forward, the wind whipped away the oxygen. His arms tightened to hold me close to him as we went into free fall. I squeezed my eyes shut, clutching Fen and trying to focus on him instead. His heart was beating loudly; I could feel his pulse in his neck.

Just as soon as it started, all the awful sensations stopped, and I was able to suck air into my lungs once more. I pulled away from him to look around as he carefully set my feet on the ground again.

Above us, the massive branches of an enormous tree stretched across the sky. The tree towered above the others surrounding us, bathed in golden light from the suns, which were just starting to descend from their highest positions.

A few birds chirped, but I expected to see more critters than I did. It seemed oddly quiet, but having never been here before, I had no way to tell if this was normal or not. Fen was scanning the area warily, as though he too sensed something was off.

"This way." Fen nodded down a trail toward the massive tree—as large as any mountain I'd ever seen—in the not too far distance. He walked behind me, a steady stream of energy and power radiating from him. I looked around for signs of life but caught no glimpses of the birds that chirped occasionally. We walked for about ten minutes before we came across a small garden patch in the woods.

"Anais." Fen's voice had me pausing to look back at him.

"Yes?" I got closer as he kept his voice low. He scanned the trees warily. He reached out, pulling me close to him.

"No matter what they say, I want you to remember that I love you." My stomach lurched uncomfortably again at his confession. Not waiting for me to respond, he pulled me into a kiss, his hand cradling the back of my neck. This one was unlike the kisses between us so far. This one felt like he was urging me to understand his desperation, like it might be the last kiss he would ever give me. The feeling made my stomach drop, and I looked up at him with wide, questioning eyes when he pulled away, standing to his full height once more.

He silently nodded for me to continue down the trail. Be-grudgingly, wanting to stand and bombard him with questions, I turned away from him and continued down the path. My mind raced, trying to understand everything that was happening as I took in this strange new realm.

Around the bend in the trail, we came to a cottage and homestead. The roots of the giant tree grew over top of the home, grasses and flowers sprouting from the roof. Several garden patches were full of vegetables, and ravens sat on a fence around a patch of pumpkins and corn.

"Fenrir." An ethereal voice floated to us on a gentle breeze sweeping through the forest.

"Verdandi." His voice was edged with a sharpness I hadn't heard since he spoke to Tora. "I'm here to—"

"Speak with me and my sisters?" I could see her now, the beautiful woman coming through the garden from the other side. Her otherworldly beauty reminded me of Talin, but she didn't have the long, sharpened ears of a light elf.

"Come." She led us inside. Fen had to duck his head to get through the low door frame. "Sisters!" she called. "We have guests."

Inside, the house was cozy but smelled of must and earth. Cobwebs covered every corner and cranny, and the wheel I'd seen in the painting of the Norns was in the center of the room. Golden-looking thread was strewn about on the tables and across the floor, and I made sure to watch my steps for the spools that were a tripping hazard everywhere.

Two more women came into the room, both looking between us with excitement and intrigue. "Skuld, Urd," Fenrir
greeted them both, and I couldn't help flickering my gaze
between the two. Skuld looked thrilled and was smirking ma-
liciously at him. She had pearly white teeth framed by deep
crimson lips that reminded me of Asgard crimson. Her blonde
hair matched both her sisters, falling in long waves past her
shoulders. Urd was watching us both with a cold glare, hatred
clear in her eyes.

"You're here about your Fate." Skuld clicked her tongue
teasingly at us as Verdandi poured tea for everyone. I reached
to take mine, but Fen stopped me. He shook his head slightly,
making pointed eye contact with me before turning back to
the Norns.

"Yes." Fen kept every response short with them.

Skuld watched us for a long moment, her attention on me
with an intense curiosity that made my skin prickle. "Odin will
not pose a threat to Helheim City. Another Thorson poses a
greater threat to you, Fenrir." Fen frowned at her words, and I
wondered if they meant Mag. We all sat in a moment of silence,
Skuld slowly growing a smirk across her lips. "But I suppose
you're here about you *being* Fated. Right?"

I swallowed, listening carefully, not sure I quite understood
what she was saying. "Are you saying he is Fated?" I blurted
out. Fen looked at the floor.

"Yes," Skuld snapped. She fixed me with her wicked smirk.
I was going to be sick.

Wrapping my arms around myself, I fought the urge to
double over and start sobbing. Of course he was Fated. He
wouldn't have come if he didn't feel something in his intuition

telling him that. The air was becoming too thick to breathe, and my stomach gurgled with a threat of being ill.

"She doesn't know? You know, Fenrir. Hellia told you. Shall I recant the Fating for her?" Verdandi smiled innocently at me. She tipped her head to the side. Compared to both of her sisters, Verdandi looked like a summer goddess, warm and rosy, flowers tucked into her hair and a soft blush of pink across her beautiful face. I wondered if she was a death god, if she somehow drew power from my suffering.

I didn't know if I could listen to him be Fated to someone else, but I had to know. "Just tell me who it is," I moaned, not meaning for it to come out sounding so pained. Fen's head snapped toward me, and he tipped his head, watching me carefully. "Is it Erika?" I gasped, watching Skuld's smirk widen.

Verdandi spoke once more. "Anais Sutton, Demigoddess, descended from Artemis. Born in secret and given up to live among humans on Earth. The girl who always had an affinity for wild animals, particularly canis lupus. Raised to worship a god who was not her own, and now doesn't see the power flowing through her own veins. You are destined to be a goddess in the realms of Helheim, Midgard, and Olympus, representing the suns and moons, which you shall bring in full clarity to the realm of Helheim."

I sat frozen, unsure how to react. "I... What?" I asked. This was not what I expected. This was completely new information. New information that said my family was a lie. I was expecting to hear who Fen was Fated to, and instead my entire life was turned upside down. I couldn't even begin processing this information. "There must be a mistake. Are you saying my mom—"

She continued before I could get any clarification. "The Fated Mate of Fenrir Lokison." Just as soon as it had skipped a beat, my heart was racing, jumping up my throat in the form of words I couldn't hold in but couldn't bear to say. I glanced down at my arm, where the tattoo of mountains pointed toward three stars. My head whipped to him, my face slack with shock, my mouth hanging open like a fish. He was watching me, tentative, hopeful, and not at all surprised.

He knew. He wasn't surprised because he knew. This whole time. The realizations crashed over me, and I couldn't form a complete thought.

"M-me?" I asked Verdandi, turning back to her and dumbly pointing to myself. "Are you sure it's me?"

"Yes, girl," Skuld snapped, and I looked at Fen. He was monitoring my reaction closely.

This whole time. He's been lying and hiding this from me. He knew we were Fated, and he didn't say anything. Feeling like I might wretch, I stood and stumbled for the door, needing fresh air. Fen caught my arm.

"Anais, please." His voice was firm and calm. Rage flashed through me. Rage at him keeping this from me. It was obvious now that everyone knew this whole time except for me. Jerrick. Hellia. Even Mag. They all knew I was not just a normal girl from Midgard. They knew I was special to him, and he'd kept it from me the whole time.

"You knew!" I screamed at him, wrenching my arm from his grip. "You knew we were Fated, and you didn't tell me?! You knew I was a what, a fucking demigoddess? This is how I find out?" My rage made him flinch back, made my voice waver, but he still blocked my way to the door. "You knew!

You knew, and you told me you had to come here to find out if you were Fated when you damn well knew!" He was starting to shrink as my rage built.

"You needed time after Mag, after your shoulder, I—" The pleading look replaced the demanding one.

"You lied to me! For weeks!" I screamed. My hands were in my hair. Strands broke away from my skull as I tried to work through the swell of emotion coursing through me.

"I didn't lie." His steely tone and expression were unraveling quickly under my rageful glare. "I just didn't tell you. It wasn't time yet—"

"It was time when I met you! When everyone else knew but me! Even fucking *Mag* knew before me, didn't he?" Fen looked guilty but sent a glare across the room at Skuld.

"That part wasn't my fault," he growled at her. She merely flicked an eyebrow up at him, her crimson lips stretching impossibly wider in a grin.

"Don't you blame her right now!" My scolding tone made him shrink further with a guilty look. "This is between you and me. How long have you known? Did you know when I was looking for you in the hallway that morning, weeks ago?"

He looked at me before he dropped his gaze from mine, looking at the floor.

"Well, I told Hellia just about eight years ago, so..." Skuld interjected.

"You shut up," I snapped at her. "This is between me and him." I didn't care if I offended them, even if we were in their home.

Years. He'd known for years.

"How. Long. Fenrir?" I snarled. I needed to hear him say it.

"Seven years." His voice was small, and even though he stood a great height taller than me, I felt like I was towering over him now. Our audience sat silently, all three pairs of eyes flitting between the two of us. Verdandi was trying to hold in a giggle, overjoyed with the drama unfolding in their living room no doubt.

"Seven years," I repeated back to him as I folded my arms across my chest, staring him down while he looked at the floor. "You knew for seven years. When you started showing up in my dreams seven years ago. You knew my life was a lie. You knew I was destined for something unexplainable. You knew I was betrothed to you. And you didn't tell me the moment you met me?!" He lowered his head, keeping his eyes averted, reminding me of Jerrick cowering in front of him the other day.

Submitting, he was submitting to me.

"I should have," he breathed. "I'm sorry, Anais. I thought this way—"

"You thought wrong," I snarled. "Let me go." I tried to move for the door again but he blocked me.

Panic attack. I was going to have a panic attack.

"Anais, it's not safe out—" He started regaining his commanding tone.

"Oh no," I cut him off with a glare. "Liars *do not* tell me what to do. Manipulators do not get to keep me prisoner anymore!" I started to push past him. He reached out, grabbing me by the waist. Without hesitation, I had the silver knife in hand and jammed the blade into his arm. He yelped, immediately letting me go as I ripped my knife from him and stormed out the door into the garden.

Fresh air hit my lungs but did nothing to help the pressure of all the new information that was crushing me, weighing on me. I bent over, hands on my knees as my head swirled. My life was a lie. My mom was not my birth mother. I was a fucking *demigoddess*. I was Fated to the Prince of Hell. He didn't tell me any of it. None of my new "friends" told me. I was questioning what was reality, wondering who I could trust, and trying not to throw up all at the same time. The entire foundation of my life was crumbling to dust beneath me.

I felt my heart breaking. It was all a lie. Everything was a lie.

"It's not. I love you, that's not a lie." He'd followed me to the garden.

"Oh, but you lied to me straight up about not being able to hear my thoughts though, huh?" I snapped, feeling another level of anxiety crash into me. I stared down at the dirt below me, cursing it under my breath for everything I was feeling right now.

He looked guilty. "Yes. I lied about that. I didn't want you to feel like I was intruding—"

"So you'll just silently intrude." I huffed an insincere laugh.

"I can't help it! Ever since you prayed to me in Asgard, you've been shouting in my head. It's because we're Fated, and we haven't even shared blood yet. We haven't accepted Fate yet." He sounded bitter as he made his excuses. "But I didn't lie about loving you, Anais."

I whipped my head around, glaring at him over my shoulder. "You don't, though. You love me *because* we're Fated. Because three witches in the woods told you, *seven years ago*, that you loved me. You didn't fall for me." Speaking of the three witches, they were watching from the door of the cabin, not following us outside but still an audience.

"That's not true." He walked to my side, reaching out to rub circles on my back. I leapt back from his touch, not missing the sadness in his eyes when I did so. "I have fallen more in love with you every single day that I have had the privilege of being in your presence. You make me feel alive after I died long ago. You are the moon, the only source of light in this eternal night I have been living in. I want to live in your moonlight forever, *hjarta*. Please."

"Oh, stop it!" I yelled, even though I could see in his eyes he meant every word. "Stop the lies and the sweet nothings. I've had it!" I started to storm away.

"What I say is not *nothing*," he snarled, but I would not be intimidated. "You do not understand my side. You do not understand the importance of being Fated."

"I don't care! I don't care how important it is to"—I spun, sniffling and wiping angry tears from my cheek—"to continue your bloodline, or produce an heir to Hellia's throne, or, or, whatever else it means. Whatever it is this betrothal wants to use me for."

His eyes darkened and he shook his head. "That is not—"

"I don't care! Fen!" I turned my back on him again, wiping my nose on my sleeve, gripping the knife firmly in the other hand. "I am a woman from the year 2023," I said to no one in particular. I thought maybe I was talking to myself. "I do not have to accept some *wack ass* marriage proposal from a *liar*, a *monster*, and a *murderer* who insists I go against my beliefs. Against *my* moral code. Who wants me to proclaim *him* as my new *deity*. Who takes me to some *psychic witches* in the forest, who look at a *magic carpet* and tell me I have to be with him eternally!" I was screaming now. "I'm going home, I'm getting psychiatric help and medications or whatever for these hallucinations, and I'm never getting involved with another religion or mythology for the rest of my life. Fuck this!" I stormed away from him up the trail.

"Anais, stop!" The dangerous tone in his voice might've turned me around before, but I marched on, needing to put as much distance between us as possible in that moment. I heard him following, not far behind. He would be caught up with me in just steps. "STOP!" he demanded again. I flipped my finger at him without turning around.

"Hm yes, you're really showing him, Anais," a bone chilling voice cooed with mocking approval. Before I could turn to meet turquoise blue eyes, I was sent sprawling backwards.

"ANAIS!" Fen screamed, just out of reach behind me. But instead of hitting the ground, the oxygen was gone and I was free falling.

CHAPTER 33

I lay on the white and gold marble floors of Asgard again, my shoulders pressed against a floor warmed by the sun. The silver blade, still gripped firmly in my hand, glinted in the bright sunshine.

No no no! I wanted to scream, but I couldn't get any air into my lungs. Blood roared in my ears, and my heart thundered in my chest. I scrambled to get to a standing position, but a hand closed around the back of my neck before I could make it off the floor.

"Gotcha," Mag said.

I swallowed hard, trying not to visibly shake as he grabbed hold of my hair, yanking my head back so my eyes met triumphant ocean turquoise. "I missed you, Anais." He stood over me, and I snarled as he kept a firm grip on the back of my neck.

"I can't say the same," I snapped back. I swung my arm back the way Jerrick taught me, driving the blade into his thigh.

"Fucking bitch!" Mag cried out, shoving me to the ground hard enough to make me let go of the knife. I scrambled back and to my feet as he pulled the blade from his leg. Staring at me with bloodthirsty malice, he dissolved the knife in his hand, letting it crumble away to nothing. There went my last hope. I guess I'd die fighting bare handed.

"No, you fucking will not!" Fen shouted angrily in my head. *"You will stay alive for the next ten minutes while I bring Hellia there."*

Get out of my fucking head, Fen! I screamed back.

"No!" I could hear the wolf snarl in his voice.

"Is Fenrir promising to come save you?" Mag taunted, and my mind refocused on the threat at hand. He was stalking me like a cat stalking a mouse, backing me toward the corner of the room.

"That's what you want, isn't it?" I asked, looking for any escape, anywhere to run, anything to use to defend myself.

"Of course"—Mag grinned—"but I also want Fenrir to suffer. Has he told you yet about growing up in Asgard? Has he told you what it was like when we were adolescents together? Or is he keeping those secrets from you too?" He narrowed his eyes, knowing he was striking a nerve.

"We haven't known each other long enough to discuss all our childhood trauma yet." I edged sideways, hoping to break for a door that was cracked across the room from us.

He clicked his tongue disapprovingly. "Based on the conversation you were having for all of us to hear at Yggdrasil, I don't think you were planning to give him a chance to. I have to say I'm proud, Anais. Standing up for yourself, after *everything* you've been through." He smirked. "I really wish I could've watched it play out between you two. You leaving him by your own choice would hurt him far more than any pain I could ever inflict." He sighed, pressing a dramatic hand to his chest. "Alas, here we are. I suppose I will have to try my best to destroy him without your help. I would imagine we have no less than ten minutes before he's here. It's a good thing Odin was prepared for you to be here, since Tora alerted him we had you the moment you landed at Yggdrasil's realm. We're ready for your execution in the plaza now. All of Asgard is waiting."

I broke for the door, but he was too fast and far too strong for me to fend off. He tackled me with ease, his body overcoming mine with nearly no effort. I slammed to the ground, knocking the breath from me and leaving me feeling like a fish out of water for the second time in the past half an hour. He pinned me beneath him, holding me to the stone floor.

"First of all, get dressed for the occasion, *darling*." Mag snapped his fingers like a corny magician, and my clothing disintegrated from my body before crimson draped me in a scantily clad skirt and bikini top. I pushed myself up to my hands and knees, wobbling slightly.

"What is it with your Princess Leia fetish?" I growled.

"Well, she is a fantasy, isn't she?" he purred, and the gleam of a new collar in his hand caught my eye.

"No!" I screamed and thrashed against his hold on me. My fingers dug into the flesh of his arm, my nails leaving scratches on him that disappeared in moments. We wrestled on the ground for several minutes before he laid his full body weight on top of me, slipping the golden collar around my neck.

"Someone's been training you; you're putting up quite a little fight here," he chuckled.

He stood, mashing me into the ground and electrifying the collar so the familiar horrid feeling of electric current coursed through my body. I screamed, tears springing to my eyes—angry tears more than anything.

"Anais?! We're coming, hold on hjarta. Stay alive." Fenrir sounded desperate.

"You fucker!" I screamed at Mag as he grabbed the collar around my neck, hauling me to my feet again. He dragged me out the palace doors toward Palace Plaza. The sunshine was bright, and the crowd was loud as Mag hauled me through the sea of people parting for us. The statue of Odin and Frigg had been removed, leaving a stone platform above the heads of onlookers.

The audience screamed insults in a foreign language; I couldn't understand a word. My eyes darted around to all the angry faces watching me. People screamed at me, spitting, some throwing produce. I struggled against Mag, digging my feet into the ground and trying to twist away from him. Having regained some of my strength over the past weeks, I was able to at least slow his march through the crowd, but it wasn't long until we reached the stone steps. He dragged me up them, making me lurch forward and catch myself with my hands when I tripped. At the top of the stage stood Odin, with Thor and Tora at his side. Mag squeezed the back of my neck roughly, forcing me to my knees before the Allfather.

"Traitor of Asgard," Odin called, making the crowd roar with renewed vigor. "She who freed Fenrir, reuniting the wicked children of Loki so that they may complete their intended destiny as foretold by my visions." The roaring boo filled my ears as I looked out over the angry faces calling for my death. "She is sentenced to immediate death by my hand for her crimes."

"They don't want—" I tried to tell Odin, but he glared at me before repeating the last sentence in another language as Mag sent a warning shock through my collar that made me sputter and choke. The audience roared with approval.

My chances to escape, to try to stop this course of action, grew slimmer by the moment. I didn't stand a chance against any of their strength. I was stronger than when I arrived in Asgard, but I still wasn't a match for all of them. There was no way for me to fight my way out, which meant I needed to try to get off this platform and run. To stay out of their reach long enough for Fenrir to appear. Then they would have larger problems to deal with than chasing me through the streets of Asgard.

But Mag's hand was firmly clamped down on the back of my neck, and I had the collar to worry about. My heartbeat raced in my ears, the blood flow roaring.

"Over my dead body will you hurt the Princess of Helheim, you ancient piece of shit!" To the side of the stage, Jerrick threw off a red cloak. He drew every set of eyes in the crowd, including my own. "Go," he mouthed when Mag let go of me and lunged forward. I scrambled sideways as the entire plaza erupted into chaos. Jerrick shifted into a massive wolf, snapping his jaws at Mag. They tangled in battle, screams of terror and anguish filling the air around us, cries of fear at the massive wolf among the people. Warriors in every direction started rushing toward the lieutenant, drawing heavy blades.

I scrambled to my feet and darted to the edge of the platform. It was a long drop for me, but I propelled myself over the edge without hesitation. My feet hit the stone of the plaza, and I was running, stumbling through the crowd, pushing my way past people and dodging swinging blades from every which way.

Something slammed into me from behind, someone tackling me to the ground and sending me skidding across the stone. They were wrestling with me, forcing me over to face them, and suddenly I was looking up at Tora straddling me.

"Oh no you don't," she hissed. "I have just as much reason to want you dead as my brother does." She barely struggled to keep me pinned, even when I thrashed against her with all my strength.

"You're an evil bitch," I spat in her face. "How dare you convince me your brother was good, that you were good, and then let him do this to me? Fenrir is going to rip you limb from limb."

"He won't." She grinned in a bone-chillingly maniacal way. "I'm going to slit your throat and then watch him die. When you die, part of him will too. After he kills my grandfather, we'll kill you. He'll be incredibly weak, and my brother will be able to rid us all of that filthy mutt."

"She's mine to kill, Tora," Odin's booming voice sounded, and we both looked up to see the old god towering over us.

"But Grandfather," she said, her voice sickly sweet with fake adoration.

"*I* will kill her, Tora," Odin repeated. "It's me she's betrayed; she's mine to put down. Hold her there, don't let her up." He lifted an enormous ax in his hand, readying to bring it down on my neck. I shivered with terror and tried to fight against Tora as hard as I could, but it was useless to put my mortal strength against her divine power.

"Don't you dare fucking touch my Fated, Odin." Fen was there, striding toward us with shadowed fury radiating in every direction. Tendrils like smoke enveloped Aesir as he passed, and upon breathing in the darkness, they fell to the ground choking and clawing at their throats.

"It's interesting how you think you deserve a Fated at all, Fenrir." Odin lifted the ax, precariously holding it over my neck so it would surely behead me the moment he let it drop. I struggled against Tora, panic rising up my exposed throat.

"I know I don't," Fen snarled, pausing several meters away when Odin raised the ax. "However, Fate gave me one, and I will protect her with everything I am. Now step away from her and fight me. Die with honor by my hand. Don't hurt an innocent woman for following her Fate-set path before I kill you."

"Her Fate-set path was to free you so you could come kill me. That doesn't make her innocent for simply following her Fate. That makes her responsible for the lives of all Asgardians. My own life, since I assume you're going to finish me off here—this is Ragnarok, is it not?" He motioned to where brutal violence was still surrounding us, wolves fighting with Aesir and Valhalla's warriors, archers shooting into the throngs of people, an already shocking number of fighters on both sides laying unmoving on the ground. "You're going to overthrow the realm's power structure over a Fate you don't deserve, Fenrir. After years of pleading with me, telling me how you never wanted to overthrow me, never wanted to kill me, all it takes is one female for you to show your true self." Odin tsked and shook his head.

Fen snorted. "You deserve to die for what you allowed to happen to Anais while I was locked up, for allowing your grandson to harass me. So it's my Fate to kill you, hm? True, I didn't want to before, but now… I think I'm ready." He stood firm, his eyes glowing as the wolf surfaced.

In one swift movement, Odin swung the ax. Fen shifted and slammed into him. I screamed at the top of my lungs. The ax was set off course, and sliced me across the throat deep enough to draw blood but not to get my windpipe. Fen in wolf form sank his fangs into the old god, shaking his head violently and throwing Odin's body around like a rag doll. Fen gripped his neck with powerful jaws and shook again as the god struggled.

"Someone has to finish the job," Tora hissed. She was still pinning me beneath her. There was a knife in her hand, raised above her head and glinting in the Asgardian sunshine. I struggled with renewed energy, waves of power radiating from where Fen was now crushing the windpipe of the dying old man. Odin let out a final hiss and stilled in the wolf's jaws. Blood dripped down from Fen's chin, slicking his black fur.

"Use my power to get free," Fen said to me. But Mag appeared over his shoulder, tackling the wolf and sinking a blade

deep into his side. I shoved Tora, surprising her with power I shouldn't have. Shadows wrapped around my arms, crawling toward her, encircling her neck and choking her. Fen's power—he was somehow channeling through me.

I could hear the scuffle between Fen and Mag next to us but had no time to look as Tora turned the knife—the knife of Gleipner, the same knife I'd used to free Fen—to the shadows, slicing them away with ease. Without another word, she flipped the knife over, raised it high above her head again, and plunged the blade into my chest, directly into my heart.

"NO!" Fen screamed. I wasn't sure if it was out loud or in my head. I stared in shock at the hilt protruding from my chest, the sickening vibration I remembered running through my whole body.

I didn't know what I thought being stabbed would feel like, but I could never imagine the feeling of the cold, foreign object entering my body. It was a completely unique experience. The unwelcome chill of the blade pressed into parts of me that had never seen the light of day, piercing delicate flesh that was never meant to withstand being punctured.

I heard Fen screaming my name, but suddenly it sounded like he was a great distance away, his voice growing more faint by the moment. He screamed for me, over and over, until it suddenly choked off and I thought I heard him gasping. My eyes roved but couldn't find him.

I watched in slow motion as Tora stood, glaring down at me. Mag joined her side with an angry frown. My heartbeat had become painful, but mercifully, the beats were getting slower and further in between.

"That's fatal. Let her die here. We need to go." Mag shoved his sister's shoulder, seeming to break the daze she was in. His voice sounded distant too, even though he was standing right over me.

"Fine, let's go. Take the knife out or she won't bleed out before he can save her," Tora said. "Goodbye, Anais." She wrenched the knife from my chest, and blood bubbled from the wound up my throat and past my lips. Feeling like it was a dream, I lifted a hand, pressing the wound in a vain attempt to keep the blood from spilling too quickly. Tora threw the knife at my side before joining Mag in the crowd.

There was more noise now, screams reverberating down the streets. Hell Hounds and archers were barreling through Asgardians and Aesir warriors. But it all sounded far away from where I lay on the stone ground. Above me, black smoke poured into the blue sky, covering white puffy clouds.

Then Hellia was at my side, screaming Fen's name. He stood over me, blocking one of the bright suns, framed by the smoke and clouds mixing in the sky. The light was too bright, but I couldn't even move my eyelids to close them. Time slowed, and my breaths became shorter.

"Anais, drink." Fen was right next to my head. He pressed something to my lips. His wrist—his cut open, bloody wrist—was pressed against my lips, his hot sweet blood hitting my tongue. "Swallow," he demanded, looking down at me. With all the effort I had left, I swallowed the mouthful of his blood. It burned like white hot liquor going down my throat.

He leaned down, gently peeling back my fingers from my open wound. I panicked, panting as more blood pumped from my body as dark spots swam in my vision. He pressed his lips to my skin, kissing the blood that leaked out. His blood burned in my stomach, like I'd swallowed acid, and I moaned in pain as the light turned blinding. My eyes were open, but I saw nothing more. My breathing became ragged and shallow.

"Please, please don't leave me after we just found each other," he begged softly while I fought to get air. "Please don't let me be too late."

I could hear my own heartbeat making irregular noises in my chest. One of these was going to be my final breath... My lungs were getting tired.

"*Your last breath is my last breath, hjarta.*" He leaned his temple against mine, his arms tightening around my limp form.

There were so many people I was leaving behind. Kerri, Gladis, Kaylee... I'd never see them again. I hoped they knew I loved them. And him... I wasn't sure I could die without him...

After what felt like ages but was probably seconds, the noises faded, the sight didn't return to my eyes, and my breaths became less and less necessary until they just stopped.

Everything stopped. It was over.

Death was peaceful, and I found myself standing in a vast white landscape. No one was around, and when I called out, no one responded. It was quiet. I wasn't sure if I should panic or be quiet in the cavernous space. Ahead of me, slowly, a door appeared. I felt the door calling me, but as I lifted my limbs to walk forward, they were suddenly tied down, bound to something behind me I couldn't see. When I tried to walk forward again, the restraints stopped me. I looked down to see gold cuffs wrapping around my wrists and legs. They looked the same as Fenrir's gold banding, impressed into my skin like a tattoo, and ribbons seemed connected to something behind me. I turned to try to see what it was, but it was shrouded in mist. Plunging into the mist, I searched for what I was chained to, what was holding me down.

It wasn't time for me to go yet.

"*Hjarta*, can you hear me? Anais? Please. Please come back." Fenrir's voice faded into my thoughts.

I could hear him calling for me, but I couldn't seem to get control of my body just yet. I was still coming back into awareness.

"Anais," he called for me again. Slowly, with a moan from the effort, I opened one eye to daylight, slowly blinking away the darkness that had covered me like a blanket. As my vision adjusted, I could see we sat on the steps of the platform, me in Fen's lap. Around us, everywhere was a bloody mess, but the fighting was over. I was tucked close to his chest and something dripped on my cheek. Fen's face was streaming with tears.

I reached a hand up, a movement that somehow felt odd and foreign in my own body. Gently caressing his cheek, I wiped the tears away. He was everywhere around me, his familiar pine scent mixed with a tang of blood and the saltiness of the tears.

"Fen," I breathed, and he shuddered, pulling me close to his body. We remained like that for minutes, and I absorbed his tears and sobs.

"I thought I lost you," his voice broke in my ear. "You died. I thought I was too late."

"You have a knack for saving my life just in time." He gave a wet, throaty laugh, slowly leaning back from me. I caught a glimmer of gold close to his cheek as I looked into his eyes, and my attention slid to the gold cuff on my wrist. It matched his, tattooed into my skin.

"I-I'm sorry." He frowned at the gold. "I thought when Odin died they would go away... I didn't know you'd get them too when I accepted Fate." He looked down at his own wrist. My betrothal to him as Fated Mates... He accepted it.

"To save your life, Anais." His tone was apologetic, soft, and pleading for me to understand. "Please, I had to do it to save you."

"I hate to burst this bubble"—Hellia's voice was cautious but anxious—"but we need to move. Now, please." Not far from us, Asgard was in chaos. Figures ran between allies, screams reverberated off the streets, and bodies littered the ground.

Fen stood with me in his arms. "We'll talk more about it later. Okay?" I nodded, wanting nothing more than to get out of here. Around us, buildings were wrecked, and some areas were smoldering with thick black smoke pouring into the sky. Mag got away with it. He got exactly what he wanted.

"I'm going to get him, don't worry." Fen grimaced at me.

I looked at him skeptically, not sure if I liked this internal talking thing. In the books, it had always sounded so cool and intimate. Now it just felt freaky. Maybe there was a way to block it. Or maybe we would learn to like it. I wondered what else of the mating bonds I read about might be true, wanting to blush as I refused to think of some specific things in front of him.

"Jerrick," he called for his lieutenant. "I'm going to send you home with Jerrick, okay?" He hugged me tight one last time.

"Wait, what?" I protested. "Where are you going?"

"Hey Princess." Jerrick was panting when he came into view. He was drenched in blood; it ran down his temples and neck. Large clots were stuck in his short beard, but his bright eyes, still full of enthusiasm, told a different story.

"Take her home please." Fen gently passed me into Jerrick's arms. I tried to swallow down the swelling feeling of dread as he let go of me. I reached out, grabbing on to him, looking at him with wide eyes. "I'm going after Mag." His soft expression dissipated, replaced by flaming anger, his dark brows pulled low.

"He left when it started, with Tora. He's not here anymore. He never told me where he was going. He's gone. You should just take me home—" I pleaded.

"Probably Midgard," Jerrick growled. It felt weird to be carried by him instead of Fen. He wasn't as tall as Fen, and though he held me securely, it wasn't the same as my wolf-man.

"I want you to come with me. He's long gone, just come with me," I pleaded again.

"I still need to go look. I'll be there soon." He leaned over, placing a kiss on my head before nodding for Jerrick to go. We watched him turn and start running, the wolf bursting forth and tearing toward the distant cries. My heart ached with the distance already.

"He'll come back, don't worry," Jerrick assured me.

"I can walk," I protested, struggling against him.

"Nah, we're going through a seam. I got you, Princess." He grinned at me. I scowled at the new pet name.

"Stop calling me that," I snapped.

"Why?"

"Because it's annoying." I glared at him.

"But you are a Princess now, of Helheim." He said it matter of factly and then finished off with an excited grin.

"I... What?" I gaped at him.

Jerrick grinned at me excitedly. "You're Fated to the Prince of Helheim, and you accepted the Fate. That makes you the Princess of Helheim. My primary job now is protecting you as part of the royal family."

I was about to yell at him, to tell him off for calling me such an inane pet name, but the oxygen was crushed from my lungs as we stepped into a seam. Blackness swallowed us until we landed in the snow outside of the gate to Helheim City.

CHAPTER 34

"You knew," I said as Jerrick set me down and we began heading through the city toward the castle. "You knew about me and Fen, and you didn't say anything." My body felt completely healed and stronger than ever. I pushed my way through the snow easily, barefoot and wearing the outfit from Asgard. I didn't feel the cold on my skin. Instead, it felt balmy, as though I was in the tropics rather than in the freezing street of Helheim.

He threw me a guilty look. "I did know. It wasn't my place to tell you."

"You pushed us together though. You tried to get us together," I accused.

The cheeky grin returned to his face. "Yeah, well, just because I couldn't tell you didn't mean I wasn't trying to make it happen naturally. Come on. I'm a werewolf but I'm still human. I'm a sucker for a little romance story just like everyone else."

"It's not really romance if it was predecided," I grumbled as we pushed open the heavy castle doors and tracked snow into the main hall.

"It could be, if you let it. He's pretty crazy about you." He raised his eyebrows suggestively at me and I huffed.

"I thought you were my friend." I frowned at him, folding my arms across my chest. "I thought you were all my friends."

This cut him, and he flinched slightly, the smile dropping from his face as his eyes met the ground. I looked him up and down, standing bloodstained, injured himself on one shoulder with blood stuck in his hair.

"We are your friends… We've been waiting for you to join our family for seven years, Anais." My heart dropped. Some of the things he'd said started to make more sense.

"My friends would have told me that I was betrothed to the Prince of Hell." I shuffled my feet, looking at the ground.

He crossed his arms, looking down at me with more seriousness than I'd seen so far in my time here.

"Your anger isn't *entirely* fair. You're falling in love with him," he declared, watching my reaction.

"What? No I am not!" I sputtered, looking at him with outrage.

"You were before you went to the Norns. You tried to accept the Fated Mates bond yourself just the other day, when you were doing training together." I stared at him, bewildered.

"I did no such thing. I don't even know how to do it," I huffed, crossing my arms.

"You did too! He came to my room immediately after he'd just chewed me out, talking my ear off about 'she just tried to bite me' and 'I can't tell if it's really how she feels or just the mating bond trying to take effect'." My face was absolutely burning, on fire, and I knew I must be the color of a fire engine because he started to smirk. "You accept a Fated mating bond by sharing each other's blood. You'd only do that if you liked him." I wanted to smack that smug expression right off his face.

"That was before I learned that he lied to me and kept secrets. This whole time, he's been in my head, reading my thoughts. I asked him, and he lied to my face. Everyone knew, Jerrick—everyone but me. We've spent all this time messing around when I didn't know, so I couldn't make the decision about how I felt about him. Make the decision of if I want to be bound to him for all eternity. And now he's made it for me, so I'm a prisoner in this. I don't care if I showed signs of"—I was sniffling now, angry and hurt tears streaking my face—"of Stockholm syndrome or whatever before… I need to go back to my normal life. Without any of you. No gods, no werewolves, no realms. Just my normal life, that's all I want."

It was as good as smacking him. The fun had disappeared, and he had a solemn look on his face.

"He wanted to tell you—"

"Then he should have when he had the chance," I cut him off, turning toward the staircase. I was not interested in the excuses he was going to come up with for his best friend. I paused before continuing up the stairs, turning to him. "And what does '*hjarta*' even mean, anyway?"

"It means soulmate," he said.

Safely behind the door and alone, I walked to the mirror, and tried not to gag at the crimson clothing hanging from my revitalized body. I was renewed, my body entirely healed. No more scar on my shoulder from freeing Fen, no more open gaping stab wound in my chest from Tora's attack or slice on my neck from Odin. Even my finger, which had been bent since I slammed it in a door as a child, was straight as an arrow. Every scar, every blemish, even my tattoos and piercings were gone. My perfect skin was a clean slate, and it almost glowed. Gold caught my eye. Gold banding, just like Fen's, wrapped around my body. One on each wrist, a cuff around each ankle, and a band around my neck.

Dammit, I paid good money for those tattoos. I shook my head at my thoughts and looked mournfully where the book with three stars had been on my arm. *I died... I died in Asgard.* I stood, staring into nothingness, my hand wrapping around the gold on my other wrist as I held them close to my chest. *I died and I didn't see Jesus.*

My eyes slammed shut, and I grit my teeth as I felt the gold band on my skin. Suddenly I was seeing with my eyes still closed. I was running, searching through the streets of

Asgard. Searching for something, someone. Around me I heard screams, pleas of dying people. Mounted archers on wolfback tore through the streets past me as the fighting and slaughter proceeded through the rest of the city. I felt panic, some elation, but mostly anger boiling over into complete red rage. Ahead was Asgard Palace, the doors slung wide open as fighting continued inside. Racing in, I saw Hellia emerging from the staircase leading down to where Fen was imprisoned for all those years. She was helping someone, his arm around her neck as she helped the man stumble from the palace toward the exit. She was shouting at me. Around them, Hell Hounds fought viciously with Odin's men, pushing their way further into the gold palace.

My eyes snapped open once more, and I was back in my bathroom in Helheim, the sound of water filling the tub replacing the screams and destruction of Asgard.

Fen, that's what Fen was seeing. Feeling. Somehow through our bond, I could see through his eyes. I shook my head, trying to get him out of my brain.

Jerrick wasn't right, was he? Was I falling in love with him? I'd had feelings for him, some that I haven't been able to explain, but that doesn't mean I'm falling for him... Does it? He's been calling me his soulmate this whole time... How was I ever supposed to go back to normal after all of this?

"*Hjarta.*" The whisper in my ear had me jolting from bed. I'd passed out after my bath, not even having the energy to change out of my bathrobe first. Fen sat next to me, leaning down over me and gently brushing my hair back from my forehead.

"Did you find him?" I asked, sitting up and wrapping the robe tighter around myself.

"No. He was gone." He dropped his head, rubbing his temples. I wanted to reach out, to comfort him, and yet I was still so angry. We sat in silence for a moment while I tried to sort through the tangle of emotions and ignore the now desperate and completely unhinged urge to grab him and never let go again.

"Why didn't you tell me?" I finally asked. He took my hand, studying the gold around my wrist. He stroked his thumb over it gently, sending tingles up my arm that filled my entire body.

"I thought if I told you, you'd hate me. I thought you'd think I was trying to trap you ... which is exactly what you thought when you did find out." He cleared his throat, his voice low. "I thought if someone else told you—the Norns, since it's they who wove your Fate—you'd see that it was a gift and not a curse. I hoped you'd see that it wasn't me trying to do something to you, but something precious we'd been given."

"Well that was stupid," I said.

"It was." He tried to give me a small smile that I didn't return.

"How long could you hear my thoughts?" I asked.

"Since you arrived in Asgard," he answered immediately, not hesitating with any information now. "I could tell the minute you arrived, but I couldn't respond to you, or at least, I don't think you heard me until you called for me asking for help."

"No… I didn't hear you until then. So you heard everything…" I whispered, putting my head in my hands, the horrible memories flashing through my mind. He heard every time I cried for help, every time I pleaded with the Christian God, every silent prayer to die. He probably was trying to speak to me, to comfort me, but I couldn't hear it.

"Yes," he whispered back. I could tell he wanted to reach out but was resisting. Hot, angry tears coated my hands as I covered my face, and a wet sniffle escaped me, filling the silence between us.

"Who is Jacob?" he asked suddenly.

"What?" I asked, confused, lifting my head from my hands.

"'*Team Jacob*.' You say his name a lot. Was he your boyfriend before?" he asked. A small flash of jealousy crossed his eyes as he waited for me to answer. I stared at him, realizing he was jealous of a fictional character from the Twilight Saga, Jacob Black. Unable to help it, I laughed. Loudly, and hard enough to squeeze more tears from my eyes.

"What is funny, *hjarta*?" he asked, his voice serious. "Is he someone who hurt you?"

"No, he's not even real, Fen. He's a werewolf in a book series, my favorite book series, back on Earth." I wiped my cheeks with my sleeve. "What's funny is that my whole world is upside down, I just found out my mother is a goddess who abandoned me and I'm Fated to you … and you're jealous of a fictional man. Not even a man—a fictional teenager." I couldn't help more laughter shaking my shoulders at the ridiculousness of it all.

"Oh," he said, sounding embarrassed.

We sat in tense silence for another moment, the air thick and heavy with unsaid words, before noise from outside caught my attention. It was a new voice, one I hadn't heard yet. I would need to get used to being able to hear people clear across the castle. I could tell they were elsewhere, but with my new ears, it sounded like they were just outside the door.

Rousing myself, I stepped into the bathroom to change into my usual castle clothes. I gave Fen a wordless look that was halfway between a glare and a sob before walking to the door and hauling it open. The merry voices were coming from the main hall, and I followed them until I came around the corner to see Hellia standing with Jorm and Jerrick and another stranger with blazing red hair who looked so much like Jorm it was instantly obvious who he was.

"Anais! Come meet my father." Hellia excitedly pulled me over, introducing me to the infamous God of Mischief, who looked tired and weary. He gave me a kind smile anyway and extended a hand.

"I've heard about you, Fated mate of my son." I flushed. I might have corrected him, if he were incorrect.

"Thank you for freeing him so my daughter could start Ragnarok and rescue me." Hellia was beaming with pride, and the longer I looked at them all, the more obvious it was that they were family. Jorm looked like a bigger version of his father almost exactly, Hellia shared his high cheekbones, and Fen had his jawline. "It will be a long road to recovery, but I'm thankful for my family being together again so we can make a start." He hugged Hellia close to him, and Jorm actually smiled for the first time.

I nodded, watching them reconnect with a half-smile hanging on my lips. I still had so many questions, so many unknowns, not the least of which was what I intended to do with my new mate. Completely unsure, I was questioning myself—who I was, what was real and not, and where I belonged in it all.

"Here. You belong here, hjarta." Fen's voice was accompanied by warmth. I pushed away his comfort, questioning how he could be so sure. He belonged here. I didn't know if I belonged here.

"You do. With me," he tried to reassure me.

I looked up to meet his watchful eyes carefully assessing every move I made. Gently, he reached out and tipped my chin to look at him the way he'd done a thousand times over the last weeks. Leaning down, he placed a kiss on my lips. My soul was instantly set aflame, consuming my entire being with the need for him, for this connection we had. He kissed me for several more moments, and I didn't pull away.

"You always belong with me, *hjarta*," he whispered just to me.

"Anais." Hellia caught my attention amid the celebration of the small group. The happiness on her face was radiant.

"Odin is dead. Ragnarok is over. You can go home," she said with a smile so bright it was nearly blinding. The news took several moments to sink in. I was going home, and everything would go back to normal.

ACKNOWLEDGEMENTS

I cannot thank my parents enough for supporting my dreams and allowing me creative freedom from a young age. Thank you Mom and Dad for always having my back and allowing me to grow continually. I could not have done this without everything you've done for me.

Thank you to my friends who have been major supporters all the way through; some of you are beta readers, some are first copy purchasers, and others are social media cheerleaders. Each of you mean so much to me, and these drops of encouragement from all of you watered me throughout the process.

I couldn't have presented this book to readers without my wonderful editor Kelly. Thank you for encouraging me and taking such care with my book. I couldn't have asked for a better person to have on my team! If you need Kelly's superior editing skills check out kellyscriven.com.

Thank you to everyone who reads my book; I'm grateful you gave my story your time and brain space. I hope you'll continue to follow Anais' story in the Fated Trilogy.

To Hellia and Jerrick, thank you for saving me. Again and again.

ABOUT THE AUTHOR

Annabelle lives by Lake Michigan in Indiana with her parents, where she enjoys taking her corgi to the beach and making pizza every Friday night; it is her favorite food after all. One time in Italy, she ate 14 pizzas in 12 days - true story. She is an aspiring tattoo artist at a local shop and is grateful to work creatively with ink every day!

After graduating Cum Laude from Washington State University (Go Cougs!), Annabelle worked in the influencer marketing field before she took time off to travel. She has been to

15 countries so far and loves to draw inspiration for her art on her travel experiences.

Annabelle started journaling regularly at the beginning of her journey writing this book and at the end of each entry she signs off with "I love you." This book was a healing journey for her. She encourages everyone to find a way to say those three words to themselves each day in their own way.

www.ingramcontent.com/pod-product-compliance
Lightning Source LLC
Chambersburg PA
CBHW070902260626
47162CB00007B/2530

* 9 7 9 8 9 9 0 4 9 0 8 0 2 *